I0847220

Maghan Hunt

Emerging Ember

To Liam, James, Jennifer, and Kaity. Thank you for putting up with the random questions, plotting sessions, and sudden subject shifts. I couldn't have written or completed this book without you.

Prologue

1913

Ember peaked out from her hiding place behind the curtain and watched the maids scurry about the ballroom, prepping it, and the formal rose garden, for an event.

She had heard rumors from her twin a royal tea party would be happening in a few days. Ember hadn't believed him. Emerson had lied to her before about tea parties. He thought such frivolity was a waste of time and preferred nature and strategy. He often lamented the fact Ember was three minutes older, and the spare heir to the throne instead of him.

When they argued about it, Ember quite maturely stamped her foot, and demanded he stop teasing her before she stuck out her tongue at him. Emerson always told her he was preparing her for the treatment she was going to receive for being a featherbrained idiot. Meanwhile, their older brother Drystan would declare them both idiotic babies and threaten to banish them from court. Grammy Margaret said it was an empty threat, but Ember had her doubts.

A maid dropped gold bud vases on the ground, pulling Ember from her thoughts.

Emerson had been right. There was going to be a royal tea party. Daddy only ordered out the gold things when important people were coming.

Ember frowned. Why hadn't she had a new dress made for the event? Grammy and Daddy always made sure she had new dresses for important events. Mommy was usually too busy taking medicine and socializing with members of the court to pay her any mind.

As the housekeeper scolded the clumsy maid, Ember dashed from the curtain to the main staircase. Daddy was in meetings all day, but Grammy Margaret should be in her quarters. As Ember rounded a corner, she ran into Drystan.

"Oh. I'm sorry," Ember murmured.

Drystan righted her on her feet before dusting himself off. Ember would have rolled her eyes, but she was eager to get to their grandmother.

"Where are you going in such a hurry?"

"The maids are setting up for a royal tea in the ballroom and garden. I know it's a royal tea because they are using the gold," Ember explained.

"Oh, that. Yes, Father is hosting foreign dignitaries because he is announcing my expanding role as his heir," Drystan told her.

Ember's eyes widened. "Does that mean Evie will be here? I must get to Grammy and ask when my fitting is."

Drystan stared at Ember for a moment before throwing back his head in laughter.

"What?" Ember was puzzled by his reaction.

"Princess Evelyn will be in attendance, but you aren't invited. You and Emerson will be in the nursery where the babies belong."

Ember gaped at him. "We are not babies, Drystan! Even if Emerson isn't invited, I should be there because I am second in line."

Drystan glared at Ember. "Yes. I am aware of the line of succession. Regardless, you aren't invited."

"But that's not fair!"

"It's completely fair! You are seven and I am fourteen. There is a large gap between us and you're also a girl."

"What does that mean?" Ember demanded placing her hands on her hips.

Drystan rolled his eyes. "Your place is planning social events, making pretty samplers, gossiping, and eventually marrying well. Not conducting important matters with visiting dignitaries."

Ember was stunned. Grammy Margaret had been queen for years before stepping down. She always said Ember's role in Parley needed to be bigger than just planning parties and marriage. It had seemed like Daddy and Drystan had agreed with this, so why was Drystan questioning the order of things now? She could do more than play with dolls and embroidery.

"I'm smart. I can do all the things you can do, and even do them better."

Drystan started laughing again. Ember wanted to kick him in the shin and tackle him to the ground, but that "wasn't what ladies do" and she wanted to go to the party.

"I'm going to ask Grammy about the tea party. I'm going to go," Ember declared.

Drystan's eyes narrowed. "You're not invited. You can beg and cry all you want, but I outright demanded you not be invited. So you will not be there."

Ember's lip trembled. Why did Drystan demand she not be there? "Fine. If I can't go to your stupid tea party, then I'll have my own."

Drystan started laughing again as he walked away. "Have fun with that! It'll be good practice for you so you can better serve your future husband."

Parley had been founded by pirates when they had claimed the Caribbean. Nothing they had done was traditional. It wasn't until Mommy and Drystan had started talking about respect and taking their place as a world power a few years ago that things started to shift.

Ember had found herself learning her royal duties in addition to the many skills that would make her a valuable wife. She hadn't minded, but Grammy Margaret spoke out against their ideas, citing the monarchies run by women and it being the twentieth century, whatever that meant. She also cited herself as someone who had successfully ruled Parley as a woman.

Ember glared at Drystan's retreating form and was tempted to push him to the ground. That would knock the smug look off his face. Instead, she took a deep breath and ran for her grandmother's quarters. If she couldn't go to the royal tea, then she would have her own.

A few days later, Ember was in the crown room. Her stuffed bear, King Teddy, needed a crown for the royal tea. Daddy never minded Ember using the crowns for her parties with her stuffed toys. She knew Drystan hated it terribly and the royal people around Daddy told him it was ridiculous to let her play with things worth so much money.

Daddy always told them it was all stolen anyway. After all, they were the descendants of Samuel Bellamy, also known as Black Bellamy or the Prince of Pirates, the richest pirate during the

Golden Age of Piracy in the early 1700s. Daddy thought it funny all the Crown Jewels of Parley were stolen.

Some of the items had been refined further or taken out of their original settings to be used in other pieces, but all of the original collection of jewels had been stolen. King Emerson scoffed when anyone, including his wife, made a comment about Ember losing a jewel in a crown or tiara she was playing with. He would always say the jewel could be replaced, but children were only children for so long. Besides, Ember only ever used two or three because it's all she could carry out of the room.

Ember had already grabbed her tiara and put it on her head. Now she was after Daddy's crown for King Teddy. He and Drystan weren't using any of the royal jewels today, so it wouldn't be missed if King Teddy wore it for the afternoon. Then she would put it back like she always did with no one the wiser.

Ember pushed a chair over to the display case. She was careful to lift the glass out of the way. As she reached for the crown, a voice startled her from behind.

"What are you doing?"

Ember put a hand to her heart as she glared at Drystan in the doorway.

"King Teddy needs a crown. I always use Daddy's crown, so I was getting it so I can finish getting ready for my tea party. Princess Evie said she is coming to my party," Ember announced triumphantly.

Drystan rolled his eyes and walked over to the display case. "Princess Evelyn is the spare heir to a bankrupt kingdom like I care what she does. And you're not using Father's crown."

"I am too using Daddy's crown. I always do. He doesn't care."

Drystan put the glass back over the crown. "He may not care, but I do. That will be my crown one day and I don't want you playing with it as you declare your stupid stuffed bear king."

Ember stamped her foot on the chair she was standing on. "But it's not your crown, Drystan. It's Daddy's and he doesn't care!"

"It's going to be mine and I do! Use one of yours or don't. I don't care, but you aren't using the crown the sitting king of Parley uses for your stupid tea party!"

Ember glared at Drystan before climbing down from the chair. She grabbed the wagon she had been using to pull her toys and had been going to use for the heavy crown.

"You keep it, Drystan. King Teddy doesn't want to use the crown of a bully anyway."

"I'm not a bully, Ember. You're being a petulant little baby."

"No, Drystan. You're a bully and King Teddy doesn't like bullies. He never wants to wear your crown again. Instead, I am going to make him the most sparkly crown in the entire kingdom."

"You're impossible. And rude!"

Ember turned and stuck her tongue out at Drystan as she exited the room.

She went to the nursery and pulled out craft paper, glue, and glitter. After cutting out the crown and double-checking the fit on Teddy's head, Ember got to work with the glitter. Three containers later, Ember had ensured King Teddy's crown was the sparkliest one in the entire kingdom.

Ember walked to the greenhouse, pulling the wagon behind her. As she opened the door, Ember noticed nothing had been set up. There were linens, dishes, and cutlery on a table, but the table had not been set up. The tea and food trays were also missing.

Ember set about preparing the table. She would need to ring for a maid and request tea and food, but that was something she could do after her important guests arrived.

She had just finished when her grandmother and Princess Evelyn walked in.

"Gracious. Did you set this up yourself?" Grammy Margaret asked as Ember straightened. She had been laying out the final place setting from the chair she was standing on when her grandmother and cousin walked into the room.

Ember smiled. "Yes, Grammy. The maids must have forgotten, but I was able to set up the table. Would you like me to ring for tea?"

Grammy Margaret smiled back. "No, my dear. I'll go to the kitchen myself and request a tray. Why don't you and Evelyn catch up?"

Ember nodded. "Come, Evie. King Teddy needs to be placed in an important spot."

Margaret opened the door and was almost knocked over by an incoming maid. "Oh, beg your pardon, Your Majesty."

Margaret smiled. "It's alright. You've saved me a trip. Can you bring us tea? Ember was supposed to be having a party here. I think with the hustle and bustle of the royal tea it was overlooked."

The maid looked past Margaret, her brow wrinkled. "I do apologize. His Royal Highness, Prince Drystan, said Princess Ember had canceled her tea party, so I didn't finish setting it up."

"Oh. Well, I think Prince Drystan was confused," Margaret told the young woman. "If you could just bring the tea and some treats, I'm sure the girls will be happy."

"Yes, ma'am." The maid curtsied before making a hasty retreat.

"Grammy? Was that a maid?"

Margaret smiled before she turned. She didn't want to tell her granddaughter her older brother had tried to sabotage her tea. Drystan was getting more brazen with this new power he seemed to think he possessed. She was going to need to discuss this matter with her son. There were some things his wife Cilia and his brother-in-law Martin seemed to be working on in the shadows, and it didn't sit well with her.

"Yes, she was confused about the time, my darling."

"Oh. Well, there is much going on. I am certain it was an honest mistake," Ember declared from her seat at the table.

Evelyn giggled. "Oh, Em. I do enjoy your air of maturity."

"King Teddy is a kindly king and understands there is a larger event happening in the ballroom and garden."

"How magnanimous of King Teddy," Grammy Margaret drolled.

"How does it feel to be fourteen?" Ember asked Evelyn, who had celebrated her birthday a few months ago. She had wanted to attend Evelyn's societal debut at her debutante ball, but it hadn't been possible because of Ember's age. Drystan had gone instead.

While many members of the aristocracy didn't formally join society at debutante balls until age sixteen, this was not so for royalty, who were introduced at age fourteen. Many marriages were arranged well before the participants were of age. There was also the possibility of an infant, toddler, or child inheriting the throne from a parent. The sooner the monarch was able to make an official debut at court to join the nightly activities, the better.

Margaret studied the exchange between both girls. She sighed softly. If only Ember and Evelyn were the heirs to their respective thrones rather than their brothers. They were both more than up to the challenge and would be more compassionate than their counterparts.

A week later, it was announced Drystan was going on a trip with their father. Something about Drystan seeing diplomacy in action. Ember didn't know what that meant, just that Drystan was thrilled with his expanded role and she couldn't go.

Ember stood on the platform at the airport with Grammy Margaret. The mid-October air was unseasonably crisp and the breeze was bone-chilling. Emerson had been allowed to say his goodbyes at the palace and was sitting next to the warm fireplace coloring.

Ember wanted to color. Well, she would rather be playing with dolls. Regardless of what she did, she would be warm, and that is really what Ember wished for.

The gray clouds overhead threatened rain. Hurricane season would end in a little over a month, and Ember knew everyone would breathe a little easier whenever storms cropped up. In the meantime, she was standing on a platform in a lightweight coat with gloves, wishing the zeppelin would depart. There had been a delay because of something.

Ember hadn't been paying attention when her father had told Grammy Margaret about it twenty minutes ago. She was busy trying not to shiver or show any form of discomfort because she didn't think that would be ladylike. She didn't want a lecture about it from her mother.

Ember was tired of all the new rules of decorum her mother and instructors insisted upon so Parley could be a world player. Ember usually rolled her eyes at these announcements, which in turn, always started another round of discussions about her "uncouth" behavior.

After what felt like an eternity, the band began to play. Ember stood up straight and moved to her place in front of Grammy Margaret. She watched as her father waved to the crowd. Drystan followed at the proper distance behind him. He too was waving, but Ember knew it was only because it was expected.

Daddy genuinely cared about the people of the island nation, while Drystan saw them as something to control, to rule over, and to profit from. Her brother wasn't a horrible person, just very black and white.

Her father and brother stood on the flight deck of the zeppelin and waved to everyone who had come to see them off. Soon the helium craft would float up into the sky and spirit away her father and brother. Ember wished she could go. She loved flying in the giant airships. But as the spare, she had to stay behind in case something happened.

Ember sighed as she waved. Grammy Margaret promised hot chocolate after this. It wasn't a ride in a zeppelin, but at least it was delicious. And warm.

The tethers from the craft were released, allowing for the accent into the sky. Once at the correct elevation, the pilot began to steer toward the direction of Europe.

"Ready, my dear?" Grammy Margaret asked. She reached for Ember's hand when a popping noise caught their attention. They looked at the zeppelin, but it seemed fine.

The blast was unexpected. Ember stood in awe as she watched the boiler room of the airship explode, catching the silky material of the balloon on fire. The world was silent as the alarms on the burning machine blared while it plummeted to the earth. People on board screamed, and a few of them jumped in a bid for life.

The sound wave from the blast hit Ember's small frame, knocking her to the ground, as the world came alive. There was a cacophony of sound and action as first responders bolted to the blazing wreckage, getting as close as they dared to the scorching heat. The acidic smell of burning metal and fuel overtook the area.

As the shock wave subsided, Ember stood, eyes locking on the red and orange blaze devouring the airship, and screamed for her father and brother. She tried to run to the inferno, but Grammy Margaret scooped her into her arms and walked back towards the palace.

Ember fought her and yelled for her to put her down, but the older woman just kept walking.

Her face and manner were somber as tears streamed down her face, the only sign of her grief for the loss of her son and grandson.

That was the day King Emerson and Prince Drystan died. It was the day Ember became queen.

Chapter 1

10 years later

Ember stood on the veranda off the library as her twin, mother, uncle, and grandmother argued over her fate.

Her mother, Dowager Queen Cilia, and her brother Martin were part of the Crown Guardians, a group of five people who helped rule Parley until she was of sound mind or turned twenty-one. Never mind that she had been coronated as queen at age eight when she had been deemed of sound mind by the lords and ladies of Parley. Her mother had exploited a provision in the constitution for monarchs under the age of ten, and thus, installed the Crown Guardians. Her mother's bid for power had created a rift within the royal family, as well as the powers of government.

Whenever Ember ruled on something or signed something into law, the Guardians were there to chastise her for overreach of her powers, then they would either repeal the law or ruling, or the High Court comprised of members from the founding families would step in. It was frustrating because Ember was undermined regularly, while the Guardians had found loopholes and workarounds to pass their agenda. There was pressure on her to step up and remove the Guardians, but Ember was unsure. Was it what her people wanted? Or was it yet another bid for power by another faction of people?

Ember sighed as she listened to the arguing around a conference table near the military wing, which was Emerson's side of the palace. Their mother had wanted sherry during the course of these negotiations, so they had to accommodate her by moving to a conference room in an area where alcohol was allowed. Emerson was a stickler for the rules and wouldn't budge, especially since he had intended to prevent Cilia from drinking.

The location change had delayed these proceedings by almost an hour. Ember had moved to the balcony to take in the cooler evening air once the dinner hour had come and gone. It wasn't that she didn't care about the negotiations or who she married; rather, these meetings changed nothing. Her plan from the beginning had been to break the engagement and that hadn't changed.

The Guardians had arranged a marriage for her when she was fourteen with the second son of the American prime minister, which had been controversial from the start. Only three of the five Guardians approved the marriage. Because the patriarch of the church was a Guardian, he had recused himself because he was blessing the engagement in his capacity as head of the church. The only Guardian to oppose the arrangement was the solicitor.

Ember was furious over the engagement because she didn't have the power to break it on her own. Under Parley law, if the monarch or Crown Guardians accepted an engagement with the blessing of the church patriarch, then only the Duke of Revenge could convene the High Court and the Lessor Lords to break it. The thought behind the checks and balances had been because marriage is a sacred and serious act, and agreeing to marry shouldn't be taken lightly. She agreed. She just wished there was another way because no one had asked her what she wanted.

When Grammy Margaret had learned the news three years ago, Ember had thought she would murder her daughter-in-law on the spot. To say she hadn't been happy with the news was an understatement. Parlian royalty typically married within the United Kingdoms or Europe. There was also the matter of Ember being allowed to choose her husband. Zephyr had been introduced to her shortly after she turned thirteen years old, then the following year their engagement was announced before her debut ball. Parley and Ember never had a chance at a better option, let alone any option.

The sticking point at the moment was the original marriage contract concessions. Under the original deal, Zephyr Levan was to be made king regent rather than king consort. This meant upon marriage he would have the same powers as Ember. Prime Minister Wilson Levan didn't want to negotiate different terms because he got what he wanted, no questions asked by the Guardians. As the Director of Intelligence and Military Operations, Emerson had only been able to dissolve the original marriage terms citing national security. This had brought everyone back to the table for negotiations, which hadn't made Cilia or Wilson happy.

"Perhaps we should pick this up again tomorrow? It's well past dinner and the servants have been waiting for hours," Wilson observed.

Martin pulled out his pocket watch. "You're right. Shall we adjourn to freshen up and then convene in the dining room in a half hour?"

The trilling noise coming from Ember's mother set her teeth on edge. "It will barely be enough time for us ladies to change and freshen up, but I'm sure we can manage."

Grammy Margaret shot daggers at her mother. Ember was surprised her grandmother hadn't made some excuse to have her removed from the conversation after the second decanter of sherry had been polished off.

"It shan't be a problem for me. Although you, Dowager, have always been fond of making an entrance," Grammy Margret retorted before she hurried from the room. Her uncle, the prime minister, and mother quickly followed.

Emerson remained in the background, as did Zephyr, her apparent fiancé.

"Well, my dear Queen Ember, what do you think of our match?"

Zephyr moved to stand next to her on the veranda. She had met Zephyr four years ago after his father had been elected to a first term. His family had been the prime minister of America for two generations. Zephyr's older brother, Caelus, was expected to carry on the political legacy, while Zephyr was expected to secure the means to do so. He knew her thoughts on their match.

"If your father and brother think they will gain access to our resources to exploit them for personal gain, they may want to think again." Ember's tone was sweet but she never took her eyes off the ocean in front of her.

Zephyr chuckled before leaning over and whispering in her ear. His breath tickled the sensitive flesh and sent a shiver down her spine.

"Come now. The goal is to build a strong trade partnership. Nothing more. It's been this way for the past three years since your debut."

Ember turned her fiery jade gaze upon him. "Yes, for three years you have been foisted upon me. No one talks of anything else, and yet, no one knows the things I do as monarch."

Zephyr threw his head back and laughed. "Oh, Ember. How you do amuse me so. You host social gatherings, play queen, and keep the natives happy."

He continued, waving a hand dismissively in the air. "Your knowledge of current events, the law, and military happenings are perfunctory at best."

Ember's knuckles turned white as she gripped the railing. She took a deep breath, letting the salty air calm her. She wasn't going to let him get under her skin.

"Perfunctory? I was coronated at age eight, exactly three months after my father and brother died. I am the queen. Regardless of what some think, I know my role."

Zephyr came closer. He reached a hand up to play with a stray lock of Ember's chestnut hair. "You needn't worry about such things. Men were built to rule."

Ember lifted a well-groomed eyebrow. "Really? What of the United Kingdoms? We all answer to the High Queen, even your democracy."

Zephyr shrugged. "Confidence in her is slipping. Give it time and she will fall. When that happens, Parley will be there to fill the political void."

Ember laughed mirthlessly. "And how would we manage that? By using the natural resources you, your family, and others will be stripping from us?"

Zephyr sighed. He raked a hand through his hair.

"I already told you nothing of the sort would happen."

Ember rolled her eyes as she walked past him. She was going to her room and requesting a dinner tray. This would allow her plenty of time for a restorative soak in a bath before the food was brought. If she was lucky, she might even have time to read Evelyn's letter.

"Lie to me again, Zeph," Ember retorted as she reached for the door handle.

"I love you."

Ember paused. "You bastard," she spat before slamming the door behind her.

His laughter followed her as she retreated to her quarters.

"You don't have to bait her. We both know she is the queen, whether others want to acknowledge the truth or not," Emerson said as he emerged from the shadows.

Zephyr walked over to the table and sank into a chair.

"I know. They want to change everything about the monarchy and how it's structured. They want me to be king regent rather than king consort. If the Guardians don't achieve that goal one way, then they will another."

Emerson took a seat across from him. Zephyr wasn't the enemy. Although Ember very much viewed him as one. Emerson on the other hand knew that while Zephyr was all about protecting his self-interests, he also saw the larger picture.

Ember was the queen. They could interpret the laws and various passages however they wanted, but Sam Bellamy made it very clear how the line of succession worked. He was the first king, and founder of Parley, along with the other prominent pirates of the time. Upon his death, the crown was passed down to his eldest child. That child happened to be a male heir, but there was nothing stating a woman couldn't be queen and lead the country.

Grammy Margaret herself had been queen regent for years until the death of her husband. At that time, she had decided to step down and pass the crown to her son, Emerson, because her grief had consumed her. She had felt her heart wasn't into ruling her people, and she did not want to drag them down with her. So she stepped down as regent and passed the duty to her eldest son.

There also wasn't a stipulation of age. The law stated as soon as the heir was of sound mind they would lead the country. Of course, the court advisors, the prime minister of America, and his mother felt this was too vague. They had been making changes and stripping Ember of her power for almost a decade. The latest power grab was to install an outsider as king regent, putting him on the same level as her.

Grammy Margaret had been fighting and trying to stop them but to no avail. Once the Duke of Revenge had left the islands three years ago after the love of his life had died, it had created waves for a number of people in a number of ways. This had led to Ember's engagement to Zephyr being uncontested. The marriage renegotiations began about eighteen months ago when the original terms of the contract were brought to Emerson's attention.

The current proposition would be a lucrative deal for America; allowing the country to strip mine caymanite and pearls, as well as harvest much of the indigenous plant life, such as orchids, to secure more wealth and power. With Zephyr as king, Cilia and Wilson could do whatever they wanted. Thus, began the restructuring of Parley in a way that better benefited everyone in the world the pair was beholden to, but its citizens.

"We should go riding tomorrow, Emerson," Zephyr mused.

"Why?"

Zephyr studied his nails for a moment before responding. "It's been a while since I've been on the back of a horse. As my future brother-in-law, I think this would be a great way to bond."

Emerson shot Zephyr a skeptical look. "Fine. I have some meetings in the morning, but can manage around brunch time."

Zephyr clapped his hands together. "Excellent. Should I request a basket from the kitchen?"

Emerson pursed his lips. How long was this ride supposed to last? He may not be the king, but as the top military strategist, he was quite busy. He was trying to track down a man who didn't want to be found, as well as find a way to stop this marriage. Meanwhile, Zephyr wanted to go for a ride, have a leisurely meal, and get to know each other. Fantastic.

"Sure. Why not. It's not like I'm busy," Emerson drolled.

"Wonderful! We shall make a day of it."

The bell rang, announcing dinner. Emerson scrubbed a hand over his face.

"We best get moving. Don't want to be late," Zephyr noted.

Emerson lifted his gaze to meet Zephyr's. "Yes. I need to change my jacket and tie. I'll join you in a moment."

The other man nodded and left the room. Emerson sighed. He knew his sister was barricading herself in her room. He didn't blame her.

Attending dinner was more efficient at this point than ordering a tray to his room or office. He was buried presently under a myriad of details but didn't have time to address anything fully because his afternoons were filled with pointless negotiations, which would be the death of him.

He stood and walked to the door. The target of Emerson's investigation had dropped off the face of the earth months ago. It would keep a few more days.

Chapter 2

"We need him."

Ember sighed as she brushed her hair in preparation for bed.

Emerson had delivered her tray and told her the happenings at dinner, which was more of the same polite, stilted conversation that surrounded her outside of the negotiations. Grammy Margaret had also declined to dine with everyone, so Ember felt heartened to know she wasn't the only person at her breaking point.

Regardless of how the Crown Guardians, and others, felt or viewed her duties, she still needed to perform them. Sitting in negotiations almost every day of the week for hours at a time left little energy or time to devote to anything else, like tenant and landlord disputes, spats between lords, foreign policy, economic matters, keeping up on the current affairs in Parley and abroad, in addition to the usual requests for her to attend charity functions and other events. The discussions hammering out her marriage to Zephyr were ridiculous at best and ludicrous at worst.

The country was preparing for the tenth anniversary of her father and brother's deaths, as well as her decade-long reign a few months after that. All her focus should be on those celebrations rather than preparing for a wedding in nine months that no one in

Parley wanted. A wedding she wanted nothing to do with and had been trying to find a way out of. Ending the engagement put her one step closer to her independence as a monarch.

"I know, Em. The only thing I can think of to stop them is to convene the High Court, which is something that hasn't been done in at least a century for a monarch's marriage," Ember said.

"Desperate times, Your Majesty," Emerson quipped.

Ember's gaze shot up to her twin's in the mirror. The dark circles under his eyes and the tight lines around his mouth told her he was as exhausted as she was. His annoyed tone was as familiar as this discussion.

"Do you know where Kieran is? Of all the High Court, he is the most important."

"Don't you think I don't know that?" Emerson hissed. "If I didn't have to be at those absurd negotiations, I could find him faster."

Ember sat down with her hair brush. "He's usually not unreachable for more than a few months at a time. Have you asked his sisters? Aren't they at Blackstone Manor in Nassau?"

"That was the first place I went! The estate is in disrepair because the money isn't there anymore. His father and grandfather neglected the property. Taking the money and using it for their every whim."

Kieran Edmund Wolf Thache was the tenth Duke of Revenge and held the only other title on the same level as Ember and Emerson. Three years ago, Kieran had lost the love of his life, Willow. This loss was the catalyst for Kieran relinquishing his military duties to become a mercenary, and leaving Parley, as well as his duchy and tenants.

The Duchy of Revenge was comprised of the island chain of the Bahamas and given to Edward Thache, Jr., better known as the pirate Blackbeard. When their seven-time great-grandfather, Sam Bellamy retired as Black Bellamy, he did so by taking over the Caribbean islands. This angered the whole of Europe.

Not only had Black Bellamy, Blackbeard, Calico Jack, Anne Bonny, Mary Read, Black Bart, and Olivier Levasseur, also known as The Buzzard, become some of the richest pirates by robbing these countries, but they poured salt in the wound by kicking them out of the Caribbean, which they renamed Parley. Other pirates joined them and retired to the various islands. Many were given titles along with their land, but none held as much power as the seven founding families.

Each island was its own recognized state and they had a representative, typically the descendent of the retiring pirate who held the title of either baron or viscount. However, with over 100 islands making up the kingdom of Parley, it had been necessary to leave major world decisions to the founding families. Of course, if enough of the smaller lords didn't agree with the direction, they could appeal the decision.

All the lords would convene to hear all sides of the matter, and then everyone voted. Sometimes the founding families were overruled, other times they won the vote. But the most important thing was everyone in Parley had a voice, and people felt things were fair and this maintained confidence in their government.

"Ember, are you even listening to me?"

Her brother's annoyed tone brought her back to the present. Kieran was off the grid when she and Parley needed him the most. Willow's unexpected death had destroyed him. His overall disinterest in his military career, duchy, sisters, and life was creating complications she couldn't afford.

"Sorry, Emerson. Do we know if he took a contract?"

Emerson glared daggers at her before snorting. "Does he even work off contracts anymore, Ember? I warned you — no — told you he was flirting with the grey area! His last kill was some prince in Africa! I'm not sure how deep I want to dig into that because I'm scared of what I'll find."

Ember hung her head. He was right. He had warned her and argued with her about Kieran's work as a mercenary on more than one occasion, especially over the past year. Willow had been his compass. She had kept him from drifting too far into the dark. Ember could see now how naïvely hopeful she had been to think Willow's memory would keep Kieran from getting into trouble.

"If he killed the prince then I'm sure it was justified. He only kills the dregs of society."

Emerson stared open-mouthed at her.

"What?" Ember asked.

"Are you serious? He killed a damn prince!" Emerson roared.

Ember winced. Her twin hardly ever yelled or really let his emotions overtake him. He was clearly livid with Kieran and her. At the same time though, how was she supposed to control him? Demand he change career paths? Their ancestors were pirates for god's sake.

"Enough! I am your queen before I am your sister."

"Then damn well start acting like it!"

Ember threw her hairbrush down onto her vanity and whirled to face him. The same fiery jade eyes stared back at her as she looked up into his face.

"How! They are trying to take everything, Emerson! Everything! What am I to do?"

The anger between them seemed to evaporate as her words sank in. Emerson raked a hand through his hair and fell into a chair near the fireplace.

Ember studied him. They had the same jawline and nose. Despite being fraternal twins, they shared many similarities. The only obvious difference between the pair, aside from their gender, was their hair color. Ember's was a dark chestnut, while Emerson's was jet black, which was a trait of the Bellamy line.

"Take the trip," Emerson conceded.

"Excuse me?" Ember asked as she pulled herself from her thoughts.

"Take the trip to visit Evelyn for her birthday. I'll stay here and gather the rest of the High Court. Then we'll be ready for Kieran's arrival," Emerson explained pinching the bridge of his nose.

"You thought visiting Geneva right now was a bad idea. Grammy Margaret as well. What's changed?" Ember eyed him with suspicion.

Emerson stared at the fireplace surround as the silence stretched between them. Ember moved to sit in the chair across from him. Emerson warred with himself over how much he should reveal to her regarding information his intelligence officers were hearing. He was sure she would be surprised by the number of things he kept from her.

Often after a brief investigation, it became clear the information was speculation, rumor, hearsay, or not worth the time of the monarch. After all, she paid him and other advisers to handle daily tasks. This meant handling a good portion of the military and intelligence happenings with Ember none the wiser.

"Evelyn's birthday celebration is in a few weeks. The remembrance for Dad and Drystan is in October, followed by the celebration of your reign for a decade in January. I've been speaking to the head of security for Geneva for a few weeks now, and after working out the logistics, you can take an airship there for the festivities."

So matter of fact. No emotion in any of those words. Emerson almost seemed resigned to some fate she didn't yet understand and wasn't sure if she wanted to. She would go insane if she had to filter through even a quarter of the information he had to in a day.

"You didn't think I would be safe in Geneva, which is why I wasn't going. What's changed?"

Emerson dropped his head in his hands. "Ember, I don't think you're safe anywhere at the moment, but I'm becoming more certain by the day that if you stay in Parley, with your current predictable schedule, I'll lose you."

Tears fell from Ember's eyes. After the death of their father and brother, Emerson devoted himself to being the best bodyguard and strategist Parley had ever seen. He felt he had failed them by not seeing the danger, despite having only been seven when they died.

Ember knew he still had an open investigation into the zeppelin explosion. Emerson had never completely believed it was an accident. There had been a time when the investigation had consumed him, but then something shifted within him. Ember wasn't sure what, just that his focus turned more to living and protecting her.

"I'm not enough to keep you safe anymore, Em. My attention is split in too many directions at the moment, and I'm not ruling out that it isn't on purpose. I won't lose you —" His voice broke.

Ember leaned forward and grabbed his hands. His eyes glistened with unshed tears.

"It's okay. It's going to be okay. I'll work on finding Kieran. He's my problem. If he's home, he can help you as well as me. You create my schedule for the next few weeks until I leave for Geneva."

Emerson wiped his eyes. "I'm going to talk with our grandmother in the morning before I call her brother, King Andrew of Astonia. He recently announced Evelyn as the heir to his throne rather than her mother, and he put together a solid security detail for her in advance."

"Are you hoping he can spare a few extras?"

"Yes. I need help once you return from the trip. I won't let pride or arrogance or anything get in the way of your safety. I won't make the mistakes Father's team did," Emerson vowed.

Ember smiled wobbly. "I know you won't. I love you."

Emerson stood and pulled Ember into a tight hug. "I love you too."

The humid late June air slammed into Emerson as he and Zephyr rode their horses to the spot along the cliffs overlooking the harbor in Careen, the capital city of Parley, located on the island of Cuba. He still wasn't sure what the American wanted to discuss, but he was willing to play along to find out.

Upon arriving at the clearing, Zephyr dismounted and walked toward the edge of the cliff. Below was the crystal clear water of the Parley Sea. Several ships were in the harbor, including a number of naval ships. The people dotting the piers, working and going about their lives, looked like ants from this distance.

Emerson grabbed their mounts and tied them to a nearby post. He grabbed the picnic basket and set it on a table under the gazebo. The fragrance of the butterfly jasmine climbing the structure was a nice change from the musky, tobacco scent of his office.

"This view never gets old. I see why your father built a discreet little hideaway here."

Emerson didn't respond. He truly didn't care why his father did what he did. What he wanted to know was what Zephyr wanted. Why did he want to meet with him?

"Yes, the view of the harbor is splendid," he retorted. "Why are we out here?"

Zephyr laughed. "You are so serious for seventeen. Sometimes I forget how young you are. Let's eat and then we can discuss business."

Emerson rolled his eyes. Zephyr was twenty-one with golden brown hair that complimented his sun-kissed skin. He was athletic, tall, eloquent, and had this way of making you feel like the only person in the world when he spoke to you. He had amber eyes that shifted in intensity with his mood.

It was because of this charismatic personality Emerson remained guarded around him at all times. Women practically threw themselves at him. Even Ember had admitted he was devilishly good-looking, and that his freckles added to his boyish charm.

Until four years ago, Emerson had believed Zephyr lived a charmed life by all verified accounts. However, when Zephyr was seventeen he was framed for a crime his older brother Caelus had committed. It had led to a dark eighteen-month period for the young man. When Emerson investigated him further, he learned it wasn't the first time Zephyr had been framed for Caelus's crimes. This had shocked him and had him trying to discover what else he didn't know about the Levan family.

As Zephyr prattled on about heaven knew what during the meal, Emerson busied himself with prioritizing his agenda for the rest of the day and week in his head. He hadn't gotten to the top of intelligence for queen and country because he was a prince. He had earned it, especially because he was so young. If his being guarded and silent with his queen's fiancé bordered on rude, that wasn't his problem. That's how everyone stayed alive.

Finally, Zephyr crumpled his cloth napkin and threw it on the table. Emerson perked up and leaned forward. He was eager to learn the reason he was dragged out on a ride and a picnic.

"How does Parley get its pearls?"

Emerson sat dumbfounded for a moment. This was about pearls? The meeting Zephyr had thrown together on a whim to better get to know him, his future brother-in-law, was about pearls?

"I could not possibly have heard you correctly. Did you seriously just ask me how Parley gets pearls?" Emerson was seething with rage. This spoiled dignitary didn't have things to do, but he damn well did.

"Yes. The pearls Parley has are the finest in the world. Is there some secret to it?"

He was serious. Zephyr wanted to know about the pearl trade from the head of military strategy and intelligence of Parley.

"This is an *astounding* waste of my time. Do you know that? I have a security plan to finalize for Ember's trip to Geneva in a few weeks, and another to plan for the remembrance ceremony in four months. Not to mention the day-to-day happenings as people come in and out for that event," Emerson railed at the young man, who seemed nonchalant about everything in life.

Emerson continued his rant, ignoring the lack of reaction on Zephyr's part. "I have to keep Ember safe, as well as every noble, visitor, and citizen of this country. I am constantly looking into possible threats against us. Meanwhile, you want to discuss pearls!"

Emerson stood from the table. He was out of there. He had things to do and Zephyr was not high on the list of priorities. If he hurried back, he might be able to reach King Andrew or the head of his security.

"You don't happen to get them from an underwater kingdom of say merpeople?"

Zephyr's words froze Emerson in place. He turned to find the young man casually studying his fingernails while he leaned back in his chair.

"What did you say?"

Zephyr stood and walked over to Emerson. "I asked if Parley gets its pearls from mermaids and mermen."

Emerson stared blankly at Zephyr for a moment before bursting into laughter.

Zephyr waited for his laughter to quiet.

"Oh, that's too good, Zephyr. No, the natives train dolphins and crabs to scour the sea floor for the rarest pearls in the entire ocean," Emerson retorted, sarcasm dripping from every word.

"Lie to me all you want, Emerson. I know what I saw."

Emerson kept an amused smile on his face. He would never tell Zephyr how they harvest pearls. He also sincerely doubted any of the natives told him a thing. This meant someone was careless. However, Emerson wasn't worried. Who was going to believe there were merpeople in Parley without proof?

"And what did you see, Zephyr?"

"I saw a child run into the ocean and then transform and swim away. Her parents noticed me too late. They said nothing, but I could see the terror in their eyes."

Of course, it was a child. Emerson knew of only one family in Careen who lived near the ocean with their small daughter. They were Native and Mer.

Of course, it had to be Zephyr who stumbled upon the centuries-old secret of Parley. This was an entirely new complication he didn't need. Ember and Grammy Margaret were going to panic when they heard the news, but he didn't need to tell them right away. He was supposed to meet with both of them at some point during the next week, he would just slip it into conversation and be done with it.

Emerson kept smiling even though he wanted to punch the man in his smug face.

"What's your point? Are you going to tell your father? Then we can have countries descend upon us, trying to discover these supposed 'merpeople,' and destroy everything in the process," Emerson observed.

"I won't say anything. You trust me more than Ember does, and I know it's still very little at best," Zephyr conceded.

"True. You also sound touched in the head, with your talk of an underwater kingdom."

Zephyr sighed and nodded. He looked back to the ocean and harbor. He watched the breeze play with the palm trees, and caress the lilies and ferns dotting the cliff's edge. He knew he sounded insane. He had tried to come up with a million rational explanations for what he saw, but the simplest answer was there was another species of half-human half-fish creatures living in the ocean.

Emerson stared at him in silence, waiting for him to continue. Zephyr chewed on his lower lip. Should he put all his cards on the table? He needed help. Caelus was doing far more in Belize than visiting his girlfriend. Due to his proximity to Central America, it would be an easy task to pin the activity on him, like they did before.

"I don't want to marry Ember. I would love nothing more than for her to find a way to break the engagement," Zephyr confessed as he scrubbed a hand through his hair. "I'll be the first to say I shouldn't bait her the way I do because I do enjoy her company. Sometimes she's the only sane person I can talk to. We're just wrong for each other."

Emerson stayed silent and watched as Zephyr paced back and forth before him.

"I was over in that area of Careen because my father and brother are trying to purchase a pearl farm as well as a caymanite mine. I learned of this by accident, so I wanted to investigate because Ember is right, we all know it, my father and Parliament will exploit everything they can."

"Foreigners aren't allowed to own pearl farms or mines in Parley. It's a matter of national security," Emerson said with a frown.

Zephyr shrugged. "I'm not sure how they are going about doing any of this. I only know what they are doing. And if there really are merpeople, then I hate to think what they'll do to them."

Emerson studied Zephyr's face and body language. His tone wasn't threatening, just a matter of fact. He also seemed resigned to whatever fate befell him. Knowing the extent to which Wilson had gone to save Caelus in the past, something big had to be looming on the horizon for Zephyr to confide in him.

"Why are you telling me this?" Emerson was skeptical there wasn't some ulterior motive.

"Because at some point I'm going to need a favor and protection."

Emerson scrubbed a hand over his face. "What did you do?"

"Nothing. It's my family's dirty laundry. Things seem to be closing in on Caelus. He's caught up in drug dealing if what my grandma is telling me is correct. This means marriage to Ember is my way out, but if that doesn't happen, then I'm the scapegoat. Again."

Emerson knew the eldest son of the prime minister was something of a wild child. Caelus liked to party hard, entertain women, and spend money on things that may or may not always be legal. Wilson also had no problem bailing him out of trouble, even at the expense of his younger sons. It was well known Zephyr had been framed for Caelus's most horrific crime to date, but very few knew of the petty thefts, drug charges, and battery charges Zephyr and his younger brother Neil took the rap for. This illustrated the lengths Wilson would go to protect his golden child.

"Marriage to Ember saves you at the cost of Parley. Who is blackmailing your family?"

Zephyr toed the ground. "The better question is who *isn't* blackmailing my family."

"Damnit." Emerson ran a hand through his short beard.

"You don't have to help me. I won't say anything about the merpeople. People would think I'm crazy. I'll try to find another way."

Emerson watched as Zephyr deflated before him. The young man seemed to be out of moves to play. He could have kept all the information to himself regarding his father's plans and what he had seen. Instead, Zephyr had come to him and then tried to poorly leverage the information to help keep him and Parley safe. This confirmed to Emerson what he had known all along — Zephyr was a good person who hid behind a carefree persona to keep people at bay.

"Why come out here to tell me all this?"

Zephyr looked surprised. "Because the walls in the palace have ears."

Emerson already knew that, but he was glad to hear Zephyr was also aware of this. It gave him some peace of mind knowing Zephyr paid attention to his words, actions, and surroundings. Whenever he needed to discuss something of great importance with Ember, it was done on the move or in their private section of the palace because Emerson didn't always trust those mingling around his office.

Emerson looked up at the sky and then let out a deep sigh. God help him, he hoped he didn't regret what he was about to do.

"Keep Ember safe until she leaves for Geneva and I'll protect you when the time comes."

Zephyr's eyes widened at his declaration. "Truly?"

Emerson ran his hands through his hair. "Yes. You have my word."

Chapter 3

Ember wasn't sure what had gotten into Zephyr. Or Emerson for that matter. Suddenly, Zephyr wouldn't leave her side and Emerson thought this was fantastic. She was either losing her mind or living in an alternate reality. There didn't seem to be a third option.

As she reached for the cake samples, Zephyr slapped her hand away. She arched an eyebrow at him. Who in their right mind would do that to the sitting queen? Ember was both amused and annoyed by his actions. What in the devil had gotten into him?

"Allow me, Your Majesty."

He took a bite of each sample, waiting a minute between bites before moving on to the next sample. Ember's eyes narrowed as she watched him. What on earth was going on?

"They are safe for your consumption, my darling," Zephyr smiled at her.

"Of course they're safe. What is *wrong* with you?" Ember seethed. Her patience for having a taste tester was wearing thin. She just wanted this task to be done. It was hard enough planning the food for the remembrance without the added interruption of Zephyr's antics.

She grabbed a fork and took a bite of each sample. When she reached for the water, Zephyr grabbed a glass and poured from the pitcher, drinking from the glass first, before handing it to her.

"I want the lemon cake with raspberry filling and chocolate buttercream with a milk chocolate ganache," Ember told the royal baker. The sooner the food decisions were made, the faster she could move on to something else.

"Yes, Your Majesty."

Ember turned, grabbing Zephyr's hand. "My darling Zeph, let's take a stroll in the garden. It is such a lovely day, and the roses are in bloom."

Before he could speak, Ember all but dragged him from the room, through the Goody Rose Garden, and straight to the fountain in the middle.

"What is going on, Zephyr? And don't tell me nothing. You have been tasting my food, drinking from my glass, and acting bizarre for a week now," Ember hissed.

She was careful to keep her voice down so the sound of the water falling from the fountain would obscure her words should anyone decide to try to listen. The gentle scent of rose filled the air, which took the edge off her mood.

"I don't know what you're talking about," Zephyr deflected.

"Cut the nonsense. Tell me what is going on."

Zephyr stared into her eyes for a moment before letting out a sigh and sitting on the edge of the fountain. He motioned for her to sit next to him on the cool marble expanse.

"Emerson asked me to be more vigilant when I'm with you," Zephyr admitted.

"And you think you're being discreet when you shove my hand out of the way or grab the fork from my fingers? Or refuse to let me drink from my glass?" Ember observed.

Zephyr's cheeks flushed red. "I'm sorry. I've never had to protect anyone before."

Ember let out a short laugh. She closed her eyes and shook her head. Emerson had failed to mention his agreement with Zephyr, more than likely because he wanted to have some fun and see how things progressed. These little antics at times were proof his playful nature still existed.

"Why would you? You're a prime minister's son. You have a protection detail."

The pair sat in silence, each retreating to their thoughts. Ember studied the various colored roses around the garden. This garden had been created in the mid-1700s by Black Bellamy for his wife, Goody, to celebrate their tenth wedding anniversary. It was also named in honor of her.

The first bushes planted had been the original white tea roses from China. This was followed by cabbage roses from North America, which gave the garden its floral scent. Everyone knew the most fragrant roses originated from North America, or so she had been told. From there, Sam had allowed Goody to pick and plant whatever roses she wanted in her garden.

A second rose garden dedicated specifically to tea roses had been added by their great-great-grandson for his wife in the early 1800s for their tenth wedding anniversary. This was where all formal teas took place in the kingdom of Parley, and was near the formal atrium and ballrooms.

No expense was spared in the creation of the formal atrium, which was accessible by either ballroom and the formal dining room. The fourth wall of the atrium was actually a gate that gave access to the tea garden. In addition to the tea roses, there were herbs planted throughout the planters to create the tea blends served at the events, as well as the daily blends at the palace.

"Why does Emerson trust you?"

Zephyr shot her a sad grin. "Because I warned him about something my father was doing. He agreed to help me if I protect you."

"But why? What if you get hurt or are killed?"

Zephyr shrugged. "I'm used to being second fiddle. My life matters very little in comparison to those I'm meant to support."

Ember jumped away from him slightly at his words. They stung her heart with their truth.

She studied Zephyr's profile. He was handsome, charismatic, intelligent, and interesting. If their engagement hadn't been arranged, maybe she would have considered him a worthy suitor rather than the enemy. Underneath all the bravado and arrogance was a kind, insecure soul similar to her own.

Emerson had told her a few times Zephyr wasn't the enemy, the situation was. Sitting next to him on the fountain, Ember understood what her twin had perceived so clearly.

She grabbed Zephyr's hand and laid her head on his shoulder. He flinched and stiffened at the sudden contact. After a minute he relaxed and squeezed her hand briefly.

"So, how goes breaking our engagement? Are you making any progress?"

Ember barked out a laugh. "Oh, Zephyr. I don't know what to say."

He turned and smiled at her. "You can tell me you're close to ending this farce."

Ember closed her eyes. "It's nice to hear you think it's a farce too. But no. I haven't made any meaningful progress yet. I'm looking for someone."

"Kieran Thache?"

She nodded into his shoulder. "Yes. He's the only person who can convene the High Court in certain circumstances, like breaking an engagement blessed by the Guardians and the patriarch of the church. It's how Parley was set up and part of the checks and balances."

Ember chewed on her lower lip for a moment before adding, "Although, there is a contingency in place if he can't be found. It's never been used before, and I don't want to be the first monarch to call for it."

"The High Court is one of the things my father, your uncle, and your mother haven't been able to figure out how to disband," Zephyr mused.

"I know. They are our only hope at the moment."

Silence settled over them again. The steady flow of water from the fountain created a peaceful backdrop to the white, pink, lavender, red, and yellow hues of the garden. The breeze was cooler, but neither minded. It was a nice respite from the summer heat.

"I heard Kieran killed an African prince and then dropped off the map."

Ember huffed out a breath. "You're the second person to tell me that in a matter of a few weeks."

"No one actually knows who killed the prince," Zephyr admitted hastily. "He was a horrific man, not many, if anyone, is mourning his passing. He was also from some obscure European country and a lower member of the aristocracy. I doubt a war will be waged over his demise."

Ember sighed as she rubbed her forehead with her fingers. "Kieran was sticking to political enemies of the Crown and fugitives. Then a few years ago the love of his life died and his soul went with her."

Zephyr nodded. "That's understandable."

"Still, I thought he would be home for the anniversary. It's a milestone and I need him here to maintain appearances. It's been almost three years since I've seen him, and six months at least since his last letter."

Kieran was seven years older than her. In a few short months, he would be twenty-five. Despite being born outside wedlock to his father's mistress, Kieran was the firstborn and had been raised a duke. He knew his duty. He had vowed to never embarrass her when he pledged his loyalty to her at her coronation. If he didn't turn up soon, then he would do just that, and on the world stage no less.

His absence would be a silent reminder she had no control over her lords despite being the reigning monarch. Her fear was it would help pave the way for the prime minister to further argue her incompetence. If he could turn the lords and citizens against her, then he and Cilia could continue utilizing the power of the Guardians to get everything they wanted.

"Is there anything I can do to help?" Zephyr offered.

Ember sucked in her lower lip. She had about three months until the remembrance ceremony. Her options were limited to going over everything Emerson had gathered or trying to get a message to him, which he had been ignoring for some time now. The first option would take more time than she had due to her social engagements and responsibilities. For the second option to work, she would need to know where he was, unless…

"You need to commission his services. I'm sure Emerson would know how that works," Ember exclaimed jumping up from the fountain. She was excited by this new idea. Why hadn't she thought of this weeks ago?

Ember took off through the garden with a singular purpose — finding Emerson so Zephyr could put out a commission to kill someone.

Zephyr quickly caught up to Ember as she strode through some hallway. He was slightly winded.

"Kieran only takes commissions to kill corrupt leaders or to locate dangerous fugitives and bring them in dead or alive," Zephyr whispered as he kept an eye on their surroundings. "Who would I even commission to kill?"

Ember's jade eyes sparkled. "Your father."

Zephyr stumbled at her words but recovered quickly. "What?"

Ember ignored him as she moved through the main hallway to a staircase tucked away near the servant areas of the palace. She climbed to the second floor with Zephyr in tense silence.

It was clear by his reaction he didn't like her plan. She couldn't blame him though. Mercenaries and government agents were a messy business. Ember didn't know much about them and preferred to keep it that way.

Emerson on the other hand knew about them. If something ever happened with one of the operatives, he would step in and fix it. This left Ember with the ability to deny any knowledge of the operation if the newspapers or radio outlets caught wind of it. Things only became national or international news when they went bad. Ember appreciated being able to deny knowledge of something publicly while making heads rolls in private.

Once they were in the military wing, Ember took another staircase which led to the offices occupied by the top brass and her brother. People in the hallway paused to acknowledge her presence as she strode past them, straight into Emerson's office.

"I need a word with you," Ember declared while her twin glared at her.

"That would be wonderful. Can I pass you to my secretary to get this arranged? My queen has just entered my office," Emerson told the person on the other end.

Greer, her brother's secretary, picked up the line and continued the phone call with the Astonian Security Council. Emerson folded his arms across his chest and waited for his sister to speak.

"I need your help," Ember announced.

"So I surmised when you waltzed in here." Emerson's tone was flat. His eyes were hard and narrowed in her direction. Ember brushed it off.

"Zephyr needs your help hiring a mercenary to kill his father."

Emerson's gaze shot to Zephyr who was looking at the floor, trying not to draw attention to himself. "Why?"

"Kieran only takes private contracts. I figured Zephyr could hire him to kill Wilson, who is one of the dregs of society," Ember explained. "It fits his pattern. Then when he takes the job, we'll know where he is and bring him home."

Her twin sat dumbfounded in his chair for several beats. His gaze darted back and forth between the pair. Was she serious? Zephyr looked nauseous while Ember looked annoyed.

Emerson shook his head. "I'm sorry, you want to do what?"

"I already explained it to you," Ember snapped. She was tapping her foot as she waited for his answer. She didn't know the first thing about contracting hits using mercenaries. That was more his territory.

Emerson looked back and forth between the pair and then started laughing. Of course, his sister would think putting out a contract kill on a famous world leader would get Kieran out of hiding. No one in their right mind would contract a hit like that, let alone respond to the request.

"I don't know why you're laughing! You're the one who is concerned about his work lately. Wouldn't this be right up his alley?" Ember folded her arms across her chest as she glared at her twin.

"He's a mercenary, not an idiot. So, no. Talking to someone about taking a contract that would amount to a world war is not Kieran's typical work."

Emerson loved his sister. She was a never-ending well of amusement. Wait until he told their grandmother. She would be in hysterics much like he had been.

That said. Ember's idea wasn't completely without merit. He turned and opened a drawer in the cabinet behind him. Emerson rifled through the files before pulling one out.

"What's that?" Zephyr asked. Ember was annoyed with Emerson. He knew she would give him the silent treatment until he made amends. However, she surprised him. Apparently, she wasn't giving up her idea without a fight.

"Zephyr can contract a hit on me. It would appear to be a credible threat and Kieran would come back to keep me safe."

There was a smug hopefulness in Ember's posture, tone, and expression. She wasn't going to drop this until he put it to rest, and then pushed her in the direction he wanted. Two birds, one stone.

Rumors were circulating about the revival of a century-old revenge plot. He didn't put much stock in the report, but if Ember thought this would lead to Kieran's return, and get her to stop suggesting murdering world leaders, then it was a win-win. Emerson shook his head and set the file down. He perched on the edge of his desk facing his sister.

"I hate to burst your bubble…"

"No, you don't."

"There have been several credible threats to your safety and life over the past few years, and Kieran hasn't come home," Emerson told her. "You're just not that important."

A sharp pain lanced through Ember's heart, but she pushed it aside. He had to be joking. Ember narrowed her eyes. "People have threatened my life — the life of his queen — and he ignored it?"

"It's not like he hasn't lifted a finger to help us when there are threats to your life. He just doesn't come back to the islands because of it." Emerson shrugged.

Two bright red spots appeared on Ember's cheeks. She felt her life should mean more to him than it did. They had helped each other through their darkest life moments for heaven's sake. The least he could do was help ensure the threats to her life amounted to nothing.

Zephyr cleared his throat. Sensing Ember's anger and hurt regarding Kieran, he decided to redirect the conversation back to the matter at hand. "So, to recap here, Kieran isn't dumb enough to take a contract to kill my father, and threats to Ember's life won't work either."

Emerson nodded. "Correct. But that doesn't mean Ember's idea is completely without merit."

Ember perked up. She folded and refolded her hands a few times before picking some imaginary lint off her skirt. "Really?"

Emerson rolled his eyes. His sister was so predictable and easy to read. Validate her ideas and all is forgiven.

"Yes, Your Majesty." That comment earned him a glare. He didn't care though. Someone had to ruffle her feathers and give her a hard time every so often to keep her on her toes.

Emerson hopped off his desk and grabbed the file he had retrieved earlier.

"Oh good. Can we finally know what's in the file folder?" Zephyr was eager to move past talk of contracting a murder, even a fictitious one.

Emerson thumbed through the pages, and murmured something, before grinning widely.

"This is everything you need to get started on the contract you are putting out, Zephyr. Inside is everything you need to destroy the Thache legacy and duchy's reputation."

Ember gapped at her twin. "I don't want to destroy them! I want him to come home. Besides, how does destroying the Thache legacy and reputation bring him home? He turned over the daily operations to his sisters."

Emerson shook his head. Then he cast his gaze upwards like he was praying for patience.

"Because you are threatening the two people he actually cares about. His sisters. Harming the family's reputation will hurt his sisters too," Emerson declared. Triumph illuminated his features.

Zephyr glanced through the file while Ember rolled her eyes. She was irritated her twin was able to find a way to execute a version of her plan. Although, Ember's sour mood began to lift. Emerson had worked for months to locate Kieran and had never thought of putting out a contract to get him to come home.

Emerson's eyes narrowed as he watched Ember's frown become a smirk. "Why are you suddenly so chipper?"

"Because you didn't think of hiring Kieran to bring him home and I did."

Emerson sighed. He was loathed to admit she was right in ways. He had tried to lure Kieran home using contracts months ago, but it hadn't worked. If he admitted he had already tried contracts, she would be sulking for days and would never believe this plan would work. As Emerson had listened to Ember, he realized he hadn't tried blackmail to get Kieran home.

Emerson had been burning the candle at both ends for months. Blinded by constantly putting out fires, he had been too close to more than one situation causing him to miss some obvious problem-solving. Like threatening and blackmailing Kieran to come home.

"You're right, Em. You came up with an idea I hadn't thought of," Emerson admitted. Let Ember believe what she wanted. The end result was all that mattered.

He pulled out his pocket watch, the one their father had given him at birth, and let out a long sigh. Emerson ran a hand through his hair.

"I have a meeting in a few minutes, so if you both can kindly take the file and leave, that would be great." Emerson made a shooing motion toward the door.

Ember pecked her twin on the cheek before flouncing out of the room and down the hall. Zephyr scurried after her, careful to conceal the folder.

"Where are we off to, Your Majesty?"

Ember paused at the end of the corridor. Her brows knit together as she bit her lip. Where could they go? She did not want anyone with the American delegation observing them with whatever Emerson had given them. She also didn't trust any of the servants or guards to not have been paid off.

"I don't know," Ember mumbled.

Zephyr was aware of their surroundings and the people walking around, as well as the ones who had taken notice of their presence. Environmental awareness had kept him alive, indispensable at times, and given him valuable information to use against others a time or two.

"My darling. If I may be so bold. The cliffs are stunning in the evening with the summer sunset, are they not? Do you want to picnic and stargaze with me?"

Ember smiled. "Oh, Zeph! That's perfect! Let me change. Can you get the horses ready while I tell the kitchen?"

Zephyr playfully tapped her nose with his finger. "Yes, I can. I'll change for riding and help the grooms ready our horses."

Ember squeezed his hand pulling him closer. She raised herself on her toes to brush a kiss against his cheek and whispered, "You remove anything from the file, I'll kill you."

Zephyr chuckled. "I'll see you in an hour."

Chapter 4

A security detail had insisted on accompanying Zephyr and Ember to the cliffs. It had taken an extra hour to leave. Neither was happy about this turn of events, but they weren't worried. Once the meal was finished, they would move over to the cliffs and slip away while dinner was cleaned up by the kitchen staff Ember insisted come along. If they were forced to have a security detail, then Ember would utilize her staff to her advantage.

Ember and Zephyr dismounted and walked over to the table under the gazebo. The light fragrance of the butterfly jasmine added to the romantic atmosphere of the sun setting on the ocean. Ember sighed quietly. If only she felt something for her dinner companion.

Zephyr pulled out Ember's chair before sitting across from her. The kitchen staff busied themselves with unloading dinner and crafting the plates. One of the footmen opened the wine and poured them each a glass, while the other footmen lit lanterns and handled the horses.

Ember's mouth lifted slightly as she watched Zephyr's indecisiveness as to whether he should drink from both glasses or leave it alone. She decided to save him by taking a sip.

She lifted an eyebrow after a moment as if to say I told you so. Zephyr let out a deep sigh and seemed to relax slightly until he realized he wasn't watching the food preparation. She covered his hand with hers and gave him a reassuring squeeze.

"Emerson sent me a note before we left. He told me I should share it with you at dinner." Ember was hoping to distract Zephyr. She wasn't worried about being killed by her staff or her citizens. It was when food wasn't prepared by her people that she was more cautious and on edge. Everyone was keenly aware of what the stakes were.

"Really? Did he give you a specific course of the meal and time in which to read it?"

Ember threw back her head and laughed. "No, he didn't. You're spot on though! He controls everything and directs every one. Spontaneity isn't in his nature."

Zephyr chuckled. "Was he ever spontaneous?"

The jovial light flickered out of her eyes as she bit her lip. "Before the zeppelin explosion. After that, a switch flipped inside him. The playful, fun-loving Emerson was replaced by a stoic soul determined to never let anything like that happen again."

Zephyr cleared his throat before taking a sip of his wine. He didn't know what to say. He could have kicked himself for forgetting about the explosion. It had just been nice to have a brief, unguarded moment with Ember. These moments between them, where conversation flowed freely, had become something of a rarity as the years passed and the pressure to marry increased.

Fortunately, the staff saved him. They began setting down dishes in front of them, as well as their place settings. A footman served them before fading into the background with the others.

They sat in silence for the first few courses, but once the main course was served, Zephyr found the silence suffocating.

"I can't take it anymore," he declared.

Ember's fork paused mid-bite. "Excuse me?"

"What does the note say?"

"Oh. The note. I forgot about it."

Zephyr scrubbed a hand over his face, while Ember set down her fork and reached into her jacket pocket for the slip of paper.

Ember shot Zephyr a coy look as she cleared her throat. He rolled his eyes and smiled.

"It says, 'Enjoy the play. E.'"

Ember flipped the card over looking for more writing. Then she handed it to Zephyr. He looked it over and then pulled out a lighter to add heat to the note in case Emerson thought he was being clever by using invisible ink. Yet, nothing happened.

"What is *that* supposed to mean?" Zephyr asked handing the note back to Ember.

"I have no idea."

"Are we supposed to attend a play? Or maybe a moving picture?" Zephyr motioned for the staff to clear dinner and bring out dessert.

"Maybe we should look in the paper to see if there is a production or something," Ember suggested.

Zephyr nodded. "I didn't bring a newspaper with me in anticipation of Emerson's scavenger hunt, so we'll have to wait until we get back."

Ember snorted a laugh. "Oh, Zeph, how could you not know Em was going to do this?"

"It always gets me balled up that you two have the same nickname."

Ember shook her head slightly, confused by the sudden subject change. "What?"

"You both call each other 'Em' and I understand why. It's the first two letters of both your names, but it still confuses me for a moment."

"Oh. Yes, we do have the same nickname. It comes in handy at times."

"I bet it does."

Ember smiled at the footmen. "Can you leave the coffee and treats, please? We are going to take in the view before dessert."

Zephyr helped Ember from her chair before walking towards the cliffs.

"You have it with you right?"

Zephyr clicked his tongue. "Of course, Your Majesty. I like not being shoved off a cliff."

Ember chuckled. She turned to him, looping her arms around his neck. Zephyr leaned down and kissed her on the forehead. They could feel the eyes of those watching them.

"Oh no! Zeph! My ring," Ember shouted in distress.

"Your ring?" Zephyr asked confused by the sudden outburst.

"Yes! I need light. Now!"

Zephyr ran towards the gazebo, but the staff were rushing out with lanterns. Footmen and maids were asking questions and trying to console Ember over the loss of this ring.

"I need all hands on deck looking for it! You! Over there! Yes, you! Do you think I'm speaking for my health? Help look for it!"

Zephyr realized she was yelling at the security detail and was impressed. She hadn't told him her plan. Before he knew it, everyone they had brought was looking along the cliffs for this ring he wasn't even sure existed.

Ember wrapped herself around his arm and tugged him slowly away from the commotion she had created. They hurried single file down a narrow path that led to the beach. Once on the beach, Ember led him to a well-hidden cave. They walked in silence for a few minutes in the dark.

Ember stopped abruptly causing Zephyr to crash into the back of her. She didn't care as she reached around in the darkness for the matches and lanterns she knew were hidden there.

Zephyr blinked a few times as his eyes adjusted to the dim light. He took in the carvings and paintings on the walls, the chiseled-out stone benches to sit on, and the animal pelts. There was also a deep pool of water in the far corner.

"What is this place?"

"It's one of the caves the Taino used for meetings with the Me — members of the tribe," Ember explained. She had been distracted with lighting the lanterns she had almost told Zephyr about the Mer. She focused on her task of lighting the lanterns around the room and keeping her mouth shut.

Zephyr shot her a look. "Is it okay that we're here?"

Ember waved a hand. "We are fine here. Not many people know about the various caves on the islands. We unfortunately don't know much about the Taino in general."

"Why's that?" Zephyr asked while studying the images on the wall near her.

She motioned for him to sit beside her. "Because of globalization. When Christopher Columbus landed in Parley in 1492, there were at least a million Taino. But then diseases wiped them out, and those who lived mingled with other tribes and people coming into the area to survive. Their culture is all around us, even if we can't understand it yet."

Zephyr lightly traced the images and words. The history of the Taino was sad, but a familiar one shared by all the American tribes. However, they were survivors. They learned to adapt and overcome despite the odds. Rather than see these brave people as victims, Ember always felt they should be seen as the victors. They lost everything in ways, but over four centuries later, they were still alive. Highlighting the resilience of the Native Americans in general.

"Let's see the file." Ember's words pulled Zephyr back from his study of the walls.

He stood and took off his jacket before untucking his shirt from his back and producing the file. Ember snatched it from his hands and began reading it while he put himself back together.

Ember looked over the pages muttering to herself before starting over. Zephyr watched her as he sat back down. He tried to catch a glimpse of the pages he had briefly scanned in Emerson's office, but she kept flipping through them too quickly.

Ember handed him the file in a huff after a moment. Zephyr was surprised to discover there were only seven pages. He knew the file had been thin and contained a few papers, but he thought there might be a little more to work with.

Each of the pages had names on them, but he was confused. It was just names, as well as a faded advertisement. There was also another piece of paper, which looked like some kind of invitation for some event hosted by one of the former dukes of Revenge.

"What is this? I don't understand. We had to be secretive and ditch a security detail for five pages of names? And this flyer or whatever." Zephyr ran a frustrated hand through his hair.

Ember sighed. "Don't forget the invitation." That remark earned her a glare from her companion. "I don't know what it is. I also don't know what the names mean."

She stood and began pacing. Why would Emerson give her pages of names, some kind of advertisement, and an invitation? How was this supposed to help her bring Kieran back? How were they supposed to contact him using this? From the look of the names on the pages, these people were dead. That thought gave Ember pause.

Why would Emerson give her names of dead people? That didn't make any sense. Ember reached for the file and Zephyr handed it over. She grabbed the first page and read the name: Edward Thache, Jr. She looked at the names beneath his as realization dawned on her.

"Zeph, this is Kieran's family tree." Her eyes began to scan the names. There had to be something there. Emerson wouldn't just give them a list of names if they didn't serve a purpose. As she reviewed the other pages, she realized only the first few pages were some kind of family tree. The other names were maybe a guest list of some kind. Either way, there wasn't a clear connection she could see between the pages of names.

Zephyr and Ember scanned the names and rescanned them several times, but nothing stood out. They studied the invitation and then the flyer. Nothing jumped out at them, other than the knowledge the party, or whatever the event was, had taken place in 1803.

The invitation was faded and smudged, so not much could be read. The flyer was in a similar state. Ember wasn't certain if they were connected. She also wasn't sure if the family tree was to help identify the duke at the time or for some other purpose. As for the other names, they meant nothing to Ember, and she couldn't make out about half of them.

Ember sighed and set down the file. Leave it to Emerson to give them a mystery rather than a straightforward path. Zephyr scrubbed a hand over his face before standing to stretch. He walked around the cave and studied the petroglyphs on the walls. Ember watched him.

There had to be something important within the pages Emerson had given them, but Ember set those thoughts aside for the moment. Something else was nagging at her, and it had to do with Emerson and Zephyr's blossoming friendship.

Emerson didn't trust many people with his intelligence files, yet he trusted Zephyr. Why? Ember was still puzzled by that. Zephyr had said it was because he told her brother something his family was planning. It must have been something major. Even if the intelligence file was a low-level one, Emerson had still trusted an outsider with the contents.

"Why does Em trust you? He doesn't trust just anyone, and yet, he trusts you."

Zephyr continued to look over the carvings, running his fingers lightly over one that looked like a fish. He had a puzzled expression on his face.

He sat down across from her. She could tell he was thinking, trying to decide how much to tell her, and whether he could trust her.

"I know how Parley gets the pearls from the ocean."

Ember's breath caught in her throat. Surely he didn't mean… No, he couldn't know. Emerson would have told her about something this big… However, they hadn't been able to meet in private over the last week because a new matter needing undivided attention seemed to crop up every second of the day for him and her.

"My father and brother, along with a few other Americans, are trying to purchase pearl farms and caymanite mines. I know only citizens of Parley are allowed to own them. I was curious and decided to explore the information in the letter that was delivered to me by mistake rather than my father. I came upon a family playing by the beach and then saw this child transform."

Zephyr shrugged and then held up his hands helplessly. "I didn't know what to do. So, I told Emerson about it."

Ember closed her eyes and leaned back against the cool rock. Blackmail. Zephyr was blackmailing Emerson over the merpeople. She had to hand it to Zephyr. She hadn't seen that coming from him.

"What did you demand in exchange for your silence?"

Zephyr remained quiet for a few minutes. Ember opened her eyes and looked at him. The hurt on his face shocked her. Regret slammed into her. She shouldn't have been so hasty in her rush to judgment and assumption of the worst.

Ember stood and sat down next to him. She reached for his hand but he brushed her away. Emerson wouldn't have trusted someone blackmailing him. She knew that. Her carelessness with her words would be the death of her.

"You didn't ask for anything. That's why Em trusts you, and I wrongly assumed the worst because I've wrongly judged you from the moment we first met. I pegged you as a playboy, despite our conversations over the years, and look for evidence to prove myself right whenever I can."

Zephyr shot her a sad half-smile. "I'm used to it. I mean I went to prison for drugs and womanizing. Why wouldn't I be another selfish playboy, thumbing my nose at the consequences?"

"You shouldn't have to be 'used to it' and your prison sentence was a sham. I'm truly sorry. I can't say I won't stick my foot in my mouth again, but I'll try," Ember promised.

"Thank you." Zephyr squeezed her hand and pulled her into a side hug.

"I still don't know what those names mean," Ember admitted. "We have to get back to the palace soon."

Zephyr nodded. "Hold on a second. Emerson's note."

"What about it? He said to enjoy the play. I don't see what that has to do with Kieran's family tree or the other names."

Zephyr turned to face her. "What if the flyer is an advertisement for a play? It's faded, but it looks like it was from a show of some kind. What if a play was written about the Thache family? Or one of them was an actor or something?"

Ember rolled this information over in her mind. "You know what? I have no idea, but it's as good a lead as any."

"How would we go about finding this information? If we start asking questions about the Thache family it's going to be obvious."

"Emerson isn't going to be able to help us... But we could do as he suggested and enjoy a play," Ember smiled.

Zephyr grinned too. "Sounds good to me, Your Majesty. Shall we return?"

Zephyr stood and held out an arm to Ember who snuffed out the lights. Together, the pair slowly exited the cave.

Chapter 5

"You want to see a play? In Careen? Why?" Cilia stared dumbfounded at Ember while she continued to put jam on her toast. Her mother never understood mingling with peasants and the appeal of not having things held at the palace.

"Because we have a box at the opera house, a box at the theater, a box everywhere we could want. It's a waste of money to bring everyone here because Zeph and I want to see a play," Ember answered with a patience she didn't feel.

"The dangers of being exposed in public like that though. Think of the expense of the security needed just to take in a play," Wilson argued.

Both Zephyr and Emerson rolled their eyes at the prime minister's comment.

"We pay for the security details regardless of what I do. Spending a few thousand notes versus tens of thousands of notes is far more reasonable," Ember fired back.

Cilia set down her tea cup. Ember braced herself for some patronizing discussion about how her little brain couldn't comprehend the logistics or whatever.

"Ember, you need to be reasonable. You don't understand truly how anything relating to your security works. I don't really think you comprehend the situation," Cilia began.

Ember cut her off. "Prince Emerson, can Zephyr and I attend a play in Careen any day and time of our choosing?"

Emerson wiped his mouth with his napkin and took a long drink of coffee before responding. All eyes were on him, and his mother's eyes were on fire.

"Well, the more notice I have the better before you go off and make public appearances," Emerson drawled.

Cilia smiled triumphantly at her daughter, she was opening her mouth to speak, when Emerson continued, "But yes, I don't think it will be an issue. It's not like we don't have security plans in place for these buildings and types of outings, Your Majesty."

Ember nodded primly. "Thank you, Your Royal Highness."

Zephyr snorted a laugh at the twins' use of their titles but hid it behind a cough when his father glared at him.

"Should we call someone from the theater to come by this afternoon, my dear? They can tell us about current and upcoming shows," Zephyr suggested.

"Oh, that's a wonderful idea, my darling," Ember cooed. "I'll have my secretary make the call. We should make sure whoever it is can brief us on all the theatrical happenings in Careen and possibly the main island of Parley."

"Brilliant, my queen. Should we meet them in your private solarium for afternoon tea?" Zephyr suggested.

Cilia and Wilson glanced at each other before Wilson cast a suspicious eye on the young couple. Ember tried to spend as little time as possible in Zephyr's presence, but now wanted to see a play with him, and in public no less. It wasn't unheard of for them to do something together, but there had to be another motive, especially after last night.

"We have negotiations this afternoon. Surely your little theater trip can wait, especially after the stunt you pulled last night," Cilia scoffed.

"It was reckless what you both did last night. It won't be tolerated," Wilson added.

Emerson and Zephyr froze. A tense minute passed before Ember pushed back her chair and stood at the head of the table.

"What won't be tolerated? What stunt did I, the queen of Parley, pull?"

Cilia rolled her eyes and giggled. "Honestly, Ember. The theatrics are a little much."

Zephyr winced while Emerson sighed under his breath and ran a hand over his short beard. Ember's breathing was coming in rapid bursts. She was disrespected at every turn, and she had put up with the abuse for far too long. She needed to take back her power, but he kept silent, knowing she needed to realize she could stand on her own.

Emerson was impressed by the anger in her jade eyes. The morning light streaming in from windows picked up the red highlights in her chestnut hair, magnifying the effect of her rage. He wasn't going to intervene. His mother and the smug prime minister were about to discover Ember was learning how to fight back without him and Kieran.

"Your Majesty."

Cilia snorted. "Excuse me?"

"'Excuse me, Your Majesty.' You both have clearly forgotten who I am and by extension, your place at court. Keep going and you will find yourselves exiled from my court."

With that declaration, Ember left the room. The silence that followed was deafening, although Emerson didn't let that stop him from grabbing seconds.

"Zephyr, do you like hunting?" Emerson asked breaking the quiet.

The other man was stunned by the shift in topic. "It depends. I don't hunt for sport."

Emerson grinned as he bit into a sausage link. "Neither do I. I'll be in touch with the details."

Everyone continued to eat in silence for a few moments, before Emerson finished and added, "Why don't you check in with the queen's secretary? I think the theater is just what she needs."

"Right. The stress and all, especially with the anniversary looming over her."

"So perceptive, Zephyr. That's what I like about you," Emerson praised. He drained his coffee, wiped his mouth, and strode out the door.

"Zephyr," Wilson called out to his son from his chair.

He turned to look down the table at his father. He raised an eyebrow when the older man didn't speak right away.

"Don't get too comfortable. She doesn't have the power she thinks," Wilson warned. "Look at the legislation being passed to dismantle the antiquated laws. Soon Parley will have an infusion of people coming to enjoy the bounty the citizens have long kept to themselves."

Zephyr shook his head. "At what cost? Also, what infusion of people are you talking about? Nothing is ever enough for you. You're never powerful enough, or rich enough. Do you even know what is enough?"

Wilson took a long sip of his coffee while Zephyr studied him. He had blonde hair and the same hazel-blue eyes the women went wild for on Caelus. At 48, his father was a good-looking man in his own right. Unlike others, he took pride in maintaining his athletic physique. Zephyr knew he kept trim for his many mistresses, as well as luring other women into his orbit.

It wasn't difficult for anyone to figure out how Caelus turned out the way he had. His older brother truly was a carbon copy of their father. The only difference between the two was Caelus's arrogance and lack of regard for anything or anyone. If he wanted something, he took it. Zephyr wasn't sure where his sense of entitlement came from. All he knew was he was tired of his father and brother thumbing their nose at the consequences of their actions. They were never the ones who paid the price.

"The cost? You sound like her," Wilson scoffed. Cilia giggled next to him and Wilson shot her a sly grin. "Parley has kept its resources to itself for too long. If this tiny island nation wants a seat at the world table, then they need to open the door and let others in."

Zephyr shook his head as he chuckled to himself. "Not everything in life is for sale. Not everyone needs to dominate the world. Some people know when they're flying too close to the sun."

"An Icarus reference? Last I checked, I don't have wax wings. Instead, I have an entire country at my disposal and I'm using that to my advantage to install my son as king regent in another. Then I will have two nations at my disposal. Ember is just a child playing, pretending she has importance and power."

Zephyr nodded. He looked down at his hands and then stood to leave. He paused at the door before turning with his reply, "I don't think you have the power you think you do, Father."

With those parting words, Zephyr left to track down Ember's secretary to help them figure out why the theater was so important to destroying Kieran's family, and how they were supposed to use it to get him home.

Emerson was the last of the participants to enter the room. He was late. Rather than prioritize the marriage negotiations, he chose to plan the security detail for Ember's trip to Geneva. The trip was in a week, whereas this sham of a marriage was months away, or better yet, not happening at all.

"Finally! Do you know how long we have been waiting?" Cilia seethed from her chair.

Emerson set down his files on the table. He walked over to the sideboard and poured himself a glass of water. His footsteps echoed on the black marble floor. He knew his mother was angry about being kept waiting for an hour and not having any booze to pass the time with. It's the reason why he picked the conference room in his wing of the palace. No alcohol was allowed in the intelligence and military wing.

Rather than answer his mother, he took a seat in the navy blue velvet chair at the head of the mahogany table. Portraits of past admirals, generals, and heads of intelligence lined the olive-green walls. The statues and vases placed around the cavernous room had been plundered from various empires or recovered from the ocean floor. Even the huge Persian area rug under the table had been pillaged from somewhere.

The room was, in a way, a show of strength and superiority. The first admirals and generals of Parley were all pirates. The European nations wrote in their history books of the century-long war with the pirates where they lost the Caribbean, now known as

Parley, to ruthless, bloodthirsty men bent on the destruction of humanity.

In the Parlian history books, however, they discussed the revival and restoration of native life and freedom. There were ups and downs and rebellions during that time too. Everyone always has a different idea or view on how something should run, or what an idea or concept meant. Parley and its pirate rulers were no different.

The history of Parley wasn't perfect, but whose history was? Pirates were definitely not role models for the masses. They were some deeply flawed people who didn't always do the right things and took advantage of situations to make money. But at least they lived authentic lives. You always knew where you stood with them.

Cilia drummed her fingers against the table, while Grammy Margaret pretended to read something, but her grip on her pen told Emerson she was holding back. The prime minister and his uncle had polite smiles on their faces. Emerson wasn't fooled though, he knew they were annoyed having their time wasted. Now they knew how he felt, well, except for his grandmother. She had her own duties to perform, so she was keenly aware of the cost of these meetings. However, he had warned her he would be an hour late. She had arrived about ten minutes before him according to his secretary.

"What's on the agenda today?" Emerson asked. He clapped his hands together and opened his portfolio.

Cilia pursed her lips together. Emerson could tell her hands were shaking slightly. She was angry, but she was going through withdrawals. He pulled out his pocket watch. It had only been a few hours since she last had a drink and she was already shaking. He shook his head as he put his watch away. She was getting worse.

"You know what's on the agenda—Ember's marriage," Cilia bit out.

Emerson nodded as he flipped through a few pages and pulled a few sheets of paper out. "Yes. Well, I'm changing the agenda. We aren't going to be discussing that dreadful topic."

His grandmother smiled in amusement at his declaration, while everyone stared at him in surprise. She relaxed in her seat even.

"Something more important has been brought to my attention regarding the prime minister, his eldest son, and some members of the American Parliament," Emerson told those in the room.

"Your Royal Highness," Uncle Martin started in a placating tone, "What could be more important, pray tell, than the queen's marriage?"

Emerson's wide grin sent a chill down Cilia's spine. She sent a fretful glance to her brother and the prime minister. Grammy Margaret on the other hand, slid her items away from her and reclined in her chair. She was preparing for the show.

"National security. That's what's more important than our beloved queen's wedding." Emerson slid the papers from his portfolio down the table to the trio.

"Is it true the prime minister and his eldest son, Caelus, are trying to purchase pearl farms and caymanite mines? As well as pave the way for others in America to do the same? It is strictly forbidden for any noncitizen of Parley to own pearl farms and mines in our country," Emerson explained.

"Therefore, I'm confused, Mother, as to why you and the Guardians would be helping them try to acquire something they cannot legally own. The cost of helping foreigners acquire assets they can't own is borderline treason."

Emerson could see the wheels in Cilia's mind turning, while Uncle Martin went a ghastly shade of white. Meanwhile, the prime minister seemed bored by the conversation.

"You are ridiculous. As part of the changes over the past year, the Crown Guardians decided such a law was antiquated, therefore, we changed it," Cilia scoffed. "I do not understand what the problem is. We even made adjustments to the law based on your suggestions."

The light in Emerson's eyes took on a dangerous glow. Margaret took in the trio at the table and marveled how only Martin understood the gravity of the situation coming. Cilia was a nitwit and easily led. While the prime minister was an arrogant, calculating scumbag, who only wanted to line his pockets and secure more power.

"Yes, I'm aware of what the Crown Guardians attempted to do. I don't think many people would view rejection as an opportunity to circumvent the law. Do you know who has the final say over matters of national security? Even above the lords and ladies and our beloved queen... hmmm?"

Cilia threw up her hands. "Why are you always trying to thwart the progress of Parley? Drystan understood the sacrifices and changes that needed to be made to be a world power. Why can't you?"

The hate and rage rolled off his mother in waves. Emerson knew she would have sacrificed him and Ember to whatever god or deity she needed to in order to have her beloved firstborn child back. However, Drystan hadn't been told about the Mer, which Emerson had always found odd. It was one of the many things he was curious about, but Grammy Margaret refused to discuss. For all the information he had access to, it was frustrating when one or two of the informational pieces were missing.

"Oh, Mother. You are delusional. Father wouldn't have allowed this, and you know it."

Cilia shot up from her seat, knocking her chair to the ground, shaking a finger in Emerson's direction. "Your father has nothing to do with this! He was giving Drystan more power. He would have maintained appearances had Drystan passed this measure."

Emerson was unmoved by Cilia's outburst. He had always had his suspicions his mother had something to do with the explosion. He felt something had gone wrong in her plan, and instead of her husband dying, she lost both her husband and her son. He hadn't been able to confirm those suspicions as of yet, but he wasn't worried. The truth had a way of revealing itself.

"Careful, Mother. You don't want to say something you might regret," Emerson taunted.

Cilia picked up a glass and threw it in Emerson's direction. He didn't duck out of the way, rather he stood his ground as the glass whizzed passed his left ear. It had been so close he could hear it. The glass shattered on the wall behind him. Both Margaret and Martin made moves toward Cilia, but Emerson held up his hand to stop them.

"Let me tell you how this is going to go, Cilia. Wilson. I had already rejected this change to Parley's law on the grounds of national security when it came across my desk months ago for the third time. To learn you not only revived it for a fourth time but then found a way to circumvent me? I was impressed, to say the least," Emerson told them.

"However, I still have the final say. I rejected it again and then ensured you wouldn't be able to revive this law a fifth time. The High Court and the Lessor Lords were sent word of my decision, along with a document stating their agreement or disagreement with my decision," Emerson explained.

He put a copy of the documents sent on the table before continuing. "Based on the responses, I'll bring forth the matter to be voted on if it's too close to call. I do feel confident it will be a resounding no to passing the law. Questions?"

Martin kept his mouth shut. Cilia vibrated with rage, while Wilson's eyes took on a calculating gleam.

"You can't be serious," Wilson responded. "Myself and other members of the American Parliament are in the process of purchasing these mines and farms. We are offering more than fair compensation. Think of the political scandal regarding failed real estate deals between a major world leader and your little island nation."

"I don't care about a 'political scandal', I care about national security and the law. How the Guardians attempted to change this law is in direct violation of Parley's constitution. So the fault lies with them," Emerson smiled politely.

Wilson pushed his chair away from the table and crossed his leg over the top of the other. "Surely you wouldn't want a war on your hands all because of some antiquated law that leads to a public slight of your allies and future in-laws."

Cilia righted her chair and sat down, beaming triumphantly. Emerson snorted and remained standing. "I have all the faith in the world in Parley's navy and army. Should America decide to view my concern, the concern of our lords, and our citizens as a slight and jump to the absurdly overdramatic reaction of declaring war, then there's nothing I can do about that."

"Your military is nothing compared to the ones at my disposal. You forget I've seen your navy. It's nothing I'm worried about."

"Emerson, be reasonable," Cilia cautioned. She looked back and forth between Wilson and her son. Worry creased her brow.

"I am being reasonable. The answer is no. The sale of all mines and pearl farms to noncitizens has been halted, and the law has been repealed. Try it again, and see what happens."

Wilson exploded out of his chair and shouted obscenities at Emerson. "Listen here, you pompous little jerk! If you terminate those contracts, I will declare war! The marriage to Ember and Zephyr will be put on hold until America crushes your tiny, insignificant island chain, and you come begging for mercy. Then the marriage will happen, and Ember and Parley will be mine to control."

Cilia and Martin winced at Wilson's declaration, while Emerson never flinched. A knock at the door announced Emerson's secretary, Greer. She handed him some papers silently before leaving. Emerson glanced over the contents before smiling widely.

"I guess we'll see who has the better military," Emerson declared as he threw the confirmation of the contract terminations on the table. "Have a great day."

Emerson gathered his portfolio and left the room. His grandmother followed on his heels.

"You better have one hell of a plan," Margaret hissed.

"Of course I do," Emerson replied. "My biggest question right now is why Wilson is so desperate for money. He isn't buying the mines and farms to pad his portfolio and net worth. According to the report Greer gave me before the meeting, Wilson is purchasing them to have money. On paper he is rich, but in practice, he's broke."

"His family and his wife's family are insanely wealthy. It was a big reason for the marriage — the Levans and the McGriffs wanted to combine their wealth and power." Margaret's brow furled in thought. "Although, if I remember correctly, only the wife has full access to the McGriff fortune."

Emerson nodded as he opened the door to his office. "You would be correct. Wilson has been paying off and bribing people for a while regarding Caelus's lifestyle. I'm not sure why he doesn't cut him off. From what I've learned, Wilson has burned through his portion, as well as his mother's share, of the Levan wealth. He's been bullying his siblings into helping fund his lifestyle, but I don't think they are funneling money to him at the rate he needs."

Margaret lowered her voice as she moved forward in her chair, "So are the rumors about him blackmailing world leaders true?"

Emerson let out a deep sigh before grabbing a cigar and lighting it. He didn't smoke often, but when he did, it was always cigars. They lasted longer, had more flavor, and he only smoked them on occasion when he had a particularly stressful day or week. Based on what Greer and his other intelligence officers were finding, he was having one hell of a month.

"Zephyr confirmed as much to me. Wilson is blackmailing world leaders to help cover those blackmailing the Levan family. His wife refuses to take part in anything related to his business dealings and always has. Meanwhile, Caelus believes he's untouchable, and Wilson makes examples of Zephyr and Neil in an effort to get his wife to loosen the purse strings."

Margaret's eyes took on a distant look as she gazed out the window. Her mind processed the information her grandson had just shared with her.

"Zephyr and Neil take the fall for all of Caelus's misdeeds and crimes? Is that what you're saying? And this is a form of revenge employed by Wilson against his wife to gain more money for his illegal activities?"

Emerson took a deep drag of his cigar, running a hand over his mouth and beard, before blowing out the white smoke. "Yes."

His grandmother let out a few choice curse words and Emerson chuckled.

"That sums up my thoughts exactly."

"Does Ember know?"

"Not the full extent. I'm keeping it from her at the moment," Emerson said. "She needs to figure out if she wants to be queen or not. Until then, does it matter what Wilson does?"

He could tell his grandmother disagreed with his reasoning. Emerson took another drag before continuing, "If push comes to shove, I will have you reinstated as queen as a matter of national security. You're a Bellamy by blood and stepped down. You have more power than the Guardians realize, and as queen, you could guide Ember until she feels confident to rule."

"Emerson, I love you." He cringed mentally knowing his grandmother was going to shoot down his idea. "You and I both know Ember is more than qualified to lead, and she does daily despite being undermined. *She* needs to realize *she* has more power than she thinks she does. She needs to believe she can be queen."

"When? When is she going to realize the Guardians have the illusion of power? When is she going to be confident enough to lead?" Emerson countered.

Margaret leaned over and patted his hand. Emerson scrubbed a hand through his hair before continuing, "Before Kieran's sudden departure after Willow's death, he and I had a conversation regarding him taking more work abroad because Ember sought his counsel regarding most things. Now that he's gone, she's pulled back and has stuck to the things she feels comfortable with, but has left legislative matters to the Guardians and the the lords."

The older woman sighed. "I've been spending more time at Whydah, and you've been buried under your own tasks for weeks. This has forced her to work through her problems, Em. You had the benefit of failing, dusting yourself off, and trying again. She didn't. She's always had advisors 'teaching' her or telling her she isn't good enough. She doesn't have the confidence to lead because she's never been given the chance to fail."

Emerson thought about his grandmother's words. She was right. Nine years ago when Ember was coronated, she was deemed to be of sound mind. This meant she was the monarch, had the full powers of the title, and could do what she wanted. Grammy Margaret had selected the advisors to help Ember; however, their mother had other plans.

In public there was a united front, in private they were at each other's throats. Cilia believed Ember was too young to be the monarch. She argued Ember didn't grasp concepts like law, politics, economics, and social cues because of her age. She then pulled rank as Ember's mother and announced the formation of the Crown Guardians. For reasons known only to Margaret, she had allowed Cilia to form the Guardians rather than assert her authority.

The details were still murky to Emerson. However, what he had learned from Kieran was that both he and Margaret had decided to give Cilia what she wanted. It was their hope Ember would grow tired of her mother, her mother's ambitions, her mother's control, and declare the Guardians useless. But that's not how things had turned out.

Cilia played on Ember's insecurities, constantly comparing her to her father, causing Ember to doubt herself and her decisions.

Over the years, Cilia had convinced Ember that if she made the wrong move, the citizens would overthrow the government like what had happened to her former country of Cardia.

"Cilia and Wilson have created what amounts to a shadow government. Nothing they are doing is legal, but the longer Ember says silent, the longer she refuses to lead, the more she legitimizes the Guardians and their power," Emerson argued. "Her tin anniversary is the deadline for me. It will be our eighteenth birthday. If she doesn't step up and take back her power, I will install you as monarch."

Margaret leaned forward and patted Emerson on the hand. "If you enact your plan, you will signal to your sister you have no confidence in her ability to be queen. No confidence she can lead. *That* will devastate her more than an entire country questioning her abilities and qualifications. My advice to you is to keep building her up."

Emerson tapped the ash from the tip of his cigar into a nearby dish. "I'm trying. I truly am. She refuses to stand on her own two feet. Ember thinks she needs Kieran for everything, especially with the anniversary looming over us. In reality, she needs only herself."

His grandmother stood and gave him a sad smile. "Ember is used to being rescued by the men in her life. Your father with Drystan. Kieran after your father, and then you after Kieran's departure to say nothing of your bond as twins."

She walked to the door before continuing, "Ember is finding her voice. She has been taking on more serious duties and succeeding with complicated matters. Each win builds her faith she can do this. Each misstep and correction shows the people won't mutinize and overthrow the government. Every single person at court, minus a handful of people, has told her for a decade she wasn't qualified to lead despite her education. She will hit her breaking point, and when that happens, she will lead."

Margaret didn't wait for a response from Emerson. She left him to his cigar and his thoughts. She understood his reasoning and even applauded his commitment to Parley, but the cost of his plan was too high. Ember would come around, she just needed to be pushed out of the nest like a baby bird so she could understand she had the wings to fly.

Chapter 6

The owner of the theater and his manager were waiting in the private solarium off the garden in the family wing of the palace when Zephyr and Ember arrived.

Both people stood and bowed as Ember entered the room. Once she was seated, she motioned for the others to sit.

"Tea? Coffee? Snacks?" Ember asked.

She motioned for one of the maids to come over and serve everyone seated. Once everyone had food and drink, Ember smiled and welcomed her guests.

"Thank you both for coming. Mr. Levan and I were wondering what the latest performances were. We would love to see one."

Adam Lewis, the owner of both the Gilded Theater and the Octave Opera House in Careen, motioned to the manager, Mae O'Shea, for the current production schedule.

"We have a few different performances, but I also brought the list of current productions for all the theaters across Parley with us, as requested." Adam laid the various schedules on the table for Ember and Zephyr to look over.

Ember clapped her hands. "Wonderful! Mr. Levan also had some questions about the history of the performing arts and theater in Parley. Would you be able to answer those for us?"

Both Adam and Mae nodded enthusiastically. "Of course, we can," Adam answered.

"Anything we are unsure of, we can find out for you too," Mae added.

Zephyr and Ember spent the next few hours poring over the theater schedules and asking questions about the various productions. They learned the names of every person involved with them, as well as the history of the plays they were unfamiliar with. Zephyr made note of the days and times of the productions they wanted to attend in his notebook.

"You had mentioned Mr. Levan had some questions about the history of the theater in our island nation," Mae said.

"Miss O'Shea is one of the most knowledgeable people in all of Parley regarding the history of the performing arts. Her family has been in theater for generations," Adam bragged.

Ember shot Zephyr an encouraging smile. "Go ahead and ask your questions."

Mae moved forward in her seat and waited for him to speak.

"This might be a silly question, so forgive me, but have there ever been any notable Parlian figures in the theater?" Zephyr asked with an innocent smile.

"How so? Like members of the aristocracy or royalty?"

"Yes. I know the actors in the performing arts haven't always been viewed in a positive light in places like England, America, and so on. I am curious if that was the case for Parley as well. And then, if so, were there any public figures who helped change the thinking," Zephyr explained carefully.

Mae looked at the Adam. He nodded encouragingly.

"Well, there have been a few. Because Parley was founded by pirates, I wouldn't say actors or the performing arts were ever viewed in a negative light per se. Some establishments had questionable reputations based on the kinds of shows and clientele they attracted."

"Interesting. I have to admit, I never gave much thought to this subject until Mr. Levan began asking questions," Ember noted.

Mae smiled and seemed to relax. Ember's words put her at ease. "I can understand that, Your Majesty. Theater plays a large role in the entertainment industry of Parley, and is viewed extremely well."

Zephyr gestured to the schedules and playbills littering the table. "It is very clear Parlians enjoy their plays."

Mae grinned. "Very much so. In regards to your question about notable figures. There have been a few from the royal family, as well as the Thache, Read, Bonny, and Roberts families."

Excitement coursed through Ember at the sound of Thache. She was careful to keep her features guarded and noticed Zephyr had done the same. This had to be what Emerson was hinting at when he said to see a play.

"Who in the royal family?" Zephyr asked before turning to Ember with a sly grin and adding, "Maybe there is a famous actor or actress in the Bellamy line."

Ember giggled behind her hand. "Maybe."

"The only members of the royal family I'm familiar with are Dahlia, Lillian, and Derrick. However, they were out of the line of succession. This gave them the freedom to participate and promote artistic endeavors. Dahlia and Lillian were involved in the Careen theater in the early 1800s, while Derrick was in the late 1700s," Mae said.

Of the names given, Ember recognized Dahlia. If she remembered correctly, the woman would have been an aunt born around the turn of the 19th century. There was a scandal surrounding her, but Ember couldn't remember the details. She would have to ask Emerson or Grammy Margaret about it.

"That is so interesting. Were any of the other members of the aristocracy also not in the line of succession? Is that why they felt they could pursue an interest in the arts."

Mae thought for a long moment. "I'm not certain. However, what I can say is both the Thache and Roberts families had their share of scandals surrounding their heirs in the early-to-mid 1800s, and it had to do with the theater."

Everyone remained silent while Mae thought. She was looking off at a spot in the distance and had a frown on her face like she was trying to remember something.

"Someone in the Thache family was a playwright. I know it created a scandal in his family and for him because of his work. I believe he was a second son though, but I would have to review the history to confirm that."

"Fascinating," Zephyr remarked. "Do you know approximately when he was born? Or the titles of any of his works?"

"I don't know the titles of any of his work, but I believe he was active in the theater scene in the late 1700s and early 1800s. I can look further into it if you would like," Mae offered.

Zephyr didn't look at Ember before responding. He knew they needed to remain guarded because you never knew about people. They may say something off-hand to someone and set a chain of events in motion without knowing it.

He waved a hand dismissively. "No, don't worry about it."

Both Ember and Zephyr asked a few more questions before Adam and Mae left.

The pair were quiet for a few moments. Each in their own mind. Zephyr turned to Ember to speak when a commotion in the hall captured their attention.

Wilson stormed into the room. "We are leaving for America. Go pack your bags!"

Zephyr and Ember sat frozen in place, stunned by Wilson's presence and demand. Neither had any idea what was going on. Because they were in the private wing of the palace there weren't guards posted at the door, just at the entrances leading to the private family spaces. Wilson was known to the guards and had permission to access certain areas without permission.

The footman had left to escort Adam and Mae to the public area so they could leave. Thus, there had been no one to announce Wilson's entrance into the solarium.

"Are you deaf? I said to get up and pack your bags!" Wilson's voice boomed throughout the glass room.

Zephyr recoiled at the sound.

"What is going on?" He asked as he glanced at Ember. She seemed to be as bewildered as he was by this sudden appearance and declaration of his father's.

"It doesn't matter what has happened! When I tell you to get up," Wilson yelled stomping over to Zephyr and grabbing him. "You get up," Wilson finished, flinging the young man from the chair.

Zephyr caught himself as he stumbled forward. Guards rushed in at the shouting and toppling of furniture. They ran to protect Ember.

Wilson glared at her for a moment before he chuckled darkly. "What good lap dogs. Must be nice to always be protected from danger, or the appearance of it."

Ember clenched her jaw but stayed silent. Battles were won in silence. She wasn't giving Wilson the satisfaction of a response.

Zephyr straightened to his full height of six feet one inch tall. The hard line of his jaw told Ember he wasn't going to faithfully leave with his father, especially not after his outburst.

"What is going on, Father?" Zephyr had his arms folded across his chest. It was evident from his stance he wasn't leaving his spot without a satisfactory answer.

"We can discuss the matter in private. While you pack," Wilson bit out.

Ember looked back and forth between the two men. She wanted to leave and give them privacy, but she was afraid of what might happen to Zephyr if she left.

"Zephyr, why don't I wait for you in my private garden? You and your father can talk in here," Ember suggested. There was a flash of panic in Zephyr's eyes before he composed himself. Ember couldn't protect him from inside this room, she needed help. She also needed to find out what was going on.

Zephyr smiled at her. "That would be great, Your Majesty. Thank you."

Ember smiled back and walked out of the room into the garden. As soon as the doors were closed she turned to the guards.

"You do not leave Zephyr unguarded. Give him and his father privacy, don't rush into any room they are in, unless Wilson becomes a serious threat to Zephyr's safety. Understood?"

The men nodded. Ember turned and rushed towards her bother's office. Emerson would know what was happening. He would know how to fix this.

Chapter 7

Ember burst into Emerson's office only to find it empty. She pushed through the adjoining door and rushed into his secretary Greer's office.

"Where is Emerson?"

Greer looked up with annoyance in her eyes until she saw who asked the question. She popped to attention and curtsied. "He is inspecting the naval ships, Your Majesty."

Ember sighed. She pinched the bridge of her nose. She didn't have time to hunt him down at the moment. Why was he down with the ships?

"May I be of assistance, Your Majesty?"

Ember turned to Greer. "I'm not sure. Wilson interrupted me and Zephyr in the private solarium. He was in a rage and told Zephyr to pack. I came here to find Emerson because I have no idea what's going on."

"Oh, I can help with that, Your Majesty. Prime Minister Levan is angry because Prince Emerson vetoed the law allowing the sale of all mineral mines and pearl farms to noncitizens for the fourth time," Greer answered.

Ember bit her lip. "The fourth time? Dear God in heaven that man is nothing if not persistent and hard-headed. The rejection would explain Wilson's anger. Is that why the prime minister is leaving the country?"

The woman nodded enthusiastically. "Oh yes, Your Majesty. The prime minister all but declared war and Prince Emerson eagerly accepted the consequences. Prince Emerson directed me to set a time with you for this afternoon to discuss the matter. It's the final item on your schedule for the day."

Ember groaned and buried her face in her hands. Both Wilson and Emerson were competitive and proud. Their meeting earlier ended in a catastrophe, while the meeting she and Zephyr had had given them some promising leads. She wished her twin had come to her sooner with this information, but at least he was on her schedule. Ember rolled her eyes at the thought.

"I need to make sure Zephyr doesn't leave," Ember stated. "I already told the guards outside the solarium not to leave him unguarded. I've heard stories of Wilson's temper. I told Zephyr to meet me in my private garden after his conversation with his father. Can you wait there until either I return or he arrives and tell him I went to find Emerson?"

Greer nodded. "Of course, Your Majesty." She curtsied and then hurried off to ensure the queen's orders were followed.

When Ember caught up to Emerson, she was going to wring his neck. What was he thinking? Breaking the engagement could lead to war in a worst-case scenario, she didn't need his help ushering one to Parley's door.

Emerson was inspecting the repairs to one of the battleships when the call rang out the queen had boarded. He squared his shoulders and braced himself for the exchange and her temper.

Ember hated being the last to know about anything related to threats against Parley. He was sure she was thrilled to find out about Wilson's threat. He had been hoping the matter would keep until this afternoon because he was busy with more pressing matters. Wilson's latest temper tantrum was a footnote in his day.

"Your Majesty," murmured the crew around them. They bowed to show their respect. Emerson greeted his twin. Her jade eyes danced with anger.

"Did you forget to tell me something, Director of Intelligence and Military Operations?" Ember was seething. Members of the crew took discreet steps away from the siblings. He couldn't blame them for giving them space and abandoning him to her rage. He would have done it too had he been in their shoes.

"Prime Minister Levan has decided to depart for America. He has to inform parliament of my decision regarding several of them attempting to purchase mineral mines and pearl farms using a law I just killed for the fourth time," Emerson explained.

He turned to inspect railings on the bridge before adding with a dismissive wave, "He also threatened war, which is his favorite threat when he's in a desperate bid to demand what he wants. I may have said we have the best navy and will rise to the challenge."

"EMERSON SAMUEL ARCHER BELLAMY THE FOURTH!" He cringed at both the pitch and volume of Ember's reaction. He had expected the invocation of his full name, but not at the level in which it was delivered.

She was never going to be happy with the outcome of the meeting. The fact was, he had to act regarding the new law the Crown Guardians had signed on her behalf. A law they had found a way to pass four times. It was war with America or war with Muirgen. Seeing as how half the population of Parley was related to someone who was Mer, there would be a revolution at even a hint of hanging them out to dry.

No. If Parley was going to war with someone, it would be America. After all, their secret weapon was the Mer. Once Emerson explained to the Muirgen king about the situation, he knew he would be able to count the Mer soldiers among his numbers. The benefits of having the Mer outnumbered so many things.

"What would you have me do, Your Majesty? Hmmm? Sit on my hands and see what happens? Wait until the strip mining begins or someone discovers something they shouldn't have? It's a matter of national security," Emerson told her. "I don't know what is going on with Mr. Levan, but he's been after two things since his arrival — total control of Parley or war so he can attempt to win Parley."

"So you decided to give him what he wants?"

Emerson leaned down to grab Ember's upper arms and search her eyes. "Again, Your Majesty, what would you have me *do*? If you refuse to involve yourself in the passage of legislation, if you refuse to *lead*, then what would you have me *do*?"

Ember looked up and studied his face. She knew he was right. Wilson was going to do whatever he was going to do. He'd had his eyes on Parley from the moment he stepped off the airship five years ago. Everyone and everything is a pawn in his ambitions and greed.

Emerson was also right about her not leading. She limited his options in several ways regarding legislation when she let the Guardians rule instead of her. Ember was terrified she would be the Bellamy to lose the kingdom, either in a war or a revolution. Russia was the most recent example that came to mind. However, she couldn't criticize her twin for taking matters into his own hands and leaving her in the dark when she wasn't willing to participate.

"You're right, Em," she admitted. "I can't be angry with you if I won't get involved. Wilson caught me off guard when he burst into the solarium. He told Zephyr to pack his bags. We can't let him take Zephyr back to America, Em."

Emerson closed his eyes and sighed. "I can't make him stay if he decides to go back to America with his father. However, we will protect him if he chooses to stay, and I will send someone with him if he leaves."

"I want to declare that he can't leave. I don't trust Wilson, and what if Zephyr...." Ember trailed off. She sucked on her lower lip as she looked at the ocean behind Emerson crashing into the shore.

Emerson arched his eyebrows. "Do I detect concern for your beau's wellbeing?"

Ember swatted her twin on the arm. "I'm not a monster. I don't like our situation or even his commentary at times, but I'm not soulless, and... he doesn't deserve what has been done to him. He isn't a bad guy."

Emerson chuckled quietly as he grinned at her admission. Maybe his grandmother was right. Maybe he should give her a chance to figure things out as he pushed, or shoved, her toward where he needed her to be. The fact she was giving Zephyr a chance and was concerned about his wellbeing gave him hope.

"Have a little faith in your fiancé. Just because Wilson is throwing a tantrum regarding not getting what he wants, doesn't mean Zephyr won't be able to calm him down and get him to see reason. War is a big leap to make over a dead real estate deal, especially in this day and age."

Ember thought about this for a moment. He was right. Wilson had threatened any number of things over the past six months.

Threatening war may have been a tactic he hadn't used as often, but that didn't mean Zephyr wouldn't be able to calm his father down.

Ember took a deep breath. Emerson was right. His level-headedness and logic were things she had always appreciated about him. He helped calm her emotions and see things more clearly. She had been reacting to how Wilson had acted with her and Zephyr in the solarium because it had taken her by surprise. She had never seen Wilson's anger like that before, but she knew Emerson was always ahead of most storms. Even the ones he created.

"You're right. I need to have more faith in Zephyr's charm," Ember conceded. "He does know how to handle and manage people, especially his father. If anyone can get that man to see reason, it will be Zeph."

"I'm glad you agree." Emerson motioned for the officers and crew to return. "Now, if you'll excuse me. I really do need to check the quality of the repairs."

Ember rolled her eyes. "Of course, Your Royal Highness. How dare I interfere with your inspection?"

Emerson snorted. "I'll see you at dinner, Your Majesty."

Ember turned on her heel to leave but stopped. She rushed to her twin and gave him an impulsive hug. He squeezed her back briefly.

"See you at dinner," Ember threw over her shoulder as she left the ship.

As soon as she made it back to the palace, she would head to her private garden and pray Zephyr was waiting for her return. With any sort of luck, he would be able to get his father to see reason and be waiting for her in the garden.

Chapter 8

"Father, do see reason."

That remark resulted in his attaché case being thrown at his head. Zephyr caught it, along with the vulgar things his father was saying about Ember, Emerson, the entire kingdom, and lastly himself. Zephyr just sighed and set down the bag near his luggage.

He wasn't leaving. His father wasn't starting a war. He just needed to let his father vent his rage and frustration. Once he calmed down and was closer to anger rather than rage, Zephyr could reason with him.

"Why can't you be like your brother? Caelus never argues with me. He just does!"

"Yes, Cael does just 'do', which is how he finds himself in the messes you then must fix," Zephyr shot back. He was sick to death of being compared to his older brother. On more than one occasion Zephyr had served as the scapegoat to excuse Caelus's behavior.

His father stopped throwing things and paused. "Excuse me? What did you just say?"

"You heard me. Caelus doesn't think. He just acts and does whatever he wants knowing you will blame me or Neil, and sweep it under the rug. We can't have the future prime minister caught in drug scandals and rape allegations. No, that's my job. Taking the blame for his misdeeds in the press and the courts."

Wilson flew at Zephyr, pulling his son to him by the lapels of his coat. "You ungrateful little bastard!"

Wilson's face was a scant few inches from his. "Need I remind you of the privileges you had growing up? As well as the secret we keep in regard to you!"

Zephyr shoved his father away from him. "I had those privileges because *whose* money is it? It's Mother's money. Not yours. Regardless of whether I'm a product of an affair or your son, you have no choice but to keep my secret. We both know what Mother will do."

Wilson curled and uncurled his hands into fists at his side. "The scandal of my birth will be nothing compared to the gossips discussing how you couldn't keep the wealthy heiress happy in or out of bed. Not to mention the speculation of who her lover was and still is your younger brother or the la crosse player from university."

"Why you little —" Wilson lunged for Zephyr. Striking him on the left side of his face.

Zephyr absorbed the punch. He was used to the physical abuse of his father's temper. Instead of cowering or shrinking back, Zephyr chuckled. "Beating me up isn't going to solve your problems. She bore you one son and then paid back your cruelty with uncertainty regarding the rest of us. She also holds the money since you've blown through yours."

Zephyr knew Wilson wanted to kill him. He could see it in his eyes. He felt the contempt Wilson had for him in everything he did. Zephyr knew he hit a nerve when he brought up his younger brother and sister. Both of them looked like Caelus and Wilson, while Zephyr looked like their mother. Then again, Mother's lover was Father's younger brother, so he could never be certain who their father was.

"Get out of my sight," Wilson seethed.

Zephyr gave him a mock salute. "Yes, sir." Instead of pointing out that they were in his room, Zephyr strode halfway across the room before throwing over his shoulder. "You're not starting a war with Parley, and I'm not leaving even if you do. Give my regards to your cronies."

Wilson picked up a metal vase and threw it at Zephyr, who slammed the door behind him. The vase hit the door a second later, the thud echoing down the hallway as Zephyr moved to find Ember. If Kieran was who they needed, then Kieran was who they would find — together.

Wilson used the veranda door to leave Zephyr's room. The boy was pissing him off. He had no idea how things worked in this family. Since Emerson had blown up his plans to purchase mines and farms, he needed a distraction while he came up with another plan.

Once in his room, Wilson went to the phone and dialed the operator. He then gave her a number to ring. She placed him on hold while she rang the number.

After a few minutes, the operator came back on the line. "I have Mr. Caelus Levan for you. I'm patching you through now."

"Hello, Father. Was it too much to wait to phone until after breakfast?" Caelus yawned into the receiver and muttered to someone near him.

Wilson growled. "You are in California and only a few hours behind me. It's almost brunch where you are!"

Caelus chuckled. "I never get up before noon. You know that, yet, you've woken me up. I can only assume it's urgent."

Wilson rolled his eyes. Cael never appreciated the sacrifices Wilson and his grandfather had made for him to live the indulgent, entitled lifestyle he enjoyed. Without access to his wife's money, Wilson was flat broke. If it wasn't for his wealthy mistress, he wouldn't have a dime to his name.

That said, his mistress expected a pearl mine in return for her investment in his career. He had been robbing Peter to pay Paul for a decade. He had been quite successful utilizing Cael to help him set up and blackmail other world leaders for many years. However, the shoe was on the other foot now as Wilson paid up to keep Cael's transgressions from catching up to them.

His oldest son felt invincible because of the secret Cael had stumbled upon. He used that secret to blackmail Wilson into helping get him out of trouble, but the walls were closing in. Wilson was tired of prostituting himself out to wealthy widows and bored socialites for money. Cael needed to step up and do his part to save them. Otherwise, they would be the bankrupt American prime minister and his criminal, cocaine-addicted son.

"You know what, Caelus? I don't give a fig about your sleeping habits. It must be nice to live the life of a playboy," Wilson scolded.

Caelus laughed. "Not only do I hold the secrets of world leaders, I hold your secret as well. My antics and sins are nothing compared to you and your friends and your vices."

Wilson was seeing red but knew he had to keep his temper in check. He could not have his secret getting out and expect to remain prime minister. "The reason for my call is that I need you to come to Parley now. That bastard prince has killed the real estate bill for the fourth time."

Caelus was silent for a moment. "You can't seal the deal?"

"It's not a matter of sealing the deal," Wilson gritted out. "It's a matter of changing the law. Cilia understands the vision of the future, but those children of hers do not. Emerson keeps citing national security as the reason why noncitizens can't own mines or farms. He's also holding up the marriage for the same reason."

Caelus clicked his tongue. "Let me guess, you need me to come and charm Zephyr's ice queen fiancée and brother?"

"I need you to be a distraction, which is something you're good at."

Caelus sighed into the receiver. "Fine. I can be there tomorrow afternoon."

"Wonderful. I want it to be a surprise so try not to tip off to anyone that you're coming," Wilson ordered.

"I will keep my arrival quiet. I promise."

Wilson scrubbed a hand over his face. "You better. It was confirmed to me earlier this afternoon your girlfriend Bianca is now engaged to the vice president of Belize's son. She grew tired of waiting for you to commit and said there was someone else you had your eye on. Who?"

"Bianca was a bore and wouldn't put out. I found someone else to have fun with, but things went sideways. She thinks she loves me," Cael said with a sneer. "Which is why I'm in California at the moment."

Wilson let out a series of curse words. "I don't have the money to bail you out!"

"I don't need you to bail me out. I'm perfectly capable of fixing my own messes, and this one provides a better opportunity than Belize," Caelus responded.

"It had better because there isn't any money, Cael. My mistress has cut me off until I either pay her back in full or hand her the deed to a pearl farm."

Caelus's laughter was muffled. "Your mistress has your balls? Don't worry. I'll try to help you get them back."

"Just get here," Wilson seethed before hanging up the phone. He didn't need Caelus's shenanigans right now, he had enough of his own.

Chapter 9

Ember was in her private garden looking over the theater information at her outdoor desk. She had dismissed Greer upon learning Zephyr was with his father in his room, and they were locked in a heated argument.

The scent of hibiscus and orchids greeted her the moment she stepped onto the screened porch. There was a sitting area as well, but Ember had wanted to make notes on some of the documents. Depending on the weather, the oversized doors from the porch leading to the main garden area could be opened or closed. Because it was a nice day, she had the space open to the elements.

She was blessed to not have to share it with anyone at the moment. That would change once she got married. Ember shifted her gaze to the screened porch across from hers. The future king would also share this suite with her. It had been odd to be moved from the nursery to the queen's suite after her father had died. Her mother had been moved to the available dowager suite, while Grammy Margaret had stayed in the one she had been in.

Ember had had no qualms about redecorating the queen's suite. She had moved her furniture over and then brought in her dollhouse. Over the next year, Ember had turned the sitting room into a doll village. It stayed that way until she became a teenager.

When she turned 15, she had the village set up in the nursery. She then redecorated her suite to match her tastes. She sent the bedroom furniture of her childhood back to her old room. Then she went around and picked pieces she wanted in her room from the various rooms in the palace, as well as commissioned furniture from local carpenters.

The garden and courtyard had also been maintained but were overgrown in ways. She had started with the screened porch, having plants thinned to see and appreciate what was there. She then moved on to the garden surrounding the courtyard. She had added birds of paradise, orchids, and lilies for color and fragrance. The hibiscus and ferns had already been in the garden, but Ember had wanted her own touch added to everything. Except for the king's suite. She didn't go into that space, and she never sat or walked over to that porch.

The cool breeze off the ocean sent a shiver through Ember. Summer was upon them with daytime temperatures remaining in the 90s, while the nights cooled off into the 60s; however, that could change depending on the air currents. Hurricane season was also here. While they didn't see hurricanes every year, they always remained vigilant.

Foot falls on the cobblestone path across the garden pulled Ember from her thoughts. A brief muffled conversation ensued before the parlor door leading to the porch opened.

"Ember?" Zephyr called out.

"I'm right here." She replied, never taking her eyes off the papers she was reviewing.

Zephyr took a seat in one of the wicker cane chairs. His fingers tapping on the arm told Ember something was wrong. She made a note on the page she was holding before gathering the documents. If she had to venture a guess, she would say the conversation with his father had gone poorly.

No matter. She would take his mind off that by laying out the notes on the coffee table for him to review and chime in. Then they could discuss what play they wanted to see, and what to research next. Ember set everything down, before pulling on the cord to summon tea.

"Let me grab a shawl. The breeze is starting to pick up."

Zephyr made a noise of acknowledgment and stopped tapping his fingers. He picked up the theater schedule to review her notes.

"I think we should figure out the name of the plays the Thache ancestor was part of. It should give us our best—" Ember's voice trailed off as she looked at Zephyr's face for the first time since he sat down. "Oh my goodness! Zephyr, what happened?"

Ember rushed to his side. She gingerly took his face in her hands to get a better look at the bruise and black eye on his face.

Zephyr tried to brush her hands away, as well as her concern, but Ember would have none of that. "It's nothing. Father was angry and I handled it. No more talk of war, by the way," he explained pasting a smile he didn't feel onto his lips.

"This doesn't look like nothing, Zeph."

Ember's face was so close to his. She had a faint freckle near the outer corner of her left eye he had never noticed before. Her jade eyes also took on an ethereal quality when she was focusing on something. There were also flecks of grey and yellow around the pupil Zephyr noted to himself. In these quiet moments with her, it was easy to wonder what if.

"I'm ringing for the doctor," Ember announced.

"No, it's nothing," Zephyr responded. He grabbed her hand and tried to pull her back down next to him.

"I'm calling for the doctor," Ember repeated. "Then I'll call the kitchen and have them bring ice or something for the swelling."

Zephyr sighed as he watched her stride into the parlor. What would it be like to be loved by Ember? Rather than dismiss the errant thought, he embraced it. He had an idea it would be a fierce, loyal kind of love fueled by the same zest and passion she pursued everything in life with.

However, he would never be the desire of her affections. He wasn't sure how he actually felt about that knowledge. Did he want to be loved by Ember? What about Amelia back in America? She was the one who got away, and he had been trying to find a way back to her for years. Despite her parents, as well as her, believing he was guilty of the crimes he had served time for, he still held out hope they would find their way back to each other.

He let out a deep sigh and then ran a hand through his hair before picking up the theater schedule again. There were the usual classics and musicals. Zephyr leaned forward to set the schedule back on the table when a title caught his eye.

Curiosity won. He grabbed the paper again.

"Queen Anne's Return" Career Theater Association

Wasn't Blackbeard's ship's name the Queen Anne's Revenge? Zephyr paused for a moment. What was Kieran's duchy's name? Revenge?

"Ember," Zephyr called out. "Ember, come here. I think I found something."

He stood and moved for the door. Ember rushed from the room and collided into his chest. Zephyr reached out and steadied her, holding onto her arms a moment longer than necessary. He could have sworn Ember started leaning into him before she pulled herself away.

"Why are you standing up? Why aren't you sitting down?"

Ember tried to usher Zephyr back to the sofa outside, but he resisted.

"Ember, stop. It's fine," he told her. "Look at this."

Ember searched his face for a moment before she took the schedule from him. She looked it over with a quizzical expression on her face. "What am I looking at or for?"

Zephyr pointed to a title toward the bottom of the page. "What was the name of Blackbeard's ship? Wasn't it the Queen Anne's Revenge?"

Ember nodded. "You think this is the play associated with his family?"

"It makes the most sense. We can tell Emerson this is the play we want to attend. There are only a few performances left before the theater brings in the late-summer programming."

A knock on the door signaled the arrival of tea and the doctor. While the maid set up the afternoon tea, and the doctor looked over Zephyr, Ember phoned Emerson's office. She explained to Greer the day and time of the performance they wanted to attend in Careen. Greer said she would inform Emerson straight away.

Once everyone had left, Ember poured Zephyr a cup of tea and fixed him a plate.

"What did the doctor say?"

Zephyr shot her a half-smile as he snagged a shortbread cookie off the plate. "I'm fine, Em. It's not the first time, and I'm sure it won't be the last. I just need to ice my face to help with the swelling."

Ember pursed her lips. She knew it wasn't the first time Wilson had punched Zephyr. However, it was the first time he had ever used any form of violence toward Zephyr in Parley. To hear him regard what happened so flippantly was typical of Zephyr. Peace at all costs. It didn't seem to matter to him if the cost was his physical safety.

Ember took a sip of her tea. She wanted to press the issue of Zephyr's health and his relationship with his father, but instead, she decided to focus on the play.

"I told Emerson's secretary, Greer, we want to attend the performance on Friday night because I leave for Geneva a few days later. Hopefully, your face will look better by then..."

"It won't affect my ability to watch the play or help you research, so it's fine," Zephyr assured her. "We should look into the history of this play. Maybe there are others by this playwright we could get our hands on."

Ember sighed. "I just hate the gossips speculating about what happened."

"They won't point the finger at you, so don't fret."

"It's not me or my reputation I'm fretting over. It's yours."

Zephyr took a sip of tea and ignored her comment. There wasn't any point in his mind in continuing the conversation. What was done was done, and people could think what they wanted to regarding how it happened.

Ember nibbled on a cucumber sandwich. Her mind churned over all the things on her ever-increasing to-do list. She blindly reached for another item on her plate, munching on it without tasting anything.

"The remembrance ceremony is still a few months away, but I'm scared. What if it isn't enough time to get Kieran home? He would move mountains if his sisters needed him, but what if we can't figure out how to do that?"

Zephyr leaned forward and took Ember's hands in his. "We are in this together. We will research this as far as we can, and if we need help, we'll figure it out."

He could see the doubt and uncertainty clouding her eyes. He didn't blame her. A part of him wondered if this wasn't some wild goose chase Emerson was sending them on to get them out of his hair. Then Emerson could focus his attention on getting the Duke of Revenge home without his sister's interference or demands.

"Besides, you're going to Geneva in a few days to visit with Princess Evelyn. While there, you might be able to discover information not readily available in Parley."

Ember's eyes lit up. "Really?"

Zephyr smiled. "Really. You still have to be guarded, but people in Geneva might not think of your questions as anything more than curiosity. Whereas here..."

"People might think it's because Kieran is being investigated for some wrongdoing or scandal or whatever. Especially because it's me asking questions, or even you."

"Exactly."

Ember and Zephyr ate and drank tea in silence for several minutes before a brief knock on the door interrupted their solitude. Nerissa walked out onto the patio.

"Your Majesty, Prince Emerson is requesting your presence in his suite for dinner tonight. His dinner will be about an hour later than the main dinner. He needs to cancel the meeting this afternoon and hopes you understand."

"Please let him know I will be there. I won't need help dressing, so you can have the rest of the evening off," Ember told her.

"Thank you, my lady."

Ember waited until Nerissa had left before speaking. "Are you going to take a tray in your room? I can't imagine wanting to have dinner with your father after this afternoon."

Zephyr sighed and ran a hand through his hair. "I hadn't thought about dinner, but you're right. I don't care to sit across from that man and eat a meal."

"I'll make sure dinner is brought to your room. I know you're down the hall from him... do you want a new room too?"

The concern on Ember's face rendered him speechless for a moment. It had been a while since someone had been concerned about his wellbeing. The only two people in recent memory would be his mother and grandmother, but even that was a complicated lesson in self-preservation. He didn't blame either of them for it.

"Thank you for the offer, but I'll be fine. If something changes, I'll let you know."

Ember nodded and the pair began looking over the theater information and playbills again. With luck, they would figure out the connection to Kieran and the theater sooner rather than later.

Wilson had sent Cilia a missive requesting a private dinner. She had accepted and invited Martin and the patriarch of the church, Peter Stone. The trio were the core group of the Crown Guardians responsible for the sweeping changes to Parley.

Tonight's dinner would be all business. Wilson needed to discuss a workaround to Emerson's decision. There had to be one, and he would find it. He had creditors breathing down his neck and a wife who cared very little about what happened to him and Caelus. She was too focused on flaunting her relationship with his younger brother while protecting the twins from his plans. Zephyr was as much her sacrificial lamb as he was his.

If Neil married someone wealthy like Zephyr was, then his problems would be solved. He would be able to line his pockets and invest the money to grow it so he could pay off his debts and live the lifestyle he was accustomed to. He was tired of using his body to seduce women for their money. Very few of the women had been enjoyable. Most of them had been a means to an end.

Wilson finished dressing for dinner and checked his appearance in this mirror one more time. He wanted to be impeccable for his queen. After the day he had, he was looking forward to their night together.

Cilia was a vain creature who loved her booze. She was beautiful and she knew it. Wilson didn't mind their flirtation or their arrangement. She was a jealous woman, though, and often pushed for him to divorce his wife and stop seeing his French mistress.

He promised he would leave his mistress behind once he had fulfilled the arrangement they had. Cilia was motivated to make that happen. She knew Emerson killing the real estate law was a setback for their relationship. She was motivated to fix it.

Wilson walked to Cilia's suite and knocked on the door. A maid answered and ushered him to the table. He was the final person to arrive, everyone else was already seated for dinner. He bowed and kissed Cilia's hand before sitting.

"You always look smart in blue. It brings out the color of your eyes," Cilia cooed. Martin rolled his eyes, while Peter downed half his glass of wine in one gulp.

Wilson smiled at Cilia. "The blush color of your gown highlights your youthful glow, my dear. Your beauty is truly unrivaled."

Cilia giggled as she playfully swatted at Wilson. "You, sir, are nothing but a flatterer."

She motioned for the footmen to start serving the food. Another footman filled the wine glasses. When the staff had finished, she dismissed them.

"Let's get down to brass tacks, gentlemen. There has to be a way for foreigners to buy real estate in Parley. Emerson doesn't understand the ramifications of his actions. How are we supposed to grow on the world stage if we hoard our resources?"

"I agree, Your Majesty. I also have a thought on this matter," Peter said in a rush.

Wilson wanted to roll his eyes. Peter was Cilia's lap dog. He eagerly accepted scraps of Cilia's attention and flirtations because he wanted the notoriety of being her right-hand man. The man had proven useful on more than one occasion, which was why Cilia kept him around.

Cilia turned her gaze to Peter and shot him a coy grin. "What are you thinking, Peter? You come up with some of our most brilliant ideas," she purred.

Peter flushed from his neck to the tips of his ears. "W-well, only, uh, citizens can own mines and farms. Rather, n-naturalized citizens," Peter stammered.

Cilia twirled a lock of her blond hair, further distracting the man. Wilson exchanged an annoyed look with Martin. Both men knew better than to interrupt Cilia when she was having her fun. It would lead to some form of outburst he didn't want to deal with.

"I'm not following, Peter. We already know this information," Cilia pouted.

"Y-y-es. What if we made Wilson and Caelus naturalized citizens? After all, citizenship is granted through not only the government but also the church."

Everyone at the table stopped eating and stared at Peter. The man looked down at his plate and started muttering how it was just a thought.

Cilia sucked in a sharp breath and grabbed his hand, clutching it to her bosom. Her smile was wide and dazzling as she vibrated with excitement.

"Oh, Peter. You never disappoint," Cilia purred in his ear. Peter blushed from head to toe.

The man sat up straighter in his seat and began to eat with renewed vigor. "We can start the paperwork tomorrow, Your Majesty. There isn't much to it. Once Wilson and Caelus are naturalized citizens, they can buy the pearl farms and mineral mines. If they pass unnoticed by the Department of National Security, then we can do it with a few more and wait again."

Wilson had to hand it to the man. It was a clever solution. He was also smart to only do a few people at a time and then wait a few months before trying it again. If they got too greedy and pushed through too many people at once it would raise suspicions. Slow and steady wins the race after all.

"Good work, Peter." The man preened under the attention. Cilia's hand slid under the table and squeezed Wilson's thigh. He gave her a sideways glance while she grinned at him.

He knew that look. Desire coursed through his body. Cilia was elated, which meant his night with her was going to be eventful. Wilson speared a carrot as he thought about the fun they were going to have.

Chapter 10

Ember and Zephyr had decided to take brunch on her patio instead of joining everyone for breakfast. This had given her a chance to sleep in after a fitful night's sleep. The dark circle under Zephyr's not bruised eye told a similar tale.

When he had requested an audience, Ember had taken one look at him and asked how he had slept. His stomach had rumbled a short time later when they had been reviewing his notes. Ember had called down to the kitchen and requested brunch be brought up to her patio. When the maid had asked if she wanted tea or coffee, Ember immediately answered coffee.

Now the pair was sitting in comfortable silence next to each other on the veranda. Zephyr was reading a newspaper while Ember went through her morning briefings. It amazed her how natural it felt to be with him while doing something so utterly domestic as reading through the daily news and tasks.

A knock on her door pulled her from the letter in her hand and her thoughts.

"Yes?" Ember called out.

"I beg your pardon, Your Majesty," Nerrisa bashfully murmured when she saw the pair sitting next to each other.

"What is it?" Ember asked lightly.

"Dowager Queen Cilia has requested your presence at the airport this afternoon, as well as at dinner tonight, in light of Mr. Levan's brother's arrival."

Zephyr's eyebrows shot up. "My brother? Which one?"

Ember could tell from his shocked tone he had not been aware of this visit.

"I believe Prime Minister Levan said it was Mr. Caelus, sir."

The color drained from his face. Ember was concerned by his reaction. Was his brother visiting so terrible? What did he know that she didn't?

"Thank you, Lady Nerissa. I'll be sure to dress to receive Mr. Levan at the airport as well as for dinner," Ember replied, dismissing her friend.

"Zephyr?" Ember sucked on her lower lip as she took in his reaction.

He looked defeated, which was alarming because Zephyr was never defeated. Ember knew this from their countless sparing matches over the years. She would think she had the upper hand in whatever matter they were discussing or taking part in, but time and again, Zeph would come bounding back regardless of whether he won or not. He would shoot her a boyish grin, made even more innocent by his freckles, and announce he would best her next time.

This Zephyr. The colorless sheet before her was one she had never seen before. There was no drive behind his amber eyes, instead, they were flat, like he had accepted whatever fate awaited him. Was Caelus's unexpected arrival really so dire?

Ember sat next to him and grabbed the hand closest to her. It was cold and clammy to the touch. Apprehension coursed through her. He must be in some kind of shock. Maybe from his injuries, but that didn't make sense. He had only been punched in the face.

Ember leaned across the coffee table and snagged the shawl she had used the day before. She wrapped it around Zephyr's shoulders. She then took both of his hands in hers and began to rub them together.

"What are you doing?"

Ember looked up to see Zephyr's amber eyes watching her. "You're hands are like ice. I was afraid you were going into some form of shock between the news and your injury. Maybe a delayed reaction or something. I'm not a doctor."

"No, I'm fine. I'm just concerned about Cael's arrival and what that means. It had to of been planned at least a day or two in advance. He was supposed to be in Belize today or tomorrow for a week-long visit with his girlfriend," Zephyr murmured out loud. "Yet, Father said nothing to me about this change of plans."

"Maybe they wanted to surprise you?"

Zephyr snorted. His complexion seemed to be returning to normal, even if he wasn't.

He let out a curse and grabbed Ember's hands, pulling her to face him. "Do not let Caelus near *any* of the female staff or ladies or women at *all*. He can only be around men."

Zephyr jumped up from the settee and began pacing. "This is bad, Ember. This is really bad. We may need to call for —"

Emerson strode through the garden gate before Zephyr could finish his thought.

"Oh thank God!" Relief flooded Zephyr's face. "We have a situation."

"I know. Why didn't you tell me Caelus was coming? I could have been better prepared," Emerson barked at Zephyr. "When did he change his plans from Belize to Parley?"

"I didn't know until Nerissa told Ember not five minutes ago. We have to clear the palace of women," Zephyr declared before turning to face Ember. "And she needs to have a guard with her at all times, even while she sleeps. I don't trust this at all, Emerson."

Ember's brows knitted together in apprehension and confusion. Why was Zephyr acting like this over his brother visiting? Surely the rumors about Caelus couldn't all be true. After all, he was being groomed to carry on the mantel of being an American prime minister. That couldn't happen if he was embroiled in scandal every moment of the day. Although, there was the incident Zephyr served time for, so maybe he wasn't overreacting.

"I'm working on it. Greer will be by Ember's side and will serve as a temporary lady's maid. She will also be staying with her. She is well trained, and won't let anything happen to Ember," Emerson assured. "I will also be staying in the king's suite."

Zephyr let out a huge sigh. "Good. That all sounds good. What about the servants? And the citizens?"

The poor man looked to be on the verge of tears. He seemed overwhelmed by this unexpected visit. It also struck Ember how quick Zephyr was to list off what needed to happen concerning the safety of the women in not only the palace but also the kingdom. Her stomach began to churn as a wave of dread washed over her. How many of the rumors were true? Especially because Emerson didn't overreact.

"The servants have been instructed to keep all the doors locked to the quarters. Only the footman will bring things out, such as tea, breakfast, and so on. I made it clear no female servants under forty were to be seen in the palace period. I had to give a few of them temporary paid time off because they live off-site, but it's a necessary precaution."

Ember listened as her brother and Zephyr discussed other things that needed to be taken care of in advance of Caelus's arrival. It sounded like they were preparing the place for a predator. Which, if the rumors were even remotely true, is what Caelus would be considered. That thought sent a shiver down her spine.

"How long is he staying? Zephyr and I are going to the theater in a few days, and I will not miss that show over some arrogant flyboy with an animalistic reputation," Ember declared.

Emerson closed his eyes for patience while Zephyr stood stunned into silence. "I don't know how long he is staying, Em. If you miss the show on Friday, I'll make it up to you and have them perform it here. My duchy will cover the cost."

"That won't work. There are only three showings left, and then they move into the mid-summer programming. I leave for Geneva before a private showing can be arranged. Then when I come back, it will be odd to request a showing of a play that has been out of the theater for weeks, especially one titled 'Queen Anne's Return,'" Ember explained.

"Why does the…. Oh. I see," Emerson stated. He ran a hand through his hair and then over his short well-kept beard. His jaw was clenched as he stared at the ocean. Ember knew the wheels were turning in that mind of his.

"I'll make it work. God save me, but I'll make it work," Emerson told her. Him and his damn idea. If he didn't play along, she would get suspicious and question why he had her look into the matter to begin with. Then she might figure out it was a ruse of sorts while he kept the pressure on Kieran.

Ember hugged him. "Thank you. I know it seems frivolous, but I need to see that play. I'm the only person aside from you and Grammy who would understand hidden references."

"I know. I know. If it hadn't been for Kieran giving me a heads up a few hours ago, I wouldn't be as far along as I am in preparing for Caelus's visit."

Zephyr and Ember's attention turned to Emerson.

"Kieran sent word about Caelus? Then you know how to contact him?" Ember asked. Her eyes hopefully searched her twin's.

He gave her a sad half-smile. "He had someone else send the message to someone, and then they forwarded it on to me. Although, this time the message only went through about four people before it reached me. That tells me it caught him off guard too."

"Where do you think he is?" Zephyr asked.

"It would appear he's still in Africa or Asia, but for what reason, I don't know."

Ember let out a frustrated breath and stamped her foot for good measure, something she hadn't done since she was a child. "He'll warn you about questionable people, but he won't come home. Not even for me."

The hurt in her voice was palpable. Emerson regretted telling her the hard truth about Kieran's behavior. However, she had to know. To be fair to Kieran, he probably would come home if he thought a threat wasn't being taken seriously or was too much for Emerson to handle alone. But Emerson would never gamble with Ember's safety to lure Kieran back, and he knew it. That left his sisters because Emerson had major doubts about Kieran even caring about the reputation of Revenge unless it affected his kin.

He wasn't telling Ember he too was pulling out all the stops in his efforts to drag the duke home. If he failed, then hopefully the task he assigned her would yield something he could use. At the moment, Emerson wanted Ember to believe she was the only person solely dedicated to bringing him home because then she would stay out of intelligence matters.

Sensing Emerson's loss for words, Zephyr walked over to Ember and gently embraced her from behind. She jumped at the sudden contact, but let him hold her.

"Em, even if Kieran wanted to protect you himself and come home, he's more than two hours away. His giving Emerson the information as quickly as he learned of it is his way of fulfilling his duty to keep you safe. I'm sorry it doesn't look like how you want it to. I know you two were very close until Willow's death."

A tear fell from Ember's eye and landed on his hand. Zephyr stiffened slightly. She never cried in front of him, and for that matter, she never cried over him either. Maybe Kieran meant more to her than she let on, which shouldn't make any difference to him.

He wanted out of their engagement as much as she did. However, that didn't explain the ache in his heart over the thought that Ember and Kieran could have a deeper relationship. It didn't make any sense. He wanted to find a way to get Amelia back and live a quiet life in America. Not marry the queen of a tropical kingdom where his every move would be scrutinized.

The phone rang in the parlor. Emerson answered it. It was a brief conversation before he disconnected and rang someone else. A few moments later, a light knock sounded on the door. Ember could hear the faint murmur of conversation, but she didn't care.

Kieran would never come back if it were up to him. That knowledge felt like a dagger plunged into her heart. Twisting and creating fresh ripples of pain every time she learned of an opportunity he failed to take to come home.

A light breeze sent a shiver through her. She cocooned herself deeper into Zephyr's light embrace. At least she could count on him to keep her safe. He even tasted her food and drinks before allowing her to consume them. She giggled at this thought.

"What's so funny?" Ember could feel Zephyr's voice rumbling through his chest as he asked the question.

"I was just thinking of how you protect me in ways no one else ever has."

Zephyr turned her to face him. He arched an eyebrow in confusion. "And that's funny?"

"You've been tasting my food and drinks. It's a little funny."

Zephyr smiled and Ember's breath caught in her throat. It was like the sun had returned after weeks of rain. It was a radiant sight and a sign he was going to fight.

Emerson walked into the garden with Greer. "Em, Greer is going to help you get ready to meet Caelus's airship when it touches down in about an hour. Then she'll help you prepare for dinner. Because she is a member of the Read family, she'll be using her honorific of lady. She'll be acting as your lady's maid, which is beneath her status, but necessary. She'll also serve as a bodyguard of sorts until either you leave for Geneva, or Caelus heads back to America."

Ember nodded and pushed away from Zephyr. "Well, then Lady Greer. Shall we dress for the airport? If you have nothing suitable, just take something from my wardrobe."

If Greer was shocked by Ember's words, she didn't show it. She just smiled and said, "Yes, Your Majesty."

Emerson turned to Zephyr. "Come. Let's go and get ready ourselves. Ember is in capable hands."

Zephyr shot one last look to the doorway where Greer and Ember had disappeared through and sighed. Caelus was going to muck everything up, and there was nothing he was going to be able to do about it.

He sighed and followed Emerson. It was going to be a long visit regardless of the length.

The palace had been thrown into chaos with the unexpected arrival of Caelus, and the man didn't disappoint. Rather than come in on an airship, which is what everyone had been expecting, the young man piloted an airplane.

Upon leaving the cockpit, Caelus announced he was honored by the royal reception. He had bowed and kissed Ember's hand before winking at Greer. Emerson had practically growled through the remaining introductions, while their half-whit mother giggled over his flattery.

Ember would give it to the Levan family, they were all good-looking people; Caelus was no exception with his six-foot-tall athletic build complete with sandy blonde hair and blue-green hazel eyes. If Ember had to wager, she would bet many a woman had been entranced by his unique eyes.

The center near his pupils was a pear color, while the main color was sky blue and the outer ring a darker sapphire. People also claimed Caelus's eyes changed colors depending on his mood. Ember had thought that an exaggeration, although now, she wasn't so sure. Regardless, he was a very charismatic and charming narcissist with a cruel heart.

Ember walked ahead of everyone with Greer following close behind. She had dismissed the idea of taking the car from the palace down the short distance to the airport. There was a private footpath the royal family took, as well as staff or military folks. It was a far more private affair than taking the car with the flags and security announcing her presence.

The early evening heat was tolerable, especially with the breeze. Soon the sun would set, bringing the temperatures down with it. Ember had also wanted the exercise. She had been stuffed within the palace grounds for too long. Aside from her short trip down to the docks in her search for Emerson, this was the first real outing she'd had in weeks.

"Look at the gams on that dame," Caelus leaned over and whispered to Zephyr.

Zephyr didn't respond. Rather he glared murderously at his brother, whom he wished would shut up. He had already broken protocol a few times with Ember and was even now failing to comprehend the magnitude of insulting a lady in the presence of the queen.

It wasn't lost on Zephyr how rigid Ember was walking, or Greer for that matter. The sheer audacity of his brother to flirt with a noblewoman in such a manner in front of her queen and a crowned prince made his blood boil. It wasn't like they hadn't received the same education regarding etiquette.

Emerson also looked fit to be tied, which meant he heard Caelus's comment. The usually poised prince was taking deep breaths to regain control of his emotions. His brother would wrongly assume Emerson was upset because he fancied Greer and was jealous rather than comprehend the anger being directed at his disrespect and disregard of Parlian customs.

"Also, you didn't tell me your fiancée was such a dish. Maybe I should tell Father I want to marry her instead," Caelus murmured under his breath with a wink.

Zephyr rolled his eyes. At least his brother had *some* sense as to not say things about the queen loudly in her presence. "And ruin your upcoming engagement to the Central American chick? I think not," he retorted in similarly hushed tones.

Cael smirked like the cat who caught the canary. "Haven't you heard? She's engaged to some other sap, leaving me on the prowl. I'm a free man again."

"You'll have to 'prowl' somewhere else. Parley is closed to your antics."

Cael chuckled. "Sure it is."

His devil-may-care attitude was prickling Zephyr's nerves. A few days was going to be far too long a visit with his brother. Speaking of which, no one had said anything about how long Caelus's trip was supposed to be.

"How long is your stay in Parley? Father didn't say or give a reason for your sudden trip here," Zephyr observed.

Emerson's body language shifted, as he took more of an interest in the conversation between the brothers. Ember and Greer also seemed to have perked up as well.

Caelus's eyes took on a calculating gleam. "Trying to be rid of me so soon? Tsk tsk little brother. You've had ample time to savor Parley's beauty and delicacies, I've decided to see what all the fuss is about."

His nonchalance put Zephyr on edge. Caelus wasn't leaving any time soon. Judging by the looks he kept shooting towards the ladies in front of him, specifically one lady, he had his eye on the crown. The hell if he was going to sink his claws into Ember.

Zephyr forced a smile and lightness he didn't feel into his tone. "I see. Well, I do so hope you enjoy your trip. I'm sure Father and his valet will be more than willing to help educate you on proper etiquette, as well as Parlian culture and customs."

Caelus cocked his brow. "It can't be that difficult, Z. I'm sure I'll breeze through the challenge of learning what I need to. After all, you managed it," he added, playfully punching his brother on the shoulder.

"By the way, how did you manage that shiner?"

"The usual way. I was punched," Zephyr retorted.

Caelus seemed to want to pop off and say more, but then he needed to maintain appearances. He couldn't torment him and still keep up the act of being a charmer, so he wisely stayed quiet, which was fine by Zephyr. Silence enveloped the group as they made their way back to the palace to ready for dinner. Things were going to get interesting.

Chapter 11

Ember walked into her closet and tried to decide what gown she wanted to wear for dinner. Did she want to wear something shorter because of the heat? Or longer because of Caelus's reputation? For that matter, she also needed to decide on the cut of the bodice as well. Most of her dinner gowns were designed to show off her assets, not hide them.

She let out a long, deep sigh. Ember fingered several gowns before landing on a light pink one. It was form-fitting and the skirt was tea length, but it would do, especially in this summer heat. The bodice also wasn't too revealing.

Greer walked into the dressing room a moment later. She was poised with her blond hair pulled into a sophisticated bun. Her teal gown highlighted her aquamarine eyes. Her features were graceful and elegant. Ember had always admired her and had often speculated about Emerson's feelings toward his secretary. While she was a few years older than them, she complimented her brother well.

"Do you need help, Your Majesty?"

"We are alone in my dressing room. You're a member of the peerage and a founding family. It's just Ember."

Greer smiled as she walked over to a drawer and pulled out a corset. "I didn't want to assume, Ember. Will this one work? Also, is my dress formal enough? I don't want to embarrass you and His Royal Highness."

Ember hid a laugh at the use of her brother's title. Greer was truly one of a kind. "Yes, that one will work. Thank you again for lowering yourself to help me."

"Oh, I don't think of it like that. I'm a lady, so it's an honor to be of service."

Ember caught her gaze in the mirror as the other woman helped her undress so she could dress for dinner. "I appreciate it nonetheless. Also, your dress is stunning. I dare say Emerson will notice."

A blush spread across Greer's cheeks. Ember's eyes lit with excitement. "You do like him, don't you? I knew it!"

Greer ducked her head as she began lacing the corset. "I enjoy your brother's company. He's my superior and my boss. I wouldn't want to compromise our relationship, or his professional image, with speculation of an affection between us."

Ember was stunned into silence for a moment before she barked out a laugh. "Greer, I do so enjoy how you phrase things. I would be less concerned about his reputation in terms of affection and more concerned about yours. That said, I wasn't asking so I could feed the rumor mill. I do view us as friends, and I think you and Emerson are good for each other."

Greer paused in her pulling and tightening. "Truly? I often think I drive him mad because he's so serious all the time, and I try to lighten the mood at times, but then he gets more sullen."

Ember waved a dismissive hand. "That's how he is with everyone. We've all known each other and been friends since childhood, so your teasing and playfulness being tolerated on any level proves he cares about you."

"I don't think he doesn't care about me," Greer remarked. "It's more like I'm not certain he would ever return my affections because he is a prince and a duke, and I'm the third daughter of an earl."

Ember watched the young woman shrug in the mirror as she finished lacing the corset. Greer was selling herself short. She was more than good enough for Emerson, and it had nothing to do with her pedigree and everything to do with her personality and character.

"If Emerson ever rejects your affections over something as trivial as being the third daughter of an earl, please let me know. I have no qualms about setting him straight."

"Oh no, Ember," Greer rushed. "Emerson, I mean His Highness, has never treated me less than in any way. He's also never returned my affections. Rather, my aunt has advised me on my marriage prospects."

Ember lifted her arms as Greer helped slip the dress over her head.

"You father's sister? The one that's the bitter spinster?"

Greer giggled as she helped straighten the satin fabric.

"That would be the one. However, Aunt Mary isn't wrong. I should be realistic with my prospects."

Ember rolled her eyes and the pair giggled as Greer buttoned the back of the dress. "You should go after Emerson. If you fail, then maybe give in to practicality at that time. Not before."

"I'll keep that in mind."

Ember looked herself over in the mirror before sitting down at the vanity and styling her hair. She could have had Greer or a maid help her, but she usually did her own hair for dinner. She added a touch of makeup and a pair of pearl earrings before sliding on her heels.

The two women made their way to the formal dining room. In the distance, Ember could hear the dinner bell ring. She hated arriving early because that meant making small talk, but they were right on time so small talk would be limited to dining only.

Ember walked into the sitting room off the dining area. Zephyr and Emerson stood and bowed, while her grandmother nodded in her direction. Cilia wasn't waiting, which was surprising. Uncle Martin walked in a moment later and bowed. Wilson and Caelus were also absent.

"Your Majesty, should we wait for the others?" Charles, the butler, asked.

No one could eat until Ember arrived unless she had made arrangements beforehand. However, she didn't have to wait for anyone. She was tempted not to wait but decided to be kind.

"We'll wait five minutes. If they aren't here by then, we shall sit for dinner and they can join us when they arrive."

Ember sat on the settee near her grandmother and motioned for Greer to sit next to her.

"I trust Lady Read is proving competent," Emerson asked from his spot leaning against the fireplace surround.

Greer and Grammy Margaret gaped at his words while Ember raised an eyebrow. "'Competent'? Honestly, Emerson, could you be more insulting."

Her twin bristled at her words. "I meant it as a compliment. I know Lady Read is proficient in all tasks. I trust acting as your lady's maid is no different."

The stunned expression on Zephyr's face summed up the thoughts of everyone in the room.

"Dear God, man, stop while you're ahead," Zephyr cautioned.

Emerson looked genuinely confused by his words. Greer decided to save him by clearing her throat. "Thank you for your confidence in my abilities, Your Highness. It means the world you think so highly of me."

Grammy Margaret shook her head slightly as she muttered under her breath, "That's one way of looking at it I suppose."

It took all of Ember's self-control to not laugh. She was going to have a conversation with her twin about how to compliment a lady. She knew he wasn't clueless or without social graces, so she wasn't sure why he was acting so inept now.

Charles cleared his throat to get Ember's attention subtly. She smiled warmly at him. He was forever the consummate professional. He had guided her through countless dinners and events, ever watchful, and ensuring she never made a mistake.

"Shall we eat?"

Everyone walked into the dining room and took their seats. A footman filled wine glasses while the others served the first course. As they began to eat the soup, there was a commotion in the sitting room.

Ember could hear her mother's angry voice. She could only surmise it was because Ember had decided to not wait on her, Wilson, and his playboy son.

A moment later Cilia waltzed into the room and narrowed her gaze at the seating arrangements. She shook her head and waved a hand around. Ember rolled her eyes. Her mother was dramatic and thought she had power. What Cilia had was the illusion of power.

"This seating arrangement will not do, and neither will the disrespect of eating before the arrival of your queen," Cilia announced. Wilson and Caelus trailed behind her.

"Ember, you need to move from the head of the table. That is not your place," Cilia ordered. "Whoever that woman is should be down there. Emerson should also not be sitting at the other end of the table. As for Zephyr, he too is in a place reserved for honored guests, and he isn't one."

Ember ignored her mother, as did Emerson, Martin, and Grammy Margaret. Greer and Zephyr had paused in their consumption of the soup but resumed when they realized no one was moving to accommodate Cilia's demands.

"Did you hear me? This insolence will not go unpunished. Mark my words, Ember. I'm tired of your attitude and disregard for your superior," Cilia scolded.

Ember's head shot up at the last sentence. She set down her spoon and wiped her mouth. Her lips were set in a firm line. She looked up at Cilia and her guests while everyone else at the table continued to eat.

"Sit down and eat, or don't. I care not what you do, but let me make something abundantly clear to you— I am the sitting queen. I decide when we eat. I decide the seating arrangements. At dinners such as this, my title is 'Your Majesty'."

"My title is also 'Your Majesty', Ember. I fail to see your point."

Grammy Margaret set down her spoon. "Dowager Queen Cilia, my title is also 'Your Majesty', and frankly, I've held it longer than you. Sit down and shut up. Know your place."

Cilia's eyes blazed with anger. "How dare you."

Wilson wisely took her mother's arm and guided her to the seat next to Martin. Caelus kept his mouth shut as he found his seat on the opposite side of the table from his father.

The footmen served the first course to the newcomers, while everyone else moved on to the next. A tense silence filled the space. Ember's fear of making small talk had been unfounded as the silence stretched.

By the time the third course was served, everyone was on the same dish. This made life easier for the staff, but the tension was thick in the air. Cilia glared at the footman setting down her plate when he brushed her shoulder but remained silent. After a few minutes, Ember decided she couldn't take the quiet any longer.

"Your Highness, how fairs Whydah?"

Emerson quirked a brow and shook his head. "The duchy is fine. I'm planning a hunt on the estate after hurricane season has ended. Is there something you require from there, Your Majesty?"

"Not particularly. It's just been a while since I've had the opportunity to visit your estate," Ember noted.

"He has an estate and is a prince? How does that work?" Caelus asked. Then remembering his manners tacked on, "Your Majesty."

Ember smiled politely at him. At least he used her title. "The Duchy of Whydah is the title and estate given to the second royal in the line of succession. The previous duchess, my father's sister, rejected the title so it reverted to the line of the firstborn royal."

Wilson's head jerked in her direction. "Your father had a sister, Your Majesty?"

Margaret laughed. "Yes. My son had a sister and a younger brother. My daughter left Parley when she married, while my youngest son prefers a quiet life, Prime Minister."

Wilson's eyes betrayed his surprise. He had been under the impression her father had been an only child Ember realized. It wasn't a secret her father had siblings, so it was interesting he hadn't known.

"How do you balance all of your duties then, Your Royal Highness? You must be a busy person," Caelus mused.

"I have an estate manager who handles everything concerning the duchy. As for royal duties, I don't have any because I am the director of intelligence and military operations, Mr. Levan," Emerson replied.

Caelus nodded as he resumed eating. Cilia kept eyeing Greer from her spot at the table, trying to figure out who she was. By the time the dessert course was served, her mother couldn't take the mystery anymore.

"Who is she?" Cilia asked pointing at Greer with her fork.

Emerson beat Ember to a response. "Lady Read. The Earl of William's daughter. She is also my secretary and right hand."

Greer's eyes met Emerson's at his words. She gave him a small smile before taking a bite of cake. He studied her for a moment before taking a sip of coffee.

Meanwhile, Caelus's eyes moved over to Greer as well. Ember watched a corner of his mouth lift as his mind landed on a direction. It was like watching a predator find his prey and sent a chill down her spine.

"I don't know about anyone else, but I'll be excusing myself for the evening."

"What's the rush, Your Majesty? Why don't we take drinks in the parlor and get to know each other better," Caelus suggested.

"I'm afraid I have to decline. I have correspondence needing my attention."

Ember excused herself and made a beeline for her office using the servant corridor. She was hoping everyone would assume she had gone to her suite rather than her office on the other side of the palace.

Footsteps echoing in the hallway behind her signaled she wouldn't be lucky enough to get any work done. She let out a sigh. If she hadn't forgotten the correspondence earlier, she wouldn't have needed to return to her office. While she could have sent someone to fetch it, Ember had wanted a moment of solitude.

She rounded a corner and ran for her office. She carefully closed the door behind her and hid out of sight from the frosted glass along the wall. Ember kept the light off and wanted to lock the door, but it would give her away.

She held her breath as she watched the person walk up the hallway. Judging by the color of the person's clothes Ember deduced it was Caelus. He was on the prowl for a new fiancée after losing his Belizean one. His shadow passed by her door and she held her breath.

She prayed he would just keep going. Ember needed to lock not only the door to her office but also the shared door to her secretary's office. Silently, she made her way across the room and closed the door. A door opening further up the hall indicated to her Caelus wasn't giving up in his pursuit of finding her.

Ember locked the shared door as the shadow came back. He was trying the door across the hallway. She dove for her door and flipped the lock, signaling her location. The shadow came to her door and tried the handle.

"Your Majesty. Ember. Come now. We are to be family. I just want to get to know you better," Caelus coaxed. "Let me in. Who knows what kind of connection we'll have."

Her heart pounded in her ears. She walked over to her desk and grabbed the letters. The handle jiggled again.

"You're a beautiful young woman, Your Majesty. I can see why my brother is smitten with you. My evening in your presence has been delightful. Maybe we can cap it off with a drink and conversation?"

Ember edged closer to the bookcase in the corner. She was escaping using the secret passage. She would stay in the passageway until she made it to her suite. Somewhere in her memory, she recalled Caelus drugging the women he found useful so he could blackmail them in the future. She would not be one of those women.

Alarm slithered through her when she heard the sound of Caelus attempting to pick the lock. Ember triggered the mechanism and bolted into the dark tunnel. She closed the panel behind her about the same time Caelus got the door open. He was interrupted by someone a second later.

Her heart slammed in her chest as she listened to the muffled baritones. The mirror in her office allowed her to see without being seen. She could barely make out the shadowed figures in the hallway. She was safe at the moment and made quick work of locating the lantern and lighting it.

She hated two things in life — darkness and tight spaces. However, she would endure both if it meant escaping the vile Caelus Levan.

Ember watched the shadows for another moment before walking to her suite. She shuddered at the thought of his invitation. It would seem Caelus was planning to woo her while he was in residence.

Ember had teased Zephyr regarding tasting her food and drinks before, but she might utilize his services now. Suddenly his concern didn't seem quite so far-fetched.

Chapter 12

Greer had stayed with Ember the night before. The other woman had been waiting for her in her suite when Ember had all but fallen out of the passageway.

To her credit, Greer took in the shaking and pale complexion of her queen and sprung into action. She ran a bath for Ember, set out her clothing, put the correspondence on the desk, and rang the kitchen for tea.

Greer had also phoned Emerson in his suite. She knew he was temporarily sleeping in the king's suite, but he wasn't moving his things into the space. Rather, he was utilizing his suite until he went to bed because he felt it was more practical.

During her brief conversation with Emerson, she asked if he could have someone bring her night clothes and toiletries to Ember's room. This had raised Emerson's curiosity because Greer was staying in Ember's suite of rooms. Her assigned room wasn't far from Ember's, so why did she need someone to grab her items?

Emerson asked if anything had happened, and Greer told him not that she was aware of. She told him she had ordered tea, and was helping Ember with something, so she was staying the night with her. This hadn't been a complete lie. Greer had no idea what had happened to Ember, and she was helping her recover from whatever had upset her.

One thing she was keenly aware of was that she was going to protect her queen and her privacy at all costs. Even if she was guarding Ember's privacy from her brother. Greer had not anticipated Emerson being the person to drop off her items to her. Embarrassment flooded her body as she took the items, knowing he had gone through her things to retrieve what she had needed.

Awareness and heat shot to her core as their hands brushed. The connection between them had been broken when the footman arrived with the tea she had requested. Emerson had bade her goodnight and made his way to the suite door across the hall.

Over tea, Greer had gotten the story about what had happened from Ember. Dread snaked down her spine, as had fear, over what could have happened to the younger woman. Ember had then asked Greer if she would sleep in her bed with her because she was afraid if she screamed out in the middle of the night Emerson would rush in. They had also kept one of the sitting room's lights on because the darkness had made her uneasy.

Now they were sitting in the breakfast room eating. Ember wasn't as jumpy as she had been. Rather than take the head seat with her back to the door, she took the seat at the end on the opposite side. Emerson had paused in the doorway for a moment when he saw where his sister was sitting.

Instead of commenting on it, he walked over to the buffet and fixed himself a plate. Greer got up from her seat and fixed him a cup of coffee, setting it down in the open spot next to his sister before resuming her seat and her meal.

Emerson's mouth lifted in amusement. "You don't have to fix my coffee for me at breakfast, Greer. I manage to do it every morning."

"Oh... I, uh, I'm sorry." Greer lowered her head as Emerson chuckled. A thrill shot through her at the sound of her given name on his lips.

"I'm not complaining. I'm merely making an observation."

"I'm so used to fixing your coffee when you take lunch or order it from the kitchen. I'm truly sorry, Your Highness." Greer's mortification was palpable.

"Stop teasing the poor woman, Em. Also, feel free to call him by his given name. Zephyr also prefers it as well. I view breakfast in this space as private because only the people I allow in can be here," Ember told her.

Zephyr was the next person to walk into the room. He let out a big yawn as he filled a plate. "Is there coffee? Please tell me there is coffee."

Emerson lifted his mug. "Of course there's coffee. If you ask nicely, Greer will even make it for you."

Emerson's eyes danced with humor while Greer shook her head slightly and grinned. Ember watched the exchange. She had never seen Emerson this comfortable around a woman before who wasn't family. She was also excited to see him letting down his guard and acting playful. He didn't do it nearly often enough, but she was pleased he trusted Greer enough to do so.

"Is your grandmother joining us this morning?" Zephyr asked as he let out another yawn.

"No, she requested breakfast in her room. Why are you so tired, Zeph?"

He opened his mouth to reply when some scuffling in the hall caught everyone's attention. A moment later Caelus walked through the door. Ember's stomach dropped. Where the hell were the guards keeping him out?

Caelus whistled as he walked into the room. Charles the butler was on his heels. His eyes were as big as saucers. The older man bowed to Ember and Emerson, before speaking.

"I apologize, Your Majesty. Your Royal Highness. I know your preference for breakfast—" The man looked alarmed. Guilt and remorse dripped from his words like he was at fault for the misstep in security.

Ember cut him off. "It's alright. Think nothing of it."

Charles nodded as he left the room. Meanwhile, Caelus had let nothing stop him in his pursuit of helping himself to breakfast.

The panic on Zephyr's face spoke volumes. Ember could tell he was uncertain about what to do. Emerson watched his sister's reaction as clarity regarding her seating switch became evident. Poor Greer was seated across from Emerson and Zephyr. Depending on Caelus, there was a chance he would take the open seat next to her.

The silence was deafening, but Caelus appeared oblivious to it. He turned with his plate and smiled at the women, giving them a wink before walking over to take the seat next to Greer.

Ember was determined to not let Caelus ruin this meal. She looked back to Zephyr and asked her question again. "Did you have trouble sleeping last night?"

He bit his lower lip in thought like he was uncertain how to respond. "Cael and I stayed up last night catching up, Your Majesty."

Pain sliced through her at the use of her title. She so rarely enjoyed moments where she didn't have to be defined by her honorific. "How wonderful to be able to visit with your brother, Mr. Levan."

Zephyr frowned and Emerson let out a small sigh. When he figured out who was behind Caelus slipping his tail, and maneuvering around the guards, there was going to be hell to pay. He grabbed the morning paper the footman had brought for him and began skimming over the news.

"We stayed up until the wee hours of the morning discussing Parley and its delicacies," Caelus supplied shooting a roguish smile in Ember's direction.

Her skin crawled under his gaze. She wouldn't give him the satisfaction of knowing how disgusting she found him. Last night in her office had been an eye-opening experience. The man didn't have boundaries when it came to what he wanted. Caelus didn't believe in the word no.

"Maybe you and Mr. Levan can explore the marketplace. Careen is known for many things, such as food and shopping," Ember suggested. She knew regardless of where the brothers went, Emerson would have them followed to ensure nothing bad happened.

"A trip to the market does sound swell. Would either of you dames care to join us?"

Greer almost choked on her tea at Cael's use of the word dame. Zephyr glared at his brother. "Lady Read and Her Majesty aren't 'dames' and should be treated with the respect they deserve due to their status and station in life."

Caelus sighed. "You're right. I apologize, Your Majesty. Lady Read. It's just us in here, but I shouldn't have been so informal. My apologies."

He bent in his head and placed a hand over his chest like he was abashed he had forgotten himself. When he looked up to continue speaking, there was a slight edge to his gaze. "I do have a question. Don't you ever get tired of being so formal?"

"The queen decides when to dispense with formalities, not you," Zephyr hissed. His cheeks were turning red. Ember surmised it was a mix of embarrassment and anger.

"I do tire of formalities at times, Mr. Levan," Ember answered. "As for your invitation. My schedule is full until I leave for Geneva. Maybe another time."

Caelus opened his mouth to respond, but Zephyr jumped in. "I'm sure the queen has more pressing matters to attend to, both now and in the future. I can't imagine her wanting to join us on an outing."

"You should let loose, Z. If I may be so bold, your fiancée is a beauty." Caelus ducked his head, pretending to be shy about his admission. "I know that comment probably isn't proper, but it's the truth, Your Majesty. You, Zephyr, need to be more of a man of action. Do you bring her flowers? Plan private outings?"

Caelus frowned at his brother, ignoring the horrified look on Zephyr's face. "You need to show her you care. All women want to feel important and be important to their beaus. I can imagine Her Majesty is no different."

Emerson had stopped reading the newspaper at the beginning of the exchange. Her twin's eyes were hard as he glared at Caelus over the top of the paper. Zephyr was trying to control the situation, but failing because his brother thrived on being unpredictable. Ember on the other hand was curious to know where the conversation was headed because the older Levan brother was speaking about her like she wasn't sitting a few feet away from him.

"Seize the day, Z. That's all I'm saying." Caelus finished the last of the food on his plate. He took a large gulp of his coffee and set the mug down. Greer jumped slightly before stiffening next to him. He then winked at her before standing to bow to Ember and leave the room.

Emerson threw down the paper in his hands onto the table. Greer was pale and clammy next to Ember. She wouldn't meet anyone's eyes at the table. Zephyr pushed his plate away.

"I'm so very sorry. I'll keep him away from you both, I promise."

"Zeph, take me to my office."

He nodded and offered Ember his arm. Emerson was seething with rage. It was clear by Greer's demeanor something had happened. They needed privacy and Ember was going to give it to them.

Emerson wanted to know what Caelus had done to Greer to elicit the response he had witnessed. He wasn't crass enough to question the woman in the breakfast room where anyone could hear their conversation. Instead, Emerson led them to his office.

Once inside, he motioned for her to sit on the couch as he got her a glass of water and set it in front of her. He locked the door for privacy and turned on the radio to help ensure their conversation wouldn't be overheard. Then he knelt in front of her and took her hands in his.

"What did Caelus do?"

Greer's blue gaze was stormy and conflicted. She shook her head slightly and tried to smile. "I'm overreacting, Your Highness. It was nothing. I was surprised."

She was afraid Emerson might physically harm the man if she told him what he had done throughout breakfast. It was his final action that made her skin crawl and feel dirty. Caelus was a sneaky man. He could do two things at once— be charming, while also being a vile human.

"I know he did something to you under that table," Emerson calmly reasoned. "Please, Greer, tell me."

She chewed on her lower lip and watched his eyes follow her action. Her tongue darted out to moisten her lips, and she noticed his breath quicken. Was Ember right? Greer quickly rejected the thought and focused on him.

"I'll tell you if you promise not to physically hurt Caelus," Greer whispered.

The intensity of his jade gaze made her pulse quicken. Emerson may be a prince and a duke, but he was a dangerous man. He had military training and continued to hone his skills daily. He didn't need a weapon to kill Caelus, just his hands.

Emerson let out a deep sigh. "I promise I won't kill him or cause permanent damage. But I can't promise I won't physically hurt him."

"Emerson." She breathed out his name in soft anguish.

He squeezed her hands. "You know who I am. I won't lie to you."

Greer nodded as she swallowed a few times. She looked at a point beyond his shoulder because she couldn't look him in the eye and get the words out. "He... he, um, put his hand on m-my thigh..."

Her vision began to swim, so she closed her eyes because she wasn't going to cry in front of her employer, who also happened to be the crowned prince. She focused on Emerson's hands covering hers, as well as his spicy scent. He wisely stayed silent, knowing if he interrupted her, she would lose her nerve.

"H-he rubbed it up and down... squeezing every so often. T-then at the end, he, ah, well... his hand slid—" Her voice broke.

Emerson pulled her closer but she resisted and shook her head. Tears were falling down her cheeks, but she wanted to get this out and put it behind her. Then she could focus on her job duties as well as protecting her queen from this monster.

She cleared her throat, keeping her eyes closed because she didn't want to see the pity in Emerson's eyes. "He slid his hand from my thigh to rub my—"

Her eyes flew open at Emerson's growl.

"I will murder him."

She wiped her eyes with her hands as he strode for the door. She threw herself in front of him, her back slamming against the door. She winced at the pain as she grabbed his arm.

"No! No, you promised you wouldn't kill him. It wasn't that bad. I'm not worth it. Let's just forget it and move on," Greer begged.

"He put his hands on you and assaulted you. In my presence!" Emerson seethed. "I'm going to teach him a lesson he'll never forget. That smug piece of work assaulted you to send a message to me. I won't stand for it."

"No. You're going to leave it alone because you respect me and my wishes."

Emerson leaned forward. Her pulse raced at the venom in his eyes. Looking at the hard, unyielding lines of his face, Greer could very much believe Kieran wasn't the only killer in the nobility.

"Move, Greer."

She shook her head. His mouth was a scant few inches from hers. Desire spread through her as she felt the heat of his body looming over her. Kissing him would be a mistake. Yet, as she stared at his angry face, it was all she could think about. She wondered if he felt it too.

"Greer." His voice was a warning, but she brushed it aside. She reached up and laid a hand against his cheek as she caressed him.

He leaned into her touch briefly before pulling away. He ran his hands through his hair, marched over to his desk, pulled out a cigar, and walked to the balcony.

She watched as he opened the doors and then cut off the tip of the cigar before lighting it. He took a long drag before blowing out the gray and white smoke. Cautiously, Greer joined him near the railing.

They stayed like that for a few minutes until Greer broke the silence. She was the embodiment of poise and professionalism as she rattled off his schedule and collected the paperwork he needed her to handle for him.

She unlocked the door and then moved through the shared door to her office. She sat down and focused on her tasks for the day. She was grateful to put the incident from this morning behind her. Emerson would handle Caelus at some point. Greer only hoped he didn't murder him because Caelus wasn't worth the effort.

Chapter 13

Ember was sitting behind her desk, talking on the phone with her cousin Evelyn about her upcoming trip when Caelus barged into her office. Her secretary, Paul, rushed into the room and pulled him out of the space.

She could hear their voices in the next room. Judging by the tone, things weren't going well. Ember was frustrated because the guards were supposed to keep people out. Why weren't they at their post? Where was Zephyr? Why wasn't he with his brother?

A few minutes later, Ember was off the phone and calling the guard station.

"Yes, this is Queen Ember. Caelus Levan is in my office and I'm not understanding how that's possible." The person on the other end assured her guards would be there to remove Caelus momentarily.

Caelus threw open the door and turned to Paul. "Her Majesty is off the phone now. I'll only be a moment."

He closed the door in Paul's face and flipped the lock. Ember's eyes narrowed. She carefully opened the top drawer of her desk and palmed the tiny pistol she kept there.

"Why are you in my office? No one is permitted to be here without my permission."

"I do apologize for the poor timing of my visit," Caelus observed. He tried to act abashed for his actions but was failing. "I thought I would see the place where my future sister-in-law works. Learn more about what you do, and your role as a figurehead."

He gazed at her, lust in his eyes as he slowly moved over to her desk. The action was meant to showcase his toned physique. Bile rose up in her throat. Did the women fall for this act?

He lowered his voice, "Then I thought you could take the rest of the day off, and we could spend time together... getting to know each other."

Ember snorted a laugh at his suggestive tone. "I very much am not a 'figurehead' and I have work to do. I don't want to get to know you better."

Caelus took a seat on the edge of her desk while Paul knocked at the door. "Zephyr is a boy compared to me, Ember. I know how to make you feel good. Just give me a chance to prove how much better I am than my brother."

She shivered at his words. "I'm not interested. Leave."

Caelus chuckled. He reached a hand out to touch her cheek, but she slapped his hand away. A moment later, Paul burst into her office using the key and the guards were right behind him.

"Your Majesty, we apologize for the interruption."

"It's quite alright. Please escort Mr. Levan out of my office. He isn't allowed here."

The guards nodded and grabbed Caelus's arm. "No need to manhandle me. I'm leaving."

As he got to the door, Caelus turned and winked at her. "See you at dinner, Your Majesty. I'm looking forward to seeing your gams again."

Ember waited until she was certain he and the guards were gone. She picked up the phone and dialed the kitchen. "Hello.

This is Queen Ember. I need dinner for five brought to my suite tonight. I don't care if we eat in the small dining area or outside. Have the footmen set up however is easiest for them please."

Once she hung up, she dialed Emerson's extension. Greer picked up.

"Greer, please let my brother know we are taking dinner and all further meals in my suite. I do not want to be anywhere near that narcissist."

Paul sent a note to her grandmother and promised to find and inform Zephyr as well. Ember moved to the private audience room. She had important matters of state to tend to and wasn't about to let Caelus ruin her day. She and Emerson were also going to have words about the security. Someone wasn't doing their job.

"What the hell is this?" Zephyr demanded as he stormed into his brother's room. Caelus had been placed in the room next door, which adjoined his.

Caelus looked up from his spot on the bed to see what his brother had found. Zephyr was holding up a handkerchief, but what it held was anyone's guess.

"A hanky?"

Zephyr rolled his eyes. "I meant the white powder in the glass vile inside the handkerchief monogrammed with my initials in my room in my dresser."

Caelus slumped back against the pillows. His shirt was off as he rested in his room after complaining about the horrendous heat. "Don't be an idiot. It's my cocaine, but I can't very well keep it in my room, now can I? It's illegal to have it in Parley."

"So you put it in my room? Are you insane? Is there any more?"

Caelus waved off his brother's words. "No. I brought enough to get me through until this weekend when we go to Belize to celebrate that bitch Bianca's engagement. I'm just glad I don't have to marry that cow."

"I don't know what women see in you."

"They see my athletic build and classic good looks, as well as my charming personality. They can't help but want me," Caelus responded.

Zephyr marched to the door and paused. "Wait. Is this why you have been acting so strange? You've been snorting coke?"

"Yes, I've been using it. It's why I'm not a stick in the mud like you are. I don't know why you care so much."

Zephyr shook his head as he left the room and closed the door behind him. He then walked over to his bathroom and washed the white powder down the sink. He was going to apologize to everyone and let Ember know.

He was not taking the fall for Caelus's use of coke, and the antics that followed. No, his brother could atone for his sins while he was in Parley. Maybe he would finally learn a lesson.

"I can't take him anymore!" Ember exclaimed. She was ranting to Zephyr, Emerson, and Greer in her private suite. She had instructed more guards to be placed outside her quarters. She was tired of Caelus popping up unexpectedly when she was trying to handle daily tasks, and he had only been in the islands for a few days.

She made sure she had a personal security detail around her because Caelus tried to get her alone whenever he could. Ember had lost her patience when she had been accosted the night before on her way to her suite for dinner. Caelus had been trying to invite himself to her private dinner. Fortunately, Uncle Martin had come across them and taken Caelus away.

"So help me," Ember continued in her fit of rage. "I will banish him from court forever. *Forever*! And if he even thinks about inviting himself to the theater tonight, I will pack his bags and pilot the airship or plane or whatever myself! He is a nuisance and I cannot take his presence anymore."

She turned to Emerson. "Have you figured out who is helping him circumvent everyone? It has to be someone on the inside, and I'm not amused."

"Mother has been helping him," Emerson supplied.

"Cilia has been helping him? Tell me there is something you can do to punish her." Ember's eyes pleaded with his.

A sinister grin spread across Emerson's face. "Yes. I've made arrangements to have her security detail removed and placed on yours. When she goes out later to the beach with Wilson, they will only have the American detail to keep the citizens away."

"Serves her right." Ember nodded before shifting the topic back to Caelus. "That's another thing! What is wrong with him? One minute he is fine, the next he fancies himself some kind of Casa Nova, flirting and hinting at some obscene things."

"It's probably the cocaine," Zephyr muttered. "I caught him with some after his arrival and disposed of it discreetly. I've told Father he needs to ship him off to a facility to handle his addiction for however long it takes, but you can see what he thought of my request."

Ember whirled on him, while Greer took the opportunity to use Emerson as a human shield of sorts. "The cocaine? He's using illegal drugs in Parley? In my kingdom?"

Zephyr sucked in a breath and prepared to go to battle against his fiancée in an effort to calm her down. He shot a look at Emerson, whose entire plan was to let Ember rant and rave the day away.

"Ember," Zephyr started. She opened her mouth to counter, but he put his hand up to silence her. "Have him arrested for the cocaine. Throw him out of the country for the inappropriate behavior towards yourself and Greer, but please focus on the larger picture. Why is Caelus here? There has to be a larger reason. Let Emerson and Greer figure that out while we focus our attention on getting Kieran home."

Ember felt like a bucket of cold water had been thrown on her ire at the sound of Kieran's name. The lancing pain of betrayal that coursed through her took her breath away. Why wasn't Kieran here? Even if it wasn't for her, Parley needed him on more than one front. It was obvious Wilson wasn't going down without a fight.

"Fine. Is Greer coming with us or staying," Ember asked, swinging her gaze to her twin.

"Staying. I need her."

"You can have her after she helps me dress for dinner and the theater."

Zephyr looked at her in confusion. "We were only going to the theater"—

"I am *not* having dinner anywhere near that uncouth heathen," Ember hissed.

Zephyr clamped his mouth shut and nodded. "Dinner will be swell wherever we end up."

"I best not see Caelus at any point between now and my trip to Geneva," Ember grumbled.

The trio surrounding Ember waited to see if she was finished. Greer decided to brave the waters. "If I may, Your Majesty, isn't Mr. Levan leaving for Belize later this afternoon?"

Zephyr jumped in. "That's right! We were both invited to Bianca's engagement festivities. I'm missing the dinner tonight, but I'll be attending the lunch tomorrow and possibly the ball. I'll be back Sunday in plenty of time to see you off."

Ember let out a breath. "Good. I'll stay in my suite until he has left."

Zephyr turned to flee when Ember's words stopped him. "I had your things moved to your new room."

"My new room? Why?"

"Because I don't trust Caelus to not go through your things, and your former room shared a door with his."

Zephyr shot her a half smile. "Cael always goes through my things. So does my father for that matter. That's why I leave all of my notes and important papers in the bottom drawer of your writing desk on the porch."

Ember gapped at him. She wasn't surprised he knew his father and brother were going through his things, she was surprised he had taken over a drawer in her desk and she hadn't noticed.

"How do you retrieve them when we meet up?"

"Oh. I just ask a footman or a guard to look and see if the notebook with my name on the front is in the bottom drawer of your desk. They hesitate to open the drawer, so I say I will and they can watch. I only take the notebook," Zephyr explained.

"There isn't anything in the bottom drawer, or really any of the drawers aside from the top one," Ember noted.

She hadn't realized how comfortable her staff was around Zephyr. There was a level of trust there for them to let him into her private garden. They would never let him into her suite of rooms without her presence or permission, but it was curious they didn't similarly view the garden.

"They won't be in trouble, will they? I would never want to invade your privacy, and I know your feelings about this garden. I couldn't come up with a safer place for my notes, especially after Caelus's arrival," Zephyr fretted.

"No. No one's in trouble. Your new room is in Emerson's suite of rooms. I'll make sure you are given access to the garden though. Emerson and Grammy Margaret also have access to it," Ember told him.

He flashed her a quick smile, and her heart flipped in her chest.

"Thank you, Ember."

Then he was gone. Ember murmured a response as she stood there thinking through Zephyr's actions. He really did take the safety of Parley seriously. He genuinely cared, despite everything.

Emerson cleared his throat, pulling her from her thoughts. "Where are you having dinner? I need to send security ahead of you."

"Oh... ummm... Isn't there a restaurant in the hotel across the street? We can just eat there. I don't care if it's in a hotel room, the dining room, the theater, or the kitchen. I would just like a peaceful meal where a foreign dignitary's son isn't not so subtly hinting at marriage."

Emerson chuckled. "I don't know, Em. I thought the entire exchange was quite humorous."

Ember glared at her twin. "I'm so glad you enjoyed the show. Caelus giving a demonstration on proposal technique to Zephyr during afternoon tea was not amusing. Especially because we are already engaged."

Emerson's shoulders were shaking as he tried to contain his mirth. "Your face was something else when he grabbed your hand and recited Shakespeare before asking for your hand in marriage."

"Again, I'm glad one of us was entertained by his antics," Ember bit out. "Now, if you'll excuse me. Lady Greer will be helping me dress so I can have a Caelus-free evening."

Chapter 14

The theater had been a massive disappointment. The performance was wonderful and witty. Queen Anne's Return was a comedy written by no one even remotely related to Parley. Rather than leave before the performance began, Ember and Zephyr stayed. Just because it hadn't been what they were hoping for didn't mean they should leave early.

The cast and crew, as well as Adam and Mae, had been over the moon when Emerson's people called to arrange the security detail for Friday evening's showing. They had been the guests of honor. The pride of having the queen take in a performance at Careen's oldest and most respected theater was palpable.

Despite the disappointment of the play not being what they had hoped for, seeing the excitement over her presence reminded Ember that for better or worse, she was their monarch. She needed to start acting like it. She had been fearful for so long that if she made a mistake the citizens would overthrow her, but being at the theater had her questioning her fears.

Once she had returned from the theater, Greer had helped her ready for bed before retiring for the evening. Ember on the other hand had tossed and turned for hours. Sometime before dawn, she had ordered tea and then requested breakfast with the others be set up on the patio.

As the sun rose, casting a pink and orange hue over the sleeping city of Careen, she knew she was at a crossroads and had been at one for a while. She hadn't wanted to acknowledge it. It was easier to deny the Guardians weren't sabotaging her and Parley than face the reality of it.

However, with each new day came another briefing on the happenings of the island kingdom. Reading about the laws and amendments to the constitution the Guardians were proposing and passing on her behalf was alarming. The increase was disturbing, as were the proposals. She caught the headlines of the *Parlian Press*, and other newspapers in the islands, questioning where the monarch was. The opinion pieces weren't as critical as they could be, but the frustration and anger were felt in every word.

She was out of time. Her people were out of time. Ember was terrified of moving against the Guardians and making matters worse, but knowing they tried to revive the real estate law for the fourth time proved they couldn't be trusted. If Ember allowed them to keep going, then things would get worse and she might not be able to stop what happened.

Ember let out a deep sigh as Grammy Margaret walked into the garden. Zephyr, Emerson, and Greer followed closely behind.

"Come now, dear. It can't be that bad," Grammy Margaret told her as she moved to make herself a plate. "After all, we are taking breakfast in the garden, surrounded by the beauty of nature."

"And the bugs," Emerson murmured swatting a fly. Greer giggled next to him, and he shot her a scathing look. She just smiled serenely and handed him a plate.

"Coffee will perk you up," Greer mumbled to him.

"Nothing is perking me up," Emerson grumbled.

Ember watched as everyone gathered their food and sat down. The footman was efficient in his strategic placement of the beverages for each person.

Zephyr's silent and pensive mood was not lost on Ember. It had been confirmed last night when they had come home that Caelus wasn't leaving for America until Zephyr did. Wilson's smug expression, as well as Caelus's sinister grin, had haunted Ember all night. Not only did she have the Guardians to counter, but the prime minister and his son.

Cilia and Wilson had been waiting in the public parlor for their return. It was then told to Ember she would need to adjust to Caelus's presence in the islands because he wasn't leaving. It was then explained to her how childish she was acting. As her mother continued her dressing down, Wilson and Caelus had begun to relax and smile. They all felt safe and like they had won.

Uncle Martin had stumbled upon the declarations his sister was making. Apparently, he had been left in the dark regarding the trio's little ambush. Probably because they thought him a killjoy, and Wilson was trying to eliminate the competition. Either way, Uncle Martin could wisely see the contempt and storm brewing within Ember. He told Cilia to stop before bowing to Ember and apologizing for her actions.

Ember had nodded and left the room with her silence. Her father and grandmother had hammered into her to never let her anger get the better of her in public. Let fools make their statements, and then win in silence. After her father passed, it was Kieran and Grammy Margaret who helped her maintain a level head in public.

"I leave for Geneva tomorrow, but when I return I'm making more public appearances," Ember announced. "You're right, Em.

The people enjoy them, and honestly, I do too. I have missed my people."

Emerson didn't respond. He just picked up the newspaper. Greer sat across from him, while Zephyr pushed the food around his plate next to Ember. He was leaving after breakfast for Belize so he could babysit Caelus as well as celebrate Bianca's engagement. Her love story was sweet — the president's daughter meets the vice president's son and they fall in love. He was supposed to return tomorrow morning in time to see her off.

Zephyr was more withdrawn this morning than he had been in weeks. The dark circles under his eyes were telling. His posture was stiff, and his hair was disheveled from running his hands through it rather than being a fashion statement. The stern set of his jaw told Ember he was thinking, trapped within the grim realm of his thoughts.

"Zeph," Ember uttered. "It's alright. I'll make it alright."

The haunted dullness of his eyes caught her off guard. There was no light, no glimmer, no sparkle in them. Did he view things as being so hopeless? She hadn't gone over her briefings this morning, but nothing she was aware of was so dire it couldn't be fixed.

"I don't know if you can," Zephyr whispered. His smile was gut-wrenching.

Dread crept down Ember's spine. Resigned. Zephyr was resigned to his fate. He was defeated. He was out of moves and pieces on his chess board.

"What do you mean?"

Emerson threw his copy of the *New York Times* in her direction. Her hands shook slightly as she picked up the paper and read the headline aloud, "Oil field scandal linked to PM's son."

She shot Zephyr and Emerson a puzzled look before reading the front page article. The secretary of the Department of the Interior for the United States had taken money to look the other way as Zephyr sold leases to two prominent oil tycoons for oil fields reserved for the Navy. Zephyr had reportedly taken millions for the deal, then bribed officials to look the other way. Wilson had also given a statement to the newspaper saying the allegations would be looked into by the authorities and he had recused himself from the matter.

Ember threw the paper down as if it would bite her. She swallowed hard. Her heart was pounding in her chest as she realized Wilson wasn't going to stop. He was once again using Zephyr as a pawn in his game of chess. Meanwhile, Zephyr had been scrambling to outmaneuver his father, only realizing he was boxed in after he was out of moves.

Truthfully, everyone sitting at the table was out of moves in one way or another. It seemed everyone only had one piece left to play— the queen. But Ember had been reluctant to set foot on the board, scared she would mess up and make things worse.

Glancing back at the newspaper, a vise tightened around her heart. How much worse did things need to get before she stepped in? Before she claimed her birthright?

"This isn't true. They can't do this," Ember declared.

Zephyr's response was harsh. "Whose going to stop them, Ember?"

His tone was taunting. She licked her lips, looking down at her hands before responding. "It isn't fair, Zeph. I didn't realize how bad things were getting for you. I'm"—

"It's fine, Ember." She recoiled at his clipped tone.

The silence filling the space was tense and anticipatory. Being her fiancé meant Zephyr had certain protections, but he only had them in Parley. Depending on what America decided, Ember might be able to shield him, but she would have to fight the Guardians to do so. Ember bit her lower lip as her eyes moved to stare at the ocean, and her thoughts turned to him.

Ember wanted Kieran, and she needed him here. Things would be so much easier if he was by her side, protecting her like how she wanted. She let out a long sigh at that thought. It wasn't his job to protect her, it was his job to protect Parley and the Crown. He was doing that, just not how she had hoped. He couldn't hold her hand and make decisions for her for the rest of their lives.

Willow's death shattered many things for many people. The ripples from that singular event almost three years ago were still felt by Ember today, and clearly Kieran. Her death had driven him from the islands and his home. She was the only person who received any form of explanation as to why he felt the need to run and never look back. The thought of the note caused an ache in her heart, but she pushed it aside. He had needed to run, and she had been forced to understand.

Emerson would keep Parley and its citizens safe from any possible war brewing with America. Well, as safe as he could. Grammy Margaret would support her publicly no matter what and voice concerns in private. Uncle Martin might prove to be useful to have in her corner. Maybe if he had another option he wouldn't do her mother's bidding.

Even above Kieran, Ember needed the High Court. While the Duke of Revenge had the sole authority to convene the court for matters regarding the Crown, he wasn't the only person who could request a hearing to stop the Guardians — she could too.

In the history of Parley, no monarch had ever requested the convening of the High Court regarding the Crown Guardians. Emerson had told her to start acting like the queen, but she had been wallowing in self-pity. Crying over the power being stripped from her. Crying over not being respected and treated poorly by advisers and those around her. You teach people how to treat you, and Ember had always deferred to those older than her because they were supposed to know better. She taught them she was weak. She taught them she was dependent. She taught them to view her as indecisive and a child.

Meanwhile, if she were honest, she knew they had taken nothing from her. At any point in time, Ember just had to assert her authority and reclaim her kingdom, but she was scared. What if she put a target on her back and was killed? Or worse, she proved everyone who ever doubted her abilities correct, and a revolution was staged. What if she misstepped and caused a war? But what if she did nothing? What then?

Great-grandpa Sam had spent a year amassing his reputation, his fortunes, and his power so he could return to Cape Cod and marry the love of his life. He risked his life on the high seas as a pirate to prove to Goody's parents he was good enough and could care for her. Ember would not be the singular cause of the destruction of his legacy and the legacy of those who came before her some eight generations later.

Anger surged through her. If she continued to sit on her hands, then she would let the Guardians do just that, and it would be all her fault. She was a Bellamy. She was the queen! It was long past time she picked up the reigns of her kingdom and be the leader they expected and deserved. She had power. What the Crown Guardians were doing was mere child's play and easily undone. She needed to rise to the challenge and put her pieces on the board rather than sit around and wait for Kieran to save her. He wasn't coming home to rescue her any time soon, so she needed to save herself and her people.

And what of the injustice being done to Zephyr yet again? Who was coming to rescue him? No one. His mother would protect Neil and his sister, Roselyn, and she would sacrifice Zephyr in the process. Wilson would utilize this knowledge to help Caelus or himself escape this scandal. At the moment she wasn't certain who had benefited from it, and it didn't matter. Zephyr would be the victim. His life was never his own.

She studied her fiancé's features as he ate his food. The breeze played with his light brown hair as the sun caught the blonde streaks. His manner and expression were stoic. She glanced at Emerson, but he was absorbed in his task with the newspaper. If no one was going to save Zephyr, then she would.

"I am the queen," Ember stated. Determination flooded her body. She would do this. She would save Zephyr and take her kingdom back.

Utensils paused as all eyes turned to her.

"Last time I checked you were," Emerson drawled from behind his newspaper, nonplused by her sudden declaration.

"No, Emerson. I am the queen," Ember enunciated.

Emerson looked over the top of the paper at her. "Again, this is news everyone already knows. You're the queen. And?"

He cocked a brow at her. Daring her to do it. Daring her to become queen.

"And I want my damn kingdom back," Ember declared.

Emerson smiled at her before going back to his reading. "That'a girl."

Relief seemed to flood the space like everyone had been waiting on her to decide which direction she would choose. Well, the wait was over. She was taking back her home and her throne. It was time for the Crown Guardians to retire permanently.

As Zephyr reached for his cup, Ember placed a hand over his. His eyes met hers, and he cocked a brow. She gave him a small smile.

"My kingdom includes you."

Shock lit his face as he froze at her words. His Adam's apple moved up and down a few times as he processed her meaning. "Truly?" The word scarcely more than a rasp.

"Truly," Ember declared.

Zephyr turned to Emerson, who also nodded. The young man gave them both a grin as he ducked his head and resumed his meal.

Chapter 15

The Crown Guardians had not been pleased to learn Ember was going on the trip to Geneva by herself as the ruling monarch of Parley. They felt she was too young to navigate the world stage; however, Grammy Margaret had argued in her favor.

She said if Ember was never given the chance to grow and represent Parley on her own, then she would never learn. She further argued Ember would be in friendly and safe hands because both Geneva and Astonia were ruled by family members. They wouldn't let Ember fall flat on her face.

After a few days of fighting back and forth, and Grammy Margaret's threat to get the High Court involved, the Crown Guardians acquiesced at the last minute. There were several demands made, including Ember bringing Zephyr with her because "he was more familiar navigating foreign affairs abroad." Ember had rolled her eyes at this but was pleased Nerissa was in attendance on the trip. She hadn't been sure if her lady-in-waiting would be permitted and was glad she was coming.

She and Nerissa hadn't had much opportunity to visit each other over these last few months. Ember was eager to catch up with both Nerissa and Evelyn. She knew Evelyn would also be excited to see Nerissa as well.

"Your Majesty? We'll be preparing to land in Geneva in a few moments. The captain requested I ask you and Mr. Levan to take your seats," the young flight attendant explained.

"Of course. We'll do that now, won't we Zephyr?"

He managed a smile as he walked over to take a seat opposite of her. He had been quiet, barely speaking a word since it was announced he was joining her on this trip the afternoon before they left. He had been in Belize at the time for the engagement lunch and ball for Bianca. Ember had word sent to him he was going to Geneva with her, and that she would have a valet pack for him.

He had returned from Belize an hour before her scheduled departure. Footmen and airport staff made quick work of off-loading and moving the bags he and his valet needed onto the zeppelin headed for Geneva. When she had arrived a short time later, she had been surprised to see him ready and waiting, ever the image of respectability.

Ember had been sure once they boarded the zeppelin he would relax, but he hadn't. Zephyr was stoic. He had retreated into himself, and she feared it was a place not even she could reach. She wasn't worried about him making a faux pas at court because his manners and etiquette were second nature to him.

No, what she truly feared were the thoughts inside his head. They were the unseen enemy. Ember couldn't rationalize or work things out with him if she didn't know what was troubling him. Or worse, what he was telling himself. Both she and Emerson had promised to protect him, but that didn't stop him from worrying.

Zephyr tapping his fingers on the table while he stared out the window pulled her from her thoughts. Ember smiled to herself. He hated landings, which was the opposite of her: she hated takeoffs. She covered his hand with hers. When he looked at her quizzically, she smiled.

"Are you looking forward to having a break in Geneva? The weather seems like it will be really nice during our visit" Ember noted.

Zephyr shrugged. "It will be a nice change from the tropical climate, I guess."

He turned back to the window and watched as the tethers were dropped from the zeppelin to the ground. The ground crew helped guide the aircraft into the hanger and moor it before the final descent to the ground was made.

Ember and Zephyr departed the aircraft and were guided to a horse-drawn carriage. She smiled. Her cousin, King Reginald, had embraced technology only so far. He did not like motor vehicles, and therefore, still used horses and carriages. In a way, Ember was jealous.

The use of carriages and horses harkened back to a simpler time, before the boom of the Industrial Revolution in many countries. There had been differing thoughts and opinions on what was the superior technology. Places like Astonia and Geneva were a mix of steam power and tradition, while Parley saw greater benefits in diesel.

Ember was always delighted to leave Parley and see what technology and machines existed within the different infrastructures around the world. She loved seeing the evolution of technology, or the different ways it was utilized.

After an agonizingly quiet carriage ride, a footman opened the door to help Ember step down into the private garden and VIP entrance of the castle. A squeal of excitement greeted her a moment before she was captured into a bear hug.

"I'm so happy you are here," Evelyn whispered. "Things will be better now."

Ember could feel her cousin melt into her embrace as relief flooded her body. She pulled Evelyn away from her slightly and studied her face. A sad smile greeted her.

Something must be amiss with Evie's mother. She had written about the strain learning her new role as queen of Astonia had put on their already tumultuous relationship. Evie was a few inches shorter than herself and was curvy instead of the willowy thin her mother had wished for. She also had beautiful strawberry blonde hair her mother despised. She was forever comparing her to a harlot in private because of it.

Ember smiled warmly at both Evie and Zephyr. She was determined they have a fun and enjoyable two weeks together. Despite having matters needing her attention, including figuring out how to dissolve the Crown Guardians, the death of her father had taught her to live in the present. Why borrow the worry of tomorrow? It would come soon enough.

During the three-day trip to Geneva, Ember realized she needed to plan for the future, but she also needed to find joy in the present. The stress of the engagement, the remembrance ceremony, finding Kieran, and her tin anniversary as monarch were taking a toll. She wasn't sleeping well and was beginning to forget little things. This trip was a much-needed respite for many reasons

"It's a lovely day. Why don't we take in the fresh air and have afternoon tea on the veranda? I'm sure King Reginald would think it delightful," Ember suggested.

There was a brief trace of fear in her eyes before Evelyn seemed to push it away. Her mouth was open to respond when she was cut off.

"There you are, Your Royal Highness! I was wondering where you had run off to." A man in his late twenties came strolling up to Evelyn, looking her up and down like a lion his prey. Ember did not recognize the man, but she saw the stiffness of Evie's posture, and fear his presence stirred within her.

"And who might we have here? Some other young lady of the court?"

Zephyr stepped closer to Ember. It wasn't proper to embrace her or touch her in any manner while in public. Although Zephyr desperately wanted to step in front of her, or at the very least, put an arm around her shoulders signaling to this man she was off limits. Ember may never be his, but she for certain was never going to be *his* either.

"And who might you be?" Ember asked coolly.

The man puffed out his chest, while also looking down his nose at Ember and Zephyr. She was impressed by this accomplishment and amused by his assumption no one could be titled higher than him during this birthday celebration.

"I am Prince Phillip Joseph Stephen Atwood the VII of Bulgaria," he crowed. Ember held back a laugh. The man was preening like a peacock.

Zephyr bowed while Ember merely nodded. That was not the reaction Phillip had been anticipating. The friendly veneer slipped over the perceived slight shown to him by Ember. She was enjoying him believing he was higher than her on the totem pole.

"I am Mr. Zephyr Levan. I am the American prime minister's second son," Zephyr said.

Phillip's eyes were narrowed on Ember. He didn't even acknowledge Zephyr's introduction, which annoyed her. She knew his type. Phillip was used to being fawned over. He wasn't a bad-looking man. His slim and trim build probably made the ladies swoon, but his cool blue eyes seemed to match his personality and his heart.

"I am—"

"Queen Ember! I apologize for not being here for your arrival. Word only reached me but a moment ago. I do apologize for the absence of my husband. King Reginald is handling something of great importance. I'm sure you understand," Queen Maria explained breathlessly as she greeted Ember.

Phillip's eyebrows shot up as he bowed to her.

"I didn't realize I was in the presence of a queen, Your Majesty." Phillip's eyes took on a calculating gleam. He could plot all he wanted. Ember wasn't fooled by his easy charm and good looks. He would soon learn that.

"Hello, Queen Maria. We were just going over introductions."

She nodded and waved a dismissive hand. "Princess Evelyn failed to mention you were arriving today. I would have made sure you had a more fitting welcome."

Maria eyed her daughter with a thinly veiled disdain. It was almost laughable how transparent this woman was. Maintaining her place in the world was all that mattered. If Ember remembered correctly, Maria had been hopeful for an engagement between Evie and Drystan. That dream, like so many others, died that cold, dreary October morning.

Maria looked Zephyr up and down before dismissing his presence altogether.

"Come, Your Majesty. Let's take tea in the sunroom and let the servants sort out the baggage," she said with a pointed look at Zephyr.

"Lady Nerissa will be joining us as well as my fiancé," Ember told the group.

"Oh, and when will your fiancé be arriving?" Queen Maria asked.

"Mr. Levan is my fiancé," Ember said in a stiff tone.

Maria's mouth gaped open for a moment at her loss for words while Phillip took a renewed interest in Zephyr. Both remained silent. An awareness washed over Maria's features as if she had remembered, on some level, hearing about her engagement.

"Princess Evelyn, Lady Nerissa, Mr. Levan, and I were going to take afternoon tea on the veranda. It will be nice to take in the fresh air after being aboard the airship for a few days," Ember announced. It was a dare directed toward Maria. The older woman's lips thinned for a moment before she slipped back into her role as a gracious monarch.

"Oh, how delightful," Maria exclaimed. "The heat is too much for my delicate constitution, but I'm sure Prince Phillip would love to join your impromptu tea."

"Wonderful," Ember responded with the same false excitement in her tone. Maria was taken aback for a moment. Good, Ember thought. Better to establish boundaries early on than later in a more public setting.

Zephyr followed behind the royals as they walked to the veranda for tea. Ember knew he would much rather unpack and settle into his suite of rooms than engage in an afternoon social event. It's what she would like to do as well, but they didn't have that luxury. Once Nerissa ensured things were settled with their footman and the baggage, she would join them. In the meantime, they would sit for tea and visit until she arrived.

Ember noticed her security detail, as well as Evelyn's, keeping an eye on their group by following at a discreet distance. Emerson had told her Evelyn had a private detail nicknamed the "Queen's Men" that Great-Uncle Andrew, the king of Astonia, had created to keep her cousin safe. While Ember had bodyguards, she didn't necessarily have a core group of six men dedicated to her person.

Emerson had hand-selected her security detail for this trip, which totaled twelve personal bodyguards. The Bellamy's had a core group of people dedicated to the royal family. The bodyguard duties shifted amongst the group of about forty men comprising the royal detail.

That said, Emerson did say Uncle Andy and his head of security had agreed to loan them two members of Evie's detail upon their departure. No one had said why, and Ember had decided not to ask. Ignorance was bliss in that regard. She was always a target because she was a queen. However, somethings she left to her twin in order to keep her sanity.

Ember shifted her attention back to the group, catching snippets of small talk. While some might view this tea as a waste of time, Ember was keen to learn who Phillip was. She would pepper Evelyn with questions later as to why she was tense around him. For now, Ember planned on enjoying herself, while learning all the latest gossip from the various kingdoms and countries.

Chapter 16

It had been a week since her arrival in Astonia. Ember could now see why Emerson, Grammy Margaret, and Uncle Andy had insisted she take the trip. Up until the final moments of her departure, she had been hesitant. She knew trips and social engagements were part of her royal duties, but she never wanted her people to think she was more interested in being a socialite rather than a monarch like her mother.

Instead, the Parlian newspapers had praised the trip. They had deemed the trip a power move by her, asserting herself as the monarch on the world stage without guardians to back her up or undermine her authority. They viewed it as a chance for her to get her wings and fly. She just hoped she didn't disappoint them.

This trip was also an eye-opener in terms of how other countries viewed not only Parley and her reign as queen, but Astonia, Geneva, and Evelyn. While the Astonians were grateful King Andrew skipped his daughter as monarch, he had skipped his son as well in the line of succession. It was understandable because his son had left the country a few decades before, saying he was abdicating the throne. He hadn't been heard from since. Uncle Andy had then named Evelyn as heir over Maria, and

Evelyn's brother Thad, which had put additional targets on her back.

Ember needed to take back her power from the Guardians, not just for herself, Zephyr, and her kingdom, but also for her allies as well. There were great odds Evelyn was going to need her help in the future against Bulgaria and a few others.

The High Queen within the United Kingdoms was facing challenges from a few countries in the alliance, and also European and African countries. If Ember wasn't in complete control when something happened, she would have to rely on Emerson and the High Court, while she battled the Crown Guardians.

It was a battle she wouldn't have to worry about if Kieran was home because he could enact the emergency powers given to the Duchy of Revenge. However, he was somewhere out there, Ember mused as she watched the sunlight play on the ocean from the picture window in her room. She let out a deep sigh. When she returned to Parley, she was going to need to make a move to dissolve the Guardians. It was going to be difficult, but it was necessary.

A light knock on the door pulled her from her thoughts. Nerissa had already attended to her for the morning, so she wasn't sure who was visiting her.

"Come in," Ember called out as she walked into the sitting room from the small study.

Zephyr entered with three men she recognized from Evelyn's personal detail. The expressions on their faces were grim. Zephyr wouldn't look her in the eye, and two of the men fell back behind the man she assumed was the leader.

Ember took a seat and then motioned for the leader and Zephyr to sit. The other two men remained by the door. She hadn't had the luxury of being introduced to them. Despite being bodyguards for the future queen of Astonia, they all held titles in recognition of their service to the Crown.

"To what do I owe this honor…." Ember trailed off for a moment. "I do apologize, and mean no disrespect, but I don't know any of your names. I've heard them, but we've never been properly introduced."

The man smiled. A glimmer of amusement lit his eyes. "You're every bit as gracious as Princess Evelyn and Mr. Levan said you would be, Your Majesty."

The leader motioned to the men by the door. "The one on the left is Ian Masters and the one on the right is Evan McClintock. I am Rhys Houndson."

Ember beamed. "It's a pleasure to meet you all." Her mood shifted though when she remembered they knocked on her door for a reason. "How may I assist you? I assume there is a purpose for this visit."

Rhys smiled politely. "There is. I have been instructed by Prince Emerson to give you this letter. He trusted no one else to get the missive to you. So you know it's authentic he said to remind you of hot chocolate in October."

Trepidation slammed into Ember like a rouge wave. It had to be serious if he was using that authentication code. Her hands shook slightly as she reached for the letter. She took deep breaths in and out to try to steady herself.

"Zeph," she whispered. "How bad is it?"

She turned to face him, but he wouldn't meet her eyes. She took his hand in hers and squeezed it briefly. He still wouldn't look in her direction.

The back of her eyes burned, but she took a deep breath. Queens didn't cry. And if they did, they didn't do it in front of others.

She broke the seal of the letter and scanned the contents. A surge of anger shot through her. She read the letter a second and third time to ensure she comprehended the subject matter of every word and line.

Caelus had been caught by the Cuban police with cocaine while he was trying to forcefully convince a baron's daughter to join him on some joyride with a royal car. The baron's daughter's only crime was being in the wrong place at the wrong time.

Lady Lianna Thornton had been returning to her hotel after taking in a performance at the theater when she had caught Caelus's eye. He pulled alongside her in the car and started flirting. The young woman flirted back but kept walking. Caelus got out of the car about a block from her hotel.

Lady Lianna refused his advances. She told him about her fiancé and wished him a good evening. When she started to walk away, things escalated, ending with the police intervening after a very public ruckus.

Ember pinched the bridge of her nose as she rested her face in her hand. The newspapers had picked up the story and were claiming a double standard because Caelus hadn't been arrested. Meanwhile, the baron was fit to be tied regarding the matter with his daughter, as well as the damage to her reputation because the press had discovered her involvement. Specifically, the *Parlian Press* had discovered her identity, which had been protected due to the circumstances surrounding the incident.

Emerson explained he had called an emergency meeting with the High Court to weigh in on the matter with the baron's daughter, but Ember was needed for that meeting to determine what would be done to Caelus. Only the queen could strip foreign dignitaries and diplomats of their immunity. She was also the only person who could banish people from court.

Ember was livid. The owner of the *Parlian Press* was the eldest son of a viscount. Jonathon Laurent had taken the lead on this matter and was charging ahead, accusing the Crown of playing favorites by picking and choosing who the rules applied to. Ember didn't need this right now. Because of his status and station in life, it explained how he determined whose daughter had been involved. Ember was going to have words with him as well.

According to Emerson's letter, she would need to leave immediately after Evelyn's birthday ball the following evening to make it back to Careen in time to attend the meeting. She was livid about having to cut her visit one week short because Wilson couldn't get a handle on his son. She needed to have Nerissa and the footmen begin preparations to leave tomorrow night.

Ember stood and walked to the window on the other side of the sitting room. From her suite of rooms, she could see the mountains, the capital city, and the main harbor of Geneva. In all her lessons and training, nothing had prepared her for this moment. She was going to have to be the queen everyone expected her to be. Butterflies took up residence in her belly at the realization because she wasn't sure if she could do it.

The last time she had an important diplomatic matter to settle, Kieran had been by her side. As the director of intelligence and military operations at the time, Kieran had cited national security and solved the problem. Longing made her heart ache for him. Willow may have been his compass, but he had been hers. She missed the conversations. She missed the advice. Above everything though, she missed his presence.

He had an air of confidence suffused with a quiet arrogance. While everyone spoke around him, Kieran was content to listen and study them. When he spoke, it was always in a calm and measured tone, which brought her comfort and reminded her of her father. His scent also soothed her because it was uniquely his.

Most men wore some kind of cologne, but not Kieran. He could walk into a room without Ember knowing, but once she caught his scent, she could find him. It was woodsy with a hint of whiskey. Everything about it was fitting, and so very Kieran.

Where are you, Kir? I don't know how to do this without you!

Rage shot through Ember as her thoughts shifted direction. She had told that arrogant jerk, Wilson, to make sure Caelus did not have cocaine after Zephyr's admission. During their meeting, Ember had warned Wilson she would allow authorities to charge and prosecute Caelus however they saw fit if he was caught with illegal drugs, or breaking any laws. She had expressed her concerns regarding his behavior toward women, especially in light of his behavior toward her and Greer. Wilson had been dismissive of her threats, probably because the Crown Guardians were in his pocket.

She paced back and forth, working things through in her mind. Ember stared out the window one last time before letting out a deep sigh and sitting back in the chair she had vacated several minutes prior.

"It would seem myself and my entourage will be departing Geneva tomorrow evening," Ember announced. "Will we be bringing two of Princess Evie's bodyguards back with us, Mr. Houndson?"

He looked her square in the eye when he answered, "Yes. King Andrew and I had a discussion and Mr. Masters and Mr. McClintock will accompany you back to Parley."

Ember nodded. "Thank you. I know Prince Emerson greatly appreciates the assistance of having a pair of bodyguards from outside our country. I don't know his reasoning, and honestly, I don't want to. I have enough of my duties to perform."

Ember turned her attention to Zephyr. He was staring into the fireplace. Not only had he not said a word during her conversation with Rhys, he hadn't moved a muscle at all.

Lines bracketed his mouth and eyes. His skin was also pallid. Life seemed to have drained him of his usual zest and spunk. Ember had hoped this trip would restore him and give him a much-needed respite. That didn't seem to happen.

"Zeph," Ember called to him.

His eyes moved to hers. Ember let out a soft cry. He was tormenting himself with his thoughts, drowning in the sea of his emotions.

"I'll fix it, Zeph. I'm the queen. It's *my* responsibility. Caelus is *my* responsibility," Ember told him. "Once we return, I'll meet with Lord Laurent and give him a piece of my mind. I'm sure Jonathon is going to be thrilled. Then I'll attend the meeting, meet with the baron, and the lady. I'll fix it."

Zephyr's dark chuckle caught her off guard. "If Caelus is charged with anything, or my father doesn't like any part of the outcome, it'll be used as another reason to declare war on Parley. He's not pleased about the stonewalling America has received regarding their bribery investigation for the oil field scandal. Prince Emerson can't keep them at bay forever."

"Be that as it may, Caelus is not above the law. No lord or lady of my court is treated any differently than anyone else. We were born of pirates, so social ranking is meaningless," Ember said. "And you're under my protection."

Zephyr sighed and scrubbed a hand over his face. "Caelus bought more cocaine while we were in Belize for Bianca's festivities."

Ember stared dumbfounded at Zephyr for a moment before anger took over. "Are you serious? I had an audience with your father before I left regarding Caelus's drug use in my kingdom. And you're telling me Caelus bought more to bring back anyway."

"It's what he always does." Zephyr sighed and let his head fall back against the back of the chair. "I wouldn't be surprised if he also set up a shipment for his contacts in Florida. Not only does he use cocaine, he deals it as well. I'm sorry I couldn't stop him, Your Majesty."

He was sorry? He traveled to and from Belize, where he was all day Saturday, before returning in time to accompany her on this trip. Meanwhile, Caelus hadn't been set to return from Belize for another few days. Caelus's drug use in her country wasn't Zephyr's fault, it was Wilson's for enabling him.

"You do not need to apologize, Zephyr. Caelus is a grown man. His actions are his own."

Zephyr snorted. Ember was confused by his demeanor. This entire trip he had been distant, including when they were researching the theater. Zephyr had gathered a ton of information they were planning to sift through on the three-day trip back to Parley, but plans seemed to be rapidly changing.

"If I may, Your Majesty," Rhys interjected. "I believe Mr. Levan is referencing being the scapegoat for his brother's antics."

This explanation further confused Ember. "Why would he be the scapegoat for Caelus's drug use? I know about the bribery, but they can't finger Zephyr for everything."

Four pairs of eyes stared at her in disbelief. "You can't be that naïve, Ember," Zephyr whispered. "Sure you remember the summer I was seventeen. I didn't see you for over a year while I took the blame for Cael's crimes."

Ember bristled at his words. "Of course I know that. I simply meant you were with me, traveling here. How could you take the blame because you left for Geneva with me."

Zephyr threw up his hands. "I wasn't even in the country for the crimes he committed the first time! I was with you, in Parley, four years ago when he was partying and assaulted the senator's daughter."

Silence greeted his declaration. Ember had been thirteen when talks of an engagement began between her and Neil, but then Zephyr had been arrested and charged with drug use, assault, battery, and kidnapping a senator's daughter. The target of her engagement had shifted and the people of Parley had been outraged when Cilia had accepted the engagement and marriage agreement.

"I've always been the fall guy for Caelus's antics, and Neil too as he got older. I served a prison sentence for him, as well as probation. I don't relish doing it again, Ember, but at the same time, why bother fighting? His misdeeds will never end," Zephyr told her. "First the bribery, then the drugs, and then they'll try to tie me to the incident in Careen."

"Even if his misdeeds never end, you taking the fall for them will if you're sent to prison. How can you be convicted if you're in a cell," Ember reasoned.

Zephyr looked at her with tired eyes. "Again, Your Majesty, I wasn't in America four years ago when I was convicted and paid for his crimes."

He continued with a distant look in his eyes, "I thought there was still hope of marrying Amelia because while our engagement was only speculation, there was an understanding. I wasn't engaged to you yet because Mother was insisting you marry Neil. You were only thirteen and he was fourteen. While an engagement to you had been brought up, it wasn't a serious thought. Then I was tried and convicted for Cael's crime, and that ended any chance I had with her."

Amelia was the one that got away for Zephyr. Ember knew this because he had mentioned it once, off-handedly, a few years back. She had been fifteen and was talking about how much it must hurt to lose the love of your life like Kieran had. Zephyr had surprised her by telling her about Amelia.

Although he had never disclosed the entire story regarding when she had deemed him unworthy of her affections. He had just said a misunderstanding had cost him the love of his life. Lies had cost him Amelia, along with so many other things. She was surprised he was as open and carefree as he was. But then personifying a carefree, privileged playboy was a type of defense mechanism, wasn't it?

He played the role people expected of him. This allowed him to control the aspects of his personality he wanted people to see. They would think he was unguarded and treated life like a game, whereas, he was protecting himself. Zephyr was clever and used these false impressions of who he was to his advantage. Ember would have applauded him if the reason for it wasn't so tragic.

Zephyr paced the room. "I didn't return to Parley for almost fifteen months because I was in jail awaiting trial, and then in prison serving my sentence. The severity of the crimes was the reason I was never offered bail. Due to my age, they decided not to send me to a high-security prison to serve my seven-month sentence. I got to be at a minimum security facility."

He whirled to face her and the others in the room. "My reputation was destroyed. I was never invited to another state function again. No one asked after me. No one wanted to be friends with me because no one wanted to be seen with someone of my supposed ilk."

Ember sat wide-eyed for a moment. His anger was a stark contrast to the indifference he had shown up to this point. "No one wanted to be seen with you because you supposedly kidnapped and punched a senator's daughter while on drugs before crashing the car, and then served a prison sentence?"

Zephyr stared slack-jawed at her for several moments. Then he started to chuckle, slowly at first before it turned into a full-blown fit of hysteria. He doubled over in laughter, using the back of a chair to keep him on his feet. Ember shot Rhys, Ian, and Evan a quizzical look, but no one said a word.

"I don't understand what's so funny about what I said." Ember crossed her arms over her chest defensively as she watched Zephyr try to contain himself. But then he muttered something about hitting a woman and his laughter picked up again.

Ember huffed out a breath. "Mr. Houndson, can you please explain to me why what I said is so funny? I kept apprised of the story and trial. Am I misremembering?"

Zephyr stood by the window, wiping tears from his eyes as he continued his efforts to calm down. She replayed everything in her mind, including the investigative news article the *Parlian Press* had released, which detailed Zephyr's innocence and told how he had been framed.

When the article had been released, Ember had requested a copy from Jonathon personally. She had been halfway through the article when word reached her that Willow was dead and Kieran was inconsolable. It had taken her a few weeks to return to the article, but she had read every word of it despite having already been briefed on the contents of the article. She had not wanted to be uninformed when it came to her fiancé, regardless of whether she wanted to be engaged to him or not. None of this explained why her comment was so funny to Zephyr though.

Rhys hesitated a moment before answering her. "Mr. Caelus Levan stole the innocence of a senator's daughter four years ago when he forced himself upon her. Mr. Levan was drinking and using cocaine at the time. He claimed she was a willing participant, but when he told her there wasn't going to be a relationship of any kind that's when allegedly she cried foul. He punched her a couple of times, then tied her up and placed her in the back seat to teach her a lesson, before he crashed the car taking a corner too quickly."

Ember turned to stare at Zephyr. The blood pounding in her ears. Rape? Caelus had raped someone. She gripped the arm of the chair as her mind sorted the facts of the case again and again. That wasn't a detail she would have forgotten.

Zephyr knelt in front of her. "The rape was only mentioned in one news article before her father made that information disappear. It was never mentioned in the investigative piece because the focus was on how I was framed."

Ember caressed the side of his face briefly. "I'm sorry I didn't know. I assume if Mr. Houndson knows, then my brother does too. While that would have been nice to know, I can understand her father's wishes to protect her from further harm. I'm just sorry you suffered the consequences of his actions."

Zephyr had only been seventeen when his father had thrown him to the wolves for Caelus and his horrific crimes. No one had been there to protect him. There had been rumors Caelus had raped a few women, but there wasn't any hard evidence. But then Ember thought of Wilson and realized there probably was evidence. It had more than likely been destroyed to keep Caelus clean and wholesome in the eyes of the world.

Anger washed over her. Caelus was a sick human who needed to be locked away from everyone. He tried to turn her kingdom into his new hunting ground, but he overestimated Cilia and his father's influence and sway. Wilson and Caelus would get a taste of their own medicine.

"Parlians know the truth, as does much of the world, thanks to whoever funded the investigative journalist piece in the *Parlian Press*," Zephyr explained. "But Cael's crimes in Careen aren't the only reason we are here."

Rhys cleared his throat. "The American delegation arrived yesterday morning. I've noticed they have had an eye on Mr. Levan, and have been trying to get him alone."

A cold chill shot down her spine. When she had been with Evelyn at the tournament the day before, she had noticed men wearing the American security uniform. Were they trying to force Zephyr back to America while he was off Parlian soil?

"I've seen the American security members on the castle grounds," Ember replied.

Rhys nodded. "Yes. I'm not sure what their interest is in Mr. Levan, but I don't trust their motives either way."

Ember turned to Zephyr. "They can't have you. You're *my* fiancé."

What if Wilson planned to destroy Zephyr as revenge for Emerson killing the law allowing them to buy pearl farms and caymanite mines? He was the prime minister after all, and he had all of America's resources at his disposal. He could make up whatever story he wanted to justify his actions of persecuting his son.

Trepidation clawed down her spine as another possibility occurred to her — what if Wilson was destroying Zephyr to get him out of the way so he could install Caelus to the throne? He was arrogant enough to believe he could do it. He also thought he would beat Parley into submission much like King Henry VIII of England had with "Rough Wooing." When she returned to Parley, she would share her suspicions with Emerson.

A light knock on the door pulled Ember back to the present.

"Yes?" Ember called out.

"Your Majesty, I have a couple of people requesting an audience," came Nerissa's muffled response.

"I am busy at the moment going over official business. Who is requesting an audience?" Ember's stomach rolled at the request. She was on edge knowing the Americans were possibly after Zephyr. She didn't want whoever it was knowing she was already taking an audience.

She took deep breaths to calm her nerves. For all she knew it was some man or his mother sniffing about to determine how official her engagement was.

A light thud outside the door, followed by whispering put Ember on edge. She shot an alarmed look at Rhys. Evan and Ian who were standing by the door locked it before joining Rhys to guard her.

"Lady Nerissa? Is everything alright?" Ember called out. The door handle jiggled. Followed by more whispering.

Had someone knocked out Lady Nerissa and meant to accost her in her private suite? Ember didn't know who they were, but she was no longer frightened. She was a Bellamy.

"I'm ringing the servants bell. Then I'm getting my pistol, and we are going to find out who is behind that door," Ember muttered to the men.

She pulled the cord while the people outside her door did heaven only knew what. She walked into her room and grabbed her pistol from her attaché case.

"They are after me, Ember. My father sent me a wire a few days ago saying he needed me to return to America to deal with the fallout from the Navy's oil fields, Belize, and Parley," Zephyr admitted.

Ah! The reason for his somber mood clicked into place. Ember looked Zephyr in the eye. "Like I said before, I'm the queen. I'll fix this."

Banging on the outside of the door pulled her attention back to the situation at hand.

"I'm going to introduce someone to the Bellamy legacy, and show them how Parley handles threats."

Evan, Ian, and Rhys made sure she was protected, while Zephyr stood off to the side, out of sight from the door. Once in position, Ember motioned for Rhys to unlock the door. A moment later it flew open and two men stumbled in.

The click of her pistol got their attention. "Start talking. As a pirate queen, I'm quite busy, and known to be a little too trigger-happy."

One of the men laughed. He moved toward her. "Put the gun down. A dame like you shouldn't have something you don't know how to use."

Ember smiled sweetly and shot past his head into the door. "Call me 'dame' again instead of 'Your Majesty' or 'Queen Ember' and you'll see how well I use my pistol."

Both men stopped short. They took in the two men behind her and were unaware Rhys was behind them at the door. They also didn't know she rang for the servants. With luck, her guards would be here in a moment. Gunshots tend to draw attention.

"Now. Who are you? And the better question, where is Lady Nerissa?"

Neither man said a word, a commotion in the hallway and shouting signaled to Ember her guards were on their way.

"Well, if you won't talk to me, then you can talk to my men. Believe me, you *will* talk."

The bodyguards rushed into the room. The lead man barked orders to take the men into custody. Ember told him what had happened. Lady Nerissa was on the floor in the public parlor. Rhys, along with half her guards, pulled the men out of the room before the servants arrived.

Once a maid arrived, Ember ordered tea for Nerissa. Her security detail apologized for their lapse. They deferred to Lady Nerissa's judgment, not realizing the men had threatened her to gain entry. Ember knew Emerson would give them an earful and possibly demote them all once they hit Parlian soil.

When Nerissa was alert, one of the bodyguards did a quick medical check to make sure she was fine. They asked her questions about the men and learned they were American and wanted to meet with Ember to let her know about Zephyr's recent behavior.

"What would you like me to do, Your Majesty?"

Ember pinched the bridge of her nose for a moment while she thought. "Contact Emerson. Tell him what happened, and then send the mercenaries to him. They attacked a member of the aristocracy and tried to harm the queen, so I'm sure he'll throw the book at them. If only to send a message."

"Yes, Your Majesty."

"Also, no one is to know this," Ember whispered in the ear of the lead. The man nodded. "If anyone asks, make up some story. We are leaving for Parley tomorrow evening after the ball."

Ember looked at the clock on the mantle. She needed to get ready for dinner. Only one more day and then she could head back to Parley. With any amount of luck, things would go smoothly from here on out.

Chapter 17

Emerson was waiting for Ember to disembark from the zeppelin. She wasn't surprised. He was probably eager to learn the full story of the mercenaries if America had any other antics, as well as everything else he deemed important.

He would have had a few days to interrogate the hired hands, as well as the guards who had escorted the men back on the airplane. However, that wouldn't stop him from further interrogating her. Ember, on the other hand, was eager to learn more about the meeting and anything else she may have missed during her week abroad.

The American delegation had avoided Ember and Zephyr during their final day in Geneva. Ember felt this was because they were aware of the blunder their mercenaries had made. They had to know a response was coming.

"Your Majesty," Emerson greeted with a slight bow. Ember acknowledged his greeting as the pair moved to the car.

Zephyr followed a few steps behind with Evan and Ian taking up the rear. Emerson got into the backseat with her along with Zephyr and Evan, while Ian got in on the front passenger side. As soon as the doors closed, the driver pulled the car away from the curb.

"Any updates?"

"The mercenaries were not sent by America, and they weren't there for Zephyr. We are still investigating," Emerson told her.

Ember's eyes darted back and forth between Zephyr and her twin. "Okay. He wasn't the target. Who was?"

The deafening roar of silence greeted her question. As she looked at the men sitting with her and darted a glance to the front, she did a double take. They were taking the ferry? Why were they taking the ferry? What was going on?

"Emerson, who were they after?" A knot formed in her stomach. She knew the answer. Her. They were after her, but she needed him to say it. It wouldn't be real until he did.

"You. They were after you," Emerson admitted. "And I didn't see it coming." His tone was brittle. Despite his blank expression, Ember knew he was wracked with guilt.

He prided himself on being ahead of everything regarding her safety. He took zero chances. Although this trip had been considered last minute, he wouldn't have let her go if he hadn't already had what he considered to be a solid security framework. Emerson had spent the better part of two weeks meticulously accounting for her time in Geneva.

Ember took her twin's hands in hers. "Em, if something had happened, it would not have been your fault. I would not have blamed you."

Emerson fiercely shook his head. "My job, my sole purpose, as the director is to protect you first and then everyone else. I failed. I failed my queen, but more importantly, I failed my sister."

Tears brimmed Ember's eyes. "Of all the people in my life, Emerson. You have never failed me." She squeezed his hands harder to silence him. "You can not always account for all the balls juggling in the air, especially when they are not yours."

"But my team failed to protect you!"

"They made an assumption regarding the men based on Zephyr, Rhys, Evan, and Ian already being with me," Ember explained. "It was an honest mistake. It could have happened to anyone."

"You were left open, without adequate means to defend yourself," he hissed.

"You taught me how to shoot when we were ten," Ember countered. "I told you there would never be a time when I would need to know how to use a gun. You were insistent, and have been over the years, making me practice with you once a week. And guess what? You were right."

Emerson would have kept arguing, but the car stopping caught Ember's attention. "Where are we going?" She asked while trying to catch a glimpse of their location through the windshield.

This question rendered Emerson speechless. He clamped his mouth shut. This put Ember's guard up. Whatever he had planned, she wasn't going to like it.

When she saw the ferry, she understood why. He was shipping her off to one of the other islands. She thought back to the direction they had taken upon leaving the airport. Realization dawned.

Ember narrowed her eyes. "We landed on the island of Andros, didn't we? You're sending me to Blackstone Manor, aren't you? Why not send me to one of our royal properties? Why send me to Revenge?"

Emerson would send her away after this security breach, but once he investigated, he would bring her back to Cuba and the Parlian capital Careen. There wasn't any reason to send her to the Duchy of Revenge. Unless...

A glimmer of hope sparked within her. Kieran was home! He had to be home, otherwise, Emerson wouldn't send her to the Bahamas without a security detail. Especially because it was well known Blackstone was falling apart.

"He's home. Kieran is finally home," Ember's words breathlessly spilling from her.

Zephyr stiffened next to Emerson as he gave her a soft smile. "No, His Grace isn't home. Lady Vivian asked for help because she and Lady Jillian can't manage the duchy anymore and be the mistresses of their own households."

Pain lanced through her chest at his words. Ember took a quick moment to shutter her emotions. She would not let the blow to her heart be on full display.

"I thought Lady Jillian was engaged. Isn't the wedding set for next spring?" Ember could feel the car slowly moving forward onto the ferry that connected the southern part of the island to the northern half.

She was the queen! She had important matters to attend to. What about the meeting she had raced home for? She couldn't go off to Revenge and play mistress to a crumbling estate and legacy.

Emerson sighed, pulling a hand over his Van Dyke beard. "We had a tropical storm while you were away. The meeting with the High Court has been pushed back to next month in light of the damage. Blackstone isn't safe for Lady Jillian to stay at anymore, so Lady Vivian moved her to her husband's estate until she marries."

"And..." Ember gestured with her hand when her twin stopped talking. Her eyes shot to Zephyr before settling back on Emerson.

"The people of Revenge need help cleaning up and rebuilding. Lady Vivian said there wasn't the money to do it. His Grace doesn't make enough to cover this. He brings in enough money to help maintain and save up for large projects. This storm has bankrupted his duchy. No one knows it."

Ember looked up and studied the ceiling of the car for several minutes. The Crown, as well as herself, had offered Kieran the money to get things back up and running. She told him it was a loan, and he could pay it back, but that his people needed him to put aside his pride. Instead, he would leave to take another job, never answering her.

"He's going to be livid when he finds out the Crown has basically taken over Revenge," Ember observed. "How will the other lords and ladies feel about this? Their queen waltzing in and seizing a bankrupt duchy of a founding family? *That* will instill so much confidence in the monarchy."

Her sarcasm wasn't lost on Emerson. "I think you'd be surprised by their reaction. No matter though, you aren't 'seizing' the estate or the duchy, you're helping your people in place of the duke."

"What about my duties in Careen?"

"I will send a car to take you to the airfield on the southern tip of New Providence for you when you need to travel back for appearances and meetings. The private airport in Nassau isn't safe at the moment. I will make sure the briefings and daily business are delivered by the time you take breakfast."

Ember looked over at Zephyr. "Is Zeph staying with me? Or am I to be isolated?"

Emerson chuckled. "You're not in isolation. You're where you are needed the most right now. And also, where I can keep you safe."

Ember sighed. "I'm not discounting my people in the Bahamas don't need me. I just don't understand, but I trust you."

A jolt had Ember looking out the window again. The ferry had arrived on the northern part of the island. She let out a gasp. Ember had been briefed on the storm the day before, but she hadn't thought much of it because it had been one sentence. The magnitude of the storm's destruction had been kept from her, probably because an assessment hadn't been done at that point.

"All the islands in the Bahamas sustained damage," Emerson told her as she stared at the damage to the beach surrounding the ferry terminal. "They received the brunt of the storm."

Palm trees were down along the beach. Ferns, lilies, and other plants were littered all over. The terminal itself had been ripped from its foundation and parts of it were discarded on the nearby sand as the waves washed over it. Threatening to drag the remains to sea. Debris of all kinds from everyday life was scattered in the water, on the sand, in the trees, and along the road.

As the car drove gingerly along the road, avoiding branches and parts of buildings, a teddy bear caught and held Ember's attention. Whose home had the bear come from? Which child was missing this treasured item? Were they alive? Was their family?

Ember's eyes burned as the teddy bear blurred. Some Parlian child was missing that teddy bear. Without thinking, Ember moved for the door. "Stop. Stop the car," she muttered as she opened the door.

Emerson cursed as he reached for her, but she avoided his grasp and leapt from the still-moving car. She walked over and picked up the toy. She looked up the road and saw people cleaning what must have been their home.

She could hear the doors of the car opening behind her. Zephyr and Emerson were calling to her, but she ignored them. Instead, she walked towards the people. Her people. Their entire lives were in tatters after this storm. They were in hurricane season. If a tropical storm had caused this kind of damage to their lives, then what would a hurricane do?

Not only did Kieran not have the money for Blackstone, his people didn't have the money to fortify their homes. Emerson was right. She was always needed in Careen, but her people in the Duchy of Revenge needed her more.

She could hear the footfalls behind her on the cement road. The men were running towards her. She would be chastised for acting without thinking, but sometimes you needed to make your security detail earn their keep.

"Honey, I'm not seeing it. I think he's gone," a feminine voice said. The child looked up with a tear-streaked face. "Maybe we can find another in Careen after we've rebuilt."

The little boy nodded bravely as fresh tears streamed from his eyes. He couldn't have been more than five or six. Ember quickly scanned the area as she picked her way through the broken walls and rubble toward the child and his mother.

"Excuse me," Ember called out. "I couldn't help but hear that you're looking for something. May I be of assistance?"

"Oh, we are looking for a stuffed bear, but I fear it's long gone with the storm," the woman replied. "But we thank you for your kindness, miss."

Ember came into the woman's view about the same time Emerson yelled at her to stop.

"You... You are.... Your Majesty," the woman dropped into a deep curtsy and then pulled her son closer to her to help him bow. "We... we are so honored, Your Majesty, that you would come to our humble home and offer assistance."

The woman's husband and a few others came over to where they were upon hearing the commotion. Ember went to move forward when Emerson's grip locked tightly around her arm.

The fire in his eyes and clenched jaw told her he was seething with anger over her actions. Meanwhile, the others realizing both the queen and her brother, the prince, were in their presence, dropped into the proper greeting and held it.

They couldn't straighten until she acknowledged them. "Thank you, please stand. There is no need for such formality in these circumstances."

The woman looked up. "Oh, Your Royal Highness is here too." Her voice was thin and her skin pale. She was going to faint.

Ember forcefully pulled herself from her twin's hold and reached the woman's side as her knees buckled. "Oh, goodness," Ember laughed with forced lightness. "I'm not that important, and neither is he. Here let's find a place to rest."

Her husband looked around and found a mostly intact bucket. He turned it over as Ember helped the woman sit. Meanwhile, the little boy's eyes were full of wonder as he studied both Ember and her entourage.

"Your Majesty, thank you so much for coming. You must have so many other things to do, but here you are," the man said. The others nodded in agreement.

It was like a bucket of ice water had been thrown on her. These people had lost everything. All material possessions. Yet they were honored by her presence? Meanwhile, not ten minutes before, she had been questioning whether her presence was even needed or warranted because it was inconvenient for her. She had never felt so humble in her life.

"Nothing, and I do mean nothing, was more important than surveying the storm damage, and connecting with you all," Ember told them. "I'm here and will remain here until the clean-up and rebuilding is well underway."

The men and women before her nodded. There was a sheen to many of their eyes. There was also a palpable relief. Like they could breathe easier because they had a leader who would see things through to the end.

Emerson cleared his throat. "Your Majesty, I do not want to minimize or cut this moment short, but there is a schedule."

"Oh my! We don't want to disrupt your schedule, Your Majesty. I'm sure you have more important people to see than us. Like our local leaders," the woman reasoned.

Ember turned and glared daggers at her brother. To hell with his schedule.

Ember smiled. "There is always a schedule and important people, but I'm here with you all. Thus, making you important."

She then looked around. It didn't seem like this family had food, water, or even shelter. Had that been set up? If not, that needed to happen. These people could be moved to all available hotels on the different islands so they could be somewhere safe while they worked on rebuilding their homes.

"So, I have two questions for you. The first is what did your son lose? And the second is what are your names?"

"I am Harlow White, this is my husband Jacob and our son Turner. The others are our neighbors, Your Majesty. They were helping us look for Pat, Turner's teddy bear," Harlow said.

"Oh! Is this Pat? We were driving from the ferry terminal and I saw this bear on the ground, so I picked it up. Then I heard you and came over," Ember explained as she held out the bear, which was a little worse for wear. He was dirty and missing an arm, but otherwise intact.

"Pat!" Turner exclaimed and rushed forward to grab the toy. His parents were alarmed and tried to grab him, but were unsuccessful.

The boy reached for the bear and Ember handed it to him. He then wrapped his tiny arms around her legs and hugged her.

"Oh, honey. The queen is clean and we aren't…"

Harlow's voice trailed off when Ember bent down and hugged the boy back.

"I'm afraid he's missing an arm and is quite dirty from his adventure," Ember apologized.

The little boy looked down at his stuffed toy. "He is hurt very seriously. I think Mommy will have to stitch him up and make him better."

His eyebrows furrowed. "But Mommy can't because we lost everything. We got nothing left. That's what Daddy said."

There was sniffling around her, but she never took her attention off Turner. She took the boy's hands in hers.

"You know what I think, Mr. Turner. I think while all your possessions are gone, the best things still remain: you, your mommy, your daddy, and Pat."

The little boy thought on her words for a moment. He didn't understand the full weight of her words, but he understood the face value. "You're right, Queen."

Ember chuckled. "I tell you what. Pat is in serious condition. How about you and your family visit me tomorrow for breakfast or lunch or whenever you can arrive at Blackstone, and I'll have the royal surgeon fix up Pat back to top form."

His eyes widened as he giggled. "Really? You'll help Pat?"

"Of course! He's an important citizen of Parley."

Turner rushed back to his parents. "The queen is going to fix Pat!"

Harlow and Jacob hugged him as he gushed with excitement.

"Your Majesty, we would love to see you at Blackstone, but…" Jacob's voice trailed off.

"I know what you're going to say. Come as you are, and if you need traveling assistance, I can send a car. I want to know what my citizens need in regards to clean up efforts and rebuilding from my people rather than leaders."

"That would be great, Your Majesty. If you could send a car, then we would be so honored to join you for tea," Jacob said.

Ember parted ways with the Whites and walked back to the car. Emerson was silent until they started moving again.

"What on earth possessed you to be so reckless? I swear, Ember, I don't know what comes over you at times." Emerson was shaking his head. He continued on his rant, but she tuned him out.

As they made their way up the island to the ferry terminal leading to New Providence, pausing at the various obstacles, the reality of Kieran's situation sank in. The man was trying to rebuild not just his estate, but the properties and infrastructures of his tenants. If he was hiding this level of insolvency from everyone, what else was he hiding?

It was well after dark by the time they arrived on the main island and the capital of Nassau. Most of the bridges had been washed away. Emerson had put temporary structures in places ahead of her trip to help cross the islands, but downed trees and buildings, so many buildings had brought them to a standstill more than a few times.

Nassau, as well as the main island in general, didn't seem to be the worse for wear. Upon entering the city, Ember could actually believe it had been a tropical storm rather than a low-level hurricane. There were some trees down, branches scattered around the roads, and some damage to the roofs of some of the older buildings. Granted, she was viewing everything by the light of the street lamps, but people weren't sleeping outside or trying to find shelter.

"Emerson," she uttered. "Why is the damage so much less here?"

In the dim light, she couldn't tell if her twin was looking at her or not when he responded. "Kieran and his tenants agreed to put the money towards making the infrastructure improvements on the main island before working their way south was the way to go because of the tourism and number of businesses here."

Ember could see the logic in the method. Securing one island at a time would help bankroll the work on the others. However, the major flaw in the plan was the dependence and faith that the weather and storms would never turn destructive and deadly.

"Were there any deaths or major injuries?" Ember was scared to know the answer. As the queen though, she needed to know. She couldn't walk into a situation such as this and not know the answer.

"No. We were extremely fortunate. Once the storm began to pick up steam, everyone on the southern islands fled to the emergency shelters on their respective island."

Ember chewed on her lip. At least there were storm shelters. Regardless of Parley's funds, the Bellamy's had a vast fortune at their disposal. She would be taking full advantage of it too. Kieran could come home and rant and rave about it being charity until he was blue in the face. At least she would see him, she thought glumly.

When the headlights shone on the gate of Blackstone Manor, Ember sat up in her seat and rolled her window down to get a better look. Ian and Evan both got out of the car to partially carry the wrought iron monstrosities out of the driveway. Once they were back in the car, the driver began the slow accent to the house.

Trepidation slithered down her spine. The darkness around them only added to the feeling of foreboding. Ember noticed right away none of the estate's lights were on, which told her one of two things: either they weren't functioning after the storm or they had never been upgraded to function. She was fairly certain it was the latter.

When they made it to the circular drive, the headlights from the car illuminated the entrance of Blackstone. Ember let out a whimper. The once proud manor had been reduced to a shell of its former self. Parts of the roof were caving in, and it appeared some of the walls were crumbling.

If the outside was in this state, what did the inside look like? Ember shuddered at the thought. Jillian and Vivian had been living here? There must be a wing or something that wasn't caving in or falling apart. She also feared what the light of day would reveal. What other disrepair was the night hiding?

Ember climbed out of the car. Servants stepped forward from somewhere to grab their bags. Emerson directed where things were to go while she carefully explored the exterior. The landscape was overgrown, looking more like a jungle rather than the manicured gardens they once had been. It was difficult to tell if any of the landscape had been harmed by the storm because it was so chaotic.

She jumped when she felt the hand on her shoulder.

"I'm sorry," Emerson muttered.

She smiled with a hand on her heart. "It's alright. Should I ask what I've done to end up here? If it was to see the state of Blackstone, a day trip would have been sufficient. Yet, I'm to stay here?"

Ember was amused by the thought. If he thought she would put up a fight or throw a fit, he would be mistaken. While the circumstances and environment were less than ideal, she could handle it. She wouldn't cry and beg for her creature comforts. If her people needed her to be on their level, then she would live on their level.

Emerson barked out a laugh at her words. "I'm not punishing you. The public areas of Blackstone are falling apart, but most of the private areas are intact enough for you to stay here safely."

"Then why did Jillian leave?"

Emerson shrugged. "I honestly don't know. I think both women are tired of running the estate in the absence of their brother."

Ember could certainly understand why. They both had lives and responsibilities outside the Duchy of Revenge. After Vivian was married, she took on her role as a countess. Meanwhile, Jillian ran things to the best of her ability, but she had been in England for several social seasons to get a husband. In her last season, she caught the attention of a viscount.

They were happily engaged, and it was Vivian's husband's estate that was providing the dowry. Her husband was also paying for the wedding, and anything else his sister-in-law needed. Of course, it had all been kept quiet, but it must be a blow to Kieran's pride to know he couldn't provide for his tenants or his sisters.

"So, now the Crown must run the estate in the duke's absence? Do we even have an idea where he is?" Ember asked while searching her twin's face in the dim light.

Emerson answered in the order she asked. "Yes, you will run it and fix it because of national security. No, but Zephyr has made some good progress."

Emerson offered her his arm. "Come. Let's get you settled for the evening. Then I leave you in the capable hands of Ethan and Ian. They are your bodyguards for the time being."

"What about Zephyr?"

"He's coming back with me to Careen. I have a separate car we are taking back to the airport tonight. It wouldn't be proper to have the queen and her fiancé staying somewhere without proper chaperones."

Of course. What Emerson was saying made perfect sense. She was annoyed though that Zephyr had made progress and shared it with him, but not her. Maybe he just wanted to work out a few things before approaching her with what he's learned.

Ember set her thoughts aside for the moment. She would focus on getting settled because she was going to have a long stay at Revenge. And that didn't even include the other matters that had brought her home, which she needed to handle.

"Emerson, when you get back to Careen, I need you to set up a meeting with Jonathon Laurent. I don't care if it's here or there, but I need to meet with him as soon as possible."

"I'll reach out to Lord Laurent in the morning and set that up straight away."

Ember looped her arm through her brother's. "Thank you. If the time conflicts with my meeting with the Whites, then his lordship can wait for his queen."

Emerson chuckled. "I almost feel sorry for Jonathon."

Chapter 18

Ember woke the next morning unsure of her surroundings. She was lying in a large bed on sheets that were clean, but worn. She looked over to the window and remembered she was in Nassau at Blackstone.

Emerson had worked out the security details ahead of time but still needed time to investigate and clear staff that had been with Ember in Geneva. Two of those people were Nerissa and her lady's maid, both of whom were in Careen. This meant Ember had utilized one of the maids on the estate to help her undress. Mostly, she needed help getting out of her blasted corset, and back into one. If she didn't have to wear them, then she could have dressed herself.

She was currently going over her daily briefings. She had finished breakfast a while ago, and received word the Whites would join her for afternoon tea. Emerson had also sent her a missive, she would be heading back to Careen after tea to take an audience with Jonathon. She would have dinner with the family before returning to Revenge.

A knock on her door drew her attention away from the pages before her.

"Yes?" Ember called out.

"The Whites have arrived, Your Majesty," Ian replied.

Ember rubbed her eyes with her fingers. She had been reading and responding to things for hours. Ember stood and stretched before walking to the door.

"Thank you."

Ian nodded as he escorted her to the garden. Along the way, Ember had stopped a footman and requested the presence of the Royal Surgeon, who had arrived shortly after breakfast.

"Queen!" Turner shouted a few seconds before his small body launched itself onto her legs in a fierce hug. His parent's attempt to stop their son from taking their monarch by surprise failed. Harlow and Jacob were mortified by their son's actions, while Ember just laughed and hugged the boy back.

"How are you today, Mr. Turner?" Ember asked as she knelt before him.

"I'm very well, Miss Queen," Turner replied.

Ember smiled in amusement at the child before looking behind him to his parents. They addressed her properly, while Ember motioned to the new-looking seating area. If she had to wager a guess, Emerson had ordered furniture to help maintain appearances.

"Did you sleep well? Are your accommodations to your liking?" Ember asked.

"The hotel is really nice, Your Majesty. Everything and everyone has been wonderful, Your Majesty," Jacob answered.

"Please, call me Ember. I'm glad to hear the hotel is to your liking." Ember turned and motioned to the surgeon behind her. "Mr. Turner, did you by chance bring Pat with you?"

The little boy went to his mother and took the damaged toy from her. "He's right here."

"This is my personal surgeon, the very best Parley has to offer. As I promised, he will take Pat straight back and repair him while we visit and have tea."

Turner gingerly handed the teddy bear over to the doctor before turning to clutch her hand and watch the surgeon leave.

"He'll be ok, Miss Queen?" Turner's voice was barely above a whisper.

She lowered herself to look the young boy in the eyes. "I swear it on my honor as the queen of Parley. My surgeon will take the very best care of Pat."

Turner nodded. His eyes were wide with worry, but Ember knew how to fix that.

"Do you like cake? The pastry chef made petit fours."

Turner's eyes lit up as he rushed for the table. She chuckled and stood. She led Harlow and Jacob to the table to join Turner, who was loading up his plate. His parents were horrified, but Ember took it in stride. She made subtly teaching Turner proper tea etiquette a game.

Ember sat and visited with the Whites for a few hours. As the trio was preparing to head back to their hotel, the surgeon came back with a freshly laundered and repaired Pat.

"Mommy! Daddy! Pat has an arm again!" Turner threw his arms around the doctor and held him tight for a moment. The surgeon swallowed hard a couple of times before responding to Turner and taking his leave. The young boy turned and squeezed Ember's legs in a tight hug.

"I take it Pat is to your liking, Mr. Turner?"

"Very much, Miss Queen."

After a few moments, Ember escorted the Whites to their car and saw them off. But not before packing up the remaining treats from the afternoon tea to take back to the hotel. Ember also promised Turner she would visit with him and Pat in the near future. Once the car was down the drive, Ember turned to Ian and Evan.

"Give me a half hour to change for dinner and my meeting with Jonathon. I promise it won't take me long," Ember told the pair.

She turned to leave and then paused. "Oh! Make sure you're both dressed for dinner too. After all, you're nobility and my honored guests."

Ember continued to her room, stopping a footman along the way to request the maid who had been helping her dress. She didn't care if she was overdressed for her meeting with Lord Laurent, she wanted to look the part for dinner. Word had come during tea that an American judge, his wife, and their youngest daughter would be in attendance for dinner as guests of the prime minister. He had also made them comfortable in a suite of rooms as if the palace were his home and not hers.

Ember was curious as to who these mystery guests were. And how they fit into his plan and strategy, because nothing Wilson did was ever without motive.

Ember, Ian, and Evan arrived at the same time as Jonathon. He bowed to her as she walked past and led the way to her office and private audience room.

She was rounding the corner, her entourage in tow, when Wilson, Caelus, and his guests noticed her. It appeared to Ember he was leading some kind of tour through the public areas. She frowned slightly because Zephyr wasn't with them, but kept walking.

"It would appear, that Her Majesty is taking someone to task," Wilson joked in a stage whisper behind her. The laughter that followed was expected, but no less grating.

"Oh, Wilson, you are clever. Ember playing queen before dinner," Cilia trilled.

Ember's abrupt stop caused Jonathon to collide into her backside.

He bowed and took a few steps back. "I'm sorry, Your Majesty. I didn't mean"—

Ember held up her hand to stop his words as she walked back to the entrance observing the small gathering from the cover of the hallway. The laughter and mockery at her expense weren't surprising. What was surprising was how emboldened Wilson and her mother had become in her absence.

A hand on her shoulder caused her to jump slightly. She turned and saw the concern in Jonathon's expression.

"Are you alright, Your Majesty?"

Ember smiled. "Yes, Lord Laurent. Shall we? And why don't you stay for dinner? I'll have word sent to the kitchen if you're schedule will allow."

He chuckled softly. "It would be my pleasure and honor to join you for dinner."

Ember nodded and started down the hall again. Once they were in the private audience room, Ian and Evan checked the room from top to bottom for signs of anyone trying to eavesdrop. Once they signaled it was safe, Ember sat in her chair and motioned for Jonathon to sit across from her.

Jonathon took a seat. The fidgeting of his hands was the only betrayal of his nerves.

"Lord Laurent, you have caused me a great deal of trouble with your antics," Ember began. Jonathon ducked his head, his cheeks turned red as he rubbed the back of his neck. Under different circumstances, Ember would have been amused by their situation. He was almost ten years older than her. Yet, here she was, getting ready to scold him for his actions. It would have been comical if the subject matter wasn't so serious.

"As a member of the peerage you are granted access to knowledge others don't have. A prime example of this was the publishing of Baron Burroughs's daughter's name. You have besmirched her reputation to the point where her fiancé's family has called off the engagement," Ember announced. She stopped herself because she felt her temper rise with each word.

Meanwhile, Jonathon's complexion drained of color. His eyes were wide as he loosened the tie around his neck to get more air. He ran a hand over his face a few times before dropping his head into his hands. Through it all, Ember remained silent.

"I know I screwed up. The situation is all wet, and I'm all balled up about it." Jonathon looked up and searched her eyes. "Can I tell you what happened? Like my side? Then you can punish me how you see fit, but please leave the viscountcy alone."

The guilt and shame rolled off Jonathon in waves. "Of course. I would never punish the entire viscountcy based on your actions alone. I will hear your side of things. That is why I called the meeting. I have already received letters and briefings from Lord Burroughs and the French nobles. I want to hear what in the devil possessed you to do what you did."

Jonathon took several deep breaths to calm himself. "A few days after you left, Caelus was partying with other Americans who had come over from Belize. I was having a drink after work with some colleagues at a nearby bar when the ruckus broke out."

Jonathon's eyes stared at a spot on the Persian rug and he seemed to withdraw into his mind. "As I was leaving the bar, I noticed who the police were arresting. I immediately went over and questioned the officers. I assumed, wrongly as it were, the woman he was arguing with was an American."

He flinched at the memory. "That shouldn't have made a difference. I should have waited for additional information before publishing the names of anyone involved in the incident aside from Caelus Levan. Then it was announced the next morning by the Guardians that Caelus wouldn't face any charges for the cocaine because it was a misunderstanding."

Jonathon's tone took on a hard, angry edge. "I couldn't believe the Crown and the Guardians would play favorites like that. When I got the full story from the Cuban police, along with the names, I didn't think. I was blinded by my anger and the betrayal I thought you were committing against the citizens of Parley to save your future brother-in-law."

He looked into Ember's face with sorrow-filled eyes.

"After I went to press and distributed the newspaper everywhere, I had lunch with my father who told me what had happened to Lady Lianna Thornton, Baron Burroughs's daughter. He hadn't seen the paper, but I instantly knew the woman whose name I was given. Lilly Grace is Lady Lianna's nickname and middle name combined. I didn't put two and two together when I was writing the story."

Jonathon wrung his hands in front of him before springing from the chair and pacing back and forth in front of Ember.

"Her fiancé was in my office waiting for me when I returned from lunch. He all but challenged me to a duel, and I don't blame him. Next was her father, and then my own entered," Jonathon explained. His eyes had a sheen over them. "He told me how disappointed he was in me. He said he taught me better than that."

Jonathon cleared his throat a couple of times. "The worst of it all was calling on Lady Lianna. I didn't say a word, she just walked forward and hugged me. She told me it was an honest mistake and it would be alright. She wasn't angry or upset with me, which was worse."

Jonathon collapsed into the chair behind him. His head cradled in his hands.

The anger Ember had held against Jonathon vanished. Nothing she could threaten or punish him with would compare to the self-imposed punishment of his guilt. She didn't have a solution to this particular matter because there wasn't one. Only a time machine would solve this situation.

"Do you know if Lady Lianna was in love with her French fiancé and visa versa? I don't have the particulars of the match. The baron and the Comte of Nevers weren't forthcoming with that in their letters," Ember said, breaking the silence.

Jonathon swiped at his eyes. Ember could hear the dinner bell ring out but ignored it. She was pretending to be queen, after all, so they could wait. When she was in residence, no one could have dinner until she arrived unless she had indicated otherwise.

"It is— it was— an arranged marriage. Her fiancé is more embarrassed by the article and scandal, as is his family. Lady Lianna was marrying up in title, but her fiancé's family was gaining a fortune they desperately needed," Jonathon told her.

"Did she love him or was she in love with him?" Ember asked. "I know love isn't always a factor with marriages amongst nobles, but I would like to know as much as I can about her feelings at least."

"She has an affection for him. Lady Lianna's not in love with him as far as I know. I believe they viewed themselves as friends," Jonathon replied. He chewed on his bottom lip a moment before adding, "That said, her fiancé is claiming to have been head over heels for her despite his Italian mistress."

Ember nodded. It didn't surprise her that Comte's son had a mistress. It eased her mind knowing there wasn't a great love between the pair. Heartbreak could be a messy business when engagements fell apart.

Ember was about to speak when the dinner bell rang a second time, catching Jonathon's attention. Her nostrils flared and her eyes narrowed slightly. She was the blasted queen and would be there when she pleased.

Jonathon arched an eyebrow, "Are we being summoned?"

"It would appear the dowager is impatient this evening, and trying to impress the prime minister's guests," Ember answered. She was annoyed by her mother's shenanigans in general, but tonight the woman was pushing her luck. Cilia was playing her role as the spoiled socialite perfectly, putting on a show to impress people she would never look twice at if not for her lover.

Ember let out a heavy sigh. "I'm going to level with you. I already told Wilson if Caelus was caught with cocaine in Parley the authorities could charge him with whatever they wanted. However, it would seem the Guardians are determined to undermine my authority."

Jonathon digested this information. "Emerson alluded to something similar when he summoned me to his office. He said things would be coming to a head soon. I promise not to breathe a word of any of that."

Ember smiled softly. "I trust you, Jonathon. I wouldn't have said anything if I didn't."

"Can I get a hint about what's coming?" The hopeful gleam in Jonathon's eyes had Ember shaking her head and chuckling. "Please?"

"You are incorrigible, Jonathon." The pair stared at each other for a moment. Ember considered the consequences of giving Jonathon a hint about what was coming. He was a newspaperman to the core, but he was a nobleman first and foremost.

"I'm dissolving the Guardians," Ember announced.

Jonathon sucked in a sharp breath. His eyes widened as his mind whirled with the implications. A slow grin spread across his face. "If I may be so bold, it's about time. I'm looking forward to the day I can write this story. Thank you, Ember."

"Soon, Jonathon. I just hope the citizens will be as ecstatic as you," Ember quipped.

"Don't let the fear of being overthrown stop you from ruling," Jonathon encouraged. He looked down at his hands for a moment before holding her gaze as he continued, "For what it's worth, I believe in you, Ember. Your father would be proud."

Ember blinked rapidly at the sudden swell of emotion. His words touched a hidden place inside her heart. There were times she wondered if her father would be proud of her, or if he would be disappointed in her. Hearing Jonathon, someone who had known her father and had interviewed him, tell her he would be proud meant more than words to her.

She leaned forward and grasped his hand in hers, squeezing it to convey her gratitude. Her throat felt thick with unshed tears. She didn't trust herself to speak without getting emotional. The pair sat like that for a few minutes as Ember composed herself.

The dinner bell rang for a third time, shattering the moment. Aggravated didn't begin to cover the surge of emotion she felt at the moment. One did not summon one's queen.

"Do we need to go?" Jonathon asked while holding back a smile.

Ember rolled her eyes. She took a deep breath and closed her eyes briefly before refocusing on Jonathon.

"No, we will finish our meeting," Ember answered. "If they ring the damned thing one more time, my grandmother will beat someone with it, I assure you. And if she doesn't, I will."

Jonathon and the other men in the room choked back laughter. The tone shifted from amusement back to somber as the conversation moved back to the original topic of the meeting.

"You are to make a public apology sometime in the next week. I'm going to talk to Lady Lianna, and see if there is anything specific she would like," Ember explained. "I know she is twenty-two or twenty-three, and her family is worried about her marriageability."

"She's twenty-three. Perhaps, at an appropriate time, I might call upon Lady Lianna," Jonathon mused.

Ember chuckled. "Your crush on her, Lord Laurent, has been obvious, even to your queen, for a few years now. I know your intention was not to cause her harm or break off her engagement, but consider this your opportunity to get the girl and make her father happy."

"Yes, Your Majesty." Jonathon shot her a roguish grin. "Is that a direct order?"

Ember rolled her eyes as she teased back, "Let's call it a strong suggestion."

Jonathon threw back his head in laughter. "Noted, Your Majesty."

"In regards to Caelus and the Guardians, because you are a member of the peerage, I will grant you exclusive access when the time comes," Ember said. "However, Caelus is due a fair investigation like anyone else in Parley. Once the police bring forth the charges, he will have a trial and then atone for his sins like everyone else."

"Yes, Your Majesty."

Ember nodded before standing. "Shall we adjourn to dinner?"

Jonathon nodded. "I don't have the proper jacket or attire, but I will join you."

Ember dismissed his concerns. "I invited you to dinner knowing this already. I need allies as I walk into the lion's den. Dress etiquette is the least of my concerns."

Jonathon chuckled and held out his arm. "Then let's give them something to talk about," he said with a wink.

Chapter 19

"Finally! Honestly, Ember, do you have any sense of time," Cilia scolded from her place on the settee. "We've been waiting ages for your arrival."

"Call me 'Ember' one more time while scolding my behavior, and see what happens, Dowager Queen," Ember fired back. Her anger was palpable as she glared at her mother.

Cilia remained silent as she continued sipping on her sherry, refusing to make eye contact with her daughter. Meanwhile, Wilson had no qualms returning Ember's glare with one of his own. She held his gaze for several moments before he looked away.

"Whose idea was it to ring the bell thrice?" Ember asked the room. Her mother shifted in her seat while Martin glanced at his sister to see if she would own up to her actions. It surprised no one when she remained quiet.

Her American guests, on the other hand, found the display amusing and the young woman began giggling. Zephyr shot her a look while nodding his head, but the young woman just narrowed her gaze at him. It was clear she had a low opinion of him. Ember was eager to find out why.

The older man turned to Wilson and stage whispered, "Is she always so dramatic? I thought she was just a figurehead with no power?"

Jonathon stiffened next to her, his eyes widened at this declaration, and watched Ember's reaction from the corner of his eye. Ian and Evan remained silent in their corner of the room, while Emerson and Greer tried to gage Ember's temper from the corner they were standing in. Grammy Margaret and Uncle Martin shared a knowing look from the settee they were sharing.

Charles, God bless the man, stepped forward to diffuse the situation. "It was I, Your Majesty. I was asked to ring the bell three times to ensure you heard it."

Ember took a calming breath and smiled at the older man. He was going to fall on the sword for her mother and the prime minister knowing full well she could dismiss him as butler for his actions. This further enraged her; however, she kept the mask of civility firmly in place.

"Thank you. My dinner companions and I did hear it," Ember shared, smiling at the man.

Turning back to the newcomers, Ember decided introductions were in order. She clapped her hands together and gave the room a saccharine grin.

"Hello, everyone. We haven't met. I am Queen Ember Lucille Soleil Bellamy the III. I am the sitting monarch, and as Lord Jonathon Laurent, heir to the Viscount Bourchier, is aware like everyone else, I am very much not a figurehead," Ember told everyone sweetly.

Jonathon chuckled. "Only fools would think you have no power, Your Majesty. After all, you were coronated at age eight. You've been the reigning monarch for almost a decade now."

Ember could kiss Jonathon as she watched the expression on Cilia's face take on a sour note. Emerson rubbed his eyes while Greer patted his arm.

She knew her twin hated when she fueled the power struggle between herself and their mother, but she was not going to be disrespected throughout dinner. Besides, he had been the one telling her she needed to step up and be queen. He couldn't be upset when she did that at what amounted to a dinner party.

"I assume you have met my brother, His Royal Highness Prince Emerson, Duke of Whydah and the Director of Intelligence and Military Operations," Ember continued. "Next to him is Lady Greer Read, third daughter of the Earl of William."

She waved to her grandmother and uncle. "I'm assuming you've also made the acquaintance of my grandmother, Dowager Queen Margaret, and my Uncle Martin, prince of Cardia."

Her uncle's eyes flashed with surprise. Cardia had been swallowed up by Turkey during a revolution. Her mother refused to acknowledge her brother's title because the country no longer existed; however, out of respect for him and to give him equal footing socially, Ember chose to recognize his title. Cilia scoffed at the use of the honorific as she drained the glass of sherry.

Ember ignored her as she turned to her new bodyguards. She had asked and memorized the pair's titles before they left for Careen. Using everyone's title at this dinner was her power move.

"This is Ian Masters of Astonia, Earl of Northumbria. Next to him is Evan McClintock of Astonia, Earl of Somerset. Prime Minister Wilson, who are your esteemed guests?" She cocked an eyebrow, turning to him expectantly.

As Ember had listed off titles during her introductions, the mood in the room had shifted from one of superiority to one of uncertainty. She had watched the smug expressions of Wilson's guests become more guarded with every word.

"This is the honorable Judge Alexander Monroe, his wife Viola, and youngest daughter Amelia," Wilson replied with his chin high.

Ah. The treatment of Zephyr by this young woman made more sense. This was the elusive Amelia. The woman Zephyr had hoped to marry. The woman who had deemed him unworthy of her affections based on not what she knew of him, but rather what the world had said about him.

Ember took a moment to study her. She was pretty with her flawless fair skin but was nothing more than skin and bones. She looked frumpy in the drop-waist dress she was wearing, which did nothing to help her figure. Her hips appeared wider while her small breasts became nonexistent.

Ember hated the fashion the Americans had embraced. All the dresses looked like sacks with a ribbon around the waist. This look was not flattering on most women, Amelia was proof of that. The brackish color of the garment was also an unfortunate one with her complexion.

Her mouse brown hair was pulled up in an uninspired bun. This along with the dainty peridot pendent showed off her slim neck. She also wore simple diamond stud earrings in another uninspiring attempt to appear fashionable, Ember thought. Her eyes were an unusual shade of honey brown, she would give her that. But the young woman failed to capture this feature in a memorable way.

At first glance, Ember couldn't figure out what Zephyr had seen in the woman to fall in love with her. It had to be her mind or personality because it for sure wasn't her looks. Amelia had a pretty face with a frame that was reminiscent of a skeleton, and her style choices didn't help. Her sour and spiteful mood wasn't doing her any favors either.

Ember may not marry Zephyr ultimately, but he was a good man. In her court, Zephyr was the fiancé of the queen. He was treated with respect by everyone because he had earned it. He had gone out of his way to learn about the different islands, the different jobs citizens held, and what issues the citizens faced.

Then he'd had to navigate the peerage and society as an outsider without a title. He had learned about the estates and how they are managed. He learned about the issues and problems the lords and ladies faced which never impacted their tenants and citizens because that was the burden of the title.

At every turn, Zephyr had been challenged and set up to fail by the Parlians to test his mettle. Through it all, Zephyr rose to the occasion. Even when he failed, he dusted himself off and tried again. He had earned his place, and he deserved recognition of this outside of being her fiancé.

Ember let go of Jonathon's arm and moved over to Zephyr. He stood and bowed slightly in recognition of her station. Ember gave him a lopsided grin before she reached up with her left hand — showing off the impressive three-karat princess cut ruby engagement ring, which was flanked on either side by two diamonds, totaling another three karats — and kissed him on the cheek. She could hear Amelia's gasp and caught her staring at the ring.

Ember smirked at Zephyr. Surprise lit his eyes at her display of affection. He hid it quickly as he offered her his arm. "Shall we eat, my Queen?"

"Yes. I can't wait to see what chef made."

The pair led the way into the dining room. Ember made sure Zephyr sat next to her, along with Jonathon. Emerson sat down at the other end of the table with Greer and Grammy. Ian and Evan sat beside Zephyr and Jonathon.

The footmen began serving everyone at the table. The conversation was stilted at first, but as the courses continued, the guests began to relax and talk. By the dessert course, everyone was even joking. Ember was happy to listen to the conversations around her and relax for a moment instead of waiting for the other shoe to drop, which she should have seen coming.

"I may be overstepping my bounds here, Your Majesty, but isn't Lord Laurent the man spreading false information in the newspapers about Mr. Caelus Levan?" Alexander inquired, faux innocence dripping from his tone.

Jonathon dropped his dessert spoon during the question and sat slack-jawed as he stared at the American judge. There it was, the other shoe dropping, she thought dryly.

"Lord Laurent is the editor and owner of the *Parlian Press*, but I was unaware he had spread any falsehoods in his reporting," Ember responded with a coolness in her tone.

The older man at the other end of the table shook his head in disbelief.

"I guess you wouldn't seeing as who your fiancé is, Your Majesty," he quipped back.

The alarm on Wilson's face was priceless, as was the look he shot Ember. Did he honestly expect her to keep her mouth shut? There was overwhelming evidence clearing Zephyr's good name, but Wilson never acknowledged the newspaper's exposé.

Ember folded her napkin and placed it on the side of her dish. She could see the looks her staff were shooting each other. This man, a judge, felt he was above her morally, but was blissfully ignorant of the company he kept in regards to the prime minister.

"Are you suggesting the Cuban police do not know how to investigate crimes? Or that Lord Laurent and other members of the Parley press corps do not know how to read and ask questions?"

Jonathon studied the faces of everyone at the table. He reached for his wine as understanding dawned on him. Ember needed allies not just at the dinner, but within her nobility as well. She was going to defend him and his actions in public despite his misstep because she was his queen and a Bellamy. Loyalty mattered. Yet, this was just a trivial battle compared to the war she must be waging to gain full control as monarch.

"I'm suggesting nothing of the sort. I do find it rather convenient though how you overlook your fiancé's antics and poor behavior to protect his reputation," Alexander noted.

His wife and daughter softly hushed him, begging him to keep quiet. A quick flash caught Ember's attention. There was a ring on Amelia's left ring finger.

"She's engaged," Ember stated in a hushed tone. Never taking her eyes off the other end of the table. The quiet squabble would have been amusing if it wasn't so dangerous.

"No. She and Caelus eloped this afternoon," Zephyr replied, matching her tone. "No one knows. They all think they are engaged. I don't know why the urgency to marry either."

Ember looked at Zephyr and saw the pleading in his eyes. She then looked at Jonathon. He had a calculating gleam in his eyes. She knew he was figuring out how things worked, after all, it was his newspaper that had led the charge in clearing Zephyr's name. In for a penny, in for a pound, Ember sighed.

"Why would I need to hide my fiancé's actions?"

Emerson and Grammy Margaret shot her alarmed looks before looking at each other. They weren't certain if she knew the entire truth. Well, it would be a surprise for everyone.

"He has been sneaking off to Belize to purchase cocaine and party with the locals. Not to mention he is a dangerous criminal and needs help. Four years ago, he attacked and raped a senator's daughter. No one in America will associate with him," Alexander said with a sneer.

To everyone's great shock, Ember threw back her head in laughter. She had learned long ago if your actions were unpredictable people were caught off guard because they weren't sure how to respond to you — thus, giving you more control over the situation.

Alexander had been expecting to scandalize her with the information few people would have been privileged to. Even if she hadn't known the entire story, she would have never second-guessed Zephyr or his actions in public. She would have demanded an explanation from him and her brother in private but would have presented a united front in public.

"Do you honestly believe the peerage, as well as my brother, the Director of Intelligence and Military Operations, would let me marry a rapist or a drug-addicted party boy?" Ember asked lightly. However, her face was a mask of indifference.

Zephyr reached over and squeezed her hand. She could feel the clamminess of his skin and hear the increase in his breathing. He was nervous, but she was fearless. They had the truth on their side. She wasn't going to back down.

Her question caught the judge and his family off guard. They looked back and forth silently at each other before casting glances at Wilson to do something. Ember grinned widely before she leaned over and whispered in Zephyr's ear.

"Where were they married?"

He breathed back one word, "Careen."

"Good."

Zephyr gave her a puzzled look, not understanding the importance of where they married. In due time he would learn why that was important. For now, there were other matters to attend to. After another minute of tense silence, Ember decided to end this campaign of hate against Zephyr.

"Prince Emerson, what was the conclusion of the investigation into Zephyr Levan?"

Emerson glared at his twin. He was not amused by her actions. In fact, Ember would say he was livid and holding on to his composure by a thread if his clenched jaw was any indication of his mood. Well, too bad. She was tired of the whispers behind Zephyr's back whenever American diplomats and visitors were in Parley.

"Zephyr Levan could not have committed the crimes in America because he was here, in Parley, as part of the American envoy."

Emerson held up a hand when the judge moved to speak. "Furthermore, there is photographic evidence in several of the newspapers, both domestic and foreign, showing Mr. Levan dancing with Queen Ember at the midsummer's ball. It was covered in all the newspapers because Queen Ember had not been introduced formally into society at that time. Her formal coming out ball wasn't slated until January, about five or six months later. It was borderline scandalous. I deemed it ridiculous."

The color drained from both Alexander and Wilson's faces. When Wilson turned to look at Ember, she could see the fear in his eyes. She took no pleasure in it because she knew she was making a powerful enemy.

"Thank you, Prince Emerson. In regards to the incident on the street with Lord Borroughs's daughter, Lady Lianna, I'm not surprised. His behavior toward myself and Lady Greer has been abhorrent. His not-so-subtle advances have been rebuffed at every turn, and yet, he continues the behavior undeterred."

Amelia turned, eyes wide to stare at Ember. She was shaking her head no. Caelus was trying to catch his wife's attention, but her eyes were fixed squarely on Ember, as she blew up her illusions about her new husband.

"I was summoned back a week early from my trip to Geneva, celebrating the birthday and coronation of the future queen of Astonia, because of the incident with Caelus on the street."

Ember turned to look at Wilson. "I warned you what would happen after Zephyr had the good sense to confiscate and destroy the cocaine he discovered upon Caelus's arrival. I will not intervene, you have my word on that."

Ember rose from her chair. Those seated around the table hastily followed suit.

"Oh. One other thing." Ember turned to Zephyr and took his hand. "I know we celebrated your birthday last month, and I gave you cuff links, but I've been toying with this idea for a while."

She looked away from his gaze, staring at a spot on the wall behind him. "I was going to wait until after the remembrance ceremony, but I don't like the timing of it."

"The cuff links are enough, Em," Zephyr murmured to her.

A faint blush crept up his cheeks as the attention of the room fell on him. His use of her nickname in public emphasized the discomfort he felt. It was a warning of sorts to her, but she wouldn't be stopped. She knew what she needed to do.

Ember waved a hand. "I love that you believe that, Zeph."

She took a deep breath and looked him in the eyes, "As a belated birthday present, Mr. Zephyr Thomas Levan is now Viscount Montague. The title reverted to the crown a generation ago, and well... you've earned it. Happy birthday, Lord Montague. Or you can also go by Lord Levan. Whichever you prefer."

Zephyr searched her eyes and face. Confusion and awe at war with one another. He looked over at Emerson and Grammy Margaret who nodded in approval before turning to look at Jonathon who beamed at him.

"But I'm not a citizen. And... and even if I were, non-nationalized citizens can't own pearl farms or mineral mines in Parley. How can I be a lord?" Zephyr inquired with a mix of shocked confusion and curiosity.

"Because the Montague title is agriculture-related. It's known for orchids and vanilla," Jonathon answered. "Congratulations, Lord Montague. We should have lunch at the gentleman's club sometime."

Zephyr smiled warmly at Jonathon. "I would like that, Lord Laurent. Thank you."

Jonathon nodded at Emerson. "If we're lucky maybe His Royal Highness, Duke Whydah will also come."

"Maybe. Lady Greer will be able to tell you," Emerson replied. "Congratulations, Lord Montague. We will have to throw a celebratory ball. Maybe Her Majesty can help you plan one."

"Splendid idea," Ember declared. "We should get to planning that straight away."

"Unbelievable," Wilson muttered. "You're giving him a title?"

Ember looked at the man. How much of her hand did she want to play? She knew Emerson had figured out part of her motive for the timing. After all, Emerson had promised to keep him safe before she had. Zephyr more than likely wouldn't connect the dots right away.

Above all though, he did deserve it. He knew the secret of Parley and chose to protect it instead of profit from it. The title, and gift of citizenship he didn't realize came with it, was the least she could do.

"Of course. Why wouldn't I give my fiancé a title?"

"You're trying to break the engagement. You don't want to marry Zephyr, you two despise each other," Wilson declared.

Ember looked thoughtful, putting a finger to her chin. "No, I don't despise Zephyr. I despise you. I want to break the engagement because of you."

Wilson blinked in surprise. "And yet you gave him a title."

Ember shrugged. Her actions didn't need to make sense to anyone but herself.

"I don't know about anyone else, but I believe I shall retire for the evening," Ember announced. "Do the Monroes need a car back to their hotel?"

Cilia had the good sense to look abashed. Ember already knew the Monroes were staying at the palace. They had been invited to do so by Caelus and Wilson as if it were their home.

The Monroes shifted on their feet, while Caelus wouldn't meet her eyes. Wilson was also avoiding her gaze. Her Uncle Martin looked at everyone and sighed. It seemed it was everyone's responsibility this evening to cover for the arrogance of Cilia and Wilson.

"No, Your Majesty. They have rooms here at the palace. I do apologize for the oversight on my part for not informing you," Martin explained.

Ember smiled at her uncle. He was an interesting character. His place at court was precarious at best because of her mother. He wasn't malicious, and he didn't go out of his way to strip power from Ember, even though it was an outcome of his actions. He was a puppet of sorts for her mother, although lately, he seemed to be growing wary of being her pawn and babysitter.

"It's quite alright, Uncle. With all the shuffling about after my return from Geneva, it was an honest mistake," Ember observed. "Lord Laurent, let me walk you out?"

"Of course, I would be honored."

Zephyr leaned down and gave Ember a peck on the cheek. "I will see you tomorrow, Em. We can discuss the estate."

Jonathon held out an arm to Ember and she took it, exiting the room with her bodyguards in tow. She wasn't sure if anyone was aware of her current living arrangements, and she wasn't volunteering that information.

Jonathon's car was brought around and the pair said their goodbyes. A second car was brought around. Evan got behind the wheel, while Ember ducked into the private entrance to put on a men's overcoat and hat. She then strode forward, careful to stay out of the light, and got into the back.

Once they had left the private driveway, they stopped near the gate to pick up Ian.

"Did anyone notice?" Ember asked.

"I don't believe so. Emerson has taken several precautions to obscure the view of the private driveway from that wing of the palace," Evan explained.

Ember chuckled. "I would expect no less."

She leaned back and enjoyed the ride to the private airfield where she would board an airship back to Blackstone. She smiled softly. Kieran didn't know it yet, but she had plans for his estate. It could not continue in its current state. She was going to use her money to restore it, whether he liked it or not.

Chapter 20

It had been almost two weeks since Ember had arrived at Blackstone. She had visited the Whites a few times and even helped find a contractor to rebuild their home.

Ember had made a point of spending time with many of the residents of the Bahamas. Several families had come for tea or meals. She sat and listened to their suggestions regarding improvements to whichever island they lived on, as well as the entire chain. Through it all, Nerissa sat and took detailed notes.

Ember had used the Bellamy fortune to create an emergency fund rather than Parlian and Revenge monies. She had kept this information private, and limited to a handful of people. Everyone on the islands had come together quickly to find the displaced temporary housing and jobs, while teams of architects and engineers worked with builders around the clock to repair or replace infrastructure, buildings, and homes.

There was a storm watch in effect on this hot and humid Sunday afternoon, so Emerson had canceled all her appointments for the day. This had given Ember a rare day off. She had tended to her duties earlier this morning, knowing the quicker she finished reading and responding to the documents and letters, the quicker she could explore the areas of Blackstone no one would allow her in.

Evan and Ian were off with Emerson in Nassau doing God knew what. She didn't know where Zephyr was either. They were due to meet regarding the ball and his estate. The storm watch had delayed his arrival to later this afternoon. Presently, she was free of her babysitters who watched her every move. Only the usual guards were watching the property and keeping her safe.

Ember crept from her room, careful to not draw attention to herself, and made her way toward the main staircase she wasn't supposed to use. She had made sure to grab a pencil and a notebook because she was recording all the things that needed to be repaired, replaced, and possibly restored.

She descended the stairs, noting the loose or broken treads. Once in the foyer, the water damage from not just the most recent storm, but also every storm for at least half a decade, was evident. The plaster crumbled from the walls onto the floor. The torn and faded floral wallpaper kept sections in place, but it was obvious gravity and the elements were gaining the upper hand.

There was a musty, rotting quality to the air. Ember was certain the mold and decay were an extra consideration for banning her from the public areas. The instability of the structure just happened to be the most glaring problem. The unseen issues could be just as dangerous.

Ember made some notes and pushed open the ornately carved cherry wood door into the front parlor. She sucked in a harsh breath and quickly regretted it when a coughing fit took over from the dust, dirt, and debris littering the room. Sunlight poured in from the giant section of the roof and the ceiling missing due to the massive cedar tree that had crashed into the space.

The tree needed to be removed and the structure repaired. From what Ember could make out from her place by the door, a section of the exterior stone wall had caved in, and the fireplace had also sustained damage. As she recovered from her coughing fit, she pulled out a handkerchief and tied it around her face to help her not breathe in the particulates floating in the air.

Ember closed the door behind her in case anyone came into this area. She then studied her surroundings and was surprised none of the remaining Louis XIV furnishings had been removed from the space. The once illustrious gold brocade fabric covering the settee, chairs, and sofa, was stained brown in several places. The fabric also had black mold spots in various places. This told Ember the room had been abandoned long ago to time and fate.

She turned to study the walls and let out a small cry. The paintings on the walls were in abhorrent condition. Ember knew most of the masterpieces had been sold, but still, these smaller paintings by lesser-known artists were worth money and part of the Revenge legacy. The paint was chipping off, the colors were dull and dingy, and the frames were in poor condition. Regardless, Ember was going to have a team come in to remove and restore them.

As she moved from the parlor to the dining room, she noticed the tapestries were in a similar state. Tears and holes, as well as fraying, adorned the various fabrics. They too had suffered water and mildew damage. Why had no one thought to remove the furnishings, paintings, and tapestries from these rooms? Especially once it had become apparent water and the elements were coming in.

Ember sighed. The mahogany table and chairs, as well as the buffets, were going to need a good cleaning before they could be repaired. She couldn't even tell what color or type of fabric covered the seat of the chairs. After making her notes, she took a breath and squared her shoulders. There was still the study, library, duchess's parlor, duke's parlor, informal dining room, small ballroom, and grand ballroom to explore.

Ember was fearful of what she might discover in the library and study. If the books were in a similar condition to the paintings and tapestries, there may not be a way to salvage them. Water and paper were not friends. Regardless, it was clear no one else was going to evaluate the damage to Blackstone. Ember pushed forward with her task. She wasn't certain if she would finish before everyone returned, but she was determined to get as far as she could.

"You weren't in your suite earlier when Lady Nerissa went looking for you," Emerson observed as he speared a carrot with his fork. His tone was tight like he was already aware of her activities and giving her the chance to confess.

Zephyr, Ian, and Evan were also sitting around the table. They glanced at each other like they were silently communicating and preparing for what was coming.

"I was making note of the damage and repairs to be made to Blackstone. I was also making arrangements for a cleanup team to come and pull out the furniture, tapestries, and paintings. I want as many things as possible restored to their original glory."

Ember shot a defiant look at her twin, daring him to question her. The heads of the others swiveled to Emerson to gauge his reaction.

He set his fork down and wiped his mouth with his napkin. "How."

There was no question in his tone. It was flat like the line of his mouth.

"I grabbed a notebook, and pencil, and went through the rooms myself. No one else seemed interested in doing so," Ember stated before grabbing her wine glass and taking a sip. "If I'm to be living here for another month or two, then I would like the manor repaired."

"Damnit, Ember," Emerson roared. "Those rooms are off-limits for a reason."

Ember took another sip of her wine. "The tree in the front parlor drove home that point, Emerson. However, there isn't any cleanup happening here. Why?"

Emerson glared at her. They were in private in all the ways that mattered, which meant he was treating her as his sister and not his queen.

"Kieran doesn't want to clean up or repairs made until the Bahamas, as a whole, are fixed."

"Good for him. I hired workers from Central America, rather than Parley, to expedite clean up and the major repairs here," Ember explained as she resumed eating.

"Wonderful. I'm not sure how the islanders will feel about that," Emerson threw back.

"They are getting the roof and walls rebuilt. Parlians can finish and restore the inside at a later date. But we are in hurricane season, Emerson. Be reasonable and practical, like the islanders are."

Emerson threw down his napkin and stood. "It's not your house first of all. Second, it's incredibly dangerous on that side of the house! You are the queen! Parley has lost enough in the past decade. They don't need to lose you too because of *your* reckless disregard for *your* safety!"

"Three minutes," Ember muttered as she drained her glass. She motioned to the footman for more wine and to clear her plate. "Dessert?"

"Are you serious?"

"Are you done?" Ember retorted as she raised an eyebrow at him. "I was careful, Em. I'm not stupid. I didn't even attempt the duke's parlor or the small ballroom. The grand ballroom was questionable too. Read my notes."

Emerson's cheeks flushed in anger as he resumed his seat. "He doesn't want your money or interference! Why can't you let the man have his pride? And yes, three minutes and we wouldn't be having this discussion."

Dessert was brought out. Ember requested a larger portion, while Emerson finished eating his dinner. The others at the table remained silent.

"Kieran should know by now how I feel about his pride when he ignores mine," Ember responded as she ate the chocolate and rum cheesecake. She moaned in delight. Closing her eyes to savor the flavor.

Zephyr was mesmerized for a moment. Especially when her tongue darted out to capture a piece near the corner of her mouth. Ember noticed his staring and winked at him, causing him to drop his gaze to his plate.

"If I may, what does three minutes have to do with anything," Ian inquired. Emerson just glared when Ember shot Ian a half smile.

"Birth order. I am three minutes older."

"And she never lets anyone forget it," Emerson grumbled. He motioned for his plate to be cleared before dessert was set down in front of him.

He loved cheesecake, which Ember knew. It was no coincidence it was the dessert tonight. She had known he would be angry with her and wanted to soften the blow.

"You can handle the former director of intelligence and military operations," he added. "As of right now, he's all yours. Enjoy his rage."

Emerson's jade eyes twinkled at his announcement. Ember brushed off his comment as she took another bite.

"Who's that?" Zephyr asked.

"The Duke of Revenge," Evan answered.

Zephyr dropped his fork in surprise. He scrambled to catch it as it clattered against the porcelain plate. "Kieran is the person who held your job, went off the rails, and abruptly left one morning?"

Emerson ran a hand over his jawline. "I see Greer has been talking again."

"Yes, Zeph. It was Kieran. Also, don't get mad at Greer, Em. It's not a secret." Ember continued to eat her cheesecake but motioned for another glass of wine after polishing off her third glass.

"Didn't he leave a note? I thought she mentioned a note."

Ember downed half the glass of wine as soon as the footman placed it in front of her.

"No. There was no note," Ember answered too quickly.

Emerson raised a brow at her but dropped the subject. The note had been for her anyway. If she didn't want to discuss the contents then that was her business. No one else knew the details. She finished her dessert, downed the remaining wine in her glass, and stood.

"I'm tired after my exploration. I wish you all goodnight."

The men hastened to stand and bow at her departure.

Greer wasn't wrong about things and had been invaluable in helping Zephyr make progress in his investigation to get Kieran home. They had even started drafting a blackmail letter with the information they had found.

He was going to have to ask Ember privately about the note. Zephyr had avoided Ember for a few days after she had gifted him the title. Truthfully, he had also avoided his family as well. He hadn't been to his estate yet or met any of his tenants, but he knew he couldn't avoid the place forever.

He also knew he couldn't avoid Ember forever either, especially because they were engaged still. He had learned from Greer that as long as he was engaged to Ember, under Parlian law, he couldn't be extradited. This had given him some relief, especially because the Monroes and his father refused to accept Caelus was anything but innocent.

He had learned a team of lawyers had been assembled to expunge his record in America. This had taken a huge weight off his shoulders. Emerson had told him the lawyers would fight until they succeeded because failure wasn't an option. He didn't know how to feel about this situation because no one, not even his mother, had ever fought for him before.

Over the last few days, Zephyr had seen the headlines in the various newspapers around Parley after his title had been announced and they were all positive. The citizens were supportive of him and congratulated him when they saw him in public. For the first time perhaps in his life, he felt like he finally belonged somewhere.

He was grateful for the faith and trust Ember and the country had in him. He never wanted to mess that up. The reprieve of not having to follow someone's plans for his life had left him reeling at first.

Caelus and Amelia flaunting their marriage had been a difficult blow as well. Cael had taken great pleasure in the knowledge he had married Zephyr's childhood sweetheart while killing any hope of them ever rekindling any kind of relationship. Zephyr didn't know how to react or where he would go.

Once the engagement to Ember was broken, he knew he would be returning to America and an uncertain future. That changed when she gifted him a title. He could create and forge a different path.

It was obvious the Monroes believed everyone in Parley was running cover for Zephyr. Yet, somehow, Wilson had convinced the Monroes that the incident with Caelus must be a case of mistaken identity, and everything would come out in the wash. Which of course the trio ate up because what else were they going to do?

There was also the matter of his engagement to Ember. There were worse fates than being engaged to Ember, but they were going to have to define their relationship soon. He knew they were friends, but did she want to try for more? He didn't know.

One thing he did know for certain was Ember had feelings for Kieran. He didn't know what feelings she harbored for the man, but they were clear as day to anyone with eyes. It was the largest motivator for him to learn what Kieran had written in the note. Ember could say it didn't exist, but he knew better.

In the meantime, he was volunteering and helping with the cleanup effort on one of the smaller islands for a few days. It gave him another reason to avoid Ember during the day but gave him the chance to think. He was looking forward to a change of pace, and the feeling of making a difference. It also gave him the distraction he needed to avoid handling his life for a few more days.

Chapter 21

Zephyr got up early to help with the removal of the rubble off the foundation of a home on the island of Eleuthera. Clean-up in the Bahamas was going well, several damaged homes and buildings had been repaired. Residents were moving back to the islands and resuming normal life.

The focus had shifted from repairing damaged structures to clearing away the homes and buildings that had collapsed so they could be rebuilt. Zephyr relished the distraction. He didn't want to think about any of his problems or finding Kieran. Instead, he wanted to do something where he could see his efforts pay off in real time.

The sound of car doors opening and closing caught the attention of some of the workers. Zephyr ignored what was happening on the street. He and a few other workers were finishing clearing the last section of the foundation. Then they would break for lunch and attend to the demolition of half of a house.

A tree had fallen and destroyed a few rooms, but the engineers determined only those rooms needed to be demolished because the rest of the house was structurally sound. The construction foreman had saved it for the afternoon because it was expected to take only a few hours. The tree had already been removed.

"Is that the mighty Lord Montague?" The mocking tone caught his attention.

Zephyr didn't turn around. He wasn't sure why Caelus was in the Bahamas, much less on the island of Eleuthera, but he didn't care either. He had work to do. He was determined to spend this week being useful before resuming life and responsibilities in Careen.

A trilling laugh held his attention. "You slay me, Cael. Like Zephyr would ever do manual labor. He's a lord and engaged to a queen."

The men around him glanced in his direction. When Zephyr didn't respond, the others took their cues from him and ignored the visitors. If Lord Montague didn't want to engage with the Americans and would rather work, then that's what they would do.

"He's a grifter who did a bit, and has everyone fooled," Caelus quipped.

Amelia giggled while someone hushed him. "Quiet. We are here on official business. Pay attention. America is pledging money, and we need to know where the greatest need is."

At the sound of his father's voice, Zephyr stiffened. Of course, today would be the day his father would tour the storm-ravaged areas. It was only a month after the storm had hit, and much of the cleanup and work had already been paid for. He rolled his eyes.

Caelus needed a publicity stunt and a way to fix his image before the trial. Their apparent tour guide was explaining the progress being made, while a clicking noise every so often indicated pictures were being taken. Why wouldn't they have members of the press with them?

The foreman called out to the men, announcing lunch, as the last of the debris was loaded onto a wagon and hauled away. A few of the men came over to where Zephyr was standing and invited him to dine with them. He agreed and began walking with them toward the café, which had an area for the workers to clean up before eating.

"Zephyr?"

He looked up to see his father's appalled face, Caelus's smug grin, and the astonishment from Amelia and her parents. The photographer with the newspaper turned to snap a picture, but Zephyr held up a hand.

"Please, no. If you're doing a story about the progress in the Bahamas, that has nothing to do with me. I'm just a volunteer helping with clean-up," Zephyr told them. The members of the press hesitated a moment before turning away and asking questions.

"He looks like a rag-a-muffin," Caelus snickered. Amelia giggled behind her hand.

"Oh how the mighty have fallen," Amelia dramatically added.

"Enough," Wilson admonished.

"Don't be a killjoy, we're just teasing. Isn't that right, Zephyr?" Caelus challenged.

"Of course," Zephyr replied with a tight smile.

He began walking away, but Caelus kept at it with his comments. Amelia's giggling was all the encouragement his brother needed to continue, all the while ignoring their father, and even his father-in-law's, bid to stop. The cruelty of Caelus was on full display to the world.

The press was enraptured by Caelus's behavior towards his brother. The photographer was discreetly taking photos of the spectacle. Zephyr kept walking towards the cafe, ignoring the barbs from his brother.

"Regardless of his newfound fortune, he'll always be a predator," Caelus called out.

The men working with Zephyr stopped and turned to Caelus. Apparently accusing a lord of being a predator was too much. Soon the workmen were shouting and heckling Caelus, as well as Amelia who had decided to defend her new husband.

Zephyr watched in amusement. Cael and his father, as well as the Monroes, would never have faced anything like this before. Parlians were polite, compassionate people. They were tight-knit and fiercely loyal to their own. Judging by the turnout, they considered him one of them. This caused a warmth to spread through his chest. He belonged somewhere.

After a few minutes of the crowd trading insults with Cael and Amelia, Zephyr stepped in. The reporters were frantically scribbling on their notepads while photographers got pictures.

"Hey, chaps! Lunch is on me! Let's go," Zephyr shouted.

The men turned up their noses at Cael and Amelia as they met up with Zephyr to wash up and eat. It was going to be interesting to see what the papers printed about the exchange because there was no way his father was going to stop that story from seeing the light of day.

After lunch, Zephyr and the men proceeded to the last project of the day. When they arrived at the house an older woman was waiting for the crews.

"Before you tear anything down, there is a painting on the wall of the living room I need someone to retrieve," the woman announced.

A few of the men scoffed. The foreman stepped forward and explained to the woman the front part of the house wasn't structurally sound, which was why nothing could be saved. They were there to knock in the front parlor and formal dining room. They would save as much as they could from those rooms, but couldn't promise anything would or could be saved.

Zephyr listened to the men tell the woman the tree that had fallen had compromised the roof and two of the exterior walls. No one was going into the house to retrieve anything from those rooms.

The woman patiently listened to the men. After they had finished explaining the situation to the woman, she told them she understood. She then turned and began walking toward the house. She would retrieve the painting herself.

Zephyr was stunned. The men yelled after her, telling her a painting wasn't worth her life, but she was insistent this painting was priceless and she wouldn't be the generation to lose it.

"Wait! Ma'am, I'll go," Zephyr offered. All eyes were on him as silence met his declaration. A moment later, several men began to speak, arguing it was too dangerous to go in, but he waved them off.

"Where is the painting located exactly?"

"Thank you, young man. It is on the shared wall with the foyer."

Zephyr nodded before taking a deep breath. He pushed his fear and reservations aside as he walked into the house through the front door. He took a cautious step forward, beams from the attic and roof trusses littered the path forward. The floor creaked under his weight but held. The crew had been warned about the cold cellar under the house before they arrived. Zephyr did not want to fall into it if he could help it.

He continued forward, careful not to disturb the twisted and broken lumber halting his forward progress. Picking his way around everything the best he could, Zephyr reached the doorway leading to the parlor. Once he crossed the threshold, he saw the painting the woman was after. Broken furniture combined with branches and debris blocked his path.

He stood for several seconds judging how well things would hold his weight if he crawled over everything. Zephyr took another deep breath, and closed his eyes, before gingerly placing a knee on what had been a table and propelling himself forward to a gap where he could grab the painting off the wall.

The picture came free from the wall with little effort. Once he had possession of this prized object, it was a balancing act to keep from damaging it and himself. He was almost out the front door when his foot slipped. A beam shifted and trapped his low leg.

Zephyr let out a yelp as he lost his balance. Keeping a grip on the painting, he threw out his other arm to catch himself.

"Are you alright?" The woman asked.

Zephyr set the painting down in a safe place and pushed against the beam. It shifted, but not enough for him to break free. "No, I'm trapped in the foyer. I have the painting though. It's safe. Maybe someone could grab it and then possibly help me?"

The older woman popped her head through the doorway. "Oh, dear. Let me grab this and I'll tell the men to help you."

Zephyr waited as the foreman and another man came in. After a quick discussion, they figured out how to get Zephyr free without hopefully causing more things to shift in the damaged structure. The men and Zephyr lifted the beam, and he quickly pulled his lower leg out.

Zephyr limped out the front door with the help of the two men.

"Oh goodness! You're hurt. Let's get you to my hotel and call a doctor," the woman said.

An hour later, Zephyr was in a well-appointed hotel suite. He had a valet helping him clean up so the doctor could examine his lower right leg, which was starting to bruise and swell. The older woman, whose name was Olivia Wade, had ordered new clothes and dinner, in addition to the doctor. He had insisted he was fine and just needed a car back to the airfield so he could fly to his lodgings, but she wouldn't take no for an answer.

Once he was cleaned up and presentable, the doctor came into the room. He examined Zephyr's right leg and told him he had sprained both his knee and his ankle. He told him he would have crutches sent straight away because he didn't want him putting any weight on it for a few days.

After the doctor left, Olivia and the hotel staff set up dinner. Zephyr hobbled over and fell into a chair at the table.

"I apologize for my manners," Zephyr told Olivia. "Under normal circumstances, I would pull out your chair and help you sit, but I'm unable to do so at the moment."

She laughed it off. "It's quite alright, Lord Montague."

His eyes lit up in surprise. "You know who I am?"

Olivia's eyes twinkled. "I found out who you were when you entered my house."

That made sense. The men would be worried the newly minted Viscount Montague, fiancé to the queen, would be killed or brutally maimed while retrieving a painting for a woman he had never met before.

"Whatever in the world possessed you to go into the house? You're the fiancé to the queen, who would have had my hide if anything had befallen you."

Zephyr was quiet for a moment as Olivia poured them wine and removed the silver covers over their food. "Honestly? You remind me of my grandmother. She is a feisty woman and would have been like you, charging into her home to retrieve a valuable heirloom. Her safety and wellbeing be damned."

Olivia's eyes crinkled at the corners as she grinned widely. "Your grandmother sounds like an interesting person. You obviously care a great deal for her."

Zephyr put his napkin in his lap and began to eat once Olivia did. "I do. She is the only person who fights for me, and it costs her dearly in different ways."

"I've heard about you and your family. I haven't had the pleasure of making your acquaintance before, but I'm so glad to meet you now."

The pair exchanged stories and made small talk during their meal. Once they were done eating dessert, Olivia called down to the front desk for tea and clean up. After a few moments, there was a knock on the door. Olivia ushered in the staff, who set down the tea service and took away the dinner dishes.

Olivia made tea for both of them. Zephyr accepted his cup and took a cautious sip of the hot liquid. "Might I be so bold as to inquire about the painting I risked life and limb for?"

Olivia barked out a laugh. "It was painted by my great-uncle, Victor Thache, the fifth Duke of Revenge."

Zephyr began choking on his tea at her declaration.

"You... are related... to Kieran?" Zephyr managed between coughs.

Olivia jumped up to pat him vigorously on the back. Once she was satisfied Zephyr was going to live and recover from his coughing fit, she sat back down.

"Yes, Kieran and I are cousins. His great-great-grandfather is my great-uncle Warren. My Grandpa Oliver was the youngest of the three sons, and I'm his namesake," Olivia said. "No one really talks about Uncle Victor, he was exiled. The painting is one of the few things I have of his. He died when I was fourteen."

Zephyr's brow furrowed. "He was exiled? I didn't know anyone in Parley could be exiled. You're all descendants of pirates."

Olivia narrowed her eyes in thought. Her gaze on his felt like she was measuring his trustworthiness. She nodded after several moments and then took a sip of tea.

"Let me tell you about Parley's largest, but almost forgotten about scandal."

Chapter 22

Ember was standing in the front courtyard, watching the workers rehang the massive wrought iron gate. The stone pillars had been rebuilt so the gate panels could be returned to their proper place. She had added gas lighting to the top of the stone posts as well.

Emerson had complained it was ridiculous and over the top, especially because she could have used plain electricity; however, she liked the way gas lights looked. It was more dramatic like herself and Blackbeard, who was known for his theatrics.

Ember had been briefed by some of the Parlian engineers on a way to create backup power generation for people using diesel. Ember had decided to test the technology at Blackstone first. She also told the engineers involved it was a secret and upon their success, there would be a huge announcement unveiling the technology.

They had been happy to hear she approved the idea. They had also been excited by the opportunity to test the technology and work out the kinks in the real world before rolling it out to the masses. Ember loved their vision and was looking forward to the progress reports.

The gravel crunching behind her announced Zephyr's presence before he stopped next to her on his crutches. When he had returned to Blackstone last night, Ember had been horrified to learn he had been injured during the clean-up. She had fussed over him and made sure he was comfortable before she had gone to bed.

They stood in companionable silence, watching the workers hang the second panel. Once the workers finished hanging the gate, they tested it a few times before signaling to her success. Ember nodded and waved in a show of her approval.

She let out a deep breath and turned to Zephyr. "Hello, Lord Montague."

He snorted as he grinned. "Hello, Your Majesty."

"Have you been to Montague Isle? And your estate, Rosenholm Manor?"

"I have not. Greer and Emerson told me some things are needing immediate attention at the manor, but I haven't traveled there yet," Zephyr admitted. "I know it's been a week, but it seems surreal to me."

Ember chuckled. "I could see how gaining a title, estate, and tenants would be overwhelming. You deserved it, though."

Zephyr scratched the back of his neck as he ducked his head while he balanced with the crutches. "Everyone keeps saying that, but I don't know. I mean, I just did what was expected of me. The citizens like me, so I must be doing okay."

Ember watched as the breeze played with his hair. He was modest because while he may have been performing duties expected of him, it was the way he handled things. He stayed late, gave everything and everyone his full attention, and never declared any task beneath him. She had seen him in action during the clean-up over the last few weeks, he had been ready to pitch in no matter what, which was how he hurt his leg.

The front page of the newspaper also relayed the spectacle Caelus created when Wilson and the Monroes had come to the Bahamas to survey the damage. The Americans were showing concern for an ally by making sure they had enough materials and helping fund parts of the repairs and reconstruction if necessary. Ember had rolled her eyes at this explanation.

Regardless of the reasoning, Ember was irritated Caelus had decided to bait and attempt to publicly humiliate Zephyr. It hadn't gone over well with the locals, and Ember couldn't wait for the report regarding how the rest of the islands reacted to the news.

Ember pulled herself from her thoughts. "Why don't you join me for afternoon tea?"

"I would enjoy that. I can tell you what Greer and I are putting together."

Zephyr motioned for her to lead the way to the newly rebuilt gazebo in the garden. Ember had brought in the royal gardeners to remove unsafe trees and branches, as well as thin out and restore the garden. Zephyr was impressed by the progress that had been made. So far the gardeners had removed the trees and trimmed the ones that remained. He could tell the thinning of the plants was in the early stages.

Zephyr and Ember made small talk until tea was served.

"What progress have you and Greer made?" Ember poured for both of them, preparing his drink before she handed him the cup.

"We have started writing the letter to be sent to Kieran," Zephyr whispered.

Ember stopped pouring the milk into her tea at his words. She set down the porcelain creamer before taking a deep breath. She looked into Zephyr's eyes. His beautiful amber eyes glowed with excitement.

"Truly?"

Zephyr grabbed her hands. "Yes. In 1803, there was a play no one knows the name of. It was sponsored by the Duke of Revenge at the time. There were about five other members of the aristocracy, both Parlian and Mer according to Greer, who were caught up in the scandal."

Ember's heart was pounding so hard she could hear it in her ears. "The invitation?"

"It was a private, opening showing of the play here at Blackstone. It was held in the large ballroom, while the party was in the small ballroom. It was also the only performance of the play because all public showings were canceled due to the nature of the subject matter," Zephyr explained, keeping his voice and tone low. Ember leaned in closer to him.

"How did you learn about this?"

A noise from the dining room caught Zephyr's attention and he pulled away. Nerissa walked out onto the terrace a moment later with a man Ember didn't recognize.

"Your Majesty, I'm sorry for the intrusion. I didn't realize you were taking tea here in the garden," Nerissa apologized. She then ushered the man back into the dining room.

Ember shrugged off the event. She would ask Evan and Ian about the man later. Or Emerson. He would also know because he and Zephyr had decided to stay the remainder of the week and weekend. He and Zephyr were avoiding the palace because of the investigation by the Cuban police and Emerson into Caelus's behavior with Lady Lianna.

Ember refocused on the conversation, pulling Zephyr closer to her as she whispered, "How did you learn about this?"

"Remember how I hurt my leg? Well, the painting I retrieved was for Olivia Wade."

Ember gasped. "I didn't realize her home had been so severely damaged. I wonder if Vivian and Jillian know."

"I'm not sure. She was waiting for us at her house with the request to retrieve a painting. No one volunteered, and I don't blame them. But Olivia reminded me of my grandmother. I looked at the house, asked where the painting was, and prayed the entire time for God to keep me safe," Zephyr told her.

Ember smiled softly. "Of course, you went into a partially condemned structure for a painting."

Zephyr shot her a boyish grin. "I know, I'm a sucker. Anyway, after the doctor looked me over at the hotel, Olivia had dinner brought in. We got to talking and she revealed her lineage I was unaware of. But she also told me the history of the painting I had retrieved."

Zephyr paused and took a sip of tea before continuing. "Turns out the painting was done by a former duke, who was also a playwright. Victor Thache, the fifth Duke of Revenge to be specific. We then spent the evening talking about her life, the painting, and the tale of the duke the family would rather forget."

"All because you rescued a painting." Ember sat in wonder for a moment, then she launched herself into his arms, squeezing him hard. "You always do the right thing, Zephyr. I love and admire that about you. Even when I despised you for being my fiancé, I always admired your dedication to the people. You are genuine, and could never pretend not to care. Even though we both felt the engagement was a total sham, your integrity shone through no matter the task."

After a brief moment, Zephyr hugged her back. "I just did what anyone would have done in my shoes."

Ember let out a quick laugh. "How many people were standing around you declining to enter the house? No, Zephyr, you are one of a kind."

He shrugged off her praise as he ducked his head. A moment later, he grabbed a plate and began adding various items to it. Ember knew he was embarrassed and was not fond of praise or compliments. He was deflecting, and pulling her attention away from him and his actions.

"So the duke no one speaks of would be Kieran's great-great-great-grandfather?"

Zephyr polished off a couple of tea sandwiches before answering. "Actually, it's his great-great-uncle. Victor didn't have children, so the title reverted to his brother Warren, which is Kieran's line."

"Oh. I'll admit, I don't know as much as I should know about the histories of each title and how they changed hands," Ember quipped.

Zephyr rolled his eyes. "You're not supposed to know every nuance regarding every title." He popped a petit four into his mouth while Ember enjoyed his energy. He hadn't been this animated in a while. It was a nice change.

"Why does no one speak of him? What unspeakable act did he commit?"

Zephyr polished off a few more cakes and his tea before staring off into the garden. Ember made him another cup. She could hear the birds in the distance, as well as the waves of the ocean crashing against the rocks below the garden.

The peaceful setting was at odds with the information Zephyr had gathered because it would be used once again to threaten the destruction of the Thache legacy. Shattering their peace depending on how the information was presented and portrayed.

"He single-handedly ruined the lives of about five people that I'm aware of; however, there could be more," Zephyr admitted.

"After the scandal erupted, Parley almost went to war with the kingdom of Branwen, but King Lane went before both the Parlian High Court, the High King for the United Kingdoms, and the United Kingdoms High Council at the time to work out a suitable solution."

Zephyr took a sip of the freshly prepared tea before continuing. "Victor was exiled. He was permitted three weeks a year in Parley to handle estate affairs, but passed the title to his brother Warren in 1825 because he couldn't effectively manage the duchy and its tenants."

"What happened? Banishment is not unheard of, but it is extremely rare," Ember commented.

"He wrote a play criticizing not only Branwen, the United Kingdoms, Querenica, Parley, and Europe, but had taken creative liberties, shall we call them, with the truth. Those liberties were slanderous, and caused a few members of the various royal families marriage prospects and a couple trade deals," Zephyr told her.

Ember gasped. "Who else was involved?"

"There were several people caught up in the fallout because they had not been aware of the entire context of the play. Once the Parlian High Court realized that, the noose was placed around the necks of everyone who should have known better. This included Princess Eugenia, the duke's lover. She was banished from the Parlian court and the country. It was interesting trying to research her because it was like King Lane erased his sister's existence from everywhere."

Ember scrunched her face in confusion. "Research? You just found out this all last night, how are you so far in the research?"

Zephyr rubbed the back of his neck. "I asked Emerson to come to my room after you left. I explained the situation. He put me in touch with Greer on his secure line, and she researched what she could all night, while I scoured the not structurally compromised study here."

Ember shook her head. "Of course. Well, I'm glad for the progress. Although, I don't think you should have hobbled around Kieran's private study on crutches by yourself. Please continue your tale."

"Lady Isadora, the daughter of the fifth Earl of Ranger, was exiled to England. She married a viscount but never returned. Julian Asher, the owner of the Beacon Theatre in the Bahamas, left on his own. He put a manager in charge of the operations and moved to America where he married. The theater is still owned by the Ashers. The other two, Lord Atlas and Lady Odette, were of Muirgen. And no, Olivia didn't tell me where they were from."

He took another sip of his tea. "I don't know what happened to them. Greer and I couldn't find any information regarding them and the consequences. That's what led us to believe they were Mer."

Ember sat back. During his entire tale, she had been on the edge of her seat, eager to find out what Zephyr had learned from a woman she hadn't thought about in a few years. To think, if Zephyr wasn't such a compassionate sap, who despite coming from money, had no problem jumping in to fix a problem, they might still be looking for the information Emerson had hinted at.

Zephyr slid a plate of treats over to her. Ember looked down and frowned for a moment. When she looked up at him, he had a soft smile on his lips. "You skipped breakfast."

She blindly reached for the plate, grabbed something, and took a bite. It was a tea sandwich. Ember chewed as she processed the information Zephyr had shared. "Thank you. How did you know I skipped breakfast?"

"The maids know everything."

Ember ate another sandwich and washed it down with tea before resuming their conversation. "Greer is helping you draft a contract or something?"

"It's more of a blackmail letter than a contract, but whatever brings him home, right? Emerson will, of course, look it over before it is sent out into the world," Zephyr said with a shrug.

Ember brightened at his words. "Between the estate getting a makeover, and your letter, Kieran is sure to come home."

Zephyr snorted as he added more food to his plate. "I just want immunity from the ire of the Duke of Revenge. His title doesn't sound ominous or threatening in any way."

Ember giggled. "You have immunity."

Zephyr's eyes sparkled causing Ember's breath to catch in her throat for a moment. "You promise? Otherwise, you might be getting the Montague title back sooner than you realized."

"I promise," Ember replied making a cross over her heart.

Zephyr shook his head as he chuckled and ate a scone. The pair slipped into silence as they finished their meal. Ember was eager for Kieran to come home. And it would seem that might finally happen.

Chapter 23

It had been almost two months and Ember was anxious to get the entire matter with Caelus over and done with. It had taken far too long to get to this point in her opinion, but she understood the lords needing time to clean up after the tropical storm. The severe damage to the Bahamas had complicated matters; however, things were returning to normal, and this trial was a start.

The High Court had been seated in their box in the Chamber of Lords. This building with its massive audience space was used for political discussions, voting, public audiences with the citizens and the monarch, and trials involving foreign officials or members of the peerage. Members of the press were in attendance in their box.

The gallery held members of the public interested in the trial. Caelus and his lawyers were seated in a box near the floor with its own podium. The prosecution had a similar setup on the other side.

There was a private gallery with limited seating underneath the public one, and that's where the American delegation would be seated, as well as any member of the peerage interested in watching the proceedings.

Ember was waiting in her private chamber for the trumpet to blow and signal her entrance. An urgent knock on the door had her calling off the herald. An exchange of muffled voices gave way to Emerson striding into the space.

The set of his jaw and lines bracketing his mouth told Ember this wasn't a social visit. His eyes were grim. He should be in the chamber with everyone else not here trying to speak to her.

"What's wrong?" Ember asked as she curled her fingers around her throat.

"The president of Belize has sent an extradition order for Zephyr. Wilson signed off on it because he's an American citizen," Emerson announced. "They are sending agents to arrest him and take him back to Belize to face charges of assault and battery against the vice president's son during Bianca's engagement weekend back in July. I believe there are some drug charges too."

Ember closed her eyes. Wilson was sacrificing Zephyr to save Caelus, and getting back at her for not sweeping Cael's antics under the rug so to speak. If Zephyr was charged and extradited to Belize on drug charges and the attack on the vice president's son, then the case against Caelus in Parley looked like a witch hunt, regardless of the facts.

"Of course," Ember snorted. "Wilson would turn to his closest ally to save his skin."

"I also received word regarding an incident in Florida. Caelus has been selling cocaine in the States to help fuel his lifestyle because his mother holds the purse strings and has cut him off. This isn't widely known, and Wilson has been threatening his wife behind the scenes to do the right thing. Meanwhile, the American authorities are onto him, but Wilson is greasing palms for Zephyr's younger brother Neil to take the fall," Emerson explained.

"It's not going well. Wilson's wife is threatening divorce and wants Caelus in a rehabilitation facility to help him get back on track," her twin continued. "Wilson is refusing because admitting Caelus has a drug problem throws into question everything Zephyr, and the younger brother, have ever taken the blame for."

Ember collapsed into a chair. She stared at the carpet as her mind whirled. Wilson was prepared to destroy Zephyr as a way to destroy and discredit her as the queen of Parley. If he could illustrate her incompetence to her people and the world, then she would have no power. Rather, the Crown Guardians would remain in control and could continue to dismantle Parley's government as they thought they had been.

What's more, she had been clueless regarding Wilson's failing marriage. She also hadn't known Zephyr's younger brother Neil was taking the fall for some of Caelus's more recent behaviors. No wonder Zephyr had been desperate for protection.

There was still the matter of the bribery charges for the oil field. That investigation was ongoing, but Emerson had made certain someone from Parley was in America keeping detailed notes on what was happening. Now these new charges from Belize? What other things were lurking below the surface waiting to see the light of day?

Wilson's house of cards was slowly collapsing. The biggest question for Ember though was why Wilson was so desperate to save Caelus. It didn't make any sense. He had other children. Why save the one hell-bent on destroying everything?

"Does Zephyr know?"

"No. I came straight to you. There are also rumors of a kidnapping plot to retaliate against Wilson, but I don't know who the target is. I am still working to find out who is behind the rumors if they are true, and what the end goal is."

Ember's eyes burned as tears threatened to fall from her eyes. Furry consumed her. She was so tired of the constant battles. She was tired of the arrogance and manipulation of Wilson and Caelus. She was sick to death of his reach and allies. Most of all, she was tired of his sense of entitlement. He was lighting matches and didn't care what he was burning down in the process. He just wanted what he wanted.

Wilson felt like he should own everything, and heaven help anyone standing in his way. The proof of this was in everything he did. Caelus was just as bad, and worse in ways because he knew his father would be there to fix everything. He would sacrifice anything to preserve what he felt he and Caelus deserved. It was baffling.

"What do you want to do, Em?" Emerson had knelt in front of her. "I'll support you no matter what."

Ember let out a bitter laugh. "Will the citizens support me regardless of the outcomes?"

"They trust you more than you think. But you, Ember, *you* have to be a leader. You have to be the queen and pick a path and embrace where that leads. There isn't a solution that's perfect and won't adversely affect us. So, what do you want to do?"

Ember took a deep breath as tears slid down her face. Emerson pulled out a handkerchief and handed it to her. As she swiped at her eyes, Ember wished Kieran were there. As quickly as the yearning began, so did the self-loathing. She was strong and could do this. She didn't need Kieran. She had Emerson and Grammy Margaret, as well as a slew of advisors. She also had allies in the United Kingdoms and Muirgen.

"Zephyr is a citizen of Parley and is not being extradited anywhere. Wilson wants us to look inept, fine. Caelus will stand trial for his crimes in Parley, I won't interfere. Then we'll need to prepare to defend our position to the Belizean officials when they come tomorrow," Ember declared. "We have no extradition agreements with anyone, including the United Kingdoms. Taking a citizen off Parlian soil is an act of war, and will be treated as such."

Emerson nodded. "I will let the Belizean authorities know of your decision in advance of their arrival tomorrow; however, they may still send agents to test your resolve."

"I know."

Emerson gave her a quick hug before leaving the room to take his place in the chamber. Ember took a moment to gather her composure and check her appearance. She took several deep breaths before summoning the herald.

"I'm ready."

Ember was announced a moment later. She walked into the massive room looking the part of the reigning monarch with her ruby and diamond crown on her head. As she took her seat she motioned for the proceedings to begin.

Ember did a quick sweep of the room. Caelus and his lawyers were seated in a box across the room from the High Court and the prosecution. In the private gallery, the Monroes and Wilson sat together. The press were in their box, and Zephyr was seated with them next to Jonathon.

A wave of relief washed over her. She was glad Zephyr was with Jonathon in the press box. The farther away from Wilson he was the better.

Ember and the High Court listened as the charges were read out against Caelus. In matters involving foreign nationals, especially high-profile individuals, the fate was decided by the High Court and the monarch. Wilson glared at Zephyr the entire time the charges were read.

As the prosecution began opening statements, the door to the private gallery opened, drawing Ember's attention briefly. She glanced up and saw Lady Lianna was the latecomer. Judging by the dismissive looks shot in her direction, the Americans didn't know who she was.

Once the case against Caelus was laid out, his law team set to work tearing it apart. The Monroes began to relax as the lawyers viscously attacked the evidence and qualifications of the Cuban police. Their attempt to make Lady Lianna out to be a woman of loose morals didn't play well with the nobles or the public.

The prosecution requested witness testimony, as well as the investigation by Emerson, be read before closing arguments. As the testimony was read out, Lady Lianna betrayed no emotion. She was the picture of poise. Jonathon was engrossed by the proceedings on the floor and hadn't noticed her arrival. Ember was curious to see his reaction when he discovered Lianna's presence.

Closing arguments were tense in light of Emerson's findings. The evidence he had provided was ironclad and damning. It also threw into jeopardy the extradition Belize had requested because Emerson had photographic evidence of Caelus hanging out with the vice president's son during the engagement party. Zephyr was conspicuously missing from the party's guest list, as well as the photos.

"Does the High Court need time to make a decision?" Ember asked.

The six members conferred briefly before indicating they were ready to vote. It wasn't a surprise to anyone in the room when Caelus was found guilty. Emerson made sure his investigation was airtight. It had sealed the American playboy's fate. Wilson was fuming, the Monroes were horrified, and Amelia looked like she was going to be sick.

"What is the recommendation of the High Court regarding punishment?" Ember inquired.

She maintained an even tone despite the pounding of her heart in her chest. This was the moment she had been both dreading and eager for. Regardless of what the High Court said, Ember had put Parley on the road to sanctions and war by letting the trial against Caelus happen. Everything else was additional fuel for the fire.

"We are undecided. We request an adjournment until tomorrow morning when we will have our answer for Her Majesty," Vivian told Ember. She was representing the Duchy of Revenge and was the highest-ranking member of the High Court.

"Granted." Ember declared. She then turned to Caelus who didn't seem so cocky or certain of his fate. "Mr. Caelus Levan, you are under the watch and care of the Parlian Guard. You will return to the palace, where you will stay until we reconvene in the morning."

Ember then adjourned the proceedings and walked out of the room. Ian and Evan were waiting for her. They would be returning to Blackstone. Emerson and Zephyr were supposed to return as well, but she knew matters with Belize could change their plans. She wasn't worried though. Emerson would handle things like he always did. Things would be fine. She hoped.

Chapter 24

Ember was preparing for bed when Emerson and Zephyr returned from Careen. She had been surprised they hadn't gone to Whydah for the evening. Emerson had opted to move out of the palace until after the trial was over because he didn't want even a hint of impropriety. He had been splitting his time between his estate in Whydah, Blackstone, and his office for that reason as well.

Zephyr had seized onto Emerson's reasoning and logic and spun a similar tale using his status as a newly minted lord to avoid the palace. No one questioned his decision to stay wherever Emerson was at. For tonight it would seem both men were staying on at Blackstone.

Heavy footfalls announced her visitor's arrival before the knock. She opened the door and was startled to discover Zephyr on the other side.

"We need to talk," he announced. Ember wordlessly moved out of his way.

Zephyr breezed into the sitting area and started pacing. Ember sat on the settee and watched him. His hair was sticking up in all sorts of directions from running his hands through it. His clothing was rumpled, there were dark circles under his eyes, and his five-o'clock shadow was pronounced along his jaw.

It was evident he knew about the extradition order. There was no other reason for his anxiety. He was on eggshells regarding the trial, but that wouldn't have elicited this level of distress. Ember let him pace, her eyes following him as he muttered to himself occasionally. She was curious to find out what else had occurred after her departure. She knew he had dinner with the Americans while Emerson had worked through the meal.

Zephyr abruptly stopped in front of her. "He's threatening war. He has reached out to the American government and told them Cael is being railroaded. The Houses are meeting to decide what to do."

Ember nodded. "I'm aware. Wilson's favorite threat is war. Believe me, I knew very well the consequence of Caelus going on trial before the High Court."

"War, Ember. War. I don't know if he would go through with it for Cael, but I think there is a good chance he would do it," Zephyr scrubbed a hand over his face. "And what about Belize?"

Ember sucked on her lower lip, debating with herself over how much she should tell him. She had a plan and had been schooled on Parlian laws since she was a toddler. She knew what to do and how to do it. After the deaths of Drystan and her father, the law became the focus of her life.

While Emerson's education had been more well-rounded, Ember's had not. The focus for her had been laws, history, math, political matters, foreign languages, and economics. She wasn't angry about her fate, it just was what it was. She learned how to play the piano and embroidery because she needed an outlet, and that was all that was offered to her.

Zephyr and others knew about her education, but they didn't know what she had retained. Ember didn't want to fail her people. She didn't want to be the monarch who dropped the ball and plunged Parley into economic ruin. When she was younger, the laws and history were dry and boring. However, when she was about twelve or thirteen there had been a legal dispute between one of the lords and the nuns in Jamaica.

The Sisters were expanding their garden to grow extra food for the orphanage, as well as anyone in need. A business owner was disputing the property line and had gone to the earl. The matter had escalated and ended up in front of her and the Crown Guardians. The Guardians had been useless. They wouldn't take the matter up because there was nothing in it for them. Ember said she would solve the matter. She had been mocked, but the Guardians had allowed it because they thought it was cute she wanted to play queen.

Ember had gone to the convent, looked over the property, and learned about what the Sisters did. She then went next door to the business and learned about the building and how the property was used. When she was leaving, one of the nuns pulled her aside.

Sister Grace told her she was confident Ember would research the matter and come to a fair and just conclusion. At that moment she had understood the power she wielded, even as a child. She knew why her lessons were so important. As she walked to the car, she turned to look back and saw not just the nuns, but also the people on the street watching her. Regardless of the outcome, her citizens trusted her to make the right choice. It had been terrifying.

In the end, Ember had spent a few weeks researching the original property lines. She had discovered the earl had inadvertently encroached on the land owned by the church when he had allowed the business owner to expand. Once Ember brought this to his attention, he made things right by offering the Sisters a larger piece of land less than a mile down the road for a community garden.

The earl explained he wasn't able to do anything with it because of its odd size and where it sat in relation to the neighborhood and businesses around it. The nuns had been thrilled. Because of this matter, Ember understood the power of knowing the laws, and how that knowledge benefited her people.

Zephyr looming over her pulled her back from her thoughts. He was a bundle of nervous energy at first glance, but Ember knew if she looked harder, she would find evidence of fear too. She couldn't fault him for either emotion. She too was terrified. What if she made the wrong decision? What if she destroyed Parley? Her people would follow her, trusting her to make the right choice, until she proved herself unworthy. Then they would turn on her, and she wouldn't blame them. It was her greatest unspoken fear.

"Belize can't have you, I won't allow it. If America decides war is the only solution, then we go to war, Zephyr," Ember declared.

Incredulous, he stared into her eyes. "Do you hear what you're saying?"

Ember stood. Zephyr was almost a head taller than her so she had to look up when she spoke. "You are innocent. No one in Parley will want to see you sacrificed for the sins of another. I'm certain of that. I know we are in uncharted waters, but I need you to trust me," Ember pled.

"I sincerely doubt the Parlians would relish going to war over your former fiancé," Zephyr scoffed. "Regardless of my innocence. Let me go, Ember. Save yourself and your people."

The final comment sparked her temper. She was tired of people telling her what to do. She was tired of no one having faith or confidence in her abilities. She was tired of feeling powerless despite being the monarch. Ember had power, she was in charge; and yet, no one saw that. They still saw her as a child dressing up and pretending. Well, this was her chance to showcase her power and authority on a world stage.

"No." Ember stared him down. Neither one broke eye contact with the other.

"First, you are innocent, and I will not send you off to pay for the sins of your detestable brother. Second, no one dissolved our engagement. Not the High Court. Not me. It is still as legally binding now as the day it was made," Ember explained.

Zephyr raised an eyebrow but made no move to speak. This had Ember seeing red. How dare he just give up. How dare he not believe in her ability to protect him. How dare he not trust her. That knowledge cut her deep to her core. They had been growing closer and leaning on each other in their quest to bring Kieran home. They were friends.

"Despite the trial and the evidence, Amelia and her parents are still standing by Caelus. I had dinner with them a few hours ago. They think Emerson's report is more about an axe to grind against Wilson than Caelus doing anything wrong!"

"Of course, they are standing by him, he's Amelia's fiancé in their eyes because no one is aware of their elopement. They have no choice but to stand by him," Ember reasoned. "If they turn against him, how would that look? The stakes are higher for them, especially Amelia. Do you think she wants to explain to her parents her poor judgment in marrying someone of his caliber?"

Zephyr snorted as he threw himself onto the settee. "Of course, she would look for the best in him. She never questioned the story regarding me. But golden boy Caelus? Amelia can't defend him while defaming everyone else fast enough. Have you seen the papers?"

The bitterness in his tone wasn't astonishing. It was to be expected. What was unexpected was his anger and anguish over Amelia's actions. Ember knew he still had feelings for the woman, but she had assumed it was because there wasn't closure. She didn't realize it was because he still carried a torch for her.

Ember had been trying to build him up because she knew he was insecure, guarded, and jaded due to his family and upbringing. Once she had decided to trust him, she had decided to create a new identity for him. An identity outside of his family and their influence, something that was his. She could see how naïve that thinking had been. If she could just build him a new life and identity, then what everyone else thought of him wouldn't matter. She was a fool to have thought it would be that easy.

Zephyr was the only person who could give himself an identity. He needed to believe in himself as much as everyone else did. If he didn't value who he was as a person, then it didn't matter what Ember gifted him or what titles she adorned him with, because he never thought he was enough.

"I have seen the papers. They are included in my daily briefings. Amelia can profess his innocence from the rooftops, but that doesn't make it so. I'm sorry she didn't believe in you, Zephyr. I'm sorry her faith and conviction in your character didn't mirror your own regarding her. But you have to fight," Ember begged.

"Why? Who wants to be friends with someone who has anger problems and can't control themselves? Who wants to marry someone convicted of forcing themselves on women?"

The full force of his temper was directed at her. Ember didn't shy away from it. If making Zephyr angry and challenging him got him to fight, like it always did, then that's what she would do. He pushed himself off the settee and loomed over her.

"No one, Ember! No one wants to be friends with someone accused of heinous violence against women. No one wants to be friends with someone with a hair-trigger temper. And now, no one will want anything to do with me after what happened in Belize coupled with the bribery scandal," Zephyr shouted.

Caelus had gone too far in Central America. He was jealous Bianca had dropped him as a beau and found someone new. Rather than celebrate the happy couple, Caelus decided to try to win back Bianca so he could be the one to abandon her and walk away. His plan hadn't worked out too well.

Caelus's delusions were fueled by cocaine and ended with Bianca's fiancé pulling Caelus off her as he tried to strangle her for refusing him. Then he got into a brawl and punched the vice president's son in the face several times before bodyguards pulled him off. He was thrown out of the country immediately. A part of Ember was dumbfounded Belize was helping Wilson frame Zephyr for the incident.

How in the dickens anyone in the situation could finger Zephyr as the villain was beyond Ember's comprehension. They had already been on their way to Geneva by that point. Her assumption was blackmail. Wilson had to have some kind of leverage to get everyone involved in the situation to go along with his scheme. She wasn't sure why he was so hell-bent on preserving Caelus's character and reputation because it was obvious to anyone who had ever met the man that he was a sociopath.

This conversation with Zephyr was leading nowhere fast. She was going to have to fight for him, on his behalf, whether he wanted her to or not. He was beaten down in so many ways until he was allowed to trust and believe in himself, he was going to surrender to his fate of injustice.

Zephyr, it seemed, had given up. Given up on his life, his new title, and clearing his name. A name, that if not exonerated, could drag her and Parley down with it. She wasn't sure she could rankle his temper enough to get him to rise to the challenge of saving himself. But she was damn well going to try.

"You selfish ass," Ember spat. "You will not destroy the reputation of the viscountcy of Montague, the Crown, or Parley because some woman you love or loved thought the worst of you and got away. Honestly, you deserve better, Zephyr, especially if she chose Caelus. Besides, I don't need one more man abandoning me in life because of some woman!"

Zephyr winced. Maybe he had been licking his wounds and nursing his pride since the announcement of Caelus and Amelia's engagement in the papers, and subsequent elopement. There was genuine happiness on her face every time she was around Cael. It was clear she was in love, even if Cael's motives were less pure. If Zephyr were honest, he knew she had never looked at him the way she did his brother. That stung his pride and hurt his feelings because he had thought Amelia had understood what he suffered at the hands of his father and brother. Clearly, she did not, or simply didn't care.

A reporter for the *New York Times* had come to Parley a week ago to cover the engagement. The story recounted the whirlwind romance, which the reporter compared to a fairytale. Little did they all know it would one day soon become a nightmare.

"I'm not Kieran, Ember. I'm also not you. But don't forget, it wasn't until recently you decided to start fighting back. I've been fighting back my entire life, and look where it has gotten me. So forgive me if I try to mitigate disaster by following their script. I've learned the consequences of challenging them, especially now that Father has another country involved."

Ember was struck by his words. Self-preservation? That's what he thought his actions were. From where she stood, she could see his logic and understand his reasoning, but how much worse could Wilson make things for Zephyr if he didn't follow along? Short of a life sentence in some hell hole, things couldn't get much worse.

"Trust me. Can you do that, please? If you can't even believe and trust I have a plan to keep you safe, then how can my citizens?" Ember stared into his haunting amber eyes.

When Zephyr remained quiet, she reached out a hand toward him. He stared at it for a moment before taking it and pulling her into a hug. Ember stiffened against his solid chest for a moment before she surrendered to the warmth of his embrace. His heartbeat was strong in her ear as she took a deep breath. Rose and oud. Ember smiled to herself, his scent was masculine with a hint of the rose water he used after shaving.

"I trust you, Em," Zephyr whispered.

Ember leaned back. His gaze darkened as it locked onto hers before lowering to her mouth. Ember sucked in a sharp breath as anticipation skirted down her spine. He dropped his arms to grip her hips firmly, holding her in place. Her heartbeat pounded in her ears. Was Zephyr going to kiss her? Like actually kiss her?

Slowly he lowered his mouth to hers, giving her time to push him away. Ember took in a shuddering breath before closing the distance. Warmth gradually spread through her body as she processed the sensation of his lips against hers.

After a moment, Zephyr raised his hands to cup her face gently and deepen the kiss. His tongue dueled with hers as heat settled into her core. Ember brought her hands up around his neck and played with his hair. The move brought her closer to his body, causing Zephyr to moan lightly against her lips. Several minutes passed before Zephyr pulled back and broke off the impromptu make-out session.

Both of them were breathing heavily. His eyes were hooded with desire. Ember kept an arm around his neck while her other hand rested against his chest. Her knees felt weak and unstable as the blood in her body rushed to areas she had never thought of. She licked her lips and Zephyr let out a soft moan.

Ember giggled. "That was unexpected."

Zephyr closed his eyes and shook his head. "Unexpected is an understatement."

Ember slowly freed herself from his hold. She hadn't thought much of being in her nightdress and robe when she had answered the door. However, she was feeling rather exposed in the thin material, especially in light of Zephyr's desire.

Zephyr raked a hand through his hair before scrubbing his face with both. Ember watched him. She knew he wouldn't do anything to her, she just wished she could read his emotions more easily in this situation. Having a glimpse into the inner workings of his mind might help her sort out whatever she was feeling.

Over the years, Zephyr had inspired any range of sentiments and feelings; however, desire had never been one of them. They had flirted. There had been kisses here and there, but never anything like what they had just shared.

Zephyr pulled himself together. He cleared his throat a few times before he spoke. "Well, I think I should be getting to bed. Big day tomorrow."

Ember nodded as she watched him leave the duchess suite she occupied. She let out a deep sigh. She finished getting ready for bed, replaying the kiss over and over again.

Things with the Guardians and Caelus were about to come to a head. Ember knew what she had to do regarding both. She even had a plan for how to handle things with Zephyr. But that kiss just made matters with Zephyr a whole lot more complicated.

As Ember climbed into bed and began to drift off, all she could think about was the feeling of Zephyr's soft lips against hers. She turned onto her side and knew she was in trouble.

Chapter 25

Ember had been warned before she arrived at the Chamber of the Lords that the Crown Guardians were asserting their power regarding the trial against Caelus. Both the American and Parlian press had reported on the matter in the morning edition.

Rather than strike in anger, Ember was curious to see what law or reasoning the Guardians were going to use. She was prepared for their stunts. In a few days, she would play her hand and end this farce once and for all. In the meantime, she wanted to see what they did. To be fair to the five people who comprised the Guardians, it wasn't every member trying to thwart her every move, just three.

The herald proclaimed her arrival as she walked into the room, Ember took note of the private gallery. The Americans were in the front row, Lianna was with Jonathon and Zephyr in the press box, while members of the public filled every available seat. The Guardians were in their box across from the High Court, while Caelus and his law team, as well as the prosecution, were on the floor front and center.

Ember shot a glance at Emerson, who was seated on her left. His jaw was clenched the only physical indication of his mood. He and Jonathon knew she was going to make an announcement in a few days. It was her hope the people wouldn't riot and overthrow the government beforehand.

"Lady Vivian," Ember called out. "Has the High Court decided the sentence for Mr. Caelus Levan?"

Before Vivian could answer, Cilia stood. Ember arched an eyebrow. Like her, Cilia was wearing a crown signaling her status and station. Her mother appeared to be sober, which meant she was planning a power play and needed to be in control of all her faculties. It wouldn't do to be a blathering idiot while asserting a power she didn't hold.

"The High Court's sentence isn't important. As the Guardians of the ruling monarch, we are stepping in because this trial could greatly impact the future of Parley. We don't think the High Court fully grasps the ramifications," Cilia announced.

Vivian looked at Ember, and she nodded for the woman to sit down. Meanwhile, Uncle Martin, the solicitor, and financier looked fit to be tied over Cilia's actions. Ember thought that was interesting. Had Wilson and Cilia once again gone off script? It was something the pair seemed to be doing more frequently lately, bolstered by the assumption they were untouchable.

"What ramifications might those be, Dowager?" Ember inquired.

Cilia preened under the attention. Her inflated sense of importance was on display for all to see. Ember gritted her teeth. Soon she wouldn't have to deal with her mother's theatrics.

"War," Cilia proclaimed. She paused a minute relishing the silence surrounding her statement. "America has decided it will declare war if anything comes from this ludicrous trial. Prime Minister Levan spoke to the Guardians this morning about the matter."

Citizens began murmuring in the gallery. Ember knew America wasn't going to declare war over Caelus. Despite Wilson's threats, Ember had spoken to members from both houses of the American parliament before arriving. They assured her war wasn't on the table, rather there could be trade ramifications and sanctions, but nothing as dramatic as war. However, Ember wasn't going to stop the show Cilia was about to regal everyone with.

"Oh, dear. War? Are they really threatening war?" Ember sat forward on her throne. She made sure to keep her tone curious rather than mocking.

Emerson snorted next to her and Ember shot him a sideways glare. Cilia was never great at detecting sarcasm. Ember's questions were all the encouragement the woman needed to detail the plan America was going to implement should Caelus be charged.

"Therefore, Mr. Levan will be set free. Furthermore, there will be corrections issued by the newspapers for besmirching his good name," Cilia concluded with a flourish of her hands.

Emerson choked on a laugh, deftly hiding it behind a cough. Ember took a moment to compose her irritation over her mother's words. The citizens and the press were going to soundly protest these leaps in logic. She let out a deep breath, pretending to have pondered on these supposed consequences.

"Let me make sure I'm understanding your words," Ember stated. "It is the decision of the Guardians to free Mr. Caelus Levan by overturning the decision of the High Court, based on an investigation by not just the Cuban police, but also His Royal Highness, Prince Emerson, Duke of Whydah and Director of Intelligence and Military Operations. Is that correct?"

Cilia eagerly nodded. Ember had wanted to give her mother a chance to recognize she was undermining the authority of not just her daughter and the High Court, but also her son. Judging by the vacant look on Cilia's face Ember should have saved her breath.

"Yes. It is also our intention to allow the extradition of Mr. Zephyr Levan to Belize to face the charges brought against him," Cilia all but bragged as she clasped her hands together. "After all, he is an American citizen and not our concern."

At Cilla's declaration, agents for the Belizean government walked into the press box and went straight for Zephyr. The crowd gasped and began to shout. Ember cursed soundly in her mind. Her mother was overstepping her reach and pushing her to show part of her hand sooner than she had been anticipating. It didn't matter though. Of all the pieces in her big announcement, Zephyr's citizenship was the least important.

"Do not touch him," Ember commanded. Her voice was steady and her tone lethal as she glared at her mother. Cilia lifted an eyebrow in return.

"He's an American. It's none of our concern," Cilia countered with a shrug.

"Mr. Levan is my fiancé. He's protected," Ember bit out. Her use of mister rather than his title was intentional. She wanted to play her cards close to her chest so to speak.

Ember was fuming at Cilia's sense of superiority, but also grateful she had listened to her instincts and moved up the timing of her gift of a title to Zephyr. It was a minor consolation in this moment.

Judging by Cilia's coy grin, she knew something Ember didn't. Unease washed over her. Even Emerson was rigid next to her, which meant he was possibly unaware of their mother's actions as well. What had she done?

"The engagement was broken this morning in light of his actions in Belize," Cilia gloated. Arrogance illuminated her eyes.

The agents moved to grab Zephyr, but Ember shot them a murderous glare. The lead agent backed off but stayed close.

"How was the engagement broken? America can deem the engagement over on their end, but in Parley, there were legal documents signed. They can't just be terminated. If the monarch or guardians of the monarch and the patriarch agree to the union, then only the Duke of Revenge can convene the High Court to break it," Ember countered.

"National security is the other way the engagement can be broken," Cilia replied sweetly. "The Guardians do not need the Duke of Revenge to break the engagement if it is for national security."

Emerson growled low in his throat. A flash of alarm shot across Cilia's features at the noise before she pushed it down and resumed her air of conceit. Cilia and the others were out of line. The financier and solicitor shifted in their seat and looked anywhere but Ember, signaling to her they had no part in this new tactic. Even Martin looked uncomfortable, but he would have given Cilia the numbers she needed because what choice did he have?

"That is incorrect, Dowager. The Guardians do not have the power or authority to intervene on matters of national security, or dissolve royal engagements they made," Ember fired back. She was seething with rage and would much rather be standing than sitting, but that would give Cilia the dramatic response she was looking for.

"Wrong," Celia began. "Two years ago, the Guardians changed the law regarding how royal engagements and marriages were enacted and dissolved. We have the power."

The smug glance Cilia shared with Wilson wasn't missed by Ember. They thought they had won. They thought they could change the constitution without anyone else's input. Fools. The hushed whispers of the crowd fueled their sense of superiority.

Ember smiled and snickered softly. "You think you're so clever, Dowager. The Guardians do not have the power or authority to change the constitution of Parley without the lords and citizens having input. The monarch marriage clause isn't a law the Guardians can change to suit them, it is an article in the constitution."

Ember looked up at the Belizean agents. Her jade eyes danced with rage. Cilia's lips thinned into a line as she realized she had overplayed her hand and lost against her daughter in public.

"Lord Zephyr Levan, Viscount Montague, is a citizen of Parley and my fiancé. Touch him and I *will* declare war against Belize. Right here. Right now," Ember asserted.

"He's a citizen of Parley?" The lead agent asked as he scrambled away from Zephyr.

Cilia's mouth was a gape briefly before she shut it. The wheels of her mind were spinning, although Ember doubted she was following much of anything or formulating any kind of clever comeback.

"Yes. He was bestowed the title of Viscount Montague. That makes him a citizen of Parley, as well as America. As long as he is in my country, he is under my protection and care."

Ember met and held Wilson's glare during her explanation. She could see the flush of anger rise to his cheeks. She wasn't sure what his end game for Zephyr was, but now he knew her motivation for gifting Zephyr a title.

Truthfully, by this afternoon, the entire kingdom would know. Yes, Zephyr had earned the title, but more than that, it gave him citizenship without them marrying. This offered him a protection being her fiancé didn't.

"You gave him citizenship?" Cilia's outrage was evident in her tone as well as her stiff posture. It was like she was trying to hold her fury inside, but needed to maintain her image.

"I didn't give him citizenship, it was included with the title. It's the only way a noncitizen of Parley can hold an agricultural title. Upon his acceptance of the title, which he signed the following day, he was made a citizen of Parley and Viscount Montague."

Ember shrugged at the end of her statement. It wasn't her fault her mother and Wilson hadn't understood the full implication of her gift. For a couple of people determined to strip her of her power, they had some glaring holes in their knowledge of Parlian law.

"End this now, Ember. The citizens are getting restless," Emerson muttered under his breath. His eyes were scanning the room for threats to her safety.

Ember glanced around the chamber, taking in the mood and atmosphere of those in it. The citizens were going to protest, possibly riot, and she could only pray they didn't revolt. She just needed her people to trust her for a few more days. She hadn't given them much of a reason to trust her, but maybe they would humor her.

"The Guardians have decided to clear Mr. Caelus Levan of all charges. That decision will stand until the High Court and Lesser Lords can convene in a week. Therefore, you are free, but can't leave the country. This session is adjourned," Ember concluded.

She stood and made her way to her antechamber. She knew Emerson would be hot on her heels as soon as he could break away. Zephyr, Jonathon, and Lianna would more than likely follow.

She was surprised when the aforementioned trio requested an audience first and not Emerson. Her twin was probably preoccupied with fielding questions or any number of things.

As soon as Zephyr entered the room, he rounded on Ember. "You made me a citizen? Was that the motivation for the title? You decided to plan your power move without consulting me like everyone else in my life?"

Ember braced herself against the onslaught of his words. That last question was more of an accusation and it hit its mark. She fought the urge to rub the center of her chest to ease the pang of hurt and guilt she felt there.

"The motivation for the title was exactly what I said it was at the dinner. It is a gift and recognition of your hard work. I wanted to give you an identity outside of me," Ember reasoned. "The citizenship piece was a bonus of sorts, and added insurance that you would have the freedom to make your own decisions."

Zephyr stared at her for a moment. Jonathon and Lianna were standing near the door and seemed ready to bolt at a moment's notice.

"Why didn't you tell me about the citizenship when you gave me the title? Because from where I'm standing, it looks like you're trying to control my life as much as everyone else," Zephyr accused.

"When the paperwork was presented for you to sign, the citizenship was listed as being part of the title. I didn't think to highlight it because I wrongly assumed you would know that, and also because I didn't want Wilson aware of it," she admitted.

Ember stood and held up her hand to cut off his words. "You can relinquish the title at any time, but Zephyr, I'm not trying to control you. I'm trying to protect you the only way I know, while also giving you a home."

Zephyr sucked on his lower lip. Tension filled the room, especially as he weighed Ember's words. He wanted to believe her, but he had been used so many times before. Ember had never used him, but the knowledge didn't give him peace.

Jonathon cleared his throat. "If I may be so bold as to interject. Her Majesty is fiercely loyal to those she loves. When she gifted you the title, regardless of motive, she cemented your legacy and importance within Parley. Look at how fiercely the people defend you."

Lianna nodded in agreement. "The people love you, Zephyr. They don't view you as an outsider, so her actions signal to everyone she doesn't view you as one either."

Zephyr sank into a chair and put his head in his hands. Ember knelt in front of him.

"I understand your hurt and anger, and can appreciate it in ways you don't know, but for four years I have watched and sat in silence, observing your role in your family and America. Frankly, I found it appalling," Ember confessed. "My motivation in giving you the title was because I wanted to give you a home and something you controlled. Citizenship is another layer of protection, but you deserve the chance to show the world who you are outside of the people you're meant to support."

Zephyr's eyes had a sheen over them as he searched her face and turned her words in his mind. He closed his eyes and took a few deep breaths before opening them and holding her gaze.

"I'll admit I'm relieved to be a citizen, and I believe your explanation. I was hurt at first because I thought you were trying to one-up my father. I have also been fearful of your reasoning for giving me the title," Zephyr admitted.

Jonathon and Lianna shot each other a quizzical look before Jonathon spoke, "Why would you be fearful of her reasoning?"

A heavy silence filled the room. Ember stood and turned to Jonathon and Lianna.

"Zephyr knows about Parley."

It took a moment before understanding washed over the pair.

"Before you ask, he was investigating something and saw a Mer child transform. He told Emerson his findings and mentioned the child. Zephyr has told no one and asked for nothing in exchange for his silence," Ember explained.

Zephyr snorted. "I didn't ask for 'nothing'. I asked for protection, but not in exchange for the Mer child. Rather it was because of the matter I had told him about, which involved my father."

"And when you heard about the citizenship you thought the title was motivated by the agreement with Emerson," Jonathon deduced.

"Yes. I want you to know I didn't blackmail anyone. I would sound like a lunatic if I spoke of the Mer, and I gave Emerson the information before he ever agreed to help me."

Jonathon chuckled. "I never for a moment thought you blackmailed anyone. As far as I'm concerned, you came by your title honestly, Lord Montague. You have integrity, and when Her Majesty saw a chance to reward you, she took it."

Lianna nodded her head. "I agree. The Bellamys have always rewarded loyalty and integrity. You're not the first outsider to encounter the Mer. It does happen on occasion, and they are always thought of as being touched in the head."

"I've wondered about this, but do the royal spouses know about the Mer?" Zephyr asked.

"Not always. Dowager Queen Cilia was never told of the Mer or Muirgen; however, I have my suspicions my uncle knows," Ember replied.

"Aren't there stories about the Mer though? I swear I've heard fairytales about them around the various islands," Zephyr inquired.

"There are stories. Cilia believes it's nonsense from the island natives, as well as the Native Americans. The Chippewa have tales warning young girls to be careful bathing in water because mermen would come and watch them," Ember said. "Because Parley is a blend of cultures, we have lots of tales about a variety of monsters and creatures. The Mer happen to be real, but that doesn't mean all the stories are."

Shouting and heavy footfalls in the corridor caught everyone's attention. A moment later, Emerson entered the room with Ian and Evan. They quickly secured the door behind them. Emerson then strode over to the other door and ensured it was locked.

"What's going on?" Ember asked. She was mildly alarmed by Emerson's actions. The commotion in the hallway seemed to be increasing.

"The citizens in the gallery have decided to protest their displeasure with the Guardian's decision by storming the building we are currently in," Emerson explained in a rush.

Chapter 26

Ember stood frozen in place as she watched her brother do a sweep of the room, making sure no one could enter the space. Once he was satisfied, he turned to face her and continued his explanation.

"The number of citizens inside is growing because of those who were standing outside waiting for the sentence to be read."

Ember jumped at the pounding on the door. Jonathon put Lianna behind him as they moved to the middle of the room. The shouting on the other side intensified.

"Are we trapped?" Lianna squeaked out.

Jonathon pulled her into a side hug as she began to shake. He absently rubbed a hand up and down her arm to comfort her.

"No. Since you are here, you will be evacuating the premises with us," Emerson responded. "I trust you both not to say a word regarding what you're about to see."

Jonathon and Lianna nodded. Emerson walked over to the paneling in the corner of the room, after a moment, a hidden door slid open. Ian and Evan went into the corridor first, followed by Ember and Zephyr. Emerson motioned for Jonathon and Lianna to follow before he entered the space and sealed the door.

Darkness filled the void for a moment until Ian and Evan lit the lanterns. They passed one back to Emerson before silently moving through the secret passageway. Every so often, shouting could be heard as they continued toward their destination.

Soon the walls became cement and the outside world could no longer be heard. The group moved through the tunnel's narrow twists and turns for what felt like an eternity. The stagnant air was suffocating and infused with the heat and humidity of the tropical nation.

Tight spaces didn't usually bother Ember, so long as she wasn't in them for very long. But the longer they were in the emergency tunnel system, the more time she had to dwell on the events leading to using them. As well as why she hated them — Drystan.

She could feel small tremors seizing her body. Her breathing became rapid as the walls closed in around her. Her limbs felt heavy as the blood seemed to rush from her body. She stumbled and caught herself a few times, forcing herself to continue forward. She knew Zephyr was behind her somewhere, as were the others, but that didn't matter... She was four years old, screaming at the top of her lungs for someone to let her out of the wardrobe Drystan had stuffed her into, while he and his friends laughed at her terror.

Emerson, sensing more than seeing, knew when Ember's mind began to wonder to the incident with Drystan. He recalled knowing something was wrong with his twin. He had tried to get the nanny to take him to where his older siblings were, but she had insisted on staying in the playroom.

Emerson had snuck out when the nanny had gone to get him a snack and headed toward the ballroom. He paused when he thought he heard crying in the direction of the guest suites. He followed the sound of Ember's terrified screams until he found the bedroom Drystan and his friends had trapped her in. He ran and got their father.

King Emerson had stood in the doorway for a second before striding in, and throwing open the door to the wardrobe, which had broken. Grammy Margaret had it repaired after the incident, which was an odd thing to recall in a time like this. Emerson had glared at his brother as he ran after their father as fast as his little legs could to make sure Ember was okay.

She was huddled in the corner. Her face was red and tear-streaked and her breathing came out in rapid bursts. Her small body quaked in fear. She hadn't realized the closet door was open until their father had picked her up. She had clutched to him like her life depended on it.

When she opened her eyes, Emerson stared up at her from their father's side. Relief had flooded her features as she took a deep breath. The tears began to fall again at that point, but silently. King Emerson's voice roared in anger as he demanded an explanation from the boys. When none was offered, he punished all of them.

From that day forward, Ember didn't sleep in the dark by herself. To this day there were still moments when Ember would leave a light on to sleep. Mostly when she was under tremendous amounts of stress. It had taken her years to overcome her terror of being in confined spaces, but they still bothered her more than she let on to anyone. They also never spoke of the incident, which few people remembered.

Emerson spoke to her in soothing tones as her breathing became louder and she tripped again. "We are almost to the end, Em. You can do it."

When she didn't respond, Emerson called out to Zephyr. "I need you to find her and help her, Zephyr. Em doesn't do well in confined spaces."

Zephyr nodded and then realized no one could see him. "I'll catch up to her. I didn't know she hated tight spaces."

Emerson didn't offer a response and no one asked for further clarification. Zephyr strode forward in the dim light. He hadn't realized how far behind Ember, Ian, and Evan he had fallen until he had to catch up. He could still see the lantern light and assumed he was close behind, but that wasn't the case. Fortunately, after a moment he caught Ember's arm.

She let out a shriek as she whipped around, smacking Zephyr hard against the chest. To his credit, and everyone else's, no one said a word. Evan and Ian paused, while Zephyr hugged Ember against him for a moment. He caught her crown in his hand as he felt it slide off her head. Rather than put it back, he decided to hold on to it for her. Once they made it out of the tunnel, he would return it.

"I have you, Ember. Take a couple of deep breaths and then we'll push forward out of here together with everyone. You're not alone," Zephyr soothed as he rubbed a hand up and down her back.

He felt something wet against his chest. Ember was crying. He was alarmed. She hated crying. She never let her emotions get the better of her in front of others or in public. He pulled her harder against him for a moment before letting go.

"How much farther, Emerson?" Zephyr asked. He held onto Ember's hand as she started forward again.

Emerson held up the lantern, looking for something on the wall or ground, and then answered, "We are only a few hundred yards from the exit."

Zephyr wasn't sure if he was lying to make Ember feel better, or telling the truth. He also wasn't going to ask. Instead, he focused on Ember and kept her calm. With their fingers laced together, he was able to rub the inside of her palm with his thumb.

After several minutes, Ember spoke up. "A few hundred yards, Emerson?"

"Yep."

After another five or so minutes of walking, Ian and Evan stopped.

"I think we're at the end," Ian called out.

Sure enough, they had finally reached the end of the tunnel. Ember was impatient to get out, she pushed her way to the front, released the lever, and darted out ahead of everyone into the safe room. Emerson handed his lantern to Ian, who extinguished the flames and returned them to the passage.

"Where are we?" Lianna asked as she took in the dark wood paneling and stone floors. The furniture was masculine and heavy. The chairs and couches were upholstered in navy blue leather which was contrasted by a light wood stain. The room was more Art Deco and modern than most royal areas in Parley.

"We are at the private lounge in the airport," Emerson replied. He walked over to a phone and dialed a number. He had a brief conversation with someone before hanging the handset back on the cradle.

"There will be a car for you and Lianna here in a few moments," Emerson told Jonathan. He then turned to Zephyr and Ember and added, "The zeppelin to take you back to Blackstone will be ready shortly. I'm walking to the palace so I can gauge the situation on the streets."

"Should I go with you or Ember?" Zephyr inquired.

Emerson turned to look at him. He wasn't sure if Ember was aware she was still clutching Zephyr's hand and he was still rubbing her palm with his thumb. Either way, she was still shaken from her time in the tunnel. He couldn't be with her, so Zephyr was the next best person to help her calm down.

"Go with Ember. If you decide you want to come back to Careen, let the pilot at the airfield know. If you'll excuse me, I have to go." Emerson ducked out of the room quickly just as the car arrived.

Jonathon promised Ember he and Lianna would head straight for the newspaper. He would ensure the stories about her announcement and the lords meeting the following week were on the front page of the evening edition, above the fold, so everyone would see it. Lianna gave Ember a quick hug before the pair left.

Evan called to Ian, Ember, and Zephyr a short time later as their small airship lowered the steps to board. It was clear to Zephyr as he helped Ember up the stairs that she wasn't present. Her mind was locked onto whatever event in the past held her captive.

The flight to the airfield in Nassau and the subsequent drive to Blackstone was quiet. Ember looked out the window while leaning against Zephyr, but she saw nothing. Instead, she was back in the closet, listening to Drystan and his friends laugh, while she prayed for someone to save her.

She never thought she would feel that level of terror again, but hearing the crowds in the corridors as she fled the audience hall brought it all back. She was a helpless child waiting for someone to rescue her all over again.

Nerissa greeted the car in the driveway. Ember told her she wanted to take a bath and then retire for the evening. Once in the duchess suite, Ember told Nerissa she would run her bath, she just needed help undressing. Once the task was complete, she dismissed her lady-in-waiting.

She grabbed her nightdress and tentatively walked to the door that connected the duke's suite to hers. She stood naked outside the door for several moments before working up the courage to enter Kieran's space.

Tears pricked the corners of her eyes as his scent greeted her. A feeling of security swept over her. She moved through the room toward his dressing room and the adjoining bathroom. She set her nightdress on a nearby bench and then turned on the water to the bath.

As the tub filled, she poked around the space in search of a washcloth and towel. She found a bar of his soap and put it near on top of the tub. She spent a few minutes exploring his bathroom, looking through the cabinets and drawers, envisioning the one person she wanted more than anything filling the space.

She turned off the faucet and climbed into the steaming liquid. Ember closed her eyes and focused on the sensation of the water moving around her. In the sanctuary of Kieran's suite, Ember surrendered to the feelings she had been fighting since entering the tunnel. Terror, grief, sadness, anger, and frustration crashed into her as the sobs claimed her. Her tears freely flowed, mixing with the water in the tub.

Ember wasn't sure how long she sat in the tub giving into her emotions for the first time in months, but she reached for the soap and washcloth, dipping them into the lukewarm water. She washed herself, enjoying the darker, masculine scent of tonka and oud. If there was only a hint of whiskey thrown in, Ember mused, then she would smell just like Kieran.

She dried off and slipped her nightgown over her head. She paused in his dressing room. Ember walked to where Kieran's night clothes were kept and rummaged for a moment before pulling out his robe. She put the garment to her nose before inhaling deeply. Wrapping the garment around herself, she cleaned up after herself before returning to her room.

There was a light knocking on the door. Ember opened the door and saw a maid on the other side. The woman asked if she wanted a dinner tray brought to her room, but Ember gently refused. She asked the maid to let everyone know she wasn't in the mood to receive visitors to her suite and bade the woman a good night.

Ember walked onto the balcony and looked in the direction of Careen. The moon was rising in the sky, reflecting off the ocean. The stars were dotting the sky as well. The calm waves were a stark contrast to the turmoil she felt. She let out a deep sigh. She couldn't see the capital city of Parley, but she was fearful of what her morning brief would say. She prayed no one would get hurt in the demonstrations she knew were happening.

Ember knew the citizens were enraged over the decision by the Guardians. She didn't blame them. She just hoped they calmed down, read the article in Jonathon's newspaper, and trusted she had a plan. She leaned forward against the railing and bowed her head.

Why would her citizens trust her? What had she done to earn their trust? She solved problems and listened to their disputes, but when it mattered and required her to go against the Guardians, Ember always remained silent. Why would her citizens believe this time would be any different?

As the tears streamed down her face, Ember looked back at the moon. She bit her lip. "I'm sorry, Daddy. You always told me I was stronger than I thought, but in the end, you had to save me against Drystan. And now? Well, I didn't fair much better against Mother and the Guardians."

Ember wiped the tears from her face. "Emerson should have been born first. I don't know how to do this without you or him or... Kieran." Her voice broke as the sobs overtook her anew.

She deserved to be overthrown. Yes, she had been a child when she was crowned queen, but it hadn't taken long for her to cower behind those meant to support her while she led. Instead, she handed Cilia everything she needed to implode Parley from the inside. How many other monarchs had been children and led better than her? Probably dozens.

Ember wasn't certain how long she stood on the balcony giving into her doubts, self-pity, and defeat as she told her dead father what a failure she was, but a shift in the wind caught her attention.

Whiskey. She buried herself deeper into Kieran's robe, taking in his scent, as a shooting star darted across the sky. A warm tingling feeling came over her and suddenly she didn't feel so alone. Ember sniffled and smiled as she closed her eyes.

Kieran believed in her, even if he wasn't here. He wouldn't be doing what he was doing wherever he was if he didn't believe in her. Grammy Margaret believed in her, as did Emerson.

Zephyr, Nerissa, Jonathan, Lianna, Evelyn, the Bahamas, and Parley's allies believed in her too. For that matter, so did her father. Even if he was no longer physically with her, the memories of him encouraging her and his unfailing support remained.

Determination filled her as hope sprang forth in her chest. Caelus, Wilson, and Cilia weren't going to win. She wasn't going to allow them to win. For better or worse, she was her father's heir. She played with the signet ring on the pinkie of her right hand. It was the same ring her father had worn. It had been recovered from the crash and given to her at her coronation.

"Thank you, Daddy."

Ember stayed on the balcony until the first rays from the sun kissed the ocean good morning before retiring to Kieran's suite. She climbed into his bed and snuggled under the blankets. All she could do was pray to God everything worked out in the end.

Chapter 27

It had been a few days since the citizens had stormed the Chamber of Lords in protest. Emerson couldn't say he blamed them. It had been mostly peaceful, with a few people getting out of hand. The Cuban police had cited those people trespassing for getting into areas that were off-limits, as well as vandalism in a few cases.

All in all, less than ten people had been cited of the hundreds that had shown up. He had directed Chamber officials to get the building cleaned and prepared for the event in a few days. Ember was making her announcement regarding her monarchal powers, as well as Caelus's punishment. He didn't think the citizens would storm the Chambers in protest, but possibly in celebration. Either way, he was preparing security plans for all outcomes.

A knock on the door pulled him from his thoughts. He frowned. He had told Greer he did not want to be disturbed. Ember would have waltzed into the room if it were her, but she was at Blackstone. That left their grandmother. Emerson sighed. Hopefully, she wouldn't bring him some new problems. He had enough of those.

"Come in." He barked out.

Emerson's eyebrows shot up in surprise when his Uncle Martin walked into the room. He had a small stack of papers in his hands. A decade ago, Martin had become an informant for the director who had held his job before Kieran. No one outside of himself and Kieran knew of Martin's spying.

Cilia believed she held the purse strings and fate of her brother, but that wasn't true. He was paid well for his work, but not well enough to make up for his reputation. Martin wanted out and had told Emerson this. He wanted a family and to stop playing the role of a meek pawn to his sister.

Emerson had agreed to help clean up his reputation and free him from his obligation once Ember took back her powers as queen. Martin had begrudgingly agreed to the terms, but Emerson knew he was interested in someone. He couldn't be a villain and win a wife in Parley.

If Martin was coming to him in the middle of the afternoon, it had to be a warning about some new plot Cilia, Wilson, and Peter had concocted. Martin hesitated at the door for a moment, sensing his nephew's mood, before shutting it and walking to the desk. Emerson motioned for his uncle to have a seat. He offered the man a cigar, which he readily accepted. Once the pair was puffing away, Martin gave Emerson the papers he had been carrying.

"What are these?" Emerson asked. He scanned the pages and saw they were naturalized citizenship forms. All babies born to at least one Parlian parent had these forms filled out and submitted. What babies had to do with national security at the moment was beyond him.

"Look carefully at the names." Martin took a deep drag off the cigar before blowing out the grey smoke. "I think you'll be interested in the last four or five pages specifically."

Emerson flipped to the back pages and scanned the names. "Son of a bitch." Rage coursed through his body. Cilia had gone too far this time in her quest to please her lover. For a woman hanging onto her title by a thread, she certainly was clueless at times.

"When did they land on this path?" Emerson shook his head as he read the names on all the forms. Noting a couple of others his uncle would have been less familiar with.

"A couple months ago. They had a dinner party shortly before Caelus arrived, who was acting as a distraction. I kept the information to myself until they made a move. Cilia and Peter hoped that you would have someone in your office approve and file these," Martin explained.

Emerson blew out white smoke as he wiped his eyes with his fingers. "I have to give them credit. It would have taken me a moment to figure out what they were up to because my attention is spread in too many directions."

"I too was impressed by Peter's gumption when he proposed it," Martin mused. "Although he stammered and stuttered his way to this proposition, hoping to impress Cilia enough for a reward."

Both men rolled their eyes. Cilia may be a drunk, but she could be cunning and manipulative when it served her purpose. Peter never had a chance because his mother had her eye on Wilson from the moment he set foot in Parley. Emerson didn't think it had taken an entire day before Cilia and Wilson were thick as thieves, tangled up in an affair. Peter had always been her useful puppet, but with Wilson on her side and in her ear, Cilia had utilized his crush on her to her advantage.

"I can't overlook this, Uncle. Surely you know that."

Emerson studied the man sitting across from him. His uncle was an unassuming man. He was in his mid-thirties. He was six feet tall, with a slim athletic build, dark blue eyes, and golden brown hair. He had lived in Parley for twenty years now. He had been fifteen when he first started as an informant of sorts regarding his sister's behavior. That was eighteen years ago.

When Cilia had revived the Crown Guardians, it had been the work of the director of intelligence at the time to get Martin placed within the group as well. The decision to not have a Bellamy as part of the five members had sparked outrage among Father's siblings with Grammy. They never understood her reasoning, and she couldn't explain it. It created a rift they still hadn't mended. Instead, Martin was given the final spot and in the process became a full-time informant for the Crown.

Cilia assumed it was Margaret, the financier, or the solicitor that squelched her plans at every turn. However, it was her brother. Uncle Martin played the role of the villain on many occasions, helping Cilia pass her legislation in a bid for more power. He was despised by most of the citizens and had a rocky relationship with Margaret and Ember.

Martin sighed as he ran a hand through his hair. "I know. This is going to make me sound like a horrible brother, but honestly, I'm glad for it. She has destroyed my chances at marriage any number of times over the years. She puts herself above everyone, and I'm tired."

"I'm exiling her permanently, along with Wilson. Truthfully, I could charge them both with treason, but I'll settle for them leaving and never coming back."

Martin sighed. "You know they won't give up that easily."

Emerson finished his cigar before snuffing it out. "I know. But this latest scheme can't be overlooked. If someone else becomes aware of it, I can't protect you if I don't punish them."

The older man smiled. "If you have to punish me too, Emerson, then I understand. I knew when I took on the role of informant that there was a good chance I wouldn't walk away unscathed. Do what you need to."

Emerson shook his head. "I'll do what I need to, but I will fight for you when the time comes. I know Kieran will too once he returns."

His uncle snubbed out his finished cigar. "How goes the progress on *that*? Any thoughts as to whether someone tied with the Revenge scandal a century ago is trying to kill Ember?"

Emerson turned to look out the French doors. He blew out a breath. The information Zephyr had uncovered was everything Emerson could have hoped for. He hadn't realized Olivia Wade had met Victor, which made sense.

The Thaches had Mer in their bloodline, so they lived longer. There wasn't a great way to bring that man up in conversation. The tropical storm and subsequent damage had been nothing short of a Godsend in the end.

"The blackmail letter has been sent off, although, sources from Astonia are saying he was captured and is being tortured along with Rhys Houndson. I don't know where or I would have sent in assets to check out the validity of the claim and rescue him."

Emerson ran a hand through his hair. He wasn't convinced Kieran hadn't been captured on purpose, which was frustrating as well. Why would he put himself in danger?

"When he comes back, lock him up. We need him to stay put for many reasons, the least his being a half-breed and the top being Ember's safety," Martin stated.

"Believe me. I haven't ruled out locking him away. Although, mine and Grammy's temper will be nothing compared to Ember's. I hope he's ready for that," Emerson drawled.

Martin threw back his head in laughter. "Hell hath no fury like that of a woman's scorn, and Ember has that in spades."

"That she does. She's in love with him," Emerson stated.

"I know." Martin studied the arm of the leather chair. "I hope it works out in the end for them because they are exactly what the other needs."

Emerson kept his gaze on the ocean outside the balcony doors. "A part of me hopes she chooses Zephyr because it would be easier and less painful; however, I have eyes. Kieran isn't as unaffected by her as he pretends to be. She was just too young, and there was Willow."

Martin let out a deep sigh. "Ah yes. Willow. The reason for him to go rogue and hide from the world."

The men lapsed into silence for a moment before Martin stood. "I best get back to Cilia like the good little lap dog I am. See you at dinner?"

Emerson chuckled. He didn't envy his uncle one bit being at his mother's beck and call. "Yes, I will see you at dinner before I return to Whydah."

Chapter 28

Emerson had assured his sister and grandmother the Chamber of Lords would be well guarded, as well as the entire building. The citizens who had protested the decision of the Guardians hadn't done any serious damage to the building. Some furniture and small items had been broken. In the week that followed, things were replaced and fixed so no one would ever know.

Meanwhile, Emerson had crafted a detailed security plan, while also setting up the radio broadcast equipment from the various news outlets to cover Ember's announcement and today's proceedings. Tickets for the public gallery had been given out the day before on a first come basis. Everyone had been screened before they were seated.

The next group to be screened and seated were those sitting in the private gallery. Emerson hadn't trusted the Americans, the Monroes, or Wilson. Lianna and her family were also seated in the area alongside Zephyr. Both Lord Burroughs and Zephyr had declined to sit with the Lesser Lords on the floor. Instead, they opted to lend their support to Lianna.

The press, the Guardians, the Lesser Lords, and the High Court were the next to file into the space. Kieran owed his sister

Vivian big time for stepping in and fulfilling the role of the Duchy of Revenge by leading the proceedings, Emerson thought as he was announced. He moved to his seat on the right of the throne.

The herald announced his grandmother a minute later. Once she was in place to the left of the throne, Ember was announced. As she entered the room, there was a murmur through the crowd. Ember was wearing their father's crown, which she had never done before. She was also wearing her red velvet and fur-lined robe.

Despite her pale coloring and slight hand shaking, there were no outward indicators of her nerves. Ember looked around the room. Hundreds of eyes were on her. In the private gallery, she saw Caelus and Amelia sitting next to each other. He had an arm wrapped around her shoulders, holding her close to his side. Zephyr was with Lianna, her family, and Lord Burroughs, which sent a clear message regarding his feelings.

She closed her eyes and took a few deep breaths before opening them and looking over to the Crown Guardians. A few members shifted in their seats under her scrutiny. Her mother looked bored, but it was evident from the way she was bobbing in her seat that Cilia was inebriated. Uncle Martin, on the other hand, was on edge. He was studying everyone around him, and his face was a careful mask of forced nonchalance. The solicitor and the financier sat looking forward, anticipating what had brought them to the Chamber of Lords.

Meanwhile, the patriarch of the church looked like he would be sick at any moment. Ember felt a small amount of glee at the thought. The man always sided with her mother and uncle, helping them push through everything they had wanted over the past nine years. As a religious leader, he should have focused on the citizens of Parley and how his choices affected them, instead of focusing on raising his own star.

"Thank you everyone for your presence today," Ember began. "With some of the recent legislation and legal decisions made by the Crown Guardians, I was alarmed.

"Several pieces of legislation were highly controversial, including a bill allowing noncitizens and foreigners the ability to purchase pearl farms and mineral mines. These new laws seemingly benefited members of the Guardians more than the citizens of Parley. To say nothing of the legal decision in regards to a criminal trial a few days ago."

Martin shot his sister a meaningful glance, but Cilia wasn't paying attention. The patriarch had his hands folded in front of him, but the pinched look on his face spoke volumes. The solicitor and the financier already knew what was coming, and they had nothing to worry about.

"But then I realized what a great opportunity these new laws and legal decisions presented to not only Parley and the world but also me," Ember stated. She could hear the murmuring pick up around the room at her words. The tension increased as the people waited to hear what she would say next.

Martin sat straighter in his seat, while Cilia smiled at her daughter. The patriarch had visibly relaxed at her words, but then Ember smiled and the man's face fell. He seemed to have figured out his fate too late. He glanced to Cilia who was still in her own world.

"I am dissolving the Crown Guardians. I am taking on the full mantel of my responsibilities, and taking back my power," Ember declared with a smirk. A startled hush fell over the crowd as Cilia's head snapped up.

"NO! You can't do that," Cilia burst out, jumping from her seat. The woman either didn't remember or didn't care about the press and her image. "You can't dissolve the guardianship. You're not twenty-one or married. I'm sorry, Ember, but you simply don't have the power to do this. You don't have the power you think you do."

"'Your Majesty' is the title one uses when addressing me, which is the same as your honorific. I do have the sole legal authority to dissolve the Guardians. However, if you choose to continue on this path of fighting me, you won't like the consequences," Ember warned.

Cilia paused for a moment before throwing back her head and laughing. "Oh, how you amuse me, Ember. The law is the law, not even you cannot change that."

"You and your lackeys clearly didn't read the law. The law reads 'until I'm of sound mind to rule.' When I was coronated at age eight, I was found to be of sound mind," Ember patiently explained. "Therefore, I've always had the sole legal authority of the sovereign to do whatever I want."

Ember held up her hand to cut her mother off. "The law also states the Crown Guardians will be dissolved regardless once I'm married or twenty-one, whichever comes first if I'm not deemed to be of sound mind before those milestones," Ember explained.

Cilia opened her mouth to speak, but again Ember cut her off and stood. "Silence! Furthermore, the law states if the Guardians fail to act within the best interest of Parley, they can be dissolved. You, Uncle Martin, and the patriarch have been denying me my power for years now, despite my being of sound mind.

"I convened both the High Court and Lesser Lords and spoke to the royal solicitor and royal financier, and all were in agreement with me. I have been acting as queen and performing my duties despite being undermined by you and your efforts. The High Court and Lesser Lords have decided to vote today on whether I rule or the Guardians do, and take the matter out of both our hands."

Ember sat back down on the throne. Her mother on the other hand remained standing. The anger and hatred for Ember were etched in her posture, as well as the lines on her face.

"You can't do this!" Cilia's scream echoed through the chamber.

Vivian took her place at the pulpit in the box where the High Court was seated. She ignored Cilia as she continued to rant and rave. Uncle Martin tried unsuccessfully to get her to be quiet and sit down, but she rebuffed his efforts.

"All those in favor of dissolving the Crown Guardians, say aye," Vivian bellowed.

The vote from the High Court was unanimous. Cilia's screaming became louder if possible. She shoved away all attempts to keep her contained in the box where the Guardians had been seated. Her manner became erratic as she narrowed her focus on Ember. Nothing around her mattered.

"All those in favor of Queen Ember taking full possession of her monarchal powers, say aye," Vivian called out again, ignoring the dramatic display of the dowager queen.

Again, the High Court's vote was unanimous. By this point, Cilia was trying to climb over the wooden barrier of her box to the area leading to the High Court. Vivian led the Lesser Lords in their vote, which was also unanimous to dissolve the Guardians and install Ember as monarch. All the while, Cilia screamed and threatened everyone.

When Vivian took her seat after the votes, Ember stood. "Dowager Queen Cilia! You will control yourself and act with some level of decorum."

"Know your place!" Cilia yelled back.

Ember knew her mother wasn't going to take the news well at all. She was even anticipating this level of rage and drama in private. She had not anticipated her mother's antics on full display for the world. She shot a glance at Emerson. His features were tight as he fought for control. They hadn't even gotten to Emerson's part of the announcement yet.

"Dowager Queen Cilia Weber-Bellamy, cease this behavior at once! You will pledge your fidelity to your queen," Ember stated. "If you fail to pledge your fidelity to me, there will be consequences. Regardless, this behavior will end."

In the gallery box, Wilson looked fit to be tied. Zephyr kept a blank expression on his face and never looked away from the chamber floor. Caelus, Amelia, and her parents looked back and forth at each other, uncertain of the events unfolding before them.

Cilia sneered. "I will never pledge my fidelity to you! It was always supposed to be Drystan! Not either of you two worthless bastards!"

"ENOUGH!" The rage in Grammy Margaret's voice bellowed throughout the entire chamber causing Ember to jump. Because she had been focused on her mother, she had not seen her grandmother stand up next to her. A hush fell over the room.

The color drained from Cilia's body. She looked terrified as she realized the danger she was in due to her tantrum. She looked around, seeming to realize where she was, who was in attendance, and how her behavior was in stark contrast to the image she had created.

"I... I didn't mean..." Cilia stammered as the older woman walked past Ember onto the chamber floor. Grammy never took her eyes off her mother. Ember shot Emerson a panicked look, while her twin just shrugged in response.

Ember had planned to banish her mother from court and sentence her to live in exile for a year if she wouldn't pledge her fidelity. Emerson had his own declaration, of which, she knew nothing, but he had said there would be consequences from him as well. Their grandmother was another matter entirely, and neither twin had anticipated her getting involved. Grammy Margaret had never liked Cilia, so Ember wasn't certain what her grandmother had in mind.

"You and you," Grammy Margaret began pointing at Cilia and Wilson. "Have two hours to leave Parley and never return. That does not include your eldest spawn, Prime Minister. Although, I'm not sure if his wife will want to stay or go."

Amelia blushed and ducked her head as her parents turned to her. Her reaction confirmed to everyone she and Caelus had married. It was evident by the look her parents traded with each other they were not pleased by this turn of events. Reporters exchanged looks with each other and scribbled down the information.

Grammy Margaret turned her attention to Cilia as she continued, "You are hereby stripped of your royal title and status. I will graciously return to you your dowry with interest so you have funds in which to live your life. No other funds will be provided to you unless Queen Ember decides to create an allowance for you."

Cilia stood in shock. Her mouth was agape. "You don't have the power to do any of what you have said. Only Queen Ember does. Besides, you have to give a reason for my exile and hatred isn't on the list."

"I have more power than you think as the six times great-granddaughter of Samuel Bellamy. While you lost all your power after my son died, I retained a fair amount of mine, because unlike you, I was born a Bellamy. I didn't marry into it," Grammy Margaret spat.

"I know his secret! I know King Emerson's secret! If you do this I will tell it to everyone. I will sell my story," Cilia threatened.

"If you sell your story or spread any tales about the late King Emerson then I will personally arrest you and have you brought before the High Court to be tried for treason," Emerson announced from his chair before Grammy Margaret could even speak.

Shock lit Cilia's eyes. "You would have me tried for treason? You're own mother?"

Emerson snorted. He didn't bother to hide the destain he felt for her. "You've never been my mother. You've been a queen, a socialite, a drunk, and a calculating debutante, but you've *never* been a mother."

The crowd gasped at his comments. Reporters were furiously writing, taking note of the action and drama playing out before them.

"Queen Margaret may not have given you a reason for her wanting to exile you and Prime Minister Levan, but I will gladly give you one for my lifetime banishment from Parley," Emerson spat.

Everyone in the audience hall began to murmur. Cilia looked around the room for a friendly face, but not even Martin offered her a sign he would help.

"What do you mean, Your Royal Highness," Cilia asked as she licked her lips.

Cilia's use of Emerson's title wasn't lost on Ember. For whatever reason, their mother was terrified of him in a way she had never been of her.

"It was brought to my attention recently that a slew of naturalized citizenship forms had been signed off on by the Crown Guardians, namely you." Cilia paled at his words. She reached out a hand behind her, catching herself on the railing of the box she had abandoned.

"What about them?"

Emerson's dark smile sent a shiver down Ember's spine. "Imagine my surprise when two of these forms landed on my desk, having been flagged by border patrol."

Cilia's legs gave out and she fell to the floor. Tears streaming down her terrified face. She had been rendered silent by the realization her actions had caught up to her.

"Upon further investigation, I learned the names of the recently naturalized citizens matched the same list of names of the people trying to buy pearl farms and mineral mines under the law I repealed for national security purposes. Imagine my dismay when I figured out who was helping circumvent my decision," Emerson growled.

"P-p-please let me ex-ex-plain the re-reasoning," Cilia stuttered.

"I do not care for the logic behind your decision. I said no four times and even sent the decision to the nobility, who also said no. You and Prime Minister Levan have committed several acts of treason against Parley," Emerson explained,

Cilia whimpered as the weight of Emerson's words sank in.

"While I could charge both you and the prime minister with treason, which is punishable by death, I have decided exile is sufficient for you both. If I ever catch either of you in Parley or off our coast, there will be consequences."

Emerson made a show of checking his pocket watch, having remained seated for the entirety of his declaration. "You have less than two hours to pack and get out of Parley. Tick tock."

He then looked up to the gallery before adding, "If I were you, I'd graciously walk away, Prime Minster Levan. Consider this your warning."

Cilia turned to Margaret and Ember, attempting one final appeal. "My country no longer exists. The rebels killed and chased my remaining family from our home country. Where am I supposed to go?'

For a moment, Ember felt a pang of sorrow for her mother. The southern part of Europe had been unstable for almost a century. Her grandfather had managed to maintain stability for some years in his country of Cardia, but when her mother was a toddler, a civil war broke out in the neighboring countries. Her grandfather had sent his children to America as political refugees.

A few years later her maternal grandmother had managed to flee before the revolutionaries had stormed the castle. Her grandfather hadn't been so lucky. He had been a political prisoner for a decade until Turkey had swallowed up the tiny nation of Cardia. Upon his release, her grandfather had gone back to the ruined castle and retrieved his stash of riches. It wasn't as much as he had hoped for, but it was better than nothing.

He had met with Grammy Margaret to arrange a marriage between Daddy and her mother. Daddy had been twenty-three at the time, while Mother had been barely seventeen. Grammy Margaret had denied the match, but something had happened. Ember didn't know what, and of the few who did, almost all were dead: except for Grammy and Mother.

Looking into her mother's fearful gaze, Ember felt a moment of pity for her. A brief moment albeit. It was dashed when Ember thought of all the times she had been afraid, and rather than protect her, her mother had forced her to keep going because it was in her best interest. Emerson was right, Cilia had never been a mother to them.

"The royal financier will ready your funds for traveling. We can hold the bulk of the money here until you find a bank you wish to use wherever you end up, but you are leaving. Where you go, I do not care," Ember stated.

Two bright spots appeared on Cilia's cheeks. "You will both live to regret this! You haven't seen or heard the last of me!"

With those parting words, Cilia marched from the room. Uncle Martin was hot on her heels. He didn't have to leave. His offenses to the Crown were far less serious. Everyone knew why Uncle Martin went along with Mother — he would have had nothing without her. And her mother had lorded it over him every chance she got.

"Come, Caelus. We need to pack," Wilson fumed. "Once we get back to America, there will be hell to pay."

Caelus snorted in agreement, shooting a dark look at Ember. "We have everything we need to destroy them."

Zephyr shifted uncomfortably in his chair. He was staying in Parley and had sent a message to his grandmother about his title and estate. He had invited her to come live with him rather than stay in America under the thumb of her oldest son. With things collapsing around Wilson, Zephyr wouldn't put it past him to use his grandmother as leverage to get him to do his father's bidding.

As Caelus stood, Ember took a deep breath to steady her nerves. Emerson gave her hand a brief squeeze, signaling his support. Her eyes burned, but she pushed it aside. She needed to focus on the task at hand.

This moment was going to be the one that could lead to war. Grammy Margaret and Emerson banishing the prime minister from Parley was enough of a political scandal. Sentencing his son was going to make things more complicated. Although she had spoken to other key figures in the American parliament, and they had assured her war would not be coming, she knew they could change their mind.

"Mr. Caelus Levan, the Crown Guardians overreached their power and authority when they dismissed the charges against you. They did not, and do not, have the legal authority to make decisions regarding criminal trials. Especially criminal trials involving foreign nationals. The power for dismissing charges and sentencing is at the sole discretion of the monarch."

Cael's eyes went wide, as Amelia paled next to him. Wilson held himself still as he listened to what Ember was saying.

"Lady Vivian, what was the recommended sentence decided upon by the High Court?"

Vivian stood and addressed Ember, "We recommend that Mr. Caelus Levan serve three years in Parlian prison for his crimes, and be banned for life from Parley."

"That's outrageous," Wilson bellowed.

"It's lenient, I assure you, by Parlian standards, Prime Minister" Ember retorted. "I agree with the High Court's recommendation. Mr. Levan will be remanded into custody tomorrow morning at the Careen Police Station. From there, he will be sent to one of the prisons to serve his sentence. In the meantime, he will be under the watch of the Royal Guard."

Wilson flew into a rage. Threatening all manner of things while Alexander attempted to calm him down and get him out of the room. Viola tried to console a sobbing Amelia, while the guards moved toward Caelus to take him into their custody.

Realizing he was losing control of the situation, Wilson turned to the one person he thought might have some power in this situation.

"Zephyr!" Wilson barked. "Do something."

Zephyr flinched. He took a deep breath and stood to look at his father and brother.

"Give everyone back home my regards. Maybe Mother can come for a visit soon. Also, prison isn't so bad. After all, I've paid for Cael's sins long enough, and so has Neil, it's about time he atones for his actions," Zephyr replied.

Wilson marched up to Zephyr, a murderous glint in his eye. "Come with me now back to the palace. We'll discuss this in private while we pack because you are coming back with me."

Zephyr gave his father a sad smile as he braced himself for what was coming.

"I'm staying. I'm Lord Zephyr Levan, the Viscount Montague, and I have an estate to run. I'm expected by my staff and tenants in a few days," Zephyr explained. "I have responsibilities. You understand."

Wilson grabbed Zephyr by the upper arm and pulled him toward the exit. Alexander fumbled to get out of the way and stand near his wife and daughter.

"We're leaving. That includes you because I can't smooth things over and fix everything without you. You're coming back to America," Wilson commanded.

Zephyr resisted his father. Pulling against his efforts to propel him forward. His actions enraged his father. "Zephyr Thomas Levan! Move yourself toward your suite and pack, or so help me,

I'm cutting you off. I don't give a flying fig what your mother thinks."

Zephyr caught Ember's eyes. His father thought if he cut him off, then he would no longer have funds and would have to sponge off Ember like a kept man. However, Ember had predicted this. He had his own money, his own house, and his own legacy because of Ember.

Furthermore, no one had disputed her actions, rather the citizens had celebrated. A warmth spread through his chest as he thought of Ember and her actions. He thought of the defense of his character by the people and smiled. He finally found what he was looking for — acceptance and a home.

"Cut me off. I don't need Mother's money. Exile me from America. I'm tired of being your puppet, and I won't be Cael's scapegoat any longer."

"You're casting your lot with them? Over family?" Caelus asked incredulously. The dumbstruck look on his face told Zephyr his older brother hadn't considered his younger brothers might want a life free of him and his antics.

Zephyr had been painted as a hunter of women and worldly pleasures for the last four years. This had cost him friends, his reputation, and even potential prospects in America. Who wanted to hire someone who chased anything in a skirt and took things too far because no was a suggestion? No one.

The woman Zephyr had been in love with had run scared from him after he had taken the fall for his brother the first time. He would never forget the terror in Amelia's eyes once she realized she was alone with someone accused of sexually assaulting a woman after he had slipped her drugs. Zephyr has gotten a prison sentence, while Cael's name splashed in the headlines as the heroic older brother chided and cautioned his younger brother over his foley.

Meanwhile, it had been Cael's foley. It was his first year in college, and he had been using cocaine for a while, but claimed it was the first time he had tried it during this incident. He said he wasn't in control of himself and didn't mean to rape the senator's daughter, but Zephyr always doubted him. Their father had told him to be more discreet next time and to stop trying to bed women in their social circles.

None of that mattered now. Once Amelia had viewed him as a monster, Zephyr had shut down. What was the point in letting people get close? They didn't know him, his personality, and his character well enough if they believed him capable of what the newspapers and tabloids said. When he had first come to Parley, he had been worried his alleged misdeeds would follow him. But they hadn't.

Someone in the intelligence community had gone on the record to defend Zephyr in the Parlian papers. There had been a large exposé and a timeline illustrating how Zephyr had been framed. In the eyes of the world, he was innocent of this crime; however, in America, he was still guilty in the eyes of everyone. To this day, he didn't know who had cleared his name three years ago, but he had always been grateful. At least when he was in the islands, or abroad, he wasn't a monster.

Amelia's cries pulled Zephyr back to the present. "Yes, I am choosing them. I would rather be poor, penniless, and alone in Parley, than rich and behind bars in America taking the fall for your crimes."

Caelus shoved his brother. "You're jealous and ungrateful. Without me, what would you really have? Amelia? She's a saucy little dish, I'll give you that. But could you make her happy?"

Zephyr's blood ran cold. He looked over at her parents, noting the shock in Alexander's and Viola's faces. Amelia stiffened at his brother's words. She looked at Caelus, and Zephyr could only hope she realized what she had married.

"What did you do to Amelia? Why did you marry her?"

"Nothing she didn't beg for," Caelus said with a wink. "Amelia is why Bianca called off the engagement. Did it matter which of them I married?"

Numbness settled over Zephyr. Amelia had been his first love. They had been practically engaged before the incident with the senator's daughter. Neil was the top consideration for the engagement to Ember because they were closer in age.

Zephyr was on the trips to Parley because he wasn't being ruled out, but his mother had argued Neil would be the better fit. Zephyr agreed with her, but his brother was in school while Zephyr was deciding what university to attend.

He had volunteered to accompany their father on behalf of Neil and see if a marriage could work. Once Zephyr had taken the fall for Caelus, his prospects in America were over. Ember became his only chance at a marriage and a fresh start despite being international news.

Amelia wasn't Cael's type, but with his brother, it was always about getting or taking what he wanted. He didn't take no for an answer. Cael was competitive and enjoyed taking away things Zephyr had or wanted. In ways, Amelia never stood a chance. Zephyr had been heartbroken when Amelia had called things off. Cael didn't want Amelia either, she was just a useful toy to hold over Zephyr and rub his face in it.

Amelia's father would avenge anything done to her. As a judge, he would be able to make charges stick. That's why he married her. Cael went too far with Amelia, and he knew it. She fancied herself in love with him. So, he would pretend to love her, then marry her, all while continuing his antics behind her back. It was the best of both worlds for him.

"Speechless?" Caelus taunted.

The guards grabbed Caelus and took him into custody. Amelia hesitated a moment before stretching up and giving him a quick kiss goodbye on the cheek. Zephyr could tell she was uncertain about the man she was tied to. However, tongues would wag if she didn't show affection for her husband before he was hauled off.

Wilson grinned darkly as he and the Monroes left. "Have fun in Parley, Zephyr."

Zephyr watched as everyone from a chapter of his life left. Rather than feel any kind of sorrow, he felt relief. However, he knew his father would be going after his grandmother. She was the only vulnerable person and bargaining chip he had in regards to getting Zephyr back to America. He needed to move his grandmother here as soon as possible.

Greer. He needed Greer right now. Emerson was busy handling matters with the Crown. Zephyr caught Ember's attention and gave her a small wave. She nodded slightly, and he slipped out, heading in the direction of Emerson's office. Both twins would be busy in the Chamber of Lords for the next several hours.

Meanwhile, he was going to pull every string available to him, call in every favor, and utilize whatever money was at his disposal to get his grandma out of America. There was no love loss between Wilson and his mother, and none of her other children would help her for fear of retribution. It was a good thing Zephyr wasn't afraid of his father.

Chapter 29

All of Zephyr's things had been moved from the palace to Rosenholm Manor on the Isle of Montague, which was a few miles off the coast of Cuba. He could see the lights of Careen and the harbor at night from the balcony off his suite, as well as the front patio and garden.

A ferry terminal, as well as a small airport on the island, facilitated travel between the two islands. There was a project proposal to put in a bridge connecting the small island to the main island so both cars and a train could go back and forth. He knew it was a project Margaret was passionate about.

The late King Emerson had been working on several transportation projects to improve travel between the islands comprising the nation of Parley when he died. Cilia hadn't been interested in continuing her late husband's work, but Margaret was determined to finish what her son had started. Zephyr was eager to learn more because as he had traveled across the islands over the last few weeks, he understood the difficulties the citizens faced and why improving public transportation was a priority.

When he had first arrived a few days ago, it had taken him almost three hours to get from Careen to Rosenholm Manner. Part of the time delay was waiting for the ferry to return, which he had missed by a few minutes. When his car finally pulled into the driveway of his estate, his staff had been waiting outside to greet their new master and lord.

Zephyr had been surprised at first but realized it was tradition. The butler, Jasper, made the introductions and assured him no one expected him to remember the names of all the staff members. Zephyr promised he would get to know them all in time. He knew several of the staff were skeptical about his declaration, but he was determined to prove them wrong.

A rapping on the study door pulled him from his thoughts.

"I beg your pardon, my lord, but Her Majesty phoned and said she will be here for dinner," Jasper informed Zephyr. "She is also planning on staying a few days. The maids are readying the VIP suite for her, and a guest suite for her lady-in-waiting."

Zephyr nodded. "Thank you, Jasper, for letting me know. Does Chef Grace know?"

"Yes, I informed her before I came to you. She will make the proper accommodations."

Zephyr smiled. Everyone on his staff was very formal with him. He hoped that as they got to know him, things would become more comfortable between them.

"Wonderful. Does she need anything? Or the maids or footmen to prepare for the queen? I can help if need be."

Jasper shook his head. "No, my lord. We have everything we need. We will do you proud. Everything will be up to snuff for Her Majesty."

"I'm sure it will be."

Jasper gave a slight bow and backed out of the room.

Zephyr looked around the room and sighed. He wasn't used to being waited on hand and foot despite having lived at the palace. It was odd to him to have servants waiting for him, in anticipation of his needs. He was used to doing things for himself, but he also understood in this world there was a hierarchy and pride in it. For those who served him, they took pride in what they did. Whether it was house chores, gardening, or his grooming, he and the estate were a reflection of their efforts.

He shook his head slightly before focusing on the architectural drawings in front of him. A few of the tenants needed new greenhouses, even though they had protested and insisted repairs would be sufficient. Zephyr brought in one of the royal gardeners and had him review the properties, greenhouses, and gardens in question. The conclusion was new greenhouses because they would be more efficient for the farmers growing the orchids for vanilla.

Zephyr agreed and made preparations for an architect to come in and review each property a few weeks ago ahead of his arrival. He had told the man to make sure each greenhouse was specific to each farmer and property. The man had argued it would cost more money, but Zephyr had asked if forcing the same design on each property would be the right call.

He pointed out that the garden area one family used for food would have to be destroyed and relocated to accommodate the greenhouse of the same scale as the other properties. The architect hadn't had a good response to that. Zephyr told him he wanted custom greenhouses for each tenant. If they could reuse the same plan at different sites then he was fine with that, but if the scale wasn't going to work then a custom greenhouse needed to be designed.

He was looking over the first of the designs that would be used on a few of the properties. Zephyr had also ordered repairs for leaking roofs, upgrades to the roads, and was evaluating the electrical system for the entire isle. He hadn't realized how much work went into running an estate, let alone one with tenants. It was overwhelming, but Emerson was helping him hire a solicitor and estate manager. When the Crown held the estate, it fell under the purview of the government. Now it was his responsibility.

Jonathon had also offered his help. Zephyr had immediately taken advantage of learning more about estates. Jonathon and his father had been a wealth of information already by helping him understand how his estate was set up, what he was responsible for, and how money came into the estate. Whenever he needed help, he would call and set up a meeting with one or both of the men. Jonathon had promised to come visit and stay a few weeks at the estate once Zephyr was more familiar with his properties and the day-to-day operations. He assured him they would go over every inch of the island to help Zephyr form a plan for the future.

Meanwhile, Ember was coming for dinner to discuss the ball, his things from America, and the arrival of his grandmother. He had collywobbles thinking about seeing her tonight. It was truly the first time he ever felt like a lord, and also the first time he was nervous about seeing her.

Zephyr stood from his desk and stretched. Heat shot through him whenever he thought about the kiss they shared. He still wasn't sure what had possessed him to kiss Ember, but it had shifted things between them. Neither of them had talked about the kiss, and while things were still comfortable between them, there was a definite awareness that hadn't been there before.

He opened the doors from his study to his garden, breathing in the scent of salt water and orchids. A scent that reminded him of Ember. Orchids were her favorite flower and she had them wherever she could. She would sit outside under the shade of a porch or gazebo to do her work whenever she was able, letting the breeze off the ocean caress her.

He hadn't realized how integrated into his life she had become until he had moved to Rosenholm. She was no longer within walking distance. While that wasn't a bad thing, it gave him time to learn about himself and grow in this new role, it was also enlightening to see how much he relied on her. He also discovered she was never far from his thoughts, which gave him pause.

Could he be falling in love with his fiancée? And if so, how was that going to work? Zephyr was positive Ember was in love with Kieran and didn't realize it. So, if he took the plunge with Ember, he needed to be prepared to face the reality of Kieran coming home, and what that meant for not only Ember but him as well.

Sighing deeply, Zephyr went back to his desk. He studied the first drawing again and looked over the site map of the properties this particular greenhouse design was going to be used at. Most of the tenants on the island didn't have phones. If he wanted feedback from the tenants on this design, he was going to have to pay them a house call. Everything regarding the drawings and proposed sites looked good to him, but he wanted to make sure the tenants agreed.

Rolling up the drawings and maps, Zephyr bellowed for Jasper. The man appeared a moment later as if anticipating the needs of his master.

"Can you have a car brought around? I'm going to visit a few of the estates ahead of Her Majesty's arrival because I want approval on these plans."

"Of course. Would you like a driver, my lord?" Jasper asked.

Zephyr started to shake his head no but realized he still wasn't overly familiar with the roads. A few of the farmers shared driveways with other properties, and he would end up hopelessly lost. He could picture his servants and tenants searching the island to find their lost lord who took a wrong turn.

"That would be swell," Zephyr replied with a smile.

Jasper bowed and scurried off. Zephyr looked at his watch. It was still early in the afternoon. He could visit both tenants and be back in time to get ready for Ember's arrival.

Zephyr quickly readied for dinner with Ember. His valet had everything waiting for him upon his arrival. He had to take a quick bath because he helped the last tenant who was installing a new fence by himself. His son was away at university and his father didn't do well in the afternoon heat, so he opted to install it on his own. Zephyr figured if they worked together they could finish the last section of the fence before dinner. So he stepped in to lend a hand while his driver kept track of the time.

His valet had no sooner put his dinner jacket on him when Jasper urgently rapped at the door to say the queen was disembarking the ferry and would arrive in ten minutes. The valet brushed off his jacket quickly before giving Zephyr a thorough once over and stepping back.

"You are ready for the queen, my lord."

"Thank you, Carter," Zephyr replied before leaving his dressing room.

He strode down the hall toward the foyer and into the driveway where his staff awaited the arrival of the queen. Jasper stood slightly behind Zephyr, who was looking in awe at his staff. They had prepared the estate in record time for Ember's arrival and still managed to change into their formal uniforms reserved for special occasions.

Zephyr held his breath as he watched the royal car come up the drive, and stop in front of him. He walked down the steps and waited for one of the footmen to open the door.

Ember had an amused smile on her lips as she took Zephyr's outstretched hand. He helped her from the car before noticing she wasn't alone. He knew Nerissa would be accompanying her, but hadn't realized the others were coming too.

"Your Majesty, welcome to Rosenholm Manor and the Viscountcy of Montague," Zephyr greeted as he bowed over her hand and kissed it.

Ember giggled, enjoying the warmth of his lips on her skin and the tingling sensation coursing through her body. "It is an honor to be here, Lord Montague."

Zephyr turned to the others exiting the car and gave each their proper greeting.

"Your Royal Highness, how delightful. I wasn't certain if you would be attending with, Her Majesty. I see you brought the Earl of Northumbria and the Earl of Somerset with you," Zephyr smiled broadly and bowed.

A wave of panic washed over him for a moment. Grace hadn't prepared dinner for five. Lady Nerissa would be following with the luggage in a few hours, so he had only told Grace there would be two for dinner.

Zephyr shot a look over to Jasper, who just smiled slightly and nodded. He took a deep breath. His staff would make sure the guests were served first, even if that meant some of them didn't get to eat the same meal. He would make it up to them.

His staff didn't flinch or balk at the unexpected guests. He surprised them when he introduced them all by name and job title. The only betrayal of their shock was the look in their eyes.

When he led his guests up the stairs, Jasper had a look of pride on his face.

The butler led the way to the formal parlor, offering drinks and refreshments before dinner. Zephyr waited a few minutes after Jasper's departure to ensure everyone was comfortable and then excused himself. He told Emerson and Ember he wanted to get their opinion on some estate business.

As Zephyr raced down the servant stairs to the kitchen, he prayed Grace had things under control for the extra guests. Fortunately, his study was near the other set of stairs the servants used so he would take those back up and grab the documents off his desk.

As he rounded the corner to the kitchen, he skidded to a halt mere inches from colliding into Jasper's back. Grace gasped and curtsied, as did the other kitchen maids.

Jasper turned and was astonished to see Zephyr behind him.

"Is something amiss, my lord?"

Zephyr shook his head. "No, I just know the staff eats whatever is prepared for the guests because it is easier for the kitchen. I wanted to make sure there would be enough food for the staff with the unexpected arrival of His Royal Highness, and the two earls."

Every eye was on him by the end of his explanation. He wanted to squirm under the weight of their stares and the heavy silence that followed. He was worried he had misspoken or insulted his chef and staff.

"I'm sorry," Zephyr mumbled. "If I've offended you and your capabilities."

Jasper was the first to recover. He cleared his throat before answering, "Chef Grace erred on the side of caution and made more food for the dinner party, anticipating there might be a change in the numbers with the Queen's entourage."

"Yes, my lord. I didn't want to let you down. I instructed the staff to make twice as much to ensure everyone was fed," Grace hastily added.

Zephyr smiled. "Wonderful. I will get out of your way then."

With those parting words, he used the other staircase, dashed into his study, and grabbed the documents before returning to the parlor.

"I apologize for leaving for so long, I had shifted some things around in my office earlier, and couldn't find the folder I was looking for," Zephyr told the twins.

Everyone brushed it off and then looked over the proposed estate plan for Montague, including upgrades and repairs to be made within the next five years. They all had an opinion on the matter, and everyone had a lively discussion regarding his choices before dinner was announced.

They moved into the dining room and continued the discussion about Montague before shifting to the happenings of Careen and Whydah as they ate. As the footmen cleared the last dinner course before serving dessert, Ember smiled and thanked the staff, which made them blush.

"Lord Montague, your chef is fantastic. She is truly gifted and I have enjoyed every dish tonight, but most especially this chocolate cake," Ember told him with a smile on her lips.

"I'm glad you enjoyed the food, Your Majesty," Zephyr replied. "I will pass along your compliments to Chef Grace. I'm sure she will be pleased."

"Will your staff be making the food for the ball?" Ember asked.

Zephyr looked up from his cake with his brows knitted. "I forgot you wanted to discuss the ball this weekend with the staff. I haven't discussed it with her, but I don't foresee any reason why she wouldn't. We may need to hire additional workers for the event, but again, it's nothing my staff can't handle."

Ember's eyes gleamed as she took a sip of her wine. With each word from his lips, the footmen around the room seemed to stand taller with the knowledge their lord valued and trusted their abilities. She was eager to discuss the ball with his butler, housekeeper, chef, and baker. It was both an introduction to Parlian society and a celebration of his new title.

"Wonderful. Why don't we meet with the various staff tomorrow morning after breakfast?" Ember asked. "If that's alright with you, Lord Montague."

Zephyr shot her a boyish grin. "You waste no time, my queen. After breakfast is fine with me, I'll confer with Jasper, my butler, to ensure everyone can attend."

"Delightful! I'm looking forward to meeting everyone."

They finished dessert in silence and then moved back to the parlor for drinks before bed. Zephyr brought over the tray of beverages he had prepared and set them on the table in front of Ember and Emerson on the settee. He passed everyone a glass before taking his and leaning against the fireplace.

"I'm dispensing with the formalities because I'm over my title today," Emerson declared before continuing, "Good work, Zephyr. Both you and Greer created a compelling blackmail letter. Remind me to never get on your bad side."

Zephyr threw back his head and laughed. "I'm glad the letter passed muster. I promise you this, I don't plan on blackmailing anyone. Ember has already promised to shield me from the Duke of Revenge."

Ian, Evan, and Emerson exchanged glances before laughing. "I appreciate your sense of self-preservation. Kieran has a reputation for a reason. I would have done the same thing in your shoes," Evan said.

Ian nodded his agreement. "Kieran and I have worked together a few times. He's intense, dedicated, and has a sixth sense the likes of which I've never seen. His ability to read people is unparalleled."

Zephyr noticed the distant look in Ember's eyes as the discussion of Kieran continued. A sharp pain lanced through his chest, and he rubbed at it. He knew the dangers of getting close to Ember romantically; and yet, he was still staying his course of courting his fiancée.

"I sent out the letter a few weeks ago."

Ember's head snapped to Emerson. Interesting, Zephyr thought, he hadn't told his twin he had sent out the letter. She didn't speak right away, instead, she took a few deep breaths and listened to what Emerson was telling the others. Her hand holding her drink was shaking slightly, the only noticeable sign the news had affected her.

Zephyr threw back his bourbon before walking over to get another glass. After he finished pouring his refill, he offered the others one and topped off their glasses. Ember didn't respond. She was staring at something on the fireplace, but the reality was she was a million miles away.

There was a lull in the conversation, so Zephyr asked the only question he cared to know the answer to. "How long do you think it will take His Grace to come home?"

Emerson's gaze narrowed momentarily as he took in Zephyr's body language and facial expression. He also glanced at Ember from the corner of his eye. She had perked up at Zephyr's question but hadn't asked her questions, which wasn't unusual.

"Honestly? I'm not sure. With luck, he'll be home by the end of the month; however, there are rumors about him being in hiding, and a few about him being held somewhere."

Emerson shrugged before taking a sip of his drink. "Time will tell," he added.

Ember's breath became heavier at the mention Kieran could have been captured. Zephyr knocked back his drink, enjoying the burn as it slid down his throat. Was he destined to fall in love with women who were emotionally attached to other men?

He froze at his thought. No. He wasn't in love with Ember, but he could fall in love with her... But he wasn't in love with her.

"Well, gentlemen, I believe I will turn in for the evening," Ember declared. The men stood as she left the room.

Zephyr's eyes followed her even after she was out of sight. Who would have thought he would have been stupid enough to fall in love with his fiancée?

Chapter 30

"Do you think you can handle the food for about one or two hundred people?" Ember asked Grace. They were sitting in the solarium after breakfast.

Jasper had gathered the head of each department within the staff. Ember had gone through them in terms of least important to most important to not waste anyone's time. The last person in the meeting was Chef Grace, who was also Zephyr's baker. This had surprised Ember because she was used to those duties being shared between two people.

Grace shot a glance at Zephyr before turning back to look at Ember. "I've never cooked for that many people before, Your Majesty. However, I know I can rise to the challenge. I've served crowds half that size, so with careful planning and preparation, myself and my staff can do it."

Ember nodded. "Do either of you have any ideas regarding the menu? The guests will be seated around various tables, so staff will serve each table. How many courses? What about dessert? Will you handle that as well?"

As she rattled off the questions, Zephyr watched Grace's expression change from one of confidence to uncertainty before settling on self-doubt. He was used to Ember peppering everyone with questions, but his staff was not used to how their queen planned events.

"We decided to open the dinner with a light appetizer, followed by a soup like clam chowder, then maybe something with fish, followed by something with crab and lobster, and then cap the dinner with dessert," Zephyr responded.

Grace shot him a smile full of relief. "Yes. Seafood is easily accessible around the islands, and something I feel confident in preparing for large groups of people. I can dress up the dishes and elevate them to be worthy of royalty."

Ember paused before responding. She knew Grace was capable and could elevate the dishes she made accordingly, but Ember wasn't certain she grasped the level this dinner and ball needed to be at. She didn't want to openly question Grace's abilities.

Zephyr could tell Ember was restraining her comments. She didn't think Grace was up to the level of an event this big. He on the other hand was tired of the pomp and circumstance that came with the upper echelons of society.

"Just say it. You don't think the menu is good enough."

Ember's gaze shot to his and saw the challenge in his eyes. She let out a small sigh before answering. "I think people are going to expect no expense be spared in your debut ball as the newly minted Lord Montague. Seafood doesn't speak to that.'

Ember smiled apologetically at Grace at the end of her statement. The young woman gave a weak smile in response. "Of course."

"Why don't I bring over the royal chef and royal baker for the evening? They know what is expected and can prepare a five-course meal worthy of the celebration and your honor."

Zephyr's lips thinned. Was she really challenging him regarding the menu of his debut ball? He waited a moment, then saw Ember carefully watch Grace from the corner of her eye. Understanding hit him. Ember was testing the young chef. She wanted to see if the young woman had it in her to politely stand up to her queen and assert herself as capable of handling the menu and event.

An awkward silence filled the room. Just when Zephyr thought Grace was going to remain silent and acquiesce to Ember, she spoke up. "Excuse me, Your Majesty. We won't need the services of the royal chef or royal baker. I'm certain they are vastly more qualified than I, but Lord Montague is placing his trust in me, and I shan't disappoint him or bring shame to him by not performing to my very best."

Grace sucked in a few deep breaths before continuing, "I will work on a dinner menu this evening and present it to you in the morning after breakfast. If that will please Your Majesty?"

Ember's lips tugged at the corners. "It does. I look forward to seeing what you come up with."

Grace nodded and rose from her seat. She was almost out the door when Ember stopped her. "Grace? Thank you for rising to the occasion and pushing back against me. It's refreshing when people go after what they want."

The tension in Grace's body seemed to evaporate. She curtsied to Ember, mumbled a thank you, and quickly strode to the kitchen.

"You had me worried for a moment with your talk of bringing people in," Zephyr noted.

"I wanted to see how badly she wanted it. She is extremely talented and I have no doubt her food will be divine regardless of what she makes." Ember responded as she made notes on the sheets of paper before her.

"She is talented. I'm glad you recognize it," he told her. "We are using the colors of Montague as the color palette for the decorations. Jasper and I decided it would be the best choice for my debut."

"I agree." Ember was distracted by her notes and checklist. It had been Zephyr's hope they would review everything for the ball, and then take afternoon tea on the veranda outside his study. Watching her read, re-read, write, and repeat the process killed any hope he had of that happening. Her mind wasn't fully focused on the task at hand, and he knew why.

"Are we done here, Em? If so, I'll get back to estate business."

When she muttered nonsense in return, Zephyr sighed and left the room. At some point she would realize he was gone, but who knew when that would be. In the meantime, he had greenhouses and orchids to plant.

Nerissa prepared Ember's tea. Something was bothering her friend, and it was evident it wasn't the ball. When she had offered to have afternoon tea with Ember, she hadn't responded one way or the other, so Nerissa decided for her.

She placed the cup on a saucer in front of Ember and then slid over the plate she made for her. Ember didn't notice, so Nerissa prepared her tea and plate before clearing her throat. She ate a sandwich as Ember pulled herself from her thoughts and looked around.

Ember took a sip of her tea and grabbed a sandwich. The pair ate in silence for several moments. When Ember finished her tea, Nerissa prepared another cup.

"Thank you, Riss. My mind isn't here. I'm far too distracted today," Ember explained.

Her childhood friend and lady-in-waiting smiled at her. "It's no trouble. The last few weeks, let alone months, have been intense. Add to it the Montague ball at the end of the month and then the remembrance ceremony a few weeks later... Well, it's understandable."

Ember grasped her hand. "Things are stressful right now, and I don't see that changing in the near future. I wish..."

Ember sighed as she let her voice trail off. Try as she might, all she wanted was Kieran home. Her singular focus on getting him back to Parley was taking a toll on her other relationships. She knew Zephyr was pulling back, and she didn't blame him.

She was balled up. Her emotions were a jumble and she was drowning in a sea of expectations with a never-ending list of problems to solve. No sooner did she fix something, than something else rose to the top. Lately, everything surrounding Belize, America, Cilia, Wilson, and Caelus was consuming too much of her time and energy. Just when she thought matters were settled, something blew up. She was on pins and needles waiting for the other shoe to drop. It had been too quiet regarding Wilson and Cilia, but Ember couldn't dwell on what they might do.

Emerson was bogged down in the details. He was doing a great job staying in the loop and keeping on top of everything; however, it would be easier if he had help. It would be easier if he had Kieran. Evan and Ian were leaving a week before Zephyr's ball. It was everyone's hope Kieran would be home by then, but no one knew for certain.

Nerissa squeezed her hand, pulling her back to reality.

"We all wish His Grace would return. I know how much you miss him, especially because you carry a torch for him."

Ember blinked a few times. Nerissa caught her off guard with her observation. Ember did have a crush on Kieran, but then when she witnessed his love for Willow and devastation over her death, she knew he would never return her feelings. She had tried to move on, and as things took a turn with Zephyr, well, Ember had been hopeful she could leave her infatuation with Kieran behind.

Ember dropped her face into her hands. "It's obvious, isn't it? It's obvious how desperate I am to have him home, and how much I care about him."

"I'm not sure if it's obvious to everyone, but it is to those who know you," Nerissa answered. "I think Zephyr has figured it out too."

"You're correct. I fear he's figured it out as well, especially after Greer told him about the note Kieran left for me," Ember admitted.

Nerissa sucked in a breath. "Not many people know about the note. You never talk about it. Not even I know what was said, and I don't need to know, it was meant for you. My point is, it was your note. Is anyone pressuring you to reveal what he said to you?"

Ember shook her head. "Not yet. I know at some point in the future Zeph will ask about it, and I don't know what to say. I don't like keeping secrets from anyone, but that note is deeply personal. Not even Emerson knows the contents."

"If that's how you want it, Ember, then you don't need to justify it," Nerissa told her. "Again, the note was for you, not for the queen and the entire country."

Ember smiled at her friend. "Thank you, Riss. I don't know what I would do without you. I also don't want to find out."

Nerissa smiled before taking a sip of her tea.

"Fortunately, you never will. You're stuck with me, I'm afraid."

Ember snagged more sweets off the tiered platter and ate one of the little cakes before speaking again. "What do I do about Zeph?"

"What do you mean? You've been working tirelessly to get Kieran home because only he can convene the High Court to dissolve a royal engagement, not a stand-in."

Ember played with the napkin in her lap, taking her time to answer. Meanwhile, Nerissa jumped to the right conclusion. She let out a gasp.

"No! Are you falling for your fiancé?" Nerissa was shocked by this revelation.

Ember hushed her. "Not so loud!"

"What has changed between you? I'll admit, Zephyr is swell and handsome. He is dreamy and many women have noticed," Nerissa mused.

"I saw him. During our time together, away from society and his father, I got an opportunity to see and know Zephyr."

"And?" Nerissa encouraged Ember to continue, as she sat forward on her seat.

Ember pursed her lips in thought for a moment. "I knew he was funny, smart, great with people, and that I could enjoy his company when he wasn't baiting me."

She paused and bit her lip, trying to figure out how to word her emotions. "He was a pain in my side, a constant reminder my power was being challenged and stolen. Then he needed me as much as I needed him. He let his guard down, and I met Zephyr for the first time. Not the Zephyr he presents to the world, but the one he keeps hidden to keep himself safe."

Nerissa cooed. "Oh! Over the last few months, there has been a noticeable shift. He has become more comfortable within Parley. I thought it was because he had been around the citizens more and saw their acceptance of him firsthand."

"I agree. I think he was reserved because he knew the engagement was contentious, and thought the citizens viewed him as an enemy, rather than someone who was a pawn in another's game," Ember surmised. "When I gifted him the title, and then he helped with the cleanup, he was able to experience firsthand what Parlians thought of him."

"They have always loved him, well maybe not at first. They despise his father and brother, but after the exposé regarding his prison sentence in America, the citizens embraced him," Nerissa said. She snagged another cookie off the tray and popped it into her mouth.

"True. He has had a lot of betrayals in his life. It's understandable why he was cautious regarding the citizens, the peerage, and even me. Everyone else controls him, or uses him to get what they want, why would Parley be any different?"

Ember grabbed the last petit four off the tray and ate it before finishing her thought. "I'm grateful he gave me and everyone else a chance to prove we are different."

Nerissa tidied up the area before ringing for a maid to clear the tea service.

"I'm happy he opened up too. He seems happier and the shadows in his eyes are less intense. He's relaxed and at ease," Nerissa observed.

Her friend's words struck her. Ember hadn't noticed he was more relaxed and carefree in public, but she wouldn't admit she hadn't paid as close attention to him as her friend had. The maid entered the room and cleared the tea service. Nerissa waited for the young woman to exit the room before asking her question.

"This brings me back to my original question, Em. Are you falling for your fiancé?"

Chapter 31

Ember sat in the war room at the palace, listening to the security report from Parley's top general, while Emerson flipped through papers. She would have thought he wasn't listening, except every so often he would ask a question regarding the report.

She was grateful to be back in Careen. She loved the Bahamas and being with her people, but she had felt isolated. After her weekend on the Isle of Montague, Emerson had informed her he had her things returned to the palace from Blackstone. The rebuilding in the Bahamas was well underway, and complete on many of the islands.

She was also happy to be away from the construction noise at Blackstone as well. Work had been going steadily to get the walls and roof fixed. There had been a brief thunderstorm the week before, and it was the first time in years water hadn't seeped through the halls, according to one of the maids. While there was still much work to be done, at least the vast majority of the structure was repaired, and the roof had been completely replaced. It was thrilling to know Blackstone was watertight once more.

The stone masons were repairing or replacing the chimneys and fireplaces this week. It was the last of the exterior repairs. While they were in a tropical climate, and it was rare to need a fire, the weather did call for it on occasion. It was also one of those ostentatious displays of wealth a duke was expected to have.

Plaster work was underway in the foyer, as was the repair work to the main staircase. Blackstone would be unrecognizable by the time Kieran returned. The thought brought a smile to Ember's lips. He was going to be livid when he saw it. She had already accounted for his stubborn nature and not wanting charity. Papers were sitting on the desk in his room outlining the terms of the money she had loaned him.

The general wrapped up his report with an expectant look on his face. Ember turned expectantly to Emerson. It wasn't like she had never participated in these reports before, but Parley had not been under the threat of war from a major world power in almost two centuries. She was uncertain what to ask or say. Rather than showcase her ignorance, she opted for silence.

"Thank you. I have no questions. Your Majesty?" Emerson said, throwing the ball back in her court.

She smiled darkly at her twin. "No. The report was quite informative and very thorough, as usual."

Emerson dismissed the man before looking up from the papers he was studying. "You didn't understand half the information he gave, did you?"

Ember sighed. "No, I didn't. I wasn't sure what to ask and didn't want to appear like a buffoon. I figured you would help me understand anything needing my attention."

Greer walked into the room, taking a file from Emerson and handing him another along with a note. Emerson ran a hand over his chin as he read the note.

"Why am I not surprised? The man clearly has more important matters to attend to," Emerson muttered as he crumpled the piece of paper and threw it in a nearby waste basket.

Why would Kieran return to Parley and take up the mantle of his military duties with the possibility of war looming? He also wasn't too concerned with Ember fixing and pouring money into Blackstone and the Bahamas. Although, the rumors circulating about Kieran being captured during some kind of assignment held some truth.

Emerson wasn't sure if his refusal to return was because he couldn't or because he didn't want to. Either way, Emerson was tired of chasing the man down. The note didn't indicate whether the blackmail letter had reached him, but Emerson would wager he hadn't received it yet judging by this response. When Kieran returned, they were having a conversation regarding his responsibilities and Emerson's expectations.

He hesitated a moment as to whether he should tell Ember but settled on keeping her in the dark. She had enough to deal with at the moment. Telling her Kieran had sent word he wasn't coming back any time soon would only upset her, and add to her worry and stress. Therefore, he would keep the information to himself and keep working to find the man.

He sighed as he rubbed his eyes with his fingers. No one had realized how far Cilia and the patriarch had gone to unravel the powers of the monarchy, and subsequently the power of the Lesser Lords and military.

Emerson had been aware of most of it because Uncle Martin was his spy, but there had been things even their uncle hadn't been aware of because Cilia had been forging signatures for a few years. Ember was discreetly repealing everything the Crown Guardians had done while restoring things to how they had been before Father had died.

"The most important part of the briefing was the end. America is not readying for war, like parliament told us before Wilson's return to America. This means you are free to go about your royal business."

"Wonderful. Maybe I'll check in with Zephyr's secretary and schedule a tea or something for later this week," Ember mused. "I worry if I don't stay on top of the planning of the ball, something will be overlooked. This is his time to shine on a world stage, and I don't want anything marring it."

Emerson nodded. "Sounds wonderfully boring. Enjoy planning the ball, and don't forget about the remembrance ceremony. I think the royal gardeners had some questions."

"I'll speak to them this afternoon. I need to discuss the flowers for Montague and then call Jasper. Between Montague and Cuba, we should have enough hibiscus and birds of paradise for the centerpieces and decorations."

"Mmhhmm." Emerson's response was as she expected. He never cared about social events. He also never appreciated the effort that went into planning them. Ember sighed and stood from the table.

She bent down and kissed Emerson on the top of his head as she headed for the door. "I'll see you tonight at dinner. Grammy Margaret should be back from Whydah this afternoon, and should be joining us."

Emerson just nodded. Ember smiled. She knew he heard her, even if he didn't respond. She walked to her wing of the palace, where the monarch's office was. She moved over to the doors on her balcony and opened them, letting in the ocean air and scent of sea salt and orchids. She loved the scent of orchids. If she had her way, she would have had them planted everywhere. Instead, they were planted in pots in the spaces she was in the most.

It was hard to imagine fall was upon them. In a few short weeks, Zephyr's ball would be held at Montague, and she could tick that off the list. The memorial celebration, which had taken up a good portion of her time lately, would be here in less than a month. Then it would be over in the blink of an eye.

It was difficult to reduce an event that had shifted and dictated the course of her life to a two-hour-long ceremony. The echoes of the explosion and subsequent deaths of her father and brother would forever follow her. It was impossible to extricate that event from her life.

The phone on her desk rang and she walked over to answer it. "Hello?"

"I have Queen Evelyn on the phone for Your Majesty. Would you like me to connect you?"

"Yes, thank you." Ember waited a moment for the operator to confirm the call had been put forth before she spoke. "Evie? How have you been?"

"Em! I've been wonderful. Being queen of my own country has been a whirlwind, but Grandpa Andy has been guiding me through it all," her cousin responded.

Ember could hear the smile in her voice. "That is wonderful news. I'm so happy you have a mentor of sorts to help you navigate the political landscape of your new country."

"It's not just Grandpa Andy helping," Evelyn confessed. "Members of my private guard have been a well of information and advice too."

The women exchanged pleasantries before the conversation turned to matters of the heart. Evelyn was the first to broach the subject.

"I see you gave Zephyr a title… Could it be because he's not the devil incarnate like Emerson and I said?"

Ember laughed. "I knew he wasn't a terrible person. I just don't like the arranged marriage, or how his father went about things. However, when we began searching for Kieran at the beginning of summer, I saw a different side to him. One who was vulnerable and willing to do the right thing, even when it put him in danger. How could I not gift him a title when he's always been loyal to me even to the detriment of himself?"

"I agree. I read in the papers what happened with Wilson and Cilia. I was shocked it was Aunt Margaret, and not Emerson, as the first person to exile them both for life."

Ember laughed. "I honestly think she beat Emerson to the punch. Grammy Margaret has despised my mother from the moment she set foot in Parley. She never thought she was good enough for the citizens of Parley, let alone my father. She saw her opportunity and took it."

Evelyn giggled. "I could see Aunt Margaret doing that. She is ruthless when it comes to protecting those she loves and her kingdom."

"I didn't know the depth of Emerson's disdain for our mother until he spoke," Ember confessed. "I knew he didn't like her or her antics, but there was a venom against her specifically I had never witnessed before."

Ember's observations were met with silence. She thought she and Evelyn had been disconnected when her cousin responded.

"Emerson is in intelligence. I would imagine he has been aware of the depths of her greed and corruption for some time," Evelyn answered. It was clear to Ember she had chosen her words carefully.

Ember weighed her response in her mind. She got the feeling there was more to the story regarding her mother than people wanted to share with her. "Do you know something about my mother I don't?"

"Yes and no. I'm older than you by seven years, so I have the benefit of time."

Ember didn't fully trust her cousin's answer, but she also wasn't going to press her for more information. At some point in time, the truth would come out about her mother. She would trust Evelyn, Emerson, and Grammy's motives for not telling her everything. One day, she would demand answers, but not now. There were more important priorities.

"You do have the benefit of time. It's difficult being the queen at times because, for as much as I know, there is still so much hidden from me."

Evelyn let out a soft sigh. "I understand exactly what you mean. I'm ignorant of many things in Astonia because I didn't grow up here. I know how to be queen, but there is a steep learning curve for politics."

"At least you avoided an engagement before leaving Geneva. I heard your mother was trying desperately to marry you off to Prince Phillip."

"She and Thad both tried to compromise me to get what they wanted," Evelyn said. "Although, there was a cost to me personally…"

"Rhys and Pierce?" Ember asked. She knew Evelyn had been in love with Prince Pierce of Scotland for as long as she could remember. Rhys was the head of Evelyn's personal guard, but Ember had heard both men went missing after Evelyn left Geneva hastily; however, one of them was found after a few days.

"Yes… Ian and Evan are supposed to be home in a week. I imagine they'll join the search for Rhys. Pierce returned to

Scotland a few weeks ago. His brother, King Richard, was overjoyed to have him home," Evelyn recounted.

"What do you think happened to Rhys? He and Pierce stayed behind in Geneva to allow your escape, correct?"

"I'm not sure, and yes. I left a few days sooner than I was supposed to because things with Phillip and Thad became volatile. Rhys made sure I made it to the boat and was settled... he promised he would come back," Evelyn recounted. "But then the ship launched from the shore and I ran to the deck in time to see Rhys and Pierce jump into a carriage and lead the guards away from us."

Ember let out a soft cry. "Oh, Evie. That must have been gut-wrenching."

"A part of me wonders if Phillip or Thad aren't behind his disappearance. Like maybe they kidnapped him... But enough about all that," Evelyn declared. "I will be there for the remembrance ceremony."

"That's wonderful! I will need all the familial support I can get that day. Especially since mother won't be here and no one knows if Kieran will be home," Ember said.

The pair talked for a few more minutes before disconnecting. Ember picked up her schedule. She didn't have the energy to handle most of the things on her list, but they needed to get done. Glancing at the list one more time, Ember steeled herself to finish everything for the remembrance ceremony.

"I was surprised to have received the itinerary for the remembrance celebration upon my return. You were busy while I was gone," Grammy Margaret commented before sipping her soup.

"I too didn't expect to receive the final schedule until a few days beforehand," Emerson added.

Ember ducked her head as she stirred her soup. She didn't want to admit she just wanted to be done with the details because the pain was too much. As the anniversary drew near, she kept thinking about the what-ifs. What if the zeppelin hadn't exploded? What if her father had delayed the trip an hour or two or an entire day? Normally she cast these thoughts aside, but this anniversary was different. It was a milestone.

Her father and brother had been dead to her longer than they had been alive to influence her. She hadn't considered things from this perspective until this anniversary because it was all anyone could speak about. Everyone kept saying how quickly the decade had gone in the wake of their deaths. In ways, Ember had to agree with them. Ten years had passed quickly. Yet, in other ways, it had been painfully slow.

There had been reminders every day of her shortcomings in comparison to her father and brother. There was also the challenge of people romanticizing the past and her father's time as monarch. For those people, Ember was woefully inadequate, and they never let her forget it. She could never learn everything she needed to fast enough.

"Ember?" She caught her grandmother's concerned gaze.

Smiling, Ember responded to everyone's silent question. "I'm fine. I am helping plan the Montague ball, and many of the tasks overlapped. I took the opportunity to complete the schedule for the anniversary while finishing the planning for Zephyr."

Her grandmother seemed uncertain about how to respond. She saw Ember's pain and knew the anniversary was a particularly difficult one. Kieran had been the one to help her get through the day in the past, but he hadn't been home in almost three years. Ember got through the day just fine, but she didn't talk about her emotions with anyone. Except Kieran. Margaret couldn't wait for that man to get home. When he did, they would be having a long chat.

Ember motioned for the footman to remove her barely-eaten soup, while another refilled her wine glass. She took a sip of the sweet white liquid, enjoying the play of flavors on her tongue before swallowing and enjoying the soft burn down her throat. The footmen would serve the main course once the others were done with their soup.

"Please let me know if changes need to be made. I'll be on the Isle of Montague tomorrow. Grace has prepared the menu and wants me to taste every single dish," Ember told the pair. "I haven't decided if I want to fly or drive."

"Driving would be the more straightforward option," Emerson replied. "But flying would be faster, so I'll make sure the pilot and crew are on standby in the morning before I come down for breakfast."

Ember smiled softly. "Thank you, Em. I told Grace I would be there around noon. I have some things I need to wrap up after breakfast, but it shouldn't take more than a few hours."

The main course was served a few minutes later. Ember picked at the food and pushed it around her plate. Margaret looked at Emerson who shrugged in response to her arched eyebrow.

Margaret sighed softly and set down her fork. "Ember, darling, what's wrong? You've barely eaten all day."

"I'm just tired. There were so many decisions to make and tasks to check off the lists. I just wanted to be done, so I pushed myself." Ember reached across and squeezed her grandma's hand. "Honestly, I'm fine. In a few days, Zephyr's ball will be over and done with, and the anniversary will follow."

"Then we have to prepare for your tin anniversary on our eighteenth birthday," Emerson reminded. "Do you want Greer and Nerissa to handle the planning?"

Ember shook her head. "No, I'll handle it."

Her twin cut into his chicken and ate a few bites as everyone slipped back into silence. He glanced up at her a couple of times as he continued to eat. He wanted to speak to her about something but was gauging her mood. After a moment he cleared his throat.

"Not to change the subject," Emerson began. Ember narrowed her gaze slightly at her twin. "What is the plan with Caelus? And let's not forget Amelia and her parents. Once it was revealed the pair were married, they opted to stay in Parley. I granted an extension of their visas myself."

Ember let out a groan. "Really? Dinner is when you pounce on me regarding that situation."

Emerson arched his brow. "I tried to reach out to you earlier, but you never responded. I need to know where you want him transferred to, otherwise, I'm picking a prison and that's where he stays for three years."

"Do you want him to stay on the main island? Or do you want to send him to one of the other islands?" Ember asked. She knew Emerson already had an opinion on which prison Caelus should be sent to. He wouldn't bring it up otherwise.

"If he stays in Cuba, I want him sent to the prison within my duchy. Otherwise, I think he should be housed in one of the prisons within the Earldom of William."

Ember wasn't surprised he picked his duchy and his secretary's father's island. If Amelia and her family stayed in Parley during Cael's sentence, they would need lodgings and permission from the lord to stay and rent a home or apartment on the island.

"Have the Monroes indicated their plans?"

"Not that I'm aware. The Earl of William said he would be willing to rent a small apartment to the Monroes, but it's on the opposite side of the island from the prison."

Ember sat back slightly as the footmen removed the dishes and readied for dessert. She knew the building the earl would put them in. It was clean and small, but below the standards the Monroes were accustomed to. She knew Emerson wouldn't be able to offer them anything better unless he allowed them to stay at his estate, which would never happen.

This meant they could either find a place to rent or ask Zephyr to help them secure lodgings. They could also ask to stay in Montague because Zephyr's estate did have a few houses available for rent. However, that was up to him. For her, it was a matter of what she wanted to deal with in regards to foreigners tied to a world leader, rather than a question of where to stick Caelus.

"Put him in Whydah. Then the Monroes can figure out if they want to rent in Cuba, ask Zephyr for help, or go home. I don't have it in me to make their lives more of a nightmare," Ember declared. "Just warn Zephyr either way. I don't want him caught off guard by Amelia."

"I'll make sure he is told of the decision before the Monroes are informed and before Caelus is moved."

Chapter 32

"**W**ere the courses to your liking, Your Majesty?"

Ember smiled warmly at Grace. She would admit she had been nervous as to whether the young chef could pull off a menu of this caliber. She was overjoyed to have been proven wrong. Grace even had a schedule regarding what could be prepared the day before and what needed to be prepared the day of. Ember knew the food would be perfect.

"Everything was delightful, and the menu you created is wonderful. I will make sure the extra staff from the palace arrives to help with the preparations. Please let me know if you need anything else," Ember told her.

Grace curtsied and murmured her thanks before leaving. Zephyr walked into the room a moment later.

"I'm glad you enjoyed the menu she prepared. She worked on it all week to ensure it was perfect for your taste test."

Ember chuckled as she stood to hug Zephyr. "It was delicious. I know your guests will love it at the ball in a few days. She is eager to please and will do you proud."

Zephyr held Ember to him for a moment longer than necessary, taking the opportunity to bury his nose in her hair and breathe in the scent of orchids. Awareness slithered down her spine as she felt his breath against her scalp. Ember pulled back and gazed into his amber eyes. She saw the lust she felt reflected back. Zephyr bent down and gave her a sweet, lingering kiss on her lips.

When he pulled back, he was grinning ear-to-ear. "How have you been, Em? It's been odd not seeing you every day."

"I've been well, and I've missed you too," Ember admitted.

Zephyr offered her his arm, and she took it. He led her out of the dining room to the garden. They strolled along the path until they reached a bench overlooking the grounds, the city, and the ocean.

The pair sat and took in the salty air coming in off the ocean. With fall upon them, the days weren't as scorchingly hot as they had been. Fortunately, the bench was shaded by a nearby cedar tree.

Ember glanced over to Zephyr and was surprised to find him watching her. She blushed slightly as she turned away. Zephyr brushed a lock of her hair behind her ear.

Ember swallowed hard at his gentle touch. Her skin tingled from the brush of his fingers. She knew he felt this attraction and pull as well. The question was what to do about it.

"Are you in love with him?" Zephyr's question was so soft, that Ember wasn't sure she had heard him. Her eyes snapped to his and found him searching her face for some insight into her mind and feelings.

Ember took in a deep breath and braced herself for his reaction. She wasn't certain if he would believe her, but she refused to lie to him. They had been through too much together.

"I don't know." Ember watched the light in his eyes dim. "I know that isn't what you want to hear, Zephyr. Kieran left after

Willow's death when I was fourteen. He and I have a complicated relationship, to say nothing of the seven-year age difference."

Zephyr ran a hand through his hair as he let out a frustrated sigh. Her answer wasn't what he wanted. He wanted her to know her feelings toward Kieran because he wanted to know what he should do.

Ember laid a hand on his arm, meeting his amber stare with her own. "I've had a crush on Kieran since I was twelve. However, he has always been in love with Willow. He still is."

Ember let out a bitter laugh as she turned to look over the city and ocean. "Even in death, I lose to her. How does one compete with a ghost? Right now, he is somewhere out there." Ember continued waving her hand, "Not giving a damn about the power I, and others, have to destroy him because all he ever cared about was her."

Tears fell from her eyes, and for once, Ember didn't stop them. She had pushed down the hurt and bitterness regarding Kieran for too long. He couldn't see anyone else through his pain. Ember wasn't his only victim, there were his sisters and his tenants as well. She knew he needed time, but he had been running for a while. And try as she might, she couldn't force him home.

Zephyr held out a handkerchief to her and she took it, gently swiping under her eyes. The irony of her situation with Zephyr had never been lost on her. If she could just let go of Kieran and fully embrace Zephyr, life would be much easier. However, her traitorous heart wouldn't give up on Kieran until she heard the words from his lips. She wasn't able to give herself fully to anyone until she knew whether there could ever be anything between her and Kieran.

Zephyr put an arm around her and tucked her into his side. Ember didn't resist. She rested her cheek on his chest and gave into the feel of his body next to hers. His warmth comforted her.

"We're a pair, aren't we? Neither of us can have who we want, and yet, neither can we bring ourselves to move on."

Ember shook her head slightly in disagreement. "That's not completely true. You've moved on from Amelia."

Zephyr kissed the top of her head. "I've only recently started to move on from Amelia. Her marrying Cael solidified to me that she never saw me the same way I saw her."

"Anyone who ever met you and then read about your crimes and believed you committed those horrific acts, never knew you. There is always an air to someone who can be so cruel, and you do not possess a cruel bone in your body," Ember declared.

She snuggled deeper into Zephyr's side. He smiled as he looked down at her. Despite their tumultuous relationship over the years, Ember had never been afraid of him. She had also never believed the worst about him.

Rather, she had viewed him as a pawn in his father's game and despised him for it. He couldn't say he blamed her. He had been a pawn in his father's game to a point because he wasn't able to break free. Ember had provided the means to help him break free from his father once and for all.

"My grandmother is moving from America to Montague," Zephyr noted.

Ember lifted her head from his chest and smiled. "That's wonderful news. I'm glad she agreed to come. I know you were worried about her and your father's possible plans for her."

"He was making moves regarding her as soon as he got back. However, she was prepared because I warned her with Greer's help. She is lying low while the movers pack her things and ready them to ship here."

"I'm glad to hear she is getting out. Wilson doesn't like to lose, and I'm not sure how he's taking the news regarding Caelus being sent to the prison in Whydah."

Zephyr didn't respond right away. "He was never going to be happy with him serving time. At least he's distracted with Cael and isn't paying attention to his mother."

"Let me know if you need me to continue to hold his attention. I hate the idea of his stopping your grandmother from coming."

"I will."

Bells tolling in the distance had Ember pulling away from Zephyr.

"I have to get back to Careen, as much as I would love to stay."

Zephyr stood and helped Ember up. "Let me walk you to the airport."

Ember giggled. She looped her arm through his and let him guide her to the airport nearby. His private landing pad on his estate was almost complete and should be ready on the day of the ball. In the meantime, Ember had driven from the airport to Rosenholm, which was only a few miles away. Ember was grateful Zephyr offered to walk her. He could always sense when she needed fresh air and a chance to stretch her legs.

They walked in silence and took the crew by surprise with their arrival. Ember felt bad about it and apologized for not letting them know she was on her way. The pilot and crew waved off her concerns and readied the airship.

All too soon, they were lifting off and flying toward Careen. Ember waved to Zephyr on the ground below and then watched him walk back to the manor. She was glad they had a chance to talk about things between them. It wasn't an in-depth conversation, but it had been a start.

"There is a tropical storm warning in effect. It's headed southwest toward us and Montague. His Royal Highness wanted me to inform you, Your Majesty," Greer said.

Ember looked over the missive that was sent by the Parlian Weather Service. She read the report twice. The storm was expected to hit the islands within the next two days. It wasn't anticipated to intensify to a hurricane at this time and would lessen the closer it got to Careen.

Zephyr's debut ball was tonight. The extra staff was already on the Isle of Montague. The festivities were being held indoors, so even if they ended up with a late September rain shower it would be fine. The airships and ferries could still run guests back and forth.

"Did you let Zephyr know?"

Greer bobbed her head. "I sent word to Lord Montague before I came to you."

"Good. I am confident the ball will be fine based on this weather report. However, if anything changes, please let me know."

"Of course, Your Majesty." Greer gave a quick curtsy before leaving the room.

Ember walked over to the window and opened it. The temperature was cooler than it had been all week, and the air was thick with moisture. A storm was coming, but that wasn't usual. Ember just prayed the tropical storm broke apart before making landfall. Either way, it was going to be a tomorrow problem because it wasn't expected until then. Why borrow trouble?

Ember was grateful the National Parlian Weather Service was on top of the storms. The weather service had been founded a century before in 1825 because of hurricanes. This was about thirty years before newspapers such as the *New York Times* began publishing daily weather forecasts.

Many of these pioneering Parlian scientists studied the skies and air currents, as well as the ocean temperatures and water currents. King Talay of Muirgen had been curious about the questions the researchers were asking his citizens. He had thrown a banquet to learn more about the research endeavor.

At this dinner, King Talay listened to how the researchers were trying to predict tropical storms and hurricanes. There had been a series of hurricanes off and on that had been deadly and destructive, wiping entire communities off the map of Parley. These cities and towns had been rebuilt over time, but it had sparked a desire to predict and warn the citizens of these events ahead of time. Having an extra day or two to prepare meant the difference between life and death, as well as the loss of homes and businesses.

King Talay had offered to have some of his advisors help because they were better able to study and collect data from the ocean to assist the Parlian researchers. This collaboration had helped push forward the Parlian meteorological sciences and given the small island nation a leg up on their counterparts.

A cool gust of wind caused Ember to shiver and pulled her from her thoughts. She studied the sky before closing the window about the same time some rapped on her office door.

"Come in," Ember called out.

"Did you hear about the weather?" Grammy Margaret asked as she swept into the room.

Ember smiled. "I did. Nothing indicates it will become a hurricane, and it's not supposed to come in until tomorrow evening at the earliest."

"Things can change. You know this," Margaret cautioned.

"I do. It's why they are informing me immediately if the weather patterns change. As of right now, the airships and ferries can still run."

Ember could tell her grandmother wanted to say more. She knew the older woman wanted her to cancel the ball. Ember had considered the idea briefly but then dismissed it. If they canceled every event over fear of a tropical storm or hurricane, then nothing would get done for half the year. Most of the storms broke up before making landfall and were nothing more than thunderstorms.

"I hope you're right. Is Emerson going with you?"

"Yes. I'm going to head up to my dressing room shortly to get ready for the ball. Greer is also coming with us. We are taking an airship," Ember explained.

"You and Emerson are taking the same vessel?" Alarm washed over her grandmother's features. It took Ember a moment to understand why.

"Yes, we are taking the same airship, but at different times. We won't be traveling together." Ember hugged her grandmother. "I'm sorry for worrying you. I shouldn't have been so careless with my words."

Margaret cupped Ember's face in her hands. "No need to apologize. If anyone understands the importance of traveling separately, it's you two."

"Are you certain you don't want to attend tonight?"

"I'm positive. I have matters of my own to see to, but do give Zephyr my regards."

Ember promised to pass on her well wishes. She stayed a few more hours in her office before heading to her suite. Emerson was doing some kind of inspections ahead of the storm and making sure everyone was in place. Greer was to make sure his suit for this evening was on the airship so he could clean up and change on the journey from Careen to Rosenholm.

Nerissa greeted Ember at her suite. "Shall we get you ready for the ball?"

"Yes. Once I'm dressed, you can send in the maid and she can do my hair while you get ready," Ember told her friend.

"Wonderful. Let's get you changed. I packed an overnight bag as well for us, just to be safe. I included enough clothing to last us a week. One of the footmen took it down to the airship," Nerissa explained.

"Thank you for your forethought. I had thought about asking you to pack a bag just in case, but then felt foolish," Ember admitted.

Nerissa giggled as she helped Ember with her clothes. "Great minds, Em."

Chapter 33

s Ember disembarked from the airship, which had landed on Zephyr's newly restored private airstrip, a murmur spread through the crowd. Zephyr approached the stairs and bowed deeply before he took her hand and pressed a kiss to the inside of her wrist, causing her to shiver with desire.

Ember's lips twitched upward at his welcome.

"Lord Montague. You are looking quite dapper."

"I am nothing in comparison to you, Your Majesty. Everything pales in comparison to your beauty," Zephyr mused with a wink.

Ember giggled at his words. "You, sir, are an unapologetic flirt."

Zephyr shot her his signature grin. The one where his eyes sparkled with mischief, and he only lifted one corner of his mouth. Her breath caught in her throat, and her knees went weak at the sight. Joy erupted in her chest because Zephyr was playful and having fun. This was a side of him she hadn't seen in a while.

"I'm only an unapologetic flirt with beautiful women, who also happen to be my fiancée and a great friend," Zephyr answered as he led her inside.

Ember chuckled softly. "It's nice to see you enjoying yourself. I've missed this side of you."

"I've missed this side of me too."

Jonathon and Lianna spotted the couple and made their way over to greet them.

"Your Majesty, your dress is stunning!" Lianna gushed after she curtsied. "Did the royal tailor make it out of silk?"

"No, she made it out of gold brocade. She wasn't certain if there would be enough fabric to make it because the merchant didn't have much left after an accident ruined much of the bolt. Fortunately, she was able to pull off this dress."

Jonathon whistled low. "That she did, Your Majesty. You truly shine tonight."

Zephyr had to agree. The silky fabric clung to her curves, giving him a new appreciation for mermaid-style gowns. The open back of the dress had been a surprise, but one he was greatly appreciative of.

Ember and Lianna enjoyed catching up with each other, and soon people began to dance. Ember danced the first waltz with Zephyr. There was also no mistaking the fire in his eyes. While he was a perfect gentleman, Ember's skin burned under his touch. Once the dance was over, he led her off the floor and to the area that had been set up for her.

Jasper came over after a few dances to let her know Emerson had arrived. Ember decided to freshen up before greeting her brother. She went to the ladies lounge and used the facilities, then checked her reflection in the mirror.

She walked back into the ballroom and didn't see Emerson, so she walked outside to the adjacent veranda. She shivered slightly noting the wind had picked up. Maybe the storm would make landfall sooner than thought. Ember didn't see her twin outside either and was turning to head back inside as the dinner bell rang when she heard whispering.

Ember cautiously inched closer to the voices.

"Are you sure?"

Ember immediately recognized Emerson's voice. From her spot hidden around a corner, she couldn't see who he was with.

"Yes, Your Highness. A man, matching the description you gave, was seen in Astonia making his way to the Bahamas earlier in the week."

Ember's heart caught in her throat. Kieran. They were talking about Kieran. He was heading back to Blackstone. She needed to get to Blackstone. Nerissa said she had packed an overnight bag, Ember would request the bag be brought to an airship at the airport...

She listened for another minute, but they had moved on to other matters. She quickly made her way to the ballroom. She needed to find Zephyr or Nerissa or Jasper... Greer spotted her first and rushed over to her.

"Your Majesty, I need to speak with you now." Greer steered her to an empty room as the other guests went to the dining room.

Once they were alone, Greer pressed a piece of paper into her hand. Ember looked down and saw the letter was from the Parlian Weather Service. Her stomach dropped to her toes as she read the contents. The tropical storm had merged with another system and was heading in their direction. They estimated it would make landfall in Cuba by mid-morning, which meant it would hit the Bahamas at least a few hours earlier.

"Please let Emerson and Zephyr know. So long as the party wraps up by midnight, everyone will make it home in time to prepare for the storm, if they haven't prepared already."

Greer nodded as she headed off to find the men. Meanwhile, Ember snagged a footman and told him she needed her overnight bag, and a ride to the airport after dinner was over. She also told him to keep it quiet because she didn't want anyone to know she was leaving due to the incoming storm and create unnecessary panic.

Was it a lie? Partly. She was leaving because of the incoming storm, and she didn't need her brother to know what she was up to so he could stop her. She would leave once the dancing resumed. There would be some nobles leaving, while others stayed, allowing her to get lost in the jumble.

Zephyr walked up to Ember and offered her his arm. "Shall we take dinner, my queen?"

Ember beamed at him. "Of course. I can't wait to see what Grace has done."

The pair walked into the room. Ember was at the head table with Zephyr, Nerissa, Greer, Emerson, Jonathon, Lianna, and a few others. As she was seated along with the others, she noticed Emerson was missing. She was going to send a footman to look for him, but he joined them a few minutes later as the first course was brought out.

The next few hours flew by as everyone enjoyed the food and wine. Ember was able to talk to and catch up with not only those she loved but also people she hadn't seen in months. In a few short weeks, she would see most of these nobles again for the remembrance ceremony, so it was nice to catch up with them under happier circumstances.

Zephyr announced to everyone the latest weather report once dinner was over. Some of the nobles who lived on the islands in the path of the tropical storm had decided to leave early, which Ember had predicted. While Zephyr's attention was diverted, Ember slipped out of the ballroom in the direction of the ladies room.

She found the footman she had spoken to earlier. "Is everything ready?"

The footman bowed. "Yes, Your Majesty. If you'll follow me, please. I have your coat and things in a private car."

"Thank you."

Ember followed the footman through the servant's quarters to where the private car was parked. The young man helped her into her coat, as well as the car. Her heart was slamming against her chest. She was worried Emerson, Zephyr, or Greer would rush out the back door at any moment.

As the car pulled away from the curb and down the driveway, the anxiety began to subside. According to the latest weather report, Ember should make it to Blackstone before the full force of the storm hit, but it was a gamble because the storm could shift or come in faster.

Emerson would be furious when he learned she was gone. He would give her another lecture on being reckless, and she would deserve it. However, she wanted Kieran's undivided attention, and a tropical storm was perfect for that. He wouldn't be able to leave until the storm passed.

Ember also knew the pilot and crew of the airship would divert to another airport if they couldn't make it to Blackstone. No one had a death wish. When her father and Drystan had gotten aboard the zeppelin that cold October morning, it had been clear skies. Then the ship exploded and they were dead. It illustrated how unpredictable life was.

Ember took a deep breath and focused on the road ahead. She pushed the dark direction of her thoughts aside. The lights came into view a few minutes later, and she could see the small airship being readied for her departure.

The driver opened the door and helped her from the car. She told him she would take her bag because most of the staff was tending to the other nobles also departing. She kept her head down, grateful her black coat hid most of her gown. Carrying her bag as she walked toward the small zeppelin reserved for her helped keep her identity quiet.

As the wind picked up, Ember's stomach began to churn. Would the airship be able to take her to Blackstone? Ember shrugged off her doubts, the pilot and crew could do it. She would be fine.

A member of the ground crew told her it would be a moment before the ship was ready to board. Ember asked to use a phone. She dialed the operator and asked them to patch her through to Blackstone, she wanted to let the staff know she was coming. However, after a few minutes, the operator came back on the line and told her no one was answering. Ember thanked the woman and hung up. No one answering meant one of two things — the phones were down or the staff was offsite since there wasn't anyone to serve.

"Your Majesty, we are ready to board." The pilot grabbed her bag and helped her to the cabin. He was surprised when she requested to go to Blackstone if possible. He told her it was possible if they left straight away, and she gave him the go-ahead. Soon they were in the air, headed east toward Naussa and the storm.

Emerson spotted Zephyr in the ballroom, he appeared to be searching for someone or something. As he walked closer, Emerson had a sinking suspicion he knew who Zephyr was looking for. Dread crept through him.

"Lose something? Or someone?" Emerson asked.

Zephyr's mood shifted at the second question. "I was looking for Ember. After dinner, I was called to see off some of my guests who wanted to make it back to their islands ahead of the storm."

Emerson closed his eyes briefly. "I haven't seen her since dinner. Although, I was pulled aside a few times by various lords. It is possible she suffered a similar fate."

Zephyr scanned the room for Ember's gold gown. The plan was to keep dancing for a few more hours and then his staff would drive those leaving to the airport.

"A few of the guests are staying here to wait out the weather, and my staff have prepared rooms and settled their luggage. I was going to ask her if she was going to stay or if she was leaving, but I can't find her," Zephyr told him. "Nerissa also doesn't know where she is."

Emerson nodded. He was only half listening to what Zephyr was saying. It wasn't that he didn't care about the nobles at this event, he just cared more about the whereabouts of his sister, the current sitting monarch.

As he and Zephyr stood surveying the room, Emerson reviewed the events of the evening in his mind before cursing under his breath. While he was talking to the officer giving him a report regarding the weather, a sighting of a man matching Kieran's description, and some other security briefings, Emerson noticed a flash of gold from the corner of his eye. He had brushed it off at the time, but now that Ember was missing, he knew his sister had been listening.

Zephyr studied Emerson for a moment. "You know where she is, don't you? She left, didn't she?"

His eyes betrayed the hurt he quickly masked, but not quick enough for Emerson not to notice. Emerson didn't want to be the person who crushed Zephyr's hope regarding Ember. He wasn't a fool. He had seen how close they had become. Even the flirting between them had changed and become more romantic in nature rather than for show.

Emerson had been hopeful at first that Ember would move on from Kieran, but once they had sent the letter, she was certain he would return. With that certainty came the uncertainty regarding her feelings for Zephyr.

"I don't know specifically where she is, but I think she left after dinner. She had received a weather report from Greer before we ate." Emerson was seething. Ember was too reckless for her own good some days. This was another example of her putting herself above the damn crown. He understood her impulse, but some days he wanted to shake her.

Jasper walked up to the pair. "Your Royal Highness. Lord Montague. The driver has just returned from the airport and wanted me to inform you Her Majesty is headed back to Careen. She apologized for leaving without a proper goodbye, but an urgent matter came up and needed her attention."

Emerson didn't betray his doubt regarding Ember's words. Instead, he pasted a polite smile on his face and thanked the butler. As soon as he was able to travel to Blackstone, he would be there. Both Ember and Kieran were going to feel his wrath. He turned to Zephyr with a lightness he didn't feel.

"Ember's on her way back to Careen, probably to oversee the emergency broadcasting ahead of the storm. Shall we enjoy the festivities? I know I promised Greer a dance, as well as Lianna and Nerissa."

Zephyr lifted the corners of his mouth in an attempt at a smile. "Of course. I think I'm on Nerissa's dance card as well."

He was too polite to call Emerson out. Everyone knew he handled the emergency broadcasting and reported to Ember about it. No, Zephyr knew where she was headed. The defeat was in the slight drop of his shoulders as he turned to walk with Emerson to join the others near the dance floor.

Chapter 34

"Your Majesty, the pilot wanted me to let you know the tropical storm has evolved into a low-level hurricane. We are heading straight for it, but we are expected to arrive at the airport near Blackstone within the next twenty minutes. We will arrive well before it is expected to hit," the stewardess informed her.

Ember figured they were heading into a hurricane. She could hear the radio operator cursing every so often and felt the pilot making adjustments.

"Thank you. You're staying at the airport hotel, right?"

The stewardess shook her head no. "The hotel is full, Your Majesty. We will stay aboard the ship and weather the storm in the hanger."

"That won't do. I won't be in residence. As soon as we land, I'm heading straight for Blackstone. You all stay in the VIP quarters at the airport. Help yourself to whatever because I am indebted to you all for flying in this weather," Ember encouraged.

"But Your Majesty, you can't walk to Blackstone in this storm. I don't think there is a driver at the airport either."

The young woman's distress over her well-being was appreciated, but Ember would make it to Blackstone come hell or high water. She would be waiting for Kieran when he returned, or surprise him if he was already home. Either way, she would have his undivided attention.

"I understand the risks and appreciate the concern. There is a tunnel system from the airport to Blackstone that I will be utilizing. I won't be out in this weather," Ember assured.

The stewardess relaxed at her words. She had been prepared to battle Ember over her safety, even if it had cost her her position. It was another reminder of the loyalty her people and staff had for her.

A particularly strong gust of wind slammed into the zeppelin. The poor woman was thrown forward, and Ember reached out and caught her, pulling her onto the couch next to her.

"Thank you, Your Majesty." The woman blushed.

"Think nothing of it. What is your name by the way?"

"I'm Lydia, Your Majesty. We were not expecting royalty on board our flight because you had your own airship."

Ember smiled as she listened to the alarms sound and the pilots yell out commands. This wasn't the first time she had flown in a tropical storm or hurricane in an airship; however, it was the first time she was flying straight towards its path.

"I left my airship for my brother. His Royal Highness was also in attendance."

Lydia nodded. Her hands clenched and unclenched in an effort to calm her nerves. Abruptly the airship lost altitude. Lydia yelped out in fear, and Ember didn't blame her. The pilot was cursing soundly, while the radio operator communicated with the ground crews that they would be making an emergency landing and would be unable to throw down the tethers due to the wind.

The pilot stopped the rapid descent as the lights of the airfield came into view. Lydia was shaking next to Ember, so she reached out a hand to comfort her.

"It will all be over soon. We are at the airport and the crews will get us situated," Ember assured her.

True to her word, the pilots landed the zeppelin on the ground a short time later. Ground crews came rushing out to help pull the ship into the hanger so it wasn't blown off the map. After several tense minutes, Ember and the crew were able to disembark inside the safety of the hanger.

Ember grabbed her bag and pulled out the key to the private VIP suite. She handed it to the pilot. "Please, stay in the suite until the storm passes. There are beds and food. Please use whatever you want."

"Thank you, Your Majesty, but where are you going?"

Ember smiled at the pilot and grabbed her bag while lifting the hem of her evening gown in her other hand. "I'm taking the private tunnel to Blackstone. I will be safe because the tunnel was repaired recently, and I won't be exposed to the elements."

The crew nodded and bowed as she began to walk away, but she turned back.

"I just want to say thank you. If there are any repairs needed to your craft, please let my secretary know. I understand flying into a tropical storm evolving into a hurricane takes skill and I asked much of you all. I will make sure your efforts are rewarded."

When the crew started to protest, Ember held up a hand. "I know you were just doing your jobs, but we all knew this storm was coming in faster and evolving. Your skills kept that craft in the air long enough to get us here. I heard the alarms. I'm under no illusions it wasn't difficult. Thus, you will all be rewarded."

There were murmurs of gratitude as Ember turned and opened the door to the tunnel system. She took a deep breath before lighting the lantern. She shifted her hem into the same hand she was holding her bag with so she could hold up the lantern. She fortified herself against the fear and the darkness and then started walking the distance uphill to Blackstone.

Home. Or at least that's what it was supposed to be. Kieran had always viewed Blackstone as more of a house after Willow died. If home was where the heart was, then his home had died along with his heart.

The hurricane was expected to make landfall sometime in the next few hours if the Parlian Weather Service could make up its mind. He had anticipated arriving in the early morning hours, but as the tropical storm grew in force, its western momentum seemed to evaporate. This had delayed the vessel he had been on by several hours. The middle of the night was not how he had wanted to arrive in Nassau.

When he had boarded the vessel in Astonia, Kieran had been grateful the crew hadn't recognized him as a duke. Instead, he was another man looking for work and passage to the Bahamas. He had paid the fee, boarded the boat, and prayed they would make it to New Providence without problem. After the ship pulled into the docks, the crew offered him shelter from the storm at the harbor house with them, but he declined.

He had slipped away toward the beach before anyone realized he was gone. The wind and rain battered his already damaged body, and Kieran prayed he would reach Blackstone before some errant piece of debris maimed him. Bloody weather service had been wrong about the speed and strength of the storm. Had they even asked the Mer? Or had they just assumed?

Kieran found the hidden stairs leading from the harbor to the cliffs above. From there, he just needed to go through the overgrown yard to the veranda either off his study or truly anywhere he could find entry at this point. His staff had probably boarded up all the areas worth saving. He was going to have to crawl through crumbling remains to get into a safe area.

After almost being swept off the stairs more times than he cared to recount, Kieran made it to the back garden. He pushed through the area, which seemed less overgrown than he remembered. But that could be because of the dark, the driving rain, the wind whipping around him, and his desperation to get inside a structure. As he made it to the back servants entrance, he was surprised to find it not braced on the inside as he pushed through the door using the key hidden within a stone in the wall.

The wind almost ripped the door from his grip, threatening to slam him and the door against the wall. After a few minutes, Kieran was able to use the last of his strength to push the door shut and get the barricade in place. He slumped against the wood and listened to the wind whistle and howl outside. Water was pooling on the floor beneath his booted feet.

His body ached anew from the battle with the storm. Kieran was certain he was probably bleeding somewhere from the injuries he had sustained during his time in captivity. He took a couple deep breaths as he debated with himself as to whether he should just walk through the kitchen upstairs to his suite soaked and leave water in his wake, or if he should strip down to his skivvies and throw his clothing in the sink.

In the end, he stripped down. He surmised his staff wasn't in residence. Someone would have come rushing to check out the ruckus he had made upon entry, as well as the noise he was making in his search for a lantern and matches. After crashing into just about every surface in the kitchen, he located one and lit it. Using the meager light, he took off his wet clothing and placed them with a semblance of care in the sink basin. Why make a mess for his staff to clean up?

Once things were settled in the kitchen, Kieran took the lantern and hobbled to his suite of rooms. The lack of cold and a draft took him off guard, but he chalked it up to exhaustion. He had managed to escape the detention facility where he had been taken and mentally tortured and abused for a few weeks.

Kieran couldn't allow Rhys to be possibly killed. Not when Rhys had agreed to spare two men to keep Ember safe while Emerson had investigated every single guard making up the Parley royal detail to ensure they were not part of the assassination plot rumors. After all, had Evan and Ian been protecting Evelyn, Pierce, and Rhys wouldn't have been kidnapped. Pierce had escaped en route to the Bulgarian prison, but Rhys hadn't been so lucky.

Kieran sighed and ran a hand through his rain-soaked hair. He paused on the stairs, gasping for breath. He didn't think his ribs were broken, just bruised. That didn't make the pain any less. It also didn't help that the left side of his torso had been grazed by a bullet during his escape, which had been fortunate all things considered. He could have been shot.

He had been relieved King Andrew had received his message regarding where Rhys was being held, and his plan for getting him out. During those few weeks, Kieran had been out of touch with the world. He hadn't known if an extraction team would be waiting for him and Rhys, or if they would be on their own. Either way, Kieran had been determined to get them out of Bulgaria and away from Phillip.

The knife wound was bleeding again. He could feel the blood trickling down his leg. He needed to push on to his room. The team Andrew had sent had been waiting where Kieran had told them to be. Rhys had been holding onto consciousness by a thread, while Kieran had maneuvered them through the forest. He had taken the brunt of the damage during the escape, knowing Rhys wouldn't last much longer as a prisoner if he didn't make a move.

Evan and Ian had greeted the men and explained the team had been in place for several days, while they had only just arrived the day before from Parley. Ian had told him Andrew didn't want to chance missing the pair in their escape attempt, so he had sent a team as soon as he received Kieran's message. Ian and Evan had been made aware of the mission as soon as Andrew had the information. However, they had been ordered to withhold the information from Emerson in case there was a spy.

On the way to Astonia, Kieran discovered someone was trying to blackmail him. He had also asked Evan and Ian some questions, confirming his suspicions there was a mole in Parley helping in the assassination attempts on Ember. This solidified his resolve to return to Parley as fast as he could, knowing he wouldn't be leaving any time soon.

As he traveled back to Blackstone, he learned of the impending war with America. After Wilson had been exiled from Parley and Caelus locked up, the American Parliament began investigating his trade deals and other business practices. What they found caused alarm; however, the people were backing the prime minister.

He was whipping the American public into a frenzy, claiming he was being used as a scapegoat and targeted by his political enemies. While the Parliament didn't want a war, Wilson was uniting his allies by any means necessary, and the masses, in support of crushing Parley and the United Kingdoms. He wasn't sure if Emerson was aware of all the facts, but he would be more than happy to fill him in after he bathed and slept.

Kieran pushed off the wall and focused on reaching the second-floor landing. He then limped down the hall to his room and shoved open the door. The scent of orchids and sea salt hit his nose instantly. It was the orchids that gave her away.

"Your Majesty," Kieran said, standing in his underwear facing his dressing room.

"Your Grace."

Acknowledgments

First and foremost, I would like to thank God for my gift of writing. I don't know what I would do with my life if I couldn't write and create worlds people enjoy spending time in.

Liam, you are my joy. Thank you for letting me be your mom. I don't know who I would have been without you, and I can honestly say I'm glad I'll never know. Reach for the stars.

Thank you to my sisters Jennifer and Kaity. I am a lot most days, and when I'm writing, I know I can be extra. You both always put up with me and help me work through writing challenges. Most of the time our workshopping sessions happen while not talking about anything related to any part of writing or my stories at all. So thank you for putting up with me.

A massive thank you to Taylor! You are a star for beta reading this manuscript. Your feedback was invaluable and helped shape this final version.

Thank you to my family and friends. Without your constant support and encouragement, I would never have pursued a career in writing, let alone fiction. Thank you for never saying I couldn't do it, and always pushing me to try.

Thank you to my loyal fans and readers! Your words of encouragement and feedback keep me going. As an independent writer and author, I wouldn't be able to do any of this without you. Thank you for joining me on this journey!

Finally, I would like to thank James. Your patience with me is a gift I treasure. Our late-night conversations mean more than words, especially when you have an early morning. You sit there and let me think out loud, and then jump in with suggestions, whether it be plot, character, or life. Thank you for making me feel safe and special, and for always making me smile. I don't know what I did in life to deserve you, but I'm forever grateful for you.

About the Author

Maghan Hunt is a native of Northern California. She is a romance writer living off coffee most days. Humor, joy, and sarcasm make frequent appearances in her writing. When she isn't plotting, she's enjoying time with her son and dog.

Maghan has an MFA in Creative Writing from Lindenwood University and received her BA in Communication Design from CSU, Chico. She is also a member of the Little Shell Tribe of Chippewa Indians of Montana. Follow her on Substack, Rumble, and Locals @TheMegLife. Or catch up with her on Truth, Instagram, Facebook, Minds, and Gettr.